DAUGHTER OF THE WIND

DAUGHTER OF THE WIND

NORA CARMODY

ACE
NEW YORK

ACE
Published by Berkley
An imprint of Penguin Random House LLC
1745 Broadway, New York, NY 10019
penguinrandomhouse.com

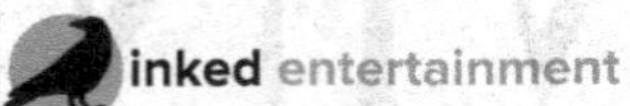

Book design by Alison Cnockaert

Library of Congress Cataloging-in-Publication Data

Names: Carmody, Nora, author.
Title: Daughter of the wind / Nora Carmody.
Description: First edition. | New York: Ace, 2026.
Identifiers: LCCN 2025024220 (print) | LCCN 2025024221 (ebook) |
ISBN 9780593955369 (trade paperback) | ISBN 9780593955376 (ebook)
Subjects: LCGFT: Fantasy fiction | Novels | Fiction
Classification: LCC PS3603.A75548 D38 2026 (print) |
LCC PS3603.A75548 (ebook)
LC record available at https://lccn.loc.gov/2025024220
LC ebook record available at https://lccn.loc.gov/2025024221

First Edition: April 2026

Printed in the United States of America
1st Printing

The authorized representative in the EU for product safety and compliance is Penguin Random House Ireland, Morrison Chambers, 32 Nassau Street, Dublin D02 YH68, Ireland, https://eu-contact.penguin.ie.

For my parents, who weren't always horse people,
but became them out of love for their daughter

AUTHOR'S NOTE

The fictional lands of *Daughter of the Wind* are inspired by events and legends from various parts of the world. None is intended as a faithful representation of any one country or culture at any point in history.

DAUGHTER OF THE WIND

1

ZARA

There was something about living under the constant threat of violence that desensitized you. Maybe it was because there were only so many times I could wake up in a cold sweat in the night, sure that *this* night would be the one where the eagle warriors would descend and destroy everything I loved. Eventually, I had to shove all those fears to the very back of my mind for my own sanity.

After years of unending war, I had to trust that my mother's ability to keep our tribe hidden was everlasting. I never thought they would find us.

I should have known better.

As the morning dawned with a red-streaked sky, I traveled the short distance from our camp to a nearby stream. My blood bay mare Shazeera carried me at a leisurely gallop—we never walked when we could race across the plains, the long grasses parting for us like waves. The sky rapidly changed to blue as the sun rose. It was empty, for the moment, of clouds, making it easy to see that no enemy would swoop down on us.

Still, with a war that had raged for over a hundred and fifty years, we could never afford to let our guard down. Even within my mother's protective wards.

Wards that wouldn't last much longer if the queen's health was any indication. As her power waned, mine was meant to replace it. When it came to the powers that should be my birthright, though, I was completely useless.

Not useless. Shazeera interrupted my thoughts with a swish of her tail. *It will come in time.*

You may be the only one left who believes that, I thought.

She shook her head, her long black mane brushing the tops of my leather-clad knees. *Considering I'm always right, isn't that all you need?*

I laughed in spite of myself. *I just wish there were some evidence of my supposed powers.*

You come from a long line of First Daughters with powerful defensive earth magic. We wouldn't have bonded if you weren't meant for greatness.

I smiled inwardly at her proud thought. Shazeera was descended from not only the greatest endurance horses, but also the fastest.

She slowed to a springy trot as the stream came into view, and before I could even let out a yelp in surprise, she continued into the water with a powerful splash, carrying me with her. As the cold water droplets hit my bare arms, goose bumps immediately sprang up. The sun had just risen, and it was still unpleasantly cool outside.

Did you think I needed a bath, or what?

A little cold water might help clear your head, she replied, before shaking off and lowering her head to drink.

It's you who isn't seeing the situation clearly, I grumbled mentally as I jumped from her back onto the bank. I wanted to avoid getting my boots even wetter than they already were.

I crouched down and cupped water in my hands to drink, closing my eyes as the refreshing coolness slid down my throat. It always tasted better fresh from the source. Rising, I scanned the distant hills to the east, where a line of trees met the plains. Beyond that rose the mountains. I couldn't see them from here, but I imagined them soaring high above the foothills, just as they did on the map my mother–Ama to me, but Queen Rana, the Queen of All Queens, to everyone else–often brought out whenever General Isa came to talk strategy. In my mind, I could see the many clusters of triangles that represented the Angora Mountains to the east, where the Zephyrian Empire's capital city of Naharu and its palace clung to the highest peak of Crane Mountain.

As the sun rose higher, warming my dark hair, I tried to imagine what it would be like to live in the forest, constantly shaded. Out on the plains, the trees were few and far between. Generations ago my people's territory had expanded as far as the Black Forest to the north and the Ridgeline Foothills to the east. Now, the enemy's territory surrounded us on three sides. Shazeera and I had explored as far as the foothills, but that had been far more dangerous than I had anticipated.

Far, far away, a giant eagle screeched, and we both froze, as we'd been trained to do from a young age. A strange tension coiled in my chest, and I couldn't say it was entirely due to fear.

I reached out with my mind to feel for my mother's protective wards as she had taught me, but as usual, I could sense nothing at all. Even the weakest earth magic user could sense the protective shields that hid our people from our enemy. The fact that I couldn't was endlessly frustrating–especially to my mother. As

First Daughter, how would I ever take over forming the wards if I couldn't even sense them?

The wards are still strong, Shazeera said gently. She knew how worthless I felt when I had to rely on her senses instead. The horses were born being able to sense earth magic—no training required. At least one of us could.

Her ears pricked toward the east as she listened for a moment, detecting another screech that I could barely make out. *The eagle is flying away from us.*

We both relaxed. It must have been a wild eagle, then. They were still dangerous, but not nearly as much as one carrying a Zephyrian rider. Our camp was currently only an hour away from the mountain foothills, where many wild eagles nested.

Just once, I would like to take a drink from this stream without worrying that a giant eagle was about to swoop down on my head, Shazeera said with an irritated swish of her tail.

Maybe none of them would be as hostile if it weren't for the Zephyrians.

The Zephyrians flew to our continent of Equnox on the backs of giant eagles a hundred and fifty years ago, from their much smaller continent of Darkhan—one of the four continents in our world. When they found our lands to be populated by mostly peaceful tribes, they returned with battalions of highly trained infantry by ship. The Angorans of the eastern mountains were the first to fall under their rule, followed by the Nazcas of the northern forests, and then the Semalians of the western coastline. Only three tribes remain free.

Once, we had been known by our individual tribes, though we were all descended from the first six daughters who had been given magic by the Earth Mother. Out of necessity, we had banded together as the Children of Earth against our common enemy. And our numbers were dwindling.

Shazeera turned her head toward our camp, growing still as though concentrating.

What is it? I asked.

Nafalla has asked us to return.

I groaned. Nafalla was my mother's bonded mare. *Ama wants to start training this early?*

Considering I couldn't even detect the wards just now, I was sure it would go as well as it ever did.

Most considered it a useful ability that the horses could all communicate with each other mentally within a short distance, especially during battle. For me, though, it was just a way for Ama to track me down quickly.

I would say we could make a run for it, Shazeera said, stepping out of the stream, *but Nafalla specifically said if we tried to skip training again, she would put me on foal duty for a month.*

I thought you liked the babies, I said as I lightly grabbed hold of her withers and vaulted onto her back.

Only from afar, Shazeera replied. *Up close, the little beasts bite and kick.*

I smiled for a moment at that image. She wasn't wrong. The foals were like long-legged toddlers with boundless energy.

But Shazeera's amusing commentary could only briefly distract me before the dread pulled me down again. Nothing made me so aware of my inability as these training sessions with Ama. Especially since every one of them had ended in embarrassing failure.

Shazeera set the pace at a fast canter, and I tried to convince myself that maybe this time I would finally tap into the power that should be my birthright.

Before it was too late.

Shazeera slowed as we entered the camp, and many called out in greeting or simply stopped and bowed their heads as we passed. Our camp wasn't the largest of all the tribes, because of the frequency with which we had to pick up and move; the Queen of All Queens moved camp frequently to change the radius of the wards' protection. But of the ten tents here, all were large, with at least two rooms in each. The largest of all, though, was the pavilion, which had three distinct points to its top and golden thread woven amongst the bright colors. It was the queen's tent, and my home.

I stood before it now, breathing in the familiar scent of sage, which wafted from beyond the doorway of the pavilion.

Well met, daughter of my heart, Nafalla's greeting passed to me through Shazeera. She dipped her head to allow me to touch her velvety nose, the soft lamplight disappearing into the deep shadows of her onyx coat.

The pavilion soared above the tips of the horses' ears, supported by light wooden rods that were flexible and strong. It created a space large enough for everyone in the camp to fit inside the main room, which served as the throne room. There were bedrooms on either side, separated by vibrant blue silk drapery. The room to the left was mine, but I knew Ama would be waiting in the throne room.

Naomi, one of Ama's guards, quietly greeted Shazeera and me with a bow as we entered.

We found Ama sitting before a bowl of polished bone, filled with burning sage. Her dark eyes, heavily lined with kohl, lit up when she met my gaze. With a smile, she gestured for me to sit. Nafalla took her place beside Ama, while Shazeera stood by my side. I tucked my legs beneath me and joined Ama on the floor of the tent, where a plush rug of many colors had been spread.

"You were up early," Ama said to me as she handed me a cup of white flower tea. The bangles on her wrists jingled pleasantly, the sound as familiar to me as my own heartbeat.

"I couldn't sleep," I admitted, taking a sip of the honey-sweetened tea.

Ama tilted her head sympathetically at me, her thick hair slipping off her shoulder. My own thick hair was tied back in a long braid. Everyone said we looked so much alike. That the blood passed down from First Daughter to First Daughter for generations was strong. We had the same golden-brown skin, deepened by the hot plains sun; high cheekbones; full lips. The same large eyes framed by dark lashes, though my eye color was a much lighter amber, where hers was a rich chocolate.

I may have looked like her on the outside, but I had none of the power given to her by the Earth Mother. At her full strength, she had been able to heal someone on the brink of death, from the inside out. She could even use her abilities offensively, by causing a wave of agony over a small battalion of soldiers, enough to cripple them.

But I couldn't even heal a scratch.

"I will admit that your power is taking longer to manifest than is common in our family," Ama said, reaching over to touch my hand, "but earth magic has always been strong in the Sorayan line. It will come. We just need to tap into it."

I glanced down at my cup with a frown. Ama believed that anything was possible if you just *tried* hard enough. And maybe she was right. Maybe I didn't put enough effort into it.

Nonsense, Shazeera said sharply. *You tried so hard to connect to your abilities last time that your nose bled with the effort.*

Yes, but I didn't pass out, so clearly I wasn't trying hard enough, I thought back with a heavy dose of sarcasm.

Shazeera snorted beside me.

"Let's begin," Ama said, and with an inward sigh, I angled my body to face her. The horsehair mantle she wore brushed against my arms as she placed her hands on mine. It was as black as Nafalla's mane and tail, as it had been taken from them over the years, and dark as Ama's own hair where it wasn't streaked with silver. My own mantle, formed from the black hairs of Shazeera's mane and tail, was much smaller, as I hadn't had as many years to add to it. "Instead of trying again to sense the protective wards, let's try to access the healing side of your magic."

I shot her a confused glance. "Aren't the wards the most important?"

"Yes, but sometimes trying a different approach can help refresh your senses."

I nodded and tried not to argue, even though we had tried this months ago and it hadn't helped. Nothing did.

"The pulse points are where you can connect with the rivers and streams of blood within someone, following it to its source. The blood will always reveal what needs to be mended, whether it is sickness or injury. Now find my pulse with your fingertips."

I did as she asked. This part was easy. Anyone could feel a heartbeat in a pulse. Her wrists were warm, her heartbeat steady, as I pressed down gently with both hands.

"Close your eyes and go into the part of you that's connected to Shazeera."

In my mind, I reached for our bond, that gleaming chain of light that was unbreakable. I could sense Shazeera's emotions—hopeful and anxious that I would finally succeed. If I went deeper, I could even sense what she physically felt. Right now, the scent of the sage filled her nostrils, the smell so much more complex than I detected. Beneath the typically herbal scent were notes of rich loam and spicy peppercorn.

"Are you there?"

"Yes," I murmured, keeping my eyes closed tightly in concentration.

"I want you to reach into yourself where that same power comes from and reach for my pulse point instead."

But when I reached for my mother's life force, the one I should have been able to sense if I had healing abilities like her, there was only darkness.

"There's nothing there," I told her, barely able to keep the frustration from my voice.

"All you can do is try again," she said gently. "Our life force shines as brightly as the sun. With your inner eye, you should be able to detect the light radiating from my bloodstream. You must reach out with the part of you that's connected to the Earth Mother."

Determination filled me. I wouldn't fail this time. I reached deep inside myself, searching for the light, and the farther I went, the more the pavilion with all its familiar scents and sounds disappeared. Even Shazeera seemed far away. My head pounded along with my heartbeat. This was usually the point where I pushed too hard and ended up with a nosebleed. But I had to keep going. I couldn't bear to let Ama down again, to see that look of disappointment on her face. I pushed past the pressure in my head and waded through the darkness in my mind, searching for any hint of magic.

Soon, I went so far I couldn't sense Shazeera at all. It was like suddenly not being able to feel my legs anymore. Fear grabbed hold of my chest, making it hard to breathe. Why couldn't I sense Shazeera?

But before I could return to the surface of my mind, the darkness cleared. I stood on top of a cliff overlooking a dark ocean, waves crashing against the rock. Above, the clouds raced across the sky as a powerful wind howled. The primal scene made my pulse jump. Wind danced over the water until it swirled around me, lifting my hair and whispering in my ear.

In all the years I had tried to reach for the earth magic Ama promised lay dormant within me, this had never happened. I only ever stumbled around in the darkness of my mind, powerless. Ever since I was little, though, I had sensed a presence in the wind, just like Ama spoke of earth magic being present in every living thing. But I had never been able to reach inside myself and make a connection with it. I stood frozen, unsure how to react. The whispers grew louder . . . I could almost make out what it was saying.

But then a voice called out to me, pulling me back to reality.

"Zara," Ama said, her eyes wide, "did you sense it? Could you see my life force?"

"I saw a powerful wind," I answered without thinking, still a little dazed from the scene. My head pounded with a splitting headache at the effort of going so deep within my own mind, but at least I didn't have a nosebleed this time. "I think it was calling me."

She dropped her hands from mine with a frown. "Tell me what you saw."

I described the stormy scene, but my words didn't seem to adequately express the depth of the power I had sensed. "It seemed like a force that could make a difference in this war."

Ama looked unimpressed. "I thought we went over this years ago. You are a First Daughter born from a First Daughter, going back generations. The power of the Earth Mother flows strongly through our veins, and it is the source of every ability I have that keeps our people safe. There may be lesser abilities in our lineage, but it is the healing and warding skills that are most needed."

"I've *tried*–"

"Our people are dying, Zara," Ama interrupted. "We've lost over sixty percent of our population, and if it keeps going like this, our entire culture will be wiped out. Years ago, I could keep nearly the entire grasslands covered by my wards," she said, sweeping her hand toward the map of Equnox hanging against one wall, "hiding us from the Eagle Riders. Now, I can barely shield our camp. So when you say you've tried–you haven't if you're wasting time trying to connect with lesser magic and ignoring the defensive abilities given to us by the Earth Mother herself."

"You're not listening to me, Ama," I said, frustration gripping me so hard my eyes welled with tears. "There *is* no other magic within me! I've spent years searching for it, and this is the first time I've found anything at all. Only the wind."

Ama's eyes flashed. "It's there! You're my daughter, so of course you have the ability. Your people need you, Zara, and you're letting them all down."

I winced like she'd physically slapped me, and Shazeera stamped her hoof and tossed her mane with an indignant snort.

She may be the queen and your mother, but she's taking it too far, Shazeera said, anger darkening her tone.

Nafalla must have heard Shazeera's words and passed them on to Ama, because my mother whipped her head around at Shazeera. "You should be using your bond as a tool to help her harness her earth magic, not indulging her in chasing after whispers of a lesser ability that will only end up costing lives."

You don't know that, Shazeera argued. *What if this magic is more powerful?*

Ama stilled. "I'm only going to say this once. To both of you. This magic is dangerous and better left alone. Or have you forgotten who it is that our enemy worships?"

The Zephyrians were called such because they worshipped the god of wind, Zephyr. As far as I knew, none of them could call on the power of the wind, but that didn't make me feel much better. The fact that I had tapped into a power associated with Zephyr, and therefore the Zephyrians, caused a prickle of unease to race over my skin.

"There is no magic besides our own," I said, because it was known that the Earth Mother bestowed powers only upon her Children.

"It wasn't always this way," Ama said. "The world was full of different types of magic once, and some of those magic lines still exist."

My eyes widened. "What do you–"

But before I could finish my question, Nasrin, one of my mother's handmaidens, rushed into the main area of the pavilion. "My queen," she said breathlessly, "a warrior and her mare were attacked by an Eagle Rider. She's dying."

I knew then that my question would go unanswered for now because Ama would never turn anyone away who needed healing. She came gracefully to her feet and gestured for me to do the same. We hurried after Nasrin, horses at our sides.

She led us past three smaller tents until we were nearly to the entrance of our camp. The other sons and daughters–mostly all healers of various strengths like my mother–surrounded the injured warrior brought in on a travois. The Queen of All Queens' camp was intentionally kept small, so we only numbered twenty-two, but with everyone shouting and talking in concern, it seemed like many more. No one was actively trying to heal the warrior right now, which meant that it was beyond their capabilities. Earth Mother willing, it wouldn't be beyond Ama's.

Someone had already hammered long poles into the ground beside the injured warrior to erect a temporary tent. Bright blue silken cloth soon soared over the injured daughter's head, shielding her from the harsh sun. We moved closer, and the crowd parted for us.

"It's Mya!" I said in a rush when I got a good look at her face twisted in pain. Mya was one of my second cousins and usually acted as a messenger between our camp and my aunt's in the Mid-Plains. Her chestnut mare Farah was small and sleek and fast. How had an eagle even caught her?

I knelt beside her and grabbed hold of her hand, but she only moaned in response. Ama knelt on the other side and put her hand gently on Mya's forehead. We both looked down at Mya's wounds. She bled heavily from a gaping gash in her abdomen that she tried unsuccessfully to hold closed with her hands. Her skin looked ashen, and her eyes had taken on the glossy look of the near dead.

Shazeera made a low, worried sound, and I glanced over at Farah. Her coat hair had turned nearly black with sweat. Foamy lather covered her chest, and her nostrils flared red. She had run herself nearly to death to bring her bonded sister here.

"You did well," Ama told her. "You got her to me in time. I can still heal her."

Farah closed her eyes in relief as Nafalla and Shazeera moved closer to her to help hold the smaller mare up.

Ama turned her attention back to Mya and moved her hands over the terrible wound. Immediately, the rich scent of freshly turned earth, bright herbs, and sweet grass filled the air.

Dani, another healer, came to her side and leaned down. "How can I assist you, my queen?"

"A spear tore through the muscles of her abdomen and pierced her intestines," Ama said quietly. "I must first push out all the blood that's pooled inside. Once I have healed her internally, she will need continued mending. You may take over at that point."

"Yes, my queen," she said with a bow of her head.

I watched Ama carefully, worrying the inside of my cheek. Her ability allowed her to channel her power into another person in order to heal them, but it took a tremendous amount of strength to keep the magic under control. Sending your own life force into another person when they're seriously injured was always a risk, because it formed a connection between the healer and the injured. If Ama didn't break the connection when she still had plenty of strength left, the other person could end up draining Ama's life force away. With the wards already draining her, Ama had to use her magic judiciously. Her solution was to use only as much magic as was required to heal the person until another healer could take over.

That was *if* she still had enough strength to end the channeling at the exact moment she chose.

Ama's expression tightened with concentration as she worked on knitting the inner parts of Mya that had been torn. It wasn't long before my mother's chest was heaving with effort. Her hands shook, and a rope of worry cinched tightly around my heart. It happened more and more lately–the physical toll on Ama when she tried to maintain the protective wards and heal anyone brought to her in danger of dying. There were healers on the front lines, too, but none of them could knit someone back together from the inside out.

Suddenly, the pleasant earthy smell of my mother's power began to fade. In its place, coppery blood scented the air. Ama's expression contorted like she was in pain, too. Sweat tracked down her face.

Mya became frighteningly still as her skin blazed hot with fever. Behind us, Farah let out a whinny that sounded like a cry.

"Ama?" I said, searching my mother's face.

"The magic is taking too much from me," Ama said, her voice strained. "I'm losing control of it."

I felt Dani's eyes on me. This is where the First Daughter should have been able to lend her own strength, allowing my mother to safely withdraw her magic. The other healers couldn't do it; only the queen or First Daughter had that type of power.

"The magic is draining your mother," Dani said to me, barely hiding the reproach in her eyes.

"Ama, I can't–"

"You *must*," she said with a hint of fear to her tone I'd never heard before.

My fingers trembled. I closed my eyes and willed myself to be able to feel *something.*

I thought about all the things Ama said I should look for: the sound of a person's blood rushing through them like a river, the bright feeling of their life force like the sun, pain and sickness in various shades of black and gray. But there was nothing. Only her skin beneath my hand. I reached deep inside me like I did just moments ago in the pavilion. I thought of the way Ama's power felt, like warm sun on soft grass.

I heard the beat of my heart and my steady breaths. I could feel my link to Shazeera like an unbreakable chain.

But there was no sunshine. No earthy sensations at all.

Only the cold, blowing wind.

Frustration surged through me so fast I felt dizzy with it. I couldn't do it. My ancestral power was completely inaccessible to me, and I feared in my churning gut that it always would be. I opened my eyes to find that in the short time I had searched fruitlessly for my nonexistent earth magic, Ama had come to look almost worse than Mya. Her face, normally glowing with vitality, appeared dry and haggard. She shook from her effort, and all the color had drained from her skin.

When I met her gaze, her eyes had an edge of panic within them.

"I can't call it back to me," Ama said through gritted teeth.

The powerful scent of the earth intensified in the air around us, only this time, it couldn't blot out the scent of blood. Not long after that, Ama began shaking violently. Not for the first time, I feared what would happen if Ama pushed herself too far. Dread knotted low in my belly, sharp and sudden.

Ama's entire body vibrated with tension, and the effort she made on Mya's behalf could be seen in every trembling muscle.

And then suddenly, Mya's eyes flew open. Mya groaned and thrashed her head. The healing process hurt like being burned, but there had been no time to offer her medicine to numb the pain.

At the same time, my mother collapsed beside her in a heap.

"Ama!" I shouted as others rushed to help. I felt for my mother's pulse, but it was so faint. My throat swelled as my eyes pricked with tears while Dani examined Ama.

Nafalla came immediately to my mother's side, watching anxiously as Dani checked Ama over.

"She's alive, but her power has been drained," Dani announced. "Let's move her to her bed."

A son named Kai—another one of my cousins, who worked as

our blacksmith and was consequently lean and strong—gently lifted Ama into his arms.

The wards, Shazeera said, and at that moment, a cry went out across the camp. My mouth went dry as my blood turned to ice water in my veins. Without the wards, the Eagle Riders finding us became more than possible.

It became inevitable.

As Dani and I flanked Kai, who was carrying Ama, Naomi strode toward us from Ama's pavilion. "The queen's wards have failed! We must leave immediately." To another guard, she said, "Summon General Isa. Her battalion is closest, and she will want to personally escort the queen and First Daughter."

"The queen will need time to recover," Dani said, brows furrowed. "We can't ask her to travel yet."

"Can you heal her enough for travel?" Naomi asked.

"Possibly, but—"

"Then we must leave as soon as General Isa arrives," Naomi said with a tone that brooked no argument. "We'll leave the breaking down of the queen's pavilion for last. Heal her as much as you can in that time."

Before Dani could even agree, Naomi strode away, barking orders at the other sons and daughters in our camp that we had to leave immediately.

"Will she be okay?" I asked Dani, reaching out and touching Shazeera's neck when she stood next to me.

Dani looked like she was having to bite back what she really wanted to say. "Her pulse is steady, but there's no way to know how long she'll stay unconscious. My power is limited, so I'll have to call on the other healers for help. And even then, we might not be strong enough to replenish even the smallest percentage of her magic stores."

I nodded, swallowing the lump in my throat. That meant Ama wouldn't be able to resume the wards anytime soon.

"Unless you think you can connect with your royal abilities and help the queen?" she asked with one eyebrow arched.

A bitter taste coated my tongue, like ash. "I would if I could."

"Then I'll have to do what I can," she said before turning back to follow Kai and my unconscious mother back into the pavilion.

I clenched my fists at my sides as tears stung my eyes. Guilt threatened to drag me under like quicksand. This was all my fault. If I had been able to connect with my power, I could have given Ama the strength she needed to maintain the wards. Now she lay unconscious, and we were all vulnerable.

Without my mother's earth magic for protection, the Eagle Riders would slaughter us all.

2

ZARA

One advantage of being a seminomadic people was that we could pack and leave quickly if needed. It took the strong sons and daughters only an hour to efficiently break down the ten tents that made up our camp, but I feared even that wouldn't be fast enough. They had left the enormous pavilion, where my mother lay deathly still, for last. Shazeera and I watched Dani and two other healers—Imani and Layla—pour their magic into Ama. Their bodies shook with the effort. Even with their power combined, as minor healers, they didn't have anywhere near the magic stores that Ama had—or even that I should have, for that matter.

Nafalla nestled close to Ama, curling her body around my mother's protectively. Tension thrummed through the air, raising the hair on the back of my neck. It felt like the terrible moment of false calm before lightning struck.

Only I knew it wasn't lightning that would strike us down from above.

Shazeera pranced in place, her anxiety mirroring my own. *Why is everyone moving so slowly? We should have been miles away from here by now! The healers are being incredibly foolish,* she added with her ears pinned back in angry frustration. *They will drain themselves and be in the same situation as your mother if they take much longer.*

They were hoping to at least reenergize her body, but she must have depleted herself more than they anticipated.

The thought brought an icy chill to my blood.

"First Daughter," Dani said, and I tensed, wary of what she would ask of me, "we cannot bring the queen back to consciousness. What would you have us do?"

I glanced at Shazeera, who tossed her head. *We must leave now.*

"The healing has taken too long," I said, ignoring the flush that came to my cheeks as I navigated the unfamiliar waters of giving orders in my mother's stead, "and the Eagle Riders could descend on us at any moment. We need to travel to safety as quickly as possible."

Dani bowed her head once. "I'll have a wagon prepared, then."

When the healers left, I went to Ama's side and touched her face. Her breaths were slow and steady, which was a comfort, but seeing her so helpless made guilt coil inside me like a serpent. "I'm so sorry," I whispered.

Nafalla nudged me gently with her nose, and tears burned my eyes. She had every reason to blame me. Every reason to be angry for my lack of power. But instead, she offered me sympathy.

Kai and his brothers arrived then to gently carry Ama out to a wagon and break down the pavilion. Shazeera made a soft beckoning noise, and I grabbed my bow with its quiver of arrows before following her outside. Once under the ominously gray sky, I pulled myself astride. Everyone else in the camp was already mounted, their horses dancing in place with obvious anxiety to start moving. Mya lay on a pallet on a small wagon pulled by a gray mare, her own horse at her side. She looked pale but alive. The healers had continued to work on her after Ama had collapsed, but she still faced many weeks of recovery.

A covered wagon, intricately detailed on the outside by gold and pulled by unbonded horses, arrived in front of the pavilion. The turquoise silk provided shade from the beating sun, and I knew the inside was already comfortably outfitted with plush fabric and pillows. Kai carefully carried Ama over to the wagon and laid her within it, where she remained unnaturally still. Nafalla positioned herself beside the wagon, where I knew she would continually check on Ama. It was beneath a bonded horse to pull things like wagons, since there were many more horses than there were my people, so the young unbonded ones were willing to help us with the more labor-intensive activities.

Vibrations under Shazeera's hooves and the sudden attention of all the horses in camp signaled the arrival of more of our tribesmen. I turned to the east, hope blooming inside me when I saw Nafalla's head and tail lift expectantly.

A band of fifteen warriors rode toward us, their horses covered in dust, as though they had traveled hard and fast. At the front was General Isa astride her gray mare Kamil, and just the sight of her unwound some of the tight knots of fear in my stomach. The general's battalion stayed within an hour or two of riding distance from Ama's camp, where they could quickly come to our aid if necessary, but also closer to the Angora Mountains and the Zephyrian capital, where they could patrol for Eagle Riders.

She rode within a few feet of Ama, and Kamil came to a full halt before both she and General Isa bowed their heads to their queen. The other warriors formed a line around us and offered the same bow of respect. Each was heavily armed, with either a bow and quiver or a spear slung on their backs, swords at their hips. Like General Isa, they all wore dark brown leather armor; only hers was intricately tooled with silver thread and had scaled pauldrons. Their horses all had protective armor on their heads, necks, and rumps—any areas that may be under threat from above.

The horsehair plume on General Isa's leather helmet fluttered in the breeze as her eyes, ringed with black, assessed the situation. She frowned when she took in my mother's condition. "How long has she been unconscious?"

"It's been almost an hour now," I said, and General Isa searched my face. I knew what she was thinking. I had failed to access my powers. But mercifully, she didn't say anything.

"The queen's retinue won't be able to travel as fast if she's in that wagon. I'll see if I can at least bring her back to consciousness," she said, swinging her leg over and jumping down from Kamil's back. General Isa was distantly related to Ama, so she could heal, too—just not as powerfully as a royal.

Gently, she placed both hands on either side of Ama's face and closed her eyes. Nafalla and Kamil stood as silent witnesses, though I saw Nafalla's dark coat twitch with nervous energy as the minutes ticked by.

Everyone around seemed to hold their breath—they probably could sense the earth magic. And then, suddenly, Ama's eyes fluttered open.

"Zara," Ama said, her voice faint.

I dismounted and went to her side, relief crashing over me like a thunderclap. "I'm here, Ama."

Her gaze shifted to just behind me. "Where are we?"

Without the tents or pavilion, we could have been anywhere

on the Equnox Plains. I thought of our location on the map in the eastern part of the Mid-Plains, a two-hour hard ride from the Ridgeline Foothills and about a hundred miles south of the Zephyrian stronghold in Naharu, nestled high in the mountains. Ama had found that staying closer to the Angora Mountains and Zephyrian territory worked to our advantage, as their scouts tended to focus on the northwestern Equnox Plains, where most of the battles were fought. But that was when we had wards that shielded us from view.

"Still at camp," I said reluctantly, and her eyes widened.

"Then we must travel to the Nazeeran Canyon under Queen Jazela's protection immediately."

General Isa swayed a bit on her feet, her face much paler than it had been. She seemed to rally her strength before nodding. "We are prepared to do just that, my queen. Do you think you are strong enough to ride?"

"If I'm conscious, I can ride," Ama said, climbing out of the wagon with assistance from Kai. But the moment she was standing, all the color drained from her face. Nafalla moved closer to Ama so that she was pressed against her side. Ama leaned heavily on her, breathing hard.

I took a step toward her in concern. "You can't ride like that, Ama," I said.

"With your permission, my queen," General Isa said, "we'll have to tie you on Nafalla."

Nafalla snorted and bobbed her head once in agreement.

"Fetch some tie-down straps," General Isa ordered one of the hovering servants, who rushed away. "That will be more comfortable for you than rough rope," she added to Ama.

"That's fine," Ama said weakly.

"Once we get you on Nafalla," General Isa said, "the safest course is for us to split you and the First Daughter up and give you both armed guards."

Ama looked at me, a crease of worry between her brows. "I don't want to be separated from Zara."

"I understand," General Isa said, "but keeping the queen and the heir together when there's this high a chance for an attack is too dangerous. I will accompany Zara myself if it makes you feel more comfortable."

"Send more warriors with Ama, then," I said, "since we all know as far as heirs go . . . I shouldn't be a high priority."

Ama's tired eyes flashed at me. "Don't ever say that, Zara. You are my daughter, and I love you. Of course I want you kept safe. You are my highest priority—whether you have powers like mine or not."

I swallowed hard as emotion rushed to the surface. I didn't know if it was the threat of imminent discovery from our enemy that had inspired Ama to say that to me, but I knew she had never made it clear before now.

Nor had she ever acknowledged the fact that I may not have earth magic at all.

I couldn't find my voice to respond, so I just nodded with tears in my eyes.

The servants returned with the wide straps, and then Kai lifted Ama gently onto Nafalla's back. They tied the straps over the tops of Ama's thighs and around her calves before crisscrossing under Nafalla's belly. Even with that small movement, Ama's lips had turned nearly white.

General Isa signaled to her warriors, and nine rode closer. "I want you to escort the queen to safety. We will all reconvene in the Nazeeran Canyon in three days. Guard her with your lives."

I mounted Shazeera, and we moved close enough that I could lean over and touch my mother's arm. Our eyes met.

"Stay safe," she whispered like a prayer, and then she slumped forward onto Nafalla's neck, completely unconscious.

"Ama!" I cried, heart in my throat.

General Isa hurried toward her and put her hand on her wrist. "She's very weak and needs more healing than we can give her right now."

"Nafalla will never be able to travel swiftly now with Ama lying on her neck like that," I said, my hand tightening on Shazeera's mane.

Nafalla is strong, Shazeera said. *She can adjust her gait to accommodate your mother. She'll likely have a terrible neck ache by the time they reach the canyon, but I'm sure she'd rather that than be separated.*

General Isa added another strap that went around Ama's upper back and around Nafalla's chest. "The queen is secure," she said. "Now we must go."

I looked at Ama, normally so vibrantly full of life that she was like the sun that everyone gravitated toward, and now so helpless and still as she lay strapped to her horse. I couldn't shake the feeling that something terrible would happen, that we stood upon a precipice and were about to be pushed over.

Nafalla will guard her with her life, Shazeera said, conveying Nafalla's thoughts to me. I had no doubt of that, but I dreaded a situation where that could be the outcome.

"I love you, Ama," I whispered, tears blurring my eyes. "Stay safe."

Nafalla nuzzled my leg before pivoting gracefully. The warriors immediately fell into a circular formation around Ama as they rode southwest.

"We will head due west," General Isa told the camp after squinting at the cloudy sky. To the five remaining warriors, she said, "Three will stay with the camp caravan, and two will accompany the First Daughter and me." The remaining soldiers divided themselves up without being specifically told who would go where.

Finally, she turned to me. "Ready?" When I nodded, she said, "Then let's move."

Kamil shot forward, while Shazeera and the other horses followed. General Isa set the pace, which was just short of neck-breaking. Every mile between us and our former camp brought thoughts of Mya and her injuries. That gaping wound had been caused by an eagle and its rider, and at any moment, they could appear.

I focused on the weak sunlight glinting off the sharp points of General Isa's sword and the spear across her back. Memories flitted through my mind of Isa's prowess with the blade, of teaching me the basics of archery and swordplay, and then drilling me on it nearly every day for years. She was my mother's closest friend, and I trusted her with my life.

More importantly, I trusted her to keep Shazeera safe.

The wind whistled loudly in my ears as we galloped. There was a strange quality to it that made me strain to hear.

The screech came soon after, far in the distance, but close enough that it would only be a matter of moments before it arrived. Shazeera's fear flooded her system, transferring to me through our bond. My own panic stole the breath from my lungs.

"One?" I asked as Shazeera and the other horses listened hard. An eagle screeched before it arrived to flush out prey—to catch the prey's frantic movement with its sharp eyes. Even surrounded by armed guards, I knew the odds of us coming through a battle with a giant eagle would almost certainly result in casualties.

Only one so far, Shazeera said, and Kamil snorted her agreement.

"I want you to run," General Isa said, her gaze never leaving the skies, though the steel-gray clouds made it impossible to see. She held a long spear with a wicked blade at the ready. The other five warriors had drawn their spears, too.

"I can help," I said, but the expression she gave me was cut from ice.

"Your duty as First Daughter is to live. Ours is to fight. You will run for the trees and leave the battle to us."

Shazeera didn't need further convincing. She sprang forward powerfully, headed east for the cover of trees.

We'd made it only a couple of lengths when a war cry split the quiet of the plains. I looked back to see Kamil holding her ground as an enormous eagle bore down on them from above. The other warriors flanked General Isa, expressions grim.

Should we turn back? I asked Shazeera, my jaw clenched so tight it hurt.

And risk your life? There is a time to stand and fight, and there is a time to run. Right now, we run, she said, continuing her ground-eating strides.

Our horses were not only faster on land than any other animal on the continent, they also had the most endurance. Across the sea, there were horses that were incapable of communication and bonding who could only gallop for a mile or two before becoming fatigued. Ours came from the very first horses created by the Earth Mother herself; along with their superior intelligence, they could run flat out for at least five miles. But even they had their limits.

Before us, the landscape changed, the relatively flat ground becoming hillier until finally dipping down into a valley. When I turned to look back, I couldn't see any of the others in the distance. Fear rose up and sank its teeth into me.

We had escaped the battle General Isa and the others were still engaged in, but it did nothing to comfort me. The tree line was still miles away, and we had very little experience with battle.

Part of our training with General Isa involved watching our warriors face down Eagle Riders, but that was from so far a vantage point that we could barely make out the giant birds in the sky—much less the smaller horses and riders. Because I was First Daughter and without offensive abilities that would be more beneficial on the battlefield, Ama and General Isa felt the risk was too great to have me any closer.

You should reserve your strength, I told Shazeera.

Not until we reach the cover of trees.

Then we heard the second screech. It came from directly above us, loud enough to turn my blood to ice.

My eyes scanned the sky desperately. Though the eagles were enormous, they could fly high, even hiding amongst the clouds. The sky was an impenetrable wall of gray, making it impossible to know if an enemy flew above us.

I pulled my bow from across my back and into my hands. Retrieving an arrow, I nocked it, my muscles tight.

It happened too fast.

One moment, there was nothing but clouds, and the next, a gigantic golden eagle was descending from on high toward us at rapid speed.

Our only hope was to make it to the tree line, but it was still at least a mile away. My legs gripped Shazeera tightly as I leaned over her neck. Her hooves thundered through my body as tall grass streaked past us.

Another piercing cry, loud enough to make my ears ring. Its wings joined the pounding sound of Shazeera's hoofbeats. *Thump, thump, thump.*

I turned to look, raising my bow and preparing to aim, but fear wrenched hold of my heart. A man crouched low over the eagle, grasping a long spear. I blinked once, hoping he would disappear into the clouds, begging for this to be an illusion. But he remained.

The truth was illuminated in the weak rays of the sun penetrating the clouds. This wasn't just a wild eagle—that would be bad enough. This was an eagle and its rider. A Zephyrian.

And we were alone.

Shazeera lengthened her strides, her whole body stretching out until it was as unhindered by the wind as possible. I leaned low over her neck to stay with her, to keep my body from dragging her back. Her mane whipped across my face.

With every stride Shazeera took, the eagle gained on us. My hand tightened on my bow. I knew we wouldn't outrun it. Our only hope was for me to shoot it down.

I sent Shazeera an image of what I planned to do so she could prepare herself for the sudden change in my weight. Bracing myself with my thighs tightly gripping her sides, I twisted my upper body sharply backward and drew my bow simultaneously, ignoring the screaming protest of my muscles.

My eyes found the place where the eagle's wing met its breast, and I sucked in my breath. The creature was massive, its wingspan easily thirty feet. It absolutely dwarfed Shazeera. Its talons were as long as daggers. When I imagined them tearing into us, a wave of terror crashed over me.

The wind whispered in my ear, even as it tore at my hair. It felt impossible, but it seemed like I could detect its desperation.

The eagle was closer now, but not enough that I could see the rider with any clarity. I did, however, see when he raised his weapon. It looked like a long pole with a noose at the end big enough to wrap around my body. Fear sliced through me, sharper than any blade. Did he want to capture me? For what purpose?

I let out my breath and then fired the arrow. It flew straight and true, but at the last moment, the eagle spun in the air to avoid it. My mouth went dry. I'd never seen an eagle make such a maneuver. I reached for another arrow as the eagle and its rider flew closer.

I fired again, but the eagle, despite its massive size, avoided it. I recognized the move as one General Isa had briefed us on. Seeing it in person, though, made my chest constrict painfully, squeezing the air from my lungs. The truth hit me like a blade to my gut. I was vastly outmatched before we had even really begun to fight back.

The eagle is too fast, Shazeera said, and even her mental voice sounded strained from exertion. *Even though it's the bigger target, your arrows will all go to waste.*

I understood her meaning perfectly as I shifted the aim of my arrow. This time, I would shoot the rider.

I let it loose, the arrow pointed at the rider's chest, but the eagle screeched and dove to avoid it.

Fueled by desperation, I fired arrow after arrow, faster than I'd ever done before, but they didn't so much as clip a feather. And I knew they would catch us. After that, I didn't dare think about what his plan was.

Too many voices in my head. Shazeera's fear, which was nothing but sharp talons and darkness, poured into my mind. My own thoughts were frantic. I wouldn't let her be killed here. And then another voice, first a whisper, but steadily growing louder. I thought of that massive, churning power I had witnessed within my own mind, and I knew it was the wind just as surely as I knew the feel of Shazeera's bond.

The eagle was close enough now to see the glint in its huge eye, to watch it stretch its talons toward my horse's flank. I continued firing, though I knew it would dodge the arrows, because it would keep it from tearing into Shazeera.

I was soon down to my last arrow. The rider knew it, too, and he urged the eagle closer.

The rider was now close enough to see his face in detail, and it was disturbingly beautiful, with strong features that made it look like he had been formed from the granite of the mountain itself. It ignited an anger in me, that he wasn't as hideous as the things the Zephyrians had done to my people. Or the things he and his eagle planned to do to us if they caught us.

Shazeera and I fell into darkness as the giant eagle completely blotted out the sun, its enormous shadow threatening to swallow us. The rider thrust his weapon toward me even as the eagle's wickedly sharp talons reached for Shazeera. Fear heightened my senses and made my thoughts race along like lightning. I told Shazeera to evade their attack, and she obeyed without question, jumping powerfully to one side, which nearly unseated me. The noose whistled past my ear, treacherously close to my neck.

I let my final arrow fly, and this time, the eagle flew too close to avoid it. Hope blossomed in my chest for one terrible moment. But then the eagle snatched the arrow out of the air with its talons, snapping it as easily as I would break a twig.

I met the rider's light-colored eyes as he raised his pole again.

Thump, thump, thump.

The eagle's wings were deafening.

I reached deep within me, the pressure building until it felt like my head would burst, but I pushed on heedlessly. I would seek out whatever power was inside me that lay dormant—lesser magic or not. Anything to save Shazeera. Time seemed to halt as I reached for the earth magic that should be mine—the wards I should be able to summon to at least shield us from this attack. Just like before, there was nothing. Only darkness. I stumbled on desperately.

Suddenly I sensed a vast power, like a thunderstorm rolling in across the plains. Wind, both from the eagle and from Shazeera, swirled around me, screaming in my ears.

Call, it said.

Call and I will answer!

I watched the eagle's talons reach for my beloved mare even as the noose began to slip over the top of me.

Do whatever it takes to live, Shazeera told me, her mind brushing against mine with a finality that felt like a blade slipping in between my ribs.

The wind cycloned around me, tearing my hair free from its bindings, ripping tears from my eyes. *No,* I thought to the eagle and its rider. *No, you will not kill her.*

I raised my arms and opened my heart to the wind. Ama had warned it was a dangerous power, but in that moment, I didn't care.

If you can understand me, I said, *then rip them from the sky.* I let out a guttural scream as power seemed to flow in me and through me as the wind responded. It pulled energy from me so hard and fast that I gasped for breath, but I would have given everything to save Shazeera.

All the wind that flowed around me like an inescapable

whirlpool burst toward the eagle and its rider. The pole with its noose was wrenched from the rider's hand, and the eagle was blown back so fiercely that its wings bent at severe angles.

With a tremendous shriek, it somersaulted through the air before finally crashing to the ground in a heap behind us. The ground shook when the eagle landed, and a wave of dust and debris rose in its wake. For an instant I thought I saw the rider wrenched from the saddle, his weapon spinning away, before the dust swallowed them both.

As Shazeera carried us far away from the scene of destruction, I watched the grounded eagle and rider for any sign of movement.

But there was none.

3

TALON

They said your life flashed before your eyes before you died. And maybe I just wasn't close enough to being dead yet, but all my mind chose to show me was the moment the girl with the staggeringly arresting features had called death upon us from the sky. Through my connection with Neo, I could see her in perfect clarity. The image of her was still burned into my retinas, dark-framed eyes blazing with fierce determination, full lips parted, chest heaving. She was as beautiful and terrible as the sudden storm she had conjured. Neo could handle powerful wind gusts that tossed smaller birds around like leaves, but he had been like a chick in storm-churned waters. Completely helpless.

Neo. Before we'd crashed, there'd been a tangle of wings and talons and feathers, and my heart turned to lead in my chest at the thought that he might have snapped his neck. It was a miracle I hadn't. But somehow, I could move my fingers and my toes, then my arms and my legs, though at least two of my ribs were fractured. As I pushed aside the cloudiness in my mind and came more fully to consciousness, I could see why I was still in one piece. Neo had broken my fall. Even now, I rested on one of his golden-brown wings, as though he'd grabbed hold of me as we crashed. He may have, but everything happened so fast that it was hard to recall clearly.

One second, we'd been closing in on the girl, and the next, we were blown out of the sky like we'd been sucked into a cyclone. I didn't know how, but I knew the wind had come from the girl. I'd been flying since I was a baby, and I'd encountered every type of wind. Updrafts, currents, gusts, even wind powerful enough to force Neo to descend to avoid it. But never had I experienced wind that sudden when we were so close to the ground.

I thought again of the girl, her eyes boring into mine, turning from the terror of someone who knew she wasn't skilled enough to save herself to steely determination. Had it all been a trick? Had she just been drawing me closer to use that strange power on me? The whole thing flashed rapidly through my mind: the girl's eyes, one slender arm outstretched—not toward me, but toward the sky itself—the resulting wind, a force so powerful it ripped through all my senses, tearing at my eyes, howling in my ears, stealing the breath from my lungs.

Powerful enough to knock a giant eagle right out of the sky.

Neo, I called in my mind, but there was only darkness at the other end of our bond, even more than when he was asleep. His chest rose and fell, so at least he was still breathing. Images of how hard he had crashed to the ground—the earth itself shaking—flashed through my mind. What if he had been injured so badly he never woke up?

After many minutes of this, I finally felt a stirring in his mind, the darkness slowly growing lighter, like the first hints of sunlight at dawn. As he swam closer to consciousness, a red haze joined the light, and I frowned as I recognized it as the haze of pain.

Neo?

I'm awake. He slowly opened his eyes. *But I wish I weren't.*

Can you move your wings?

He lifted the left gingerly with no problem besides stiffness, but the right caused him to shriek so suddenly that I grabbed hold of his wing—gently—and pushed it back down.

It's broken, he said when the pain had faded enough that he could think again.

My mind raced toward a solution to the problem at hand. Corbin and Phoenix, the eagle and rider pair we had flown a formation with, had hopefully been able to defeat the Children of Earth warriors they had encountered. I glanced up at the position of the sun in the sky, and my mouth went dry. We must have been knocked out for hours now. If Corbin and Phoenix had won their battle, they would have come for us already.

A broken wing meant we would have to walk until we were noticed by another eagle and rider scouting, and that could take days—best-case scenario. Worst was that we'd have to wait for Neo's wing to heal, which could take two to three weeks. And we were at least one hundred miles deep into enemy territory. Luckily, hollow bones meant fast healing. More than anything, though, I needed to get word to the emperor about this girl.

Her power could change everything.

The emperor will send someone to look for us, Neo said when he caught hold of the thoughts flying through my mind.

I'm just glad you're alive. I laid my hand on his uninjured wing. *We should make for the foothills for food and shelter. The last thing I want to do is sleep here on the plains, exposed.*

I agree on all counts.

Having a goal gave me something to focus on other than the fact that I had failed my mission for the first time in my life.

While Eagle Rider scouts engaged the queen's guards, I had been sent to capture the Queen of All Queens. We had flown to the exact coordinates the sorcerer had provided, but it wasn't the queen we found there.

Who was she? Not the queen, for she was too young. But she had a black headdress that only the royals wore. The First Daughter, then? Had the Children of Earth somehow kept this power hidden? And if so, what was their strategy behind it?

I turned over the possibilities in my mind as the tall prairie grass reached up to my thighs, hindering each step. Even Neo, who towered over me, struggled through the thick blades. In the distance, perhaps only a few miles, stood the tree line. This was no doubt where that girl and her horse had been headed. Beyond it rose the Angora Mountains, their silvery outlines just visible against the horizon.

Neo tried to hide it from me, but we were connected more than brothers who'd shared a womb; I felt the waves of pain crashing over him with every step. An eagle wasn't particularly fast while walking, but because of his injury, our progress was achingly slow. If any of the Children found us here, or worse, if the girl with the power over the wind returned with reinforcements, we'd be killed as easily as pigs for slaughter.

I don't appreciate being compared to a pig, Neo said huffily. *I still have talons and a sharp beak, and you have all your weapons. That's hardly helpless.*

None of those things were much help before. Have you ever heard of someone commanding the wind? Eagles had an understanding of the wind that was unmatched by any human, but I didn't think that extended to being able to control it.

He paused for a moment in walking, pretending to only be adjusting his feathers under his wing, but I knew the tide of pain had risen to the point where every step sent a stabbing agony into his broken bone. *No.*

We can stop here and rest.

One golden eye fixed on me. *No.*

I sighed but continued to take slow, plodding steps toward the foothills in the distance. We both fell silent after that, focusing on escaping the hot sun of the plains. An ache had been growing in my abdomen, dull at first, but with every breath becoming increasingly sharp. It made my vision start to blur and my breath come in pants. Neo tried to lend me strength with his uninjured wing, but I pushed him away.

At long last, we made it to the very bottom of the foothills, where thick trees provided shade and shelter, and the burbling of a creek promised cold water. Neo collapsed beside the creek, dipping his beak into the water repeatedly. I staggered toward him, eager for a taste in the hopes it would make the pain stop, even for a moment, but then I coughed. When I wiped my mouth, the back of my hand came back red.

I stared at it uncomprehendingly as the pain twisted in my abdomen enough to double me over. It was probably the lowering of my head that caused the sudden rush of dizziness, the darkening of my vision. Distantly, I could hear Neo calling me in my mind, and his shriek of surprise when I toppled to the ground like a tree.

My last thought was extremely profound:

Shit, I'm falling.

4

ZARA

Adrenaline had rushed through my veins, making my hands shake and my breaths come in pants. We had left the downed eagle and its rider miles behind us and made it to the shelter of the trees, like General Isa ordered, an hour ago, but there was still no sign of them. Had they survived their own battle?

Call, it had said.

Call and I will answer!

Had I really called forth the power of the wind? I thought of that powerful blast that tore the eagle and its rider out of the air. Of the way they'd crashed to the ground. There was no other explanation for such an impressive gust of wind—no sudden tornado from the sky. Being connected to the vastness of that ability, even for a moment, felt like it would drain away my energy until my heart stopped. My heart was beating normally now, but exhaustion wrapped around me, dulling my senses and making it difficult to sit up straight.

How could Ama have called this a lesser power? I asked

Shazeera. She shook out her mane and twitched her tail but didn't answer me. *Shazeera?*

What was the matter with her?

"Shazeera?" I whispered, but she still didn't respond.

An ill feeling of dread swirled within me, gaining momentum with every minute that I couldn't hear Shazeera through our bond. There wasn't a moment in my life when I couldn't talk to Shazeera and hear her answer in my mind. Not since I first bonded with her.

I was three years old, and Ama carried me in her lap while she rode Nafalla to the grasslands in the very center of the Equnox Plains. An ancient band of horses, descended from the very first horses created by the Earth Mother, surrounded us. They were a beautiful array of colors, from the deepest black, to rich chestnuts and bays, to shining white. Their tails were so long they dragged on the ground. In the center of these beautiful stallions and mares were the foals, happily playing.

As soon as Ama helped me down from Nafalla's back, the adult horses parted, and the foals came over to me on their impossibly long legs. I remember laughing at the way they seemed to dance around me. I wanted to join them, but they were all more interested in playing with each other than with me. But one filly left the others and came to stare at me with her big doe eyes.

Her coat was a much duller version of the deep blood bay it would eventually become, but even then, with her short, babyish mane and tail, it was beautiful. She tossed her head at me and did a playful half rear, inviting me to join her. I laughed and jumped at the chance as she led me in a game of tag. The elders looked on approvingly. And when we were so tired we both collapsed in a heap, Ama came and helped me to my feet, while the little filly's mother did the same.

The foal's mother lowered her head around her baby in an embrace, and then on shaky legs, the filly walked over to me.

She wasn't much taller than me, but she still had to lower her forehead to touch mine. The moment she did, warmth spread throughout my body—it was like waking up in the night terrified, only to be enveloped in your mother's embrace. Like the purest love. Tears streamed down my face.

I'm Shazeera, she said for the first time in my mind, and the bond between us solidified inside me.

When I felt for our bond now—that strong, seemingly unbreakable rope that connected us—it was different, no longer easily found within me. It was like it was buried deep underground, and I would have to dig for miles to find it again.

Shazeera, I said, my mental voice sobbing. Tears stung my eyes, and my throat felt thick. I placed one hand on her strong neck, the other entwined in her mane. She turned to look at me, one eye meeting mine, and I could see the fear in her gaze.

Panic surged within me so fast, the edges of my vision went dark. Then it wasn't just me. She knew something had happened to the bond, too.

Before I could say anything else, we both heard the rumbling of hoofbeats. Relief hit me when I saw General Isa astride Kamil and the others behind her, but at the same time, I tried to hide my growing panic at whatever had happened between Shazeera and me.

"First Daughter!" General Isa said, glancing at the now-empty sky before cantering toward me. "I'm sorry it took us so long to find you. You were farther south than I thought you would be."

I decided then not to tell her about our own battle. What would I even say happened? I could barely explain it to myself. "We were only concerned for you. What happened to the Eagle Rider?"

"We managed to critically injure the enemy enough to force his retreat." Her eyes narrowed. "But they'll be back. We must leave this area immediately."

Shazeera fell into line behind Kamil, and the two warriors flanked us as we kept a fast pace west. Reflexively, I kept reaching for the bond with Shazeera again, like prodding a sore over and over with my tongue. Every time I found silence on the other side, it felt like a noose slowly tightening around my neck. What had I done?

HOURS PASSED. WITH our camp location over one hundred miles from Queen Jazela's canyon city of Nazeeran, it was a hard three days on horseback. General Isa and the others didn't make small talk, so at least I was spared from having to act like I wasn't rapidly dissolving into a puddle of fear.

What if I can never talk to Shazeera again?

I had never heard of a Zephyrian being able to use magic that could cause a daughter and her horse not to be able to communicate. They were entirely without magic. That left only the wind power I had called upon. And though it had been terrible in its strength, calling upon it had also done something to the bond between Shazeera and me.

Which meant I was responsible for damaging—possibly even destroying—the bond between us.

What if I broke our bond forever?

I shuddered at the thought. I had never heard of a daughter or son breaking their bonds with their horses while they were still alive. The only time it happened was when either the human or the horse died—something that occurred far too often because of the war.

A memory hit me then, of Ama providing mental healing to a daughter named Cassia who lost her bonded mare during battle. Only it hadn't been to arrows or a sword.

Cassia's words drifted through my mind again, the pain echoing. *The eagle landed on top of my mare, and I knew it was crushing her under its weight. She screamed as its talons raked down her back. I tried to get up . . . tried to go to her. And then . . .* She'd swallowed hard, her voice thick. *The eagle sank its talons into her throat. The last thing she said to me in my mind was, "I love you. They're coming. Run. Live." It was the other Children, you see. A small group of warriors had heard my mare's screams and released a torrent of arrows on the eagle and its rider. The eagle released my mare and flew away—neither of them were even injured. They killed her as easily as a falcon kills a rabbit.*

The horror of watching the eagle's talons tear into her beloved horse must have been a soul-crushing loop in her mind. The loss of her mare had made her a shell of a person. Ama worked with her almost every day for two years before she even was able to smile again. A severed bond only made the grief harder to bear.

We lived under constant threat of this happening to cur horses or the people we loved, but the fact that I had brought this on by using a strange power I didn't understand gutted me. I couldn't blame our enemy. *I* had done this to us.

The wind whistled past my ears, cooling my sweaty neck as though trying to ease my mind. But I couldn't take comfort from it, not when there was silence at the other end of my link to Shazeera.

That night, as we camped in darkness, we didn't dare light a fire. Our horses lay on the ground, and we leaned against them for warmth. At my back, Shazeera's steady breathing was as familiar as my own, but the lack of communication between us felt like a missing limb. I gazed up at the sliver of moon and thousands of stars, glad that we didn't have more light as tears slipped down my face.

After offering me bread and honey, which I couldn't bring myself to eat, General Isa and the other five warriors fell asleep almost instantly.

I thought of Ama, with a fear that prickled over my scalp. We hadn't gone very far before we had been set upon by that first Eagle Rider. Had Ama and the others been attacked, too? Had she regained consciousness? Or was she still strapped helplessly to Nafalla? Even if Ama had woken up, without her ability to shield, she wouldn't have been able to defend herself much more than I could with a bow and arrow. Surely if the others had all been killed–if my own mother had been fatally wounded by an eagle attack–I would have sensed it. I may not have been able to wield earth magic, but I was of the Sorayan line just like all the others in my tribe. Their blood would have cried out to mine.

Or if not to mine, then at least to General Isa's.

I squeezed my eyes closed, desperately wishing I were able to discuss any of this with Shazeera. After a moment, she shifted so that her whole body was curled around mine. I wrapped my arms around her neck and pressed my face into her mane.

My mind replayed over and over what had happened with the Eagle Rider, thankful that we were alive. I prayed that the Earth Mother would allow the bond with Shazeera to be restored, even though I had used a power completely unknown to our people. I prayed that Ama and the others hadn't been attacked like we were. As always, I didn't hear even a whisper of answer from the Earth Mother.

The last of my hope unraveled inside me, thread by thread.

So that night, I prayed to anyone who would listen to please, please help me. Help my bond be restored with Shazeera. Help me to never have to use that power again.

"Help," I whispered to the wind as I finally relinquished my hold on consciousness.

IT WAS ONLY natural to have a dream about eagles after nearly being killed by one. Only, the terrible thing was, it wasn't just a dream, but a memory.

Shazeera and I had traveled to the Ridgeline Foothills over a year ago, when our camp had been stationed closer to the tree line. While Shazeera grazed beside a waterfall, I had climbed to the top and stumbled into the middle of a giant eagle's nest.

In my dream, I could see the nestlings. One of the babies peeped, a sound so small and innocent it drew me in against my will.

There were three of them, their downy fluff gray instead of the golden plumage they would have as adults. The largest of the three looked at me, its dark eyes meeting mine. It ceased peeping, and did nothing but watch me. In the dream, as in real life, I found myself reaching out to it. The truth was that I had always been drawn to all things wind and sky. And this included a morbid fascination with giant eagles.

It took a hesitant hop toward me, its gaze never leaving mine, and I didn't dare shift a muscle. I kept my hand steady as it came closer. The breeze picked up, ruffling its down and pulling more of my hair loose around my face. Another hop, and I could just feel the soft feathers of its head. I knew what was expected of me as a Child of Earth. These nestlings would only be small and helpless for a short time before growing up to become mortal threats to my people.

But I couldn't imagine causing any harm to these little ones. Instead, I gently petted the chick's soft head, and it let out a happy peep.

In the distance, a screech echoed. I froze as cold bloomed like frost across my skin.

The baby eagle jerked its head up and hopped back to its siblings, where they immediately began to let out excited screeches of their own.

The mother was returning.

Below, Shazeera let out a low, anxious sound of warning. I didn't waste any time trying to climb down the rock face; I jumped from the top of the waterfall. I hit the water with a tremendous splash, the water swallowing me greedily. I emerged with a gasp and swam to the edge of the pool, where Shazeera paced and blew powerfully from her nostrils.

We must go now. Her thoughts vibrated with anxiety. *Now, now, now.*

The screech came again, this time much closer, and Shazeera's eyes rolled in her fear.

I was out of the pool in an instant, water pouring from my body. With a movement born from years of practice, I pulled myself astride Shazeera. She took off at a gallop, careening perilously close to trees and brush. Leaves and branches stung my cheeks, but it was nothing compared to what talons would feel like if the eagle caught us.

Down, down the mountainside we went, curving around to follow the trail. The mother eagle screeched again, and when I risked a glance back, I saw that she was directly overhead—only the trees kept her from diving and grabbing us both.

She knows we're here, I thought to Shazeera. Panic closed my throat, making it difficult to speak.

Well, you were *playing with her babies in the middle of her nest,* Shazeera said, her tone only lightly admonishing.

Shame burned through me, thick and hot. *I couldn't kill them.*

I could feel the gentle brush of her mind against mine. *It would take a truly hardened heart to end a baby's life, no matter what it will grow up to be in the future.*

I wish the mother knew I spared their lives, I said as I checked the sky. The eagle kept trying to find an opening in the tree canopy.

The trail is too slow and winding, Shazeera said, abruptly turning left.

When I saw what she planned, I sat back hard on my hip bones. "No! You can't do this."

She galloped unheedingly toward the edge. *Lean back as far as you can.*

You'll break your legs, I thought back to her so that she'd have no choice but to hear me.

The ominous beating of wings battered our eardrums as the eagle brought herself closer, the trees themselves swaying beneath the power of the wind she stirred. But even the eagle was momentarily forgotten when Shazeera plunged over the side of the mountain.

With a yelp, I leaned back so far that my head and shoulders were above Shazeera's hindquarters. Behind us, the eagle dove. Shazeera galloped on, rocks and sticks flying beneath her hooves as we plummeted down the mountainside. A fallen tree lay before us, but she cleared it like it was nothing as I grabbed fistfuls of mane and wrapped my legs tightly around her belly. I didn't dare look back, but I knew the eagle pursued us—I could feel great torrents of air from her wings, and my neck prickled at the thought of her talons so close.

At last, we reached the bottom of the mountain, landing hard enough to whip me forward. For one terrible moment, Shazeera nearly stumbled, but she was fleet of foot and strong, and she gathered her hind legs under her and powered forward until we were once again flying.

On flat ground again, she lengthened her strides, her nostrils flared wide as she raced along like light dancing on water. I grabbed hold of my bow and turned, only to find the eagle dodging trees, her gaze still trained on us. She was enormous, easily five times as big as Shazeera. She blotted out the sun, bathing us in shadow.

That day, we had outrun the mother eagle. She hadn't wanted to stray too far beyond her nest, and she had turned back quickly.

But in my dream, the mother eagle transformed into the eagle and its rider that had nearly caught us. I fired arrows ceaselessly, but the eagle dodged them as though I had thrown sticks instead.

The eagle stretched out its talons and caught Shazeera's haunches. She screamed as she reared, and I was thrown free. When I crashed to the ground, I rolled to my feet, bow and arrows at the ready, but it was too late.

The eagle landed on top of Shazeera and before I could even raise my bow, it tore into her throat. My heart shattered, and I fell to my knees screaming as the blood poured out of Shazeera.

You can choose them over me, she said into my mind.

I felt something press against my leg. It was the little chick from the nest.

5

TALON

I didn't regain consciousness again until the next day. My entire body ached like I'd been beaten and then trampled. Neo and I had spent the better part of the last five years flying constant missions on behalf of the emperor, joining in battles against the Children of Earth, many of which had left me scarred from arrows or spearheads, but nothing came close to how bad I felt now.

I will carry you on my back, and we will walk until a scout sees us, Neo said, coming shakily to his feet the moment he saw I was awake.

If no one comes for us by tomorrow, I'll consider that, I lied to him. *For now, we both should lie still and rest.*

I didn't want to alarm him by admitting that I didn't think there was any way I could lift my head, much less pull myself onto his back. The rest of the day was lost in a haze of pain that made the edges of my vision dark. I drifted in and out of consciousness.

I was too weak to give it the attention it deserved, but one thought kept worming its way into my muddled mind: *So this is what dying feels like.*

Was this what it felt like for my father? Suddenly, all I wanted was to be with them: my father with his warm smile, and my mother with her gentle voice and kind eyes. My mother was far away, in our home in the mountains, but my father had been dead for a decade now. Maybe it wouldn't be long until I saw him again.

Don't even think like that, Neo snapped in my mind, but I couldn't rally myself to reassure him.

As I lay on the ground, possibly dying, I kept thinking about what brought me here.

Neo and I were in the palace court again, facing the dais of the throne. The emperor–my cousin, Altair–stood in front of the throne, his eagle, Sky, at his side. But our attention wasn't on Altair. It was on the creature masquerading as a man that joined him. Beside me, Neo spread his wings, a shriek escaping his mouth. Neo was a war eagle, too, hardened by battle. Anything that spooked him automatically put me on edge.

The man was bare-chested, clothed from the waist down in leather pants and fur boots. But it was what he wore upon his head that caused those closest to the doors to leave. On his head and back, he wore the skin of a coyote, and his face was hidden by a mask of leather, with slits for his eyes and mouth.

I'd never seen someone like him, but still I knew. We'd all grown up with the stories, the whispered tales in the dark.

It was the Devourer.

Two male servants staggered forward, each carrying the handle to a wide metal bowl. Liquid sloshed audibly within it as they placed it before the creature. I had the immediate sense that the bowl wasn't filled with water–not with the thick sound it made. My stomach dropped when I got a better look. Blood.

The creature moved forward and bathed his gray hands in the blood until they dripped with red, and the people of the court who remained in the throne room released murmurs of disgust and dismay. It spoke, but its voice was something from the depths of the underworld: whispery as dry leaves, coarse as gravel, harsh and throaty as a raven's call. It was all these things and none, and it covered my arms in goose bumps.

It fell silent, and the blood dripped back into the bowl, each drop hypnotic.

Then it began to sing, the sound hair-raising, the rhythm unusual and irregular. Its voice started out low and soft and quickly gained volume until, amidst his ululations and dripping of the blood, a dark mist spread through the throne room.

A red haze appeared before my eyes, like a veil of blood, and for one terrible moment, it was all I could see. The people around me gasped in shock, and Neo let out a screech. I knew then that we were all trapped in the same enthrallment. I expected to hear my cousin cry out loudest of all. Instead, he laughed.

"Yes," he cried. "Yes! Now you will all see for yourselves what Ozul can do."

The red mist faded; it wasn't the throne room I saw before me. Instead, it was as if I were on Neo's back, soaring high above the earth. I flew down from Crane Mountain, tracing along the spine just above the tops of the highest trees. Foothills spread out before me, and then, just over the flat grasslands of the Equnox Plains, was a small encampment. There was a pavilion—bigger than I'd ever seen—but before I could take a better look, the enthrallment ended as quickly as it began. I stumbled unsteadily as my vision returned to normal.

When I looked at my cousin, his face was one of triumph. "So close," he said to himself. "They've been only a short flight away all this time."

The High Queen of the Children of Earth—the one they called

their Queen of All Queens—had long eluded our scouts. She kept her camp hidden from view with magic. She shielded and healed her people and kept this war never-ending. And now, at last, we had her location.

It was she I had been sent to retrieve, to force a one-sided treaty that would benefit our people only, but I hadn't expected to be blasted out of the sky.

Or for her to be so young.

The girl I encountered may have been the First Daughter instead of the queen, but regardless, my people had to be warned of her power. An ability like that threatened our eagles and could turn the tide of this war against us. I had to warn the emperor.

THE NEXT DAY, just as the edges of my vision took on a weird kaleidoscope effect of red and black, we were favored by the Lord of the Skies. A rider found us, thanks to the sharp eyes of his eagle. When we didn't return that first night, the emperor gave it another day before ordering scouts to search for us. The creek kept us alive with its fresh water, but I was incapable of doing anything but lowering my face into it to drink. I couldn't hunt or fish, and none of the animals of the forest dared venture close enough to Neo to allow themselves to be caught. By the second day, I couldn't even get myself water. I lay helplessly, blood pooling in my gut, while Neo tried to will his wing to heal. The only good thing about the throbbing inside me was that it filled my stomach and made me forget it had been days since I'd last eaten.

"Commander," the scout said to me. I was too busy dying to look up and note who he was. "I'll have to leave you again for a moment so I can locate the other scout. We've brought a cot that will enable our eagles to carry Neo between us. She wasn't far. I won't be gone long." His tone was irritatingly urgent when all I wanted to do was lie here and drift off.

Talon, Neo prodded when the scout stood there waiting for my acknowledgment.

"I'll be here," I finally mumbled, giving the scout the permission he evidently needed to do his damned job.

I couldn't say what happened after that because I closed my eyes to rest them for a minute, and I didn't open them again until I was in a bed in the palace.

A medic dressed in a crisp white robe leaned over me, and I sat up so suddenly I almost slammed my head into his.

Neo's voice was in my head immediately, reassuring me that he was alive and healing.

"Commander, how do you feel?" the medic asked.

I pushed away the blankets that had been piled on top of me and stood. The medic reached out to steady me, but I waved away his assistance, ignoring the nausea coursing through my aching body from the effort it took to remain standing.

"I need to speak to the emperor. Now."

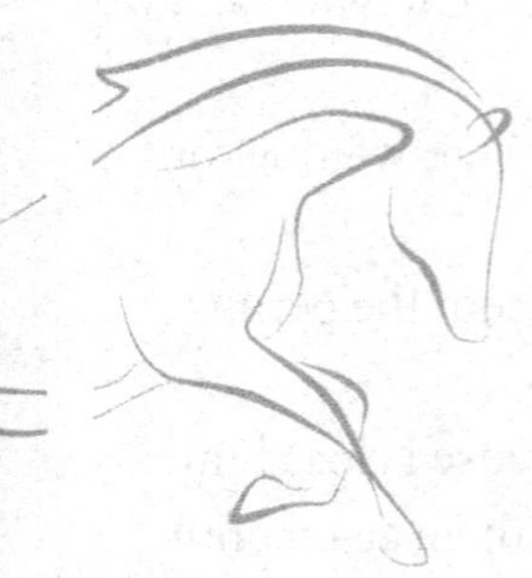

6

ZARA

The first thing I felt when I woke was a velvety-soft nose nuzzling my shoulder.

But it was when the voice flitted through my mind that I jolted fully awake. *Zara, wake up.*

Shazeera?

Shazeera pricked her ears forward and tossed her head in obvious surprise. *You heard me! At last.*

I wasted no time throwing my arms around her neck. With the eyes of General Isa and the others on me, I tried to stifle my sobs knowing that, to them, my actions had no basis.

Shazeera dipped her head to hug me back. *Thank the Mother. I thought I would never be able to speak to you again.*

I'm so sorry, Shazeera. I'll never use that power again–that's what did it, I think. Somehow opening myself to the wind stifled our bond.

"First Daughter," General Isa said gently, "is something wrong?"

I looked up to find all three of them and their horses watching me with rapt curiosity.

"I had a terrible dream," I told General Isa.

She nodded like she had suspected as much. "That's only natural given the eagle attack."

I looked at her in surprise, but then I realized she only meant the eagle and rider who attacked her and her warriors. They still didn't know about my own battle.

"Let's press on," General Isa said. "We have another full day ahead."

As we set out, the weight on my shoulders lifted, the link between Shazeera and me shimmering brightly.

Perhaps the power you channeled only silences our link for a short time.

Short? I thought back incredulously. *It felt like an eternity. I never want to go through anything like that again.*

Shazeera fell silent for a few moments, and I could tell she was turning things over in her mind. Finally, she said, *It was worth it, though, wasn't it? You knocked that monstrous bird right out of the sky.*

It was worth it this *time, and we can say that now that we're safely talking to each other again. How do we know what will happen if I try to use that power again? What if we can't talk to each other for days? Weeks? Or what if it damages our bond permanently?*

There's no way to know what it will do unless you explore the power a little more.

I knew there was wisdom in what she said, but the fear that had lived inside me for the last twenty-four hours still had me in its grip. I thought about the way it had made it difficult to draw breath, too, when I was connected to the vastness of its power. But in the end, it hadn't really hurt me. I had only felt exhausted and physically fatigued.

I had no proof that the wind power I had called upon would do anything worse than make it so Shazeera and I couldn't communicate mentally or make me tired. But I had a terrible feeling deep inside me that the more I used the unknown magic, the greater the risk.

Because the one thing I knew for certain was that magic always had a cost.

AT SUNSET ON the third day of travel, we could finally see the tops of the plateaus that formed the Nazeeran Canyon. I prayed to the Earth Mother that Ama and the others from my camp were already there, safe with Queen Jazela and our other cousins. Queen Jazela came from the Nazeeran line of earth magic users capable of causing massive earthquakes and fissures in the earth. Inspired by the landscape around the Great Twin Plateaus to the west, she had created a split in the earth that formed a massive canyon. That way, even on the relatively flat land of the plains, her people and horses could quickly escape eagle attacks by following paths down into the gorge. The many outcroppings provided cover, and there were caves that had been carved into the sides, where they could hide.

Many generations ago, before the Zephyrians came to our continent, six tribes had spread across the land. Each tribe was descended from a single daughter who had been given an earth magic gift from the Earth Mother. The Angoran tribe in the mountains could find useful minerals and precious gemstones. The Semalian tribe along the coast could transform sand into glass without having to use fire, which made them profitable with the port city merchants. The Nazca tribe in the north grew countless massive trees, creating the Black Forest. In the south, the Faridan tribe grew crops in such abundance they could feed the entire continent year-round. Each tribe had their own queen, the direct descendent of the First Daughter who was given the earth magic gifts from the Earth Mother. But it was the Sorayan tribe—my tribe—whose line produced the Queen of All Queens. This queen always had the power to heal and shield. This was the magic the Earth Mother was known for, and because of that, the Queen of All Queens was revered.

We all lived in harmony, trading resources and sharing our gifts with one another. But when the Zephyrians came, all they wanted was to conquer. Coveted for their gem-seeking abilities, the Angoran tribe were the first to fall. Fifty years later, the Zephyrians decided they needed to expand their eagle nests and conquered the Nazcas of the Black Forest. More time passed, and they spread their empire to the Semalian land on the western coastline, and created a massive settlement near the northeastern port city of Rhythos. Soon, the grassland tribes were surrounded on three sides of the continent. The Zephyrians coveted the land we roamed with our horses, wanting it for more settlements and cities. So the three remaining free tribes—the Sorayans, the Nazeerans, and the Faridan—joined forces, becoming the Children of Earth.

But it wouldn't be long until the Zephyrians overthrew us, too. They'd take over the ancient grasslands that kept our horses fed and force those of us who survived the onslaught into Zephyrian settlements until we lost our culture and ourselves.

As we passed Nazeeran Lake, which bordered one side of the encampment, a trio of riders and a line of warriors came to meet us. When I recognized Ama astride Nafalla in the middle, relief hit me so hard I nearly cried. To see her conscious and riding removed the heavy cloak of fear I'd worn since I last saw her. She didn't look completely recovered—she was still far too pale, and her shoulders slumped like she didn't have the strength to hold herself fully upright–but she wasn't almost lifeless like the last time I had seen her. Queen Jazela and her royal consort, Prince Malik, rode with her. He smiled warmly at me when he caught my eye. The prince and Queen Jazela had been together since I was a baby. This was in contrast to my mother, who had always said she had many suitors before I was born, but there had never been any that I could remember. It wasn't unusual amongst our people not to have a life partner, but lately, I had wondered more and more about the man who sired me.

As Ama rode beside Queen Jazela, the family resemblance was easy to see. Their large dark eyes were framed by long black eyelashes and thick but well-arched eyebrows. Fairly prominent yet elegantly defined noses led to full, bow-shaped lips. And though Ama and I were slightly lighter, we all shared the same golden-toned skin and thick black hair.

Ama immediately dismounted from Nafalla and came to my side as I did the same from Shazeera. She pulled me in for a tight embrace, and I noted with dismay how much weaker her arms felt around me as I breathed in the familiar scent of sage and cloves.

"Thank the Earth Mother for bringing you to me safely." She pressed a kiss to my forehead.

"Are you feeling stronger?" I asked her, taking in her too-pale skin and slightly hunched shoulders. "When did you regain consciousness?"

"Not until the second morning," she admitted, and I frowned. I had never seen my mother lose consciousness before, much less for that long. "Poor Nafalla and the others traveled through the night to keep from disturbing me. It's how we managed to arrive before you, even with everyone forced to go so slowly. But I'm regaining my strength," she said with a little squeeze to my hand when she saw my distraught expression. "Just slower than I would like."

That was the part that concerned me. What if she never fully recovered her strength this time? As that disturbing thought rattled around in my mind, Ama turned to include General Isa in the conversation. "Anything to report?" Ama asked her.

"One Eagle Rider attack, my queen."

Ama's eyes widened, and she stiffened as her gaze jumped from me to General Isa as Queen Jazela sucked in her breath in horror. "You were attacked?"

I opened my mouth to lie that I hadn't been attacked, but General Isa answered for me.

"We sent the First Daughter to safety under cover of trees while we engaged the enemy," General Isa said. "Thankfully we were still close enough to the forests of the foothills to have her run for cover."

Ama looked suddenly much paler. "Thank you all for keeping her safe." She linked her arm through mine, leaning into me a bit.

"What about all of you?" I asked, turning to look more closely at the line of warriors to see if any of them came from our camp. With relief, I recognized Naomi and Kai. "Did everyone get here safely?"

"Yes, you must have drawn the attention of the eagle scouts," Ama said with a frown.

But as horrible and terrifying as the attack from the Eagle Riders had been, I only felt overwhelming gratitude. If they had gone after Ama and the others instead, I knew she wouldn't have survived.

Don't even think about it, Shazeera said with a shudder.

The sound of a rider approaching drew our attention. When I saw who it was, a huge smile stretched across my face.

"Am I too late for the reunion?" Mariyah, Queen Jazela's daughter and my favorite cousin, asked, grinning as she rode over to me on her chestnut mare, Citrine, and dismounted.

"I'm sure we'll be around so long you'll get sick of us," I said with a laugh.

She hugged me tightly. "I wouldn't complain if you stayed forever. We hardly ever get to see each other."

It had already been an entire year since the last time I saw Mariyah. As a rule, the queens tried not to spend much time in the same place. Having two of the queens picked off would be disastrous. Mariyah was already a better heir than I was, having inherited her mother's power of summoning powerful earthquakes. It was to our everlasting regret that our enemy could fly. The infantry was susceptible to it, of course. Queen Jazela had won many battles by asking the earth to swallow whole battalions of soldiers. But the Eagle Riders were formidable. They put Queen Jazela at risk the moment she set foot on the battlefield.

"The pavilion is ready if you'd like to rest," Ama said.

Suddenly, the weight of everything—the terror of being attacked, fleeing from our home, and worst of all, losing contact with Shazeera—settled on me like iron chains. I still felt drained from the encounter with the Eagle Rider, and I wondered if summoning the wind had also taken a toll on my body in the same way my mother's magic drained her. Beside me, Shazeera drooped with exhaustion, too. "I could use a little sleep."

"Rest up, then," Mariyah said with a sympathetic look, "and we'll catch up later."

Ama sensed my change in mood like she always did and kindly led Shazeera and me to where our pavilion had been erected on the banks of the enormous lake that provided the horses with fresh water. To the west, I could just make out the craggy mouth of the Nazeeran Canyon, where it was surrounded on both sides by countless tents and pavilions. We walked through lush grass with horses grazing peacefully. I couldn't see it from here, but I knew the green landscape ended abruptly in scrubland and rocky soil that led to the Great Twin Plateaus and Little Mesa. The grass surrounding the canyon was lush for our horses thanks to Queen Samira in the south, who had used her earth magic to create this oasis for our people.

As I entered the cool, dim interior, my shoulders relaxed . . . until I caught sight of the map of Equnox. Sucking in a breath, I moved closer to it.

"The battlegrounds have spread this far south?" I asked, trepidation making my hands shake as I pointed to the red flags spread across our land.

With the Zephyrian territories marked, it was easy to see how much of our continent had been swallowed by their empire. They ruled over the Angora Mountains and Ridgeline Foothills to the east, the Black Forest to the north, and the coastal port city of Rhythos in the northeast. With the Modavian Sea to the east, our territory had shrunk to the grasslands in the middle and southern parts of the continent. To protect our people, we kept the battlegrounds to the north near the Black Forest, hundreds of miles from our encampments. But this map showed we were losing ground.

Soon, they would threaten Queen Jazela's canyon city, where the majority of our people took refuge.

Ama leveled her gaze at me, and there was so much in that look. She was the Queen of All Queens of a people on the brink of extinction. If we didn't all die in battle, then we would be assimilated by the Zephyrian Empire, losing our ability to live a nomadic life, to follow our horses across the Equnox Plains. "Yes," she said. "We don't have much longer."

And I knew what she meant. We didn't have much longer as a people if I couldn't manifest the power to shield us. With our power combined, we might have the strength to cover the plains and keep the Zephyrians out. The wards would repel eagles and infantry alike.

Looking at the map reminded me of what Ama had said before. That the world had once been full of different types of magic.

"Ama, when you said there were magic lines that still exist, how is that possible?"

"I only meant that the world once had different types of magic. Some of those ancient magic bloodlines may have even made their way into the people of this continent through the port cities long ago, but none of them were as powerful as earth magic, so they didn't matter."

"So there are others in the world with magic?" I asked, feeling like my entire worldview was being turned upside down.

She shrugged one shoulder. "Perhaps. At one time, yes." She reached out and touched my cheek. "But you are tired. We can talk about this later. Just rest now." She pressed a kiss on my forehead and turned to leave.

Thoughts raced around in my mind. Ama didn't know what the wind power could do—what would she say if she knew what had happened with the Eagle Rider?

"Ama." I craved that comfort and reassurance only a mother could give, but when she paused and looked back at me, the words evaporated off my tongue. I couldn't tell her yet. I didn't want to see the disappointment when she found out I truly couldn't channel the Earth Mother's power. For surely what happened with the wind proved that I had no connection to the earth like all the women in my line before me. I couldn't even begin to fathom the gravity of what this revelation meant.

I shook my head. "It's nothing."

She gave me that look that told me she knew that wasn't true, but she must have taken pity on the fact that I was too tired to get into it. "I love you, Zara, and I'm glad you're here safe." She laid a hand gently on Shazeera's neck and then ducked back out of the pavilion.

Without another word to each other, Shazeera and I moved to one of the bedrooms off the main space of the tent and collapsed onto a bed of azure silken pillows. Shazeera lay down beside me on a plush rug, and as I listened to her deep breaths, I knew one thing was true. I would never do anything to risk our bond again.

7

TALON

In the end, trying to get out of bed to speak to the emperor when I had internal bleeding had proved impossible. I took two steps before crashing into the medic like a falling tree. After a thorough scolding, he made me get back into bed and dosed me with a drug that made me sleep.

My injuries made it difficult at times to tell dreams from reality. Too often, I found myself flying on Neo's back, headed toward the battlefields in northern Zephyrus. One battle stood out amongst all the others, my mind insisting on reliving it many times.

I dreamed of kneeling on Neo's back, his powerful wings buffeting hard against the air current, each movement reverberating through me. The wind rushed past my ears with a roar, tearing at my hair like some wild thing. We were flying hard and fast back to the battlefields after meeting with the emperor at the palace.

Emperor Altair frequently called me from the battlefields I was supposed to be commanding to ask for my advice. He did this not because he needed my counsel, but rather because I had become something of a security blanket for him, easing his ever-present anxiety. Though lately, even I had been unable to stave off his crippling fear of failure.

We had wasted days I didn't have at the palace, when I should have been launching another offensive march from the Shendayah River Outpost to capture more ground from the Children of Earth. Slowly but steadily, we were taking over the Mid-Plains and pushing the Children farther south. Eventually, they would have nowhere left to go.

The wind became more turbulent, and Neo pumped his wings harder in answer. Muscles in my legs burned as I fought the torrents of wind that threatened to wrench me from his back. Ropes of tendons stood out in my arms as I held tight to the pommel of the flat piece of horse leather that served as a saddle—though I wouldn't dare call it that in front of Neo. In truth, it scarcely shared resemblance to a saddle for ordinary beasts, as it was wide and flat and meant for protecting Neo's feathers. We soared higher, finally breaking free of the powerful current, and I released my hold on the pommel. With the wind no longer roaring in my ears like a monster come to life, I could hear my own heart thundering in my chest as it always did when we soared high above the earth.

Once we reached the Black Forest, we turned to the south and followed the Shendayah River. After half a day's flight, we approached our southernmost outpost. With towering walls made of hardwood, the Shendayah River Outpost's rectangular base held three thousand soldiers with room for fifty Eagle Riders. We had ten other bases to house our army of thirty thousand. Even with so many soldiers, we were constantly having to recruit men and women from our conquered lands, as the army was susceptible to the devastating earthquake attacks the Children of Earth unleashed on them.

But as the outpost's wooden walls came into view, a jolt of surprise went through Neo and traveled through my legs.

What is it? I asked, knowing he could see much farther than I could.

Flying arrows, he said. *This outpost is engaged in battle.*

My mind raced through scenarios. As I was the one coming with orders to launch an offensive attack, this meant Lieutenant Callum had engaged in battle with the enemy in defense of the outpost.

Let's get a better view of it, I told Neo.

We soared over the empty outpost as Neo climbed higher and higher, gaining altitude so we could get a full view of the battle. Once Neo was level with the clouds, he glided in circles over the land below.

I took stock of the situation grimly. The first thing I noticed was the enormous fissures in the earth, deep and wide enough to swallow whole platoons of infantry. Our soldiers stood on one side of the opening in the ground, while the Children of Earth's cavalry stood on the other. They outnumbered us by nearly a thousand soldiers. The armies traded arrows on both sides of the fissure, but for now, it was creating a natural barrier. The ten Eagle Riders had split into five groups of two and were engaged in battles of their own on the other side of the opening in the earth.

How many earth magic wielders? I asked Neo.

One, he replied after a moment spent scanning the battle below. Through our connection, he sent me what he could see. The earth magic wielder was protected from aerial attacks by a copse of trees and surrounded by a small squad of cavalry.

Already lost a platoon, Neo added, scanning the fissures. Soldiers lay at the bottom, broken and bleeding, if not dead already.

Even with an earth magic wielder present, we should have mounted a superior defense with the outpost's Eagle Riders. But as we scanned the skies below, we counted only ten. There should have been fifty.

Where is Captain Suna? I demanded.

Not here. This is what happens when you promote someone simply because her father was a great leader, Neo said with an air of disgust.

Skies knew I agreed with him, but this wasn't the time to point fingers. *Then let's find Lieutenant Callum.*

After a moment scanning the ground, Neo's gaze was drawn by the golden scales of the lieutenant's breastplate, which caught the light. The emperor insisted that each and every officer–and palace guard–dressed in full golden armor whenever on duty, which always seemed excessive at best and ridiculous at worst. My own black leather armor was rustic in comparison, consisting of only a breastplate, pauldrons, and greaves atop cotton and wool. A breeze rushed over me then, rustling the feathers that covered my pauldrons, the ones given to me by Neo himself, designating my rank as an Eagle Rider.

Neo's great talons scraped across the dirt as he touched down at the back of the platoon. I slid from his back, landing with a solid *thunk* of my boots. It was a long way down–Neo was one of the biggest eagles in our aerial army. Though I was considered tall myself, I only reached the bottom of his wing.

"Commander Ramses," Lieutenant Callum said, making his hand into a fist and placing it over his heart in deference to my rank. The squad members who flanked him did the same. "I am relieved and honored to see you, sir."

"Neo and I were surprised to see you engaged in battle this afternoon, Lieutenant. We came straight from the palace with orders for offensive maneuvers, but it seems like you're already on the defensive."

"Yes, Commander. They attacked two hours ago."

I scanned the battleground before us. "How long ago did the earth magic wielder open the fissure?"

"Forty-five minutes," Lieutenant Callum said grimly.

My gaze shifted to the copse of trees that hid the earth magic user. "Another earthquake will be coming soon."

The lieutenant nodded, jaw tense. He knew the Children of Earth took an average of an hour to recharge their ability and unleash another devastating earthquake that ripped apart the ground. Thankfully we didn't seem to be dealing with a royal, who could release wave after wave of attacks before finally needing to replenish their magic.

"You're also light on Eagle Riders."

"Yes, Commander."

"Where is Captain Suna?" I asked.

"Captain Suna does not inform me of the aerial cavalry's movements," he said stiffly, "though I understand she outranks me."

"She is still required to keep you apprised of their movements so that you can plan accordingly."

"I have found they don't always follow protocol, Commander."

Captain Suna never had respect for the army soldiers, and now it has cost lives, I said to Neo.

This wasn't unheard of when it came to many of the Eagle Riders. The former emperor had made it clear that those who had the ability to bond with eagles were superior to those who couldn't, and they should be treated as such. My father's words about being an Eagle Rider drifted through my mind: *There is no greater calling or responsibility than our bond to our eagles, not be-*

cause we are better than our fellow man, but rather because we must use our strength to protect the empire.

Many Eagle Riders still felt the same as my father, but there were also those who believed they were second only to the Lord of the Skies himself and should be treated as such. Captain Suna was of the latter.

Neo puffed up the feathers of his neck, like a wolf raising its hackles. *Then it's time she answers for it.*

Agreed. But first, we must win this battle.

To Lieutenant Callum I said, "I want your platoons working to flank them on the left and right. I will send for reinforcements from Chimney Rock Outpost."

"Understood, Commander."

He saluted me, and I gave a terse nod before turning to Neo. After pulling myself into position between his wings, I called down to the lieutenant. "I'm sorry for the loss of your soldiers. You will have the protection guaranteed by the Eagle Riders—even if I have to remove Captain Suna."

His eyebrows rose slightly, and even his tone was taken aback. "Thank you, Commander."

Neo spread his massive wings, and Lieutenant Callum and his squad of soldiers hurried out of the way to avoid being buffeted by the wind. Neo launched us into the sky.

Should we fly to the Chimney Rock Outpost? Neo asked.

No, I said, *we need to lend assistance to the Eagle Riders under attack here so that we can free up one of the lower-ranking riders to go instead.*

Understood, Neo said, already scanning the battlefield.

We flew over the fissure toward the nearest Eagle Rider team, which was currently battling several squads of cavalry.

With talons extended and my bow drawn, we joined Aras

and his eagle, Baran, as they guarded the right wing of Baz and his eagle, Storm. The sounds of war, of shouting warriors and screaming horses, enveloped us. I fired arrow after arrow as Neo swooped over an entire squad, knocking horses to the ground or into the fissure their own earth magic wielder had created. The cavalry retaliated with spears and arrows, but Neo was the best flier on the continent.

He evaded and rolled, his strong feathers repelling the arrowheads easily. When we flew close enough, I struck with my own spear, killing riders within reach. Neo, Baran, and Storm formed a loose triangle with the remaining squads in the middle. The six of us coordinated our attacks so that the eagles dove with talons outstretched from three different sides, preventing the remaining squads of horses and riders from being able to successfully fire their bows. The horses reared, their eyes rolling in their heads as our eagles descended, tearing through flesh and throwing them to the ground. Simultaneously, Aras, Baz, and I attacked the riders with our bows, firing an onslaught of arrows. Combined with the aerial attack of our eagles, it only took two sweeps before the squads were destroyed.

More squads would replace them, though. They had the advantage of numbers, and I needed to change that. Rapidly.

Before the dust settled, I turned to Aras. "I need you to send for reinforcements from Chimney Rock Outpost. We'll win this battle in the next two hours with their help."

"Yes, Commander!" he shouted, and Baran took off like lightning across the sky.

The earth magic wielder will have recharged her power by now, Neo said, hovering far enough above the battlefield that no arrows could reach us.

If we kill her, this battle will be over, I said.

We both scanned the copse of trees, looking for an opening, but the magic wielder was well guarded.

Infantry to the west needs assistance, Neo reported.

I shifted my weight in the saddle. *Let's go.*

With a few powerful pumps of his wings, Neo shot across the battlefield toward the western side of the fissure. He used his momentum to swoop down on a squad, slamming his talons into the nearest horse's chest as wind from his wings buffeted them so powerfully that they stumbled to the ground. Shouts rang out as soldiers pushed forward, cutting down enemy riders from their fallen horses. Two other Eagle Riders lent their strength, and the infantry made it around the western edge of the fissure, forcing the enemy back.

The mounted riders turned and galloped south, and our soldiers pursued. But just as we made strides in flanking them, the earth beneath the soldiers' feet rumbled ominously.

Men shouted and scrambled over one another, desperately trying to get away from the earthquake. They were only seconds from it splitting open and swallowing them. Lieutenant Callum called orders from his position on the other side of the fissure, for the soldiers to move toward the enemy cavalry who would be in the safe zone.

The rumbling sound gave way to an explosive crack, and the ground split, yawning like an open grave. Neo and the other eagles dove, grabbing as many soldiers as they could and throwing them away from the new fissure, but there were too many to save. Another two hundred soldiers plummeted to their deaths before they could be snatched away from the edge.

Without even having to ask Neo, he changed direction and flew toward the copse of trees that shielded the earth magic wielder. He circled the trees, his sharp eyes seeking an opening.

A barrage of arrows forced Neo to fly higher, and he screeched down at them in defiance.

We can't get to them from above, so let's push from below, I said. *Call another eagle. We need to break through those guards.*

I'll summon Storm. He is the most capable flier.

Storm and Baz were veterans of the sky alongside Neo and me, and we'd fought side by side enough to move as one. No orders were needed.

The moment Storm appeared alongside Neo, I nodded at Baz. In the next instant, our eagles dove in unison. I stayed flush against the saddle to reduce wind disturbance, and so the sheer force of speed wouldn't rip me off his back. Just before they hit the ground, the eagles pulled up and surged toward the enemy guards.

I drew my bow but held my position.

They waited for us behind a wall of spearheads pointed right at us, but they were no match for the eagles' talons and powerful momentum. We slammed into the horses like a battering ram, causing cataclysmic injury. Storm created an insurmountable wave behind us that barreled through the other cavalry warriors who had managed to stay standing through Neo's onslaught. In this way, we punched a hole through their defensive line.

With my bow drawn, I waited for the moment when the warriors around the earth magic wielder fell. Two still stood in front of her, their spears drawn. Neo's wings buffeted them as he hovered in place, and the horses reared in the face of the powerful gusts.

I still don't have an opening, I said to Neo, tamping down my frustration.

Then I'll make one, he said and lashed out with his deadly talons.

He connected with the horse on the left side of the earth magic wielder, tearing into its neck and spraying blood in a torrent. Both horse and rider screamed as the force of the blow knocked the horse to its knees. In that moment, the earth magic wielder was exposed.

Her dark eyes widened in shock, and too late, her horse tried to turn away and flee.

I loosed my arrow, and it flew straight and true, piercing the wielder's leather breastplate and tearing through her heart. She slumped forward on her horse. Relief joined the blood pumping hot through my veins at the thought that we had saved our soldiers from another attack.

Neo soared over the carnage we'd wrought, flying higher and higher until we could see the entire battlefield laid out before us.

Something has happened to Lieutenant Callum, Neo said after a moment of turning his sharp eyes on the field below.

I looked around the area I had last seen him, and found him on the ground, surrounded by soldiers.

An arrow found its mark, I said grimly. *Let's hope he has time to be transported to a medic.*

Neo immediately flew to the other side of the fissure and landed. The soldiers parted as I slid down from Neo's back and ran to Lieutenant Callum. An arrow protruded from his chest. I knelt beside him, quickly taking stock of his injuries. He struggled to breathe, frothy blood on his lips as he lay prostrate on the ground.

"His lung is punctured," I said to the nearest soldier. "He needs immediate care by a medic."

"Yes, Commander," the soldier said, watching the lieutenant with wide eyes.

"I'll send for one of the Eagle Riders to fly him to the next closest outpost," I announced, but suddenly, Lieutenant Callum grabbed my arm.

"Trust *you*," he said, his gaze desperately holding mine. "Please," he said, but uttering the word took a toll on him. He closed his eyes, breathing harshly.

"We'll fly you to the Chimney Rock Outpost," I said.

He managed a slight nod, and then the soldiers lifted him up on a travois. The pain must have been unbearable. He lost consciousness almost immediately. Neo laid himself nearly flush to the ground so that they could more easily attach the travois to the back of the saddle. They made quick work of strapping him down so that he lay across Neo's back, directly behind me.

Low and smooth, I told Neo.

He ruffled the feathers of his neck. *No need to tell* me *how to fly.*

I'm just helpfully reminding you of our mortally wounded passenger.

He turned his head and snapped his beak in a sign of irritation. *Hold on to our passenger, then, because I'm taking off.*

But before he could, a cry rang out around us. I looked to the skies. Aras led a battalion of fifty Eagle Riders. When the enemy cavalry saw them, their horses screamed a warning, but it wasn't one of challenge. The horses turned tail and galloped away with their riders, the sound thunderous across the fissure.

"Pursue them," I told Baz, "but do not engage. Follow them until they have returned to their own territory."

"Yes, Commander," he said, and his eagle immediately flew to intercept the others.

I returned my attention to Lieutenant Callum. "Whatever happens now, Lieutenant," I told him as he still lay unconscious, "you won this battle."

And soon, Neo added, *we will win the war.*

8

ZARA

I slept through that afternoon, evening, and into the next morning. At some point, Shazeera had left to graze. Just the thought of food had my stomach growling loudly, and I found that someone had kindly left an arrangement of small plates on a tray containing my favorite breakfast foods: sun-dried fruit, bread, soft cheese, and a small silver pot of hot tea. I ate ravenously, pushing all thoughts aside and focusing on my physical needs. They pushed against the walls of my mind like a violent sandstorm, but I refused to acknowledge them.

After eating, I desperately wanted a bath. The cool fresh water of the lake would feel incredible, but for now, I cleaned my body with a soft cloth and perfumed water from my porcelain basin. I changed into a leather-and-gemstone bodice that stopped just short of my belly button, leather leggings, and tall boots. Choosing one of my simpler headpieces, with strands of silver chains and turquoise beads that hung down over my hair and forehead, I pulled my thick hair into a knot at the base of my neck.

When I pushed through the silk that separated my room from

the rest of the pavilion, I saw Ama in the main room with Dani beside her. Ama's eyes were closed, and Dani had her hand on Ama's forehead. Unease churned inside me at the sight of it. It meant my mother still hadn't recovered.

"Are you feeling unwell?" I asked Ama, coming to her side.

She gave me a wan smile. "Just fatigued. It's taking me longer to recover this time."

"Using that much magic at once put a strain on your mother's body," Dani said with a glance at me. "Especially her heart."

A cold sweat broke out over my skin at her words, and I swallowed hard. Losing the wards was bad enough, but if it cost my mother her life . . .

I couldn't even let myself think such thoughts.

"Can you recover?" I asked Ama.

Ama was quiet for a moment. "We don't have prior experience to draw on, so there's no way to know."

Her words cut deep even though she hadn't meant to hurt me. "Meaning no First Daughter has been unable to replenish the queen's energy—until me."

"This is true, but only right now. We don't know what the future holds."

Her kind tone didn't do anything to stop the burn of shame that spread through my body like wildfire. Tears of frustration abruptly filled my eyes, and I turned away, unwilling to let Ama and Dani see them. I didn't deserve their comfort.

Ama called my name as I hurried out of the pavilion, but I didn't stop. Shazeera came immediately to my side from where she had been grazing near the lake.

Your mother is descended from the strongest line. She will recover, Shazeera told me confidently.

Yes, but when? I thought again of the map I had seen when we first arrived, of the Zephyrians pushing ever closer to the Nazeeran Canyon. *It could be too late.*

Shazeera swished her tail nervously. She knew I had a point.

"Zara," a voice called, and I turned to find Mariyah and Citrine riding toward us. "You're finally awake! I was about to come and wake you up myself. Would you like to go for a swim in the lake?"

Despite everything that was happening–the flight from our camp, worry over Ama's inability to maintain the wards, and the strange wind power I had manifested–the mere suggestion of going for a simple swim put a smile on my face. "I've honestly never wanted to do anything more."

We turned and headed for the lake just beyond my pavilion, passing many guards and grazing horses. Queen Jazela had created the lake soon after splitting the earth to form the canyon, and it stretched on for miles. The feat of strength must have been staggering to watch.

It was only a short ride, and the lake spread out before us, its dark water sparkling and inviting as gentle waves licked the shore. Mariyah and I wasted no time stripping down to our underclothes and wading into it. Shazeera and Citrine joined, walking in deep enough for the water to reach their bellies.

"I brought you some soap." Mariyah handed over a thick, creamy brick of it. "You look like you could use it."

I laughed as I started scrubbing my arms, turning the suds brown. "I can't argue with you there. Apparently, I'm filthy."

My hair was worse, and since it was so long and thick, I had to wash it several times before the soap could penetrate to my scalp. Mariyah washed herself, too, just not as vigorously as I was forced to.

When we finished, we floated peacefully on our backs, our

eyes shaded by low-hanging branches. "I'm really glad you and Queen Rana came," Mariyah said. "I was so relieved to see you ride into camp."

I reached my hand out and touched hers in the water. "I'm glad, too."

She smiled at me, but then her eyes seemed shadowed. "I think we're all safer together, especially in light of what your mother and mine were talking about before you got here."

"What do you mean?" I shifted so my feet were now in the soft sand of the lake and I could see her better.

"They sensed that the Zephyrians used magic to find your camp."

A jolt of horror ran through me. "They don't have magic."

"This is definitely new," she said, treading water. "But the worst part is, it's a magic they've never sensed before."

"Then where did it come from?"

"No one knows–it shouldn't be possible," Mariyah said as a chill spread throughout my body. "Whoever it was had enough power to overcome your mother's shields."

My skin erupted in goose bumps, though the water hadn't changed temperature. "So that's how they found our camp."

"That must have been so scary when you were attacked," she said, and Citrine snorted an agreement. "We keep hearing horrible things from the battles"–she glanced behind her at the guards in the distance before dropping her voice even lower–"like that the riders have been allowing their eagles to *eat* our horses."

Both Shazeera and Citrine shuddered violently. I had heard the same thing from warriors on the front lines reporting to Ama and General Isa. All I could think about was how close that eagle's talons came to ripping into Shazeera's haunches. If it hadn't been for the wind . . .

"This war has to end." I felt sick at the thought of all the losses—both of our people and our horses.

"Queen Samira keeps saying we need a peace treaty," Mariyah said.

Samira was queen of the Faridan line of earth magic users and ruled over the southern Equnox Plains. She was the third member of the alliance that made up the Children of Earth. She had the weaker, but still important, ability of channeling the Earth Mother to encourage crops to grow, no matter the conditions. Her tribe provided all the crops needed to supply the warriors, but she rarely left the southern territory.

"It's not like we haven't tried! We've seen what happens when the Zephyrians take over a territory. They build cities and completely raze what was originally there. We already can't migrate the way our ancestors did with our horses. If they seized the grasslands and built cities, we would lose all our ancestral land."

"They would let Queen Samira keep the southern plains, though," Mariyah said with an edge to her voice. "Her crops are too valuable to raze and replace with cities instead."

And no doubt Samira would make sure she would continue to profit under Zephyrian rule. Already her territory brought in wagons of silver and gold through her lucrative trade with the port city of Rhythos. Ama had always said that Queen Samira only allied herself with us because the Zephyrians would force her to pay too high a percentage of her profits were they to take over her land.

"I shouldn't judge her, honestly," I said—mostly to myself. "At least she contributes something to our people."

Mariyah shot me a sympathetic look. "Still no powers?"

Tell her, Shazeera said. *Mariyah has always been trustworthy.*

Yes, but I don't even understand it myself.

"I haven't heard the Earth Mother's voice even once," I admitted to Mariyah, "much less been able to heal."

"It could still happen," Mariyah said, her tone full of positivity that I just couldn't relate to.

"Only you and Shazeera believe that at this point."

Shazeera flicked her ears back at me and tossed her head.

"Well, you should listen, because we're both very wise," Mariyah said with a lofty grin.

Easy for you to say, I thought and then immediately felt guilty. It wasn't Mariyah's fault her powers had manifested early. Technically she was right that I would have abilities—just nothing like what I was supposed to have.

We both fell silent after that, casually paddling in the cool water, or floating lazily on our backs. Nearby, our horses stood in the shallow part of the lake and grazed on the plants that grew at the water's edge.

I nearly fell asleep, floating on my back, when suddenly, the breeze changed. Where before it was light, it now blew hard enough to create waves on the water. Cold spread through me, and I sat up to look at Mariyah. Strangely, the water around her was unaffected, and when she turned toward me, not a hair on her head stirred. The wind blew strongly in my ears, pushing me from all directions. It felt like a hand on my back, urging me out of the water.

"Mariyah," I hedged, unsure how to tell her I felt uneasy because of the change in the wind, "I think we should head back."

She opened her mouth to reply, but a flock of birds took flight so violently from the branches of the trees surrounding us, that it interrupted her and drew the horses' attention.

Zara, Shazeera said in my mind, and there was a note of anxiety that mirrored my own. *I hear wings beating. Giant wings.*

No, I thought, *they never come here. We're too far south.*

A breeze swirled around me then, lifting the ends of my hair, and I knew . . . I knew they were coming. Mariyah and I followed our horses out of the lake, leaving in a torrent of water. We dressed hurriedly, and my fingers shook as I pulled on my clothes.

In the distance, I heard a sound that made me freeze. My inadequate human ears couldn't quite pick it up, but Shazeera's could, and the sound ripped through my mind as she transferred it to me.

It was a giant eagle's screech. And it was rapidly followed by another. And another.

Get on, Shazeera said. *Now.*

I swung myself astride as Mariyah did the same beside me. Back toward the canyon, I could see the warriors and guards scrambling to arm themselves and mount up.

Suddenly, the pounding of hooves rang out as Kamil carried General Isa to our side. "First Daughters, you must follow me to the safety of the canyon. We will soon be under attack." She handed us bows and quivers of arrows. I tried to hide my shaking hands as I took them.

We turned to look at the canyon in the distance. It was only two miles away, but right now, it seemed impossibly far.

Some of the guards who had been stationed closest to the lake now came to General Isa, led by Naomi. "We await your command, General," Naomi said with a quick bow.

General Isa turned to Naomi. "I want you and your battalion to scout for eagles. If you find them, engage. We need to lead them away from the settlement. I will take the daughters to safety."

They saluted her and galloped away. I watched them go with my heart in my throat.

The five remaining guards surrounded us as General Isa took the lead. "We'll ride for camp. If the eagles should find us, keep going. The guards and I will draw them away from you."

Mariyah and I shared a look, her eyes wide and panicked. I couldn't even let myself think of that scenario.

"Where are our mothers and Prince Malik?" I asked. "Are they safe?"

"They're deep inside the canyon by now, which is where I must get *you*—now let's go!"

As one, the horses took off at a gallop for camp. Their hoofbeats were thunderous, and the wind whipped Shazeera's mane into my face. As fear turned my insides into a quivering mass of snakes, I tried to convince myself the eagles were only passing through and hadn't even discovered us. Maybe we would make it back and never even encounter them.

That was when Shazeera heard the beat of wings in the distance, the sound of men and women shouting to be heard above the wind. She passed what she heard along to me through our link, and my mouth went dry.

Shouts of men meant these were Eagle Riders—no hope now that we had only heard wild eagles in the distance—and we still had over a mile to go.

The other horses had detected the sound, too, and were flicking their ears nervously. General Isa turned and shouted back to us, "We continue for the canyon. They may not have spotted us yet."

Our horses lengthened their strides even more, their hooves barely touching the ground before launching us forward again. All eight of us flew over the earth like we had wings.

But I knew it wouldn't be enough. I had seen for myself how

fast the eagles were. How they fell upon you like a meteor from the sky.

The wind whispered in my ears again, stronger this time, and I could almost hear it encouraging me to call upon it again, how easily I could knock the eagles and their riders down to earth.

You may have to call on the wind, Shazeera said.

Remembering how torturous it had been to not communicate with Shazeera still made my mind cloud with terror. Worse was the fear that it would be a permanent condition. I couldn't lose my bond with my heart's sister. I'd rather die. *No, I won't risk that again.*

Better to risk our ability to communicate than to watch daughters and horses be killed, Shazeera said. Before I could answer, she added, *They're coming.* Mariyah's mare turned her head in the direction of the sound, too.

That's when I looked up and saw an eagle and its rider streaking toward us out of the sky.

9

ZARA

"Go now!" General Isa shouted to Mariyah and me before her horse spun around to face the eagle and its rider along with the other guards.

Shazeera carried me toward the canyon, Mariyah's mare keeping pace beside us. Over a mile away, the settlement swarmed with frantic activity as people and horses hurried into the gorge. A line of mounted warriors fanned out around the canyon, protecting the people from the imminent attack. We just had to make it behind that line.

I dared to look back, and as I did, I let out a cry that was probably exactly what a small, helpless animal sounded like in the face of a stalking predator. Another eagle and rider had joined the first.

"Zara," Mariyah said, her voice strangled, and I turned to look at her just as Shazeera slid to a jarring halt.

A third eagle and its rider hovered just in front of us.

It was a female rider, thin and leanly muscular, her hair slicked back in a tight bun. Her face lacked any emotion—no sneer, no dark threat of violence, nothing. It was like we were so beneath her notice as any sort of threat that she couldn't even form an emotional response. I froze, muscles completely paralyzed as goose bumps rose like tiny warnings over my arms.

I couldn't even articulate *this is bad* to Shazeera. My mind just sent her various images of fleeing until she could no longer run anymore. One eagle and rider pair was bad enough, but three? There was no hope of escape.

I pushed down that terror and, in one swift movement, drew back my bow. Mariyah did the same. Before I took another breath, I let the arrow fly, straight at the eagle's breast. Beside me, Mariyah fired her arrow. The arrows blurred, and I knew the eagle wouldn't have time to dodge—they were far too close.

With a resounding *thunk*, the eagle caught both arrows with its talons.

I cried out, my gaze flying to the rider's, but she was still cold, emotionless. And then the eagle dove toward us.

Mariyah's earthquake ability would do nothing against the eagle in the air, but I knew that wasn't her only offensive power. Her hands lifted as her face took on an expression of intense concentration. She may not have had access to the massive boulders we would find west in the scrublands, but there were still plenty of stones to do considerable damage. The ground around us began to shake as all the rocks within a hundred-foot radius of us rose up. Fifty rocks the size of horse hooves flew at the eagle at such a high velocity that they struck it from the sky. It landed in an explosive heap of wings and scattered feathers, pinning its rider beneath it.

"That was incredible, Mariyah!" I told her as the horses continued unimpeded toward the canyon.

She grinned back at me, but then her face quickly took on a mask of terror. "On your left!"

I had only a breath of time to throw myself down low on Shazeera's back. Mariyah did the same, until we were both nearly hanging off the right sides of our horses. As soon as we had thrown ourselves down, the massive eagle flew over, the wind from its wings ripping at our hair and clothes.

Our horses slid to an abrupt stop, grass and debris flying up beneath their hooves. When we pulled ourselves upright again, I froze in fear as two eagles and their riders cut off our path to the canyon. Mariyah's face paled, but she raised her hands again, summoning the rock storm.

Now that Mariyah had used her power, the Eagle Rider anticipated it and immediately fired a crossbow at her. I screamed a warning, and Citrine jumped out of the way at the last moment. With a cry, Mariyah grabbed hold of her ear, which was now pouring blood. The arrow had nicked Mariyah's ear instead of her neck.

With our path to the canyon blocked, the horses were forced back toward General Isa and the guards who were struggling against three other eagles. Far in the distance, near the lake, I saw Naomi's battalion facing off against their own Eagle Riders. I saw a flash of their battle before my attention was dragged back to the enemies threatening us. Naomi had summoned a wave of hardened earth to hurl against the bird of prey with a guttural yell.

There were so many of the massive creatures–at least ten of them–that they blotted out the sun. A yawning chasm opened inside me as I thought about how deadly only *one* eagle with its rider was. I remembered stories of battle I'd been told before, how the riders let their eagles prey upon the horses. How no one was left alive.

General Isa and her warriors surrounded us, trying to keep us safe within a circle of drawn weapons. Very soon, though, each warrior was locked in a deadly battle with an eagle and its rider.

The eagle closest to General Isa let out a piercing screech and dove, talons outstretched. General Isa struck with swift precision, her spear flashing as her mare pivoted to not only the eagle, but the rider's spear as well.

General Isa stretched her hands toward the sky, her face contorted with rage as Kamil reared. A terrible screech rent the air, and the eagle closest to the general plummeted from above. The impact shook the earth.

I had never seen it used in battle before, but I knew instantly she had unleashed a wave of agony to knock the bird out of the sky. It was incredible to witness, though the ability had limits. She could target only one victim at a time, and it drained a large amount of energy. She likely wouldn't be able to cause that level of pain again right away.

I lost track of her battle when an eagle to my left attacked. Two guards came to my defense, and the sound of their swords making contact with talons and the Eagle Rider's spear rang out over the hillside. Across from me, the third Eagle Rider attacked the guards trying to protect Mariyah.

My eyes darted from battle to battle as I tried in vain to find an opening. There was too much chaos, too much movement. And I wasn't skilled enough. I was just as likely to hit an ally as an enemy.

And then the most terrible sound cut through the cacophony of blades and talons and beaks. The scream of an injured horse. A gray stallion crashed to the ground, blood pouring from his throat where it had been torn open by a powerful beak. Before the other guards could come to the daughter's aid, the Eagle Rider speared her through the heart. She fell dead upon her horse.

They will kill us all, I thought as a cold trickle of horror washed over me.

You've encountered a skilled Eagle Rider before, Shazeera said. *You brought it down with a force not even the eagles could withstand.*

I tightened my grip on her mane. *I won't use that power again. We don't know what the consequences of it might be.*

Well, we do *know the consequences if you do nothing. We will all be picked off by the eagles one by one. There are too many of them.*

Before I could argue, the eagle closest to us dove again, talons outstretched. A mare screamed, and a terrible clang of metal on metal sounded as a daughter's sword met an Eagle Rider's. General Isa shouted at the rest of us to hold our formation as she tried to lend aid to the daughter, and I continued to fire arrows, useless though I knew it to be, just to keep the other Eagle Riders distracted.

The eagle's talons rent the flesh of the mare until she collapsed in a heap. General Isa lunged with her spear, piercing the rider's side. The rider let out a ragged cry, and the eagle she rode immediately shot into the sky, carrying its rider out of the range of our weapons.

The other Eagle Riders took that moment to launch a full-scale attack, dodging our arrows and swords, and tearing into horses and daughters alike. The smell of blood and the sharp tang of fear and sweat filled the air. Many fell around us. It seemed like everyone was dying—like none of us would be left standing.

Zara, you must, Shazeera said as I reached for my last arrow.

The wind picked up, snatching at my hair and clothes like an insistent child. I wanted to push it away.

And then Mariyah's voice pierced the chaos—a raw, desperate cry that cut through me like a blade.

My head snapped in her direction, only to watch her barely fending off a rider with another wave of rocks—the effort much weaker than before as she lost strength.

Call upon me, the wind whispered.

A sob escaped my mouth, and my tears were blown away by the wind. *Shazeera,* I said.

Do it, she replied. *Our bond is stronger than this.*

The wind swirled still stronger around me, buffeting my ears, and I knew I only had to reach deep inside myself and access that power.

Mariyah's mare reared, her flinty hooves striking out against the eagle, but she was knocked easily to the ground. She and Mariyah struggled to get up.

The eagle reached for Mariyah, and I raised my eyes to the heavens.

"No!" I shouted, my arms outstretched. I sank deep inside my own mind, searching for that colossal power that hid itself within me. Faster than it had before, the wind answered my call. I begged it to save my cousin, to destroy my enemies.

One moment, the wind filled my ears, threatening to burst my eardrums, and the next, eagles and their riders were caught in a dark cyclone of power.

The sun shone brightly, not a cloud in the sky, but the cyclone as black as a thunderstorm swallowed them up. The howls of the wind were so loud that if the riders shrieked in terror, no one could hear them.

I held my arms high as the power drained away my energy. My heart beat so hard in my chest it felt like it would burst. Every muscle in my body shook with fatigue. But I didn't dare break the connection–not until the Zephyrians had been defeated. I watched as riders were torn from eagles, as wings were forcibly bent at terrible angles, and as bodies were slammed into one another until they were as broken as rag dolls.

I shifted my attention to Naomi's battle, and the cyclones

blew toward the east. Two of the eagles streaked away before the cyclones arrived, their wings pumping powerfully as they retreated. But the others were caught up just as the ones who threatened us had been.

At last, the cyclone released them, and they crashed toward the earth. They fell in a heap, eagles on top of eagles and riders, every limb and wing facing unnatural directions. At least ten Zephyrian Eagle Rider pairs were dead. A silence descended, and not a single chest of our enemy rose to draw breath. Slowly, I let my arms drop to my sides and released the power. If I hadn't been mounted, I would have collapsed in a heap on the ground. As it was, I slumped forward over Shazeera's neck, breathing hard.

Something soft and light fell on my shoulder, and I glanced over at it before looking back at the sky. It was raining golden feathers.

10

ZARA

The daughters stared at the heap of broken eagles and riders before slowly turning as one toward me. Instead of the horror and condemnation I expected to see, they looked at me with awe and more than a little hope. But when I reached for Shazeera, as reflexively as examining my own thoughts, there was nothing.

The moment I'd called the wind, I felt a pressure on the thread connecting our hearts. The cyclone had erupted from the sky, swallowing the eagles and their riders, and the thread between us felt like it had been plucked. I clutched my chest. The vibrations still hummed in my chest, and cold sweat broke across my skin at the thought that the thread might unravel.

In my mind, where there should have been Shazeera's comforting voice, there was only silence. She was there beneath me—I could still feel the warmth of her body, and the comforting sounds of her breaths, but it was as if she were a normal horse. A horse who could not communicate in words.

Soft hoofbeats made me look up to find General Isa moving closer to me. She glanced at the fallen Eagle Riders, and I could see her throat work as she swallowed hard. "First Daughter," she said, and her tone was like nothing I'd ever heard from her. She was always as unflappable and calm as still water. "That cyclone . . . Did you do this?"

I could only manage a mute nod, but my acknowledgment was enough to release something held in check by the others.

"I've never seen power like that before," Naomi said, riding toward us.

"This could change everything!" another said.

From beside the fallen guard and horse, a daughter gazed from the carnage and back to me. "Why didn't you use such a power earlier?" she asked quietly.

A lump rose in my throat. "You don't understand," I said. "There's a cost . . ." But it was hard to explain myself in the face of death, even as a bone-deep weariness settled over me, making it difficult to even hold my head up.

I couldn't bring myself to look at Mariyah. I couldn't bear it if she judged me for withholding my ability until it was too late for the many that had been killed—eleven horses and riders. I kept my gaze on Shazeera's mane, but that only reminded me that I couldn't hear her.

It was like the time when I was a child and had climbed as high as I could go in a tree. I wanted to see a bird's nest at the very top, but I put my weight on a branch that wasn't strong enough, and I came crashing down to the ground. The breath was knocked from my lungs, and I couldn't even scream. Worse, I hit my head, and the terrible ringing in my ears drowned out everyone else. I couldn't hear Shazeera or Ama. I couldn't hear anything.

It was the same now. In my mind, there was silence but for my own voice. My own stupid thoughts. Panic raked claws over my flesh, and my breaths came faster. The amount of power I had called upon this time was so much more than the first. What if I'd severed the bond this time? What if I could never communicate with her again?

I panted, lungs burning, like I was drowning on dry land. No matter how hard I tried, I couldn't draw a full breath. Sweat poured down my back, and I shook. Shazeera nuzzled me—she could sense my distress even if she couldn't hear me speak in her mind—but her touch only shattered what little control I had left. A broken sound escaped me, ragged and raw.

"Zara," a voice said, and a gentle hand touched my shoulder. I looked up to find Mariyah right beside me on her mare. "Breathe."

I took a shuddering breath, keeping my eyes on her familiar face. She stayed like that while I took several deep breaths, reminding my lungs that they still functioned.

"Better?" Mariyah asked after a moment. When I nodded, she gave me a gentle hug. "This war has taken many lives, but we're all so thankful you saved ours." She turned to the others. "We owe First Daughter our undying gratitude."

"Mariyah is right," General Isa said, bowing her head in a gesture of respect. "We are grateful for your intervention, First Daughter." She waited until the four guards bowed their heads and murmured their thanks before refocusing on the necessary tasks at hand. The fallen and their horses would need to be brought home to rest. Another guard would need to seek out the five riders who had split off from our original team. The others would accompany us back to Queen Jazela's camp.

As we prepared to leave, I turned to Mariyah and Citrine. "Is Citrine okay? I saw the eagle's talons—" I swallowed hard.

"The scratches are deep, but it's nothing a healer can't fix. She said they don't hurt so badly she can't walk."

"That's a relief," I said, even as shame clung to me like a second skin over my selfish hesitation. What if I had blasted the Eagle Riders from the sky the moment they arrived? Then there would have been zero injuries . . . and fatalities.

"You did everything you could," Mariyah said, because she could always read my moods as easily as a seer. "This loss is because of the Zephyrians–not you."

I shook my head. "I could have called that power sooner. I could have saved us all."

I could feel her eyes on me. "Why didn't you tell me you could do that?"

"I didn't know until recently," I said, keeping my voice low from prying ears. "And I didn't think I'd ever use it again."

"You've been so afraid you wouldn't have an ability to help us in this war, but look how powerful this is," she said with a gesture toward the fallen eagles and riders. "When did you first discover you could do this?"

I took a steadying breath, not used to talking about things I'd kept hidden for so long. "I've always felt drawn to the wind–ever since I was little. I could almost sense a presence, like Ama has always described about things of the earth. But I've never been able to call upon that power. Not until the day that Eagle Rider showed up."

Her eyes widened. "The one who attacked you and General Isa before you came to my camp? But that doesn't make sense. Isa acted completely stunned today."

"There was another Eagle Rider. It attacked Shazeera and me when we tried to escape–we were alone."

Mariyah grabbed my arm, mouth open in shock. "Zara, no! How horrible. You must have been terrified."

The fear of the moment when that eagle and its rider swooped down on us came back to me, choking me with its intensity. "I thought I would be captured or worse. I thought *Shazeera* would die. But then I heard the voice of the wind. It begged me to call upon it, to unleash its power."

"Was it like today? With that cyclone?"

"Yes, it just–it blasted them from the sky."

"This magic is incredible," she said in an excited whisper. "This could make all the difference–"

"It comes with a terrible price," I said, cutting her off. "It hurts my bond with Shazeera. I lose the ability to communicate with her, and–" I paused to rub my chest, where I could still feel the weakened threads that tied us together. "I'm afraid one day, I'll use that power, and it'll sever the bond between us entirely. It might already have."

Mariyah stilled, mouth open. "Oh, Zara," she said finally. "That's why you were so upset."

"Last time, we were able to talk again after a day, but that was with only one Eagle Rider. I don't know how long it'll take to recover this time."

"That's so scary. What does Shazeera think? I mean, obviously not right now, since you can't . . . Did she say anything before?"

I glanced at her, knowing she was listening. "She wanted me to unleash it and save us–even if it hurt the bond." I could feel myself tearing up again. "She's more selfless than I am. Mariyah," I said, lowering my voice, "what if this isn't a gift from the Earth Mother? Why would it hurt my bond if it was?"

Mariyah put her arm around me. "When my magic first manifested, it drained me to the point that I couldn't even lift my head afterward. But now, I can use it without getting immediately exhausted. What you did–calling the wind to knock eagles out of the sky—that kind of strength is bound to take a toll. The Earth Mother is kind. I'm sure once you get used to the ability, you'll be able to use it without the terrible consequences."

Hope bloomed inside me, but it was dampened when I thought of all the years I had never heard the Earth Mother's voice. "I'm just so scared to risk it, you know?"

Mariyah watched us, her brows drawn in sympathy. "I can't imagine, and you know I'll support you in whatever you choose to do, but I don't think the general will let this go easily." She glanced back at where General Isa was taking stock of injuries and overseeing the transport of the fallen.

I bit the inside of my lip as emotions swelled within me. We were losing this war. Every day there were more casualties, and very soon, our entire people would likely be overcome by the Zephyrians. Every peace treaty we had tried so far had failed. The problem was, we had no leverage. Why should they make a treaty with us when they could just crush us in war?

Mariyah was right. This power could make a difference—could make *all* the difference in this war—but how could I sacrifice my bond with Shazeera?

I thought of Cassia, the girl who had suffered so terribly after the loss of her mare. I thought of how tortured she was—how every day she relived those moments when her mare was preyed upon by an eagle, and now she would never see or speak to her horse again. That could be me. How would I endure it?

But how could I endure doing nothing when I had the power to help?

11

TALON

For several days, I revisited the battlefield in a dreamworld while my body slowly healed. But more than any other, I dreamed of the battle that involved the Shendayah River Outpost, and I wondered if it was because not only had Lieutenant Callum died, but Emperor Altair had refused my recommendation to strip Captain Suna of her rank and remove her from commanding any outpost. Days after that battle, Emperor Altair had summoned me to the palace for the mission that had landed me in the hospital. Captain Suna remained in charge of the Eagle Riders at Shendayah River Outpost.

The medics had drugged me with canthis root powder, which kept me unconscious. They didn't trust that I would stay in bed otherwise, and they were right. The minute it wore off and I woke up fully, I asked to speak to the emperor.

A medic with a permanent scowl shook his head and told me I couldn't leave my bed. He sent a servant to summon the emperor to come debrief me.

I wasn't sure he would come. Emperors were the ones who

did the summoning, after all, but he arrived so quickly I realized he must have been waiting in the hallway outside the clinic.

His face relaxed with obvious relief when he saw me. "It makes me happy to see you awake after so long. What happened, Cousin? I was told you crashed."

Neo's indignant screech rang out through my mind as loudly as if he were in the room with me. *I have never crashed in my life!* Normally, Neo and I kept up mental shields to keep from sharing every little thought we had with each other. But because of our injuries, we'd both been too weak to maintain them, so Neo overheard Altair's comment through our link.

"The end result was a crash, yes," I said, trying unsuccessfully to mentally calm Neo at the same time, "but that's bound to happen when a cyclone from nowhere rips you from the sky."

Altair looked stunned. "A cyclone? Since when do the Children of Earth use wind magic?"

I told him everything I knew about the girl who had called the wind—what little I had gathered from my near-death experience, anyway.

Altair's skin looked as washed out as mine by the time I finished. "And you're sure it wasn't one of the queens?" he asked.

I shook my head against the pillow. "No, she was too young. She looked like she was around twenty years old."

"Where have they been hiding a girl with power like that?" he asked. "There has never been any mention of someone who could control the wind, and even if there were, the chances of them being a Child of Earth are so slim it's laughable."

I'd wondered the same thing, so I had a ready answer. "What if she's been in training? She seemed to be of royal blood—she was dressed in gemstones, which is why I thought she was the queen."

He was quiet for so long, his expression deep in thought, that I began to slip into unconsciousness again. I startled when he suddenly spoke. "We must track her down, then. Kill her before she can grow to be a bigger threat."

I thought of the vastness of that power—how Neo's enormous wings became like a songbird's in the face of that wind. "She was young, but she was incredibly strong. Her magic blasted us out of the sky like we were dust."

"You and Neo are the best we have without question, but even still, she won't be able to take on a squadron of Eagle Riders."

A squadron meant fifteen. Fifteen may be enough, but I had my doubts. Unfortunately, I was too weak to give it much more thought. I fell asleep while Altair remained in the room with me. There were times when I crawled back to the surface of consciousness and saw him sitting at my bedside. I would have thought it was a hallucination, but the medics confirmed for me that Altair had kept vigil. It was so different from our usual relationship—I'd spent so many times during my childhood comforting him through injuries—that the accompanying lump in my throat was unexpected.

Even with the medic's intervention, I was barely able to walk unassisted for a few days. Neo, though, recovered quickly. He flew almost immediately after being mended by the medic.

In that time, the sorcerer Ozul had managed to scry the girl's location. She had made it to the Nazeeran Canyon, which wasn't the best place to stage an ambush, as it was easily defensible. There was a good chance for a successful attack, though, if she was caught outside the safety of the caverns, and this seemed like a possibility, since the horses grazed in the rich grasses surrounding the canyon. The plan then would be to wait for a sufficiently cloudy day, fly high under cloud cover, and see if an ambush opportunity presented itself.

I had argued with Altair that I should be allowed to lead the battalion, as I was the only one with firsthand experience with the strange magic. He had stubbornly refused my every request, citing my injuries as too serious to allow me to fly again so soon.

The emperor insults me, Neo said, his thoughts pushing into my mind along with his outrage.

I would think he's insulting me, I replied. *He's saying I'm too weak to participate in this mission.*

No, he's saying I'm too stupid to keep you safe.

I groaned inwardly. Eagles were very easily offended, and it didn't help when Neo eavesdropped on my thoughts.

It didn't take much to trigger a rant from him since he'd been knocked out of the sky by that wind magic, so I knew he was only getting started. With effort, I closed the door in my mind that connected us, and went to bed. I had to heal up as quickly as I could—I had a feeling this mission wouldn't go as easily as Altair assumed.

The next day, a storm rolled in on the plains, giving the eagle battalion the cover they needed. Altair summoned me to his rooms to await the news of the mission, while I tried to shake the feeling that it was doomed to failure.

"Talon," Altair said by way of greeting as I entered his sitting room. He was drinking a steaming cup of aromatic tea—I could smell its spicy scent even from the doorway. On his desk was a mess of papers, covering every inch. "It's good to see you walking around."

"Thank you, Majesty," I said, bowing. As I stood straight again, I saw a figure shift in the shadows behind Altair. My hand moved toward the hilt of the sword on my hip as my entire body tensed like a bow.

Ozul moved into the light, his head still covered with the coyote mask, chest bare despite the chill.

I didn't remove my hand from the hilt of my sword. Everything in me said being in the same room with this creature was the height of stupidity. But I tamped down my instincts to run and forced my breathing to slow. I couldn't see Ozul's eyes through the slits in the mask, but I had the sense he was staring at me. My heart rate increased.

"The mission has changed since we last spoke," Altair interrupted, and it took all my training not to flinch as his voice broke my concentration on the creature before me.

"How so?" I asked tightly.

Altair took a casual sip of his tea, as if the ghoul weren't in here, looming threateningly over us. "I asked Ozul if any of the Children of Earth had ever had wind magic, and he said no. It's incredibly rare, and none of their bloodlines have ever manifested in such a way. He wants her brought here alive."

I shifted my gaze back to the masked sorcerer. "To what end? So she can summon cyclones that pull the palace walls down around you?"

He said nothing, only continued to stare at me through the slits in his mask that were dark as pitch.

Altair answered instead. "No doubt she is extremely important to her people, and we will hold her for ransom to force their compliance."

I gaped at Altair, my hand momentarily falling away from the sword hilt. "Forgive me, Majesty, but you should have consulted me on this before the mission. Even if the aerial cavalry managed to capture her, how will they control her power?"

"Through her horse," a deep, gravelly voice said. It sounded slightly distorted coming through the mask.

I stiffened as I turned to look at the creature that called itself Ozul.

A loud pounding on the emperor's door interrupted us. "Enter," Altair said, his tone deeply annoyed.

Rhea strode into the room, her normally lightly browned skin looking pale. Rhea was one of the best scouts we had, with a real knack for reconnaissance and returning without the enemy having any idea they were being spied upon. She'd perfected the art our people had of schooling her features to appear statuesque, but now, she looked completely undone. Her hair was a wild halo around her head, having escaped its braided knot at the base of her neck, and her eyes were so wide I could see whites all the way around.

"What is it?" the emperor asked, and by his restraint, I could tell he realized as I did that something was wrong.

"Captain Suna and her squadron are all dead, Majesty," Rhea said, her voice shaky. "Their eagles, too. I saw it with my own eyes."

My eyes widened at her words, and not just because the whole squadron had been wiped out. Emperor Altair hadn't consulted me on which squadron to send on this mission. If he had, I certainly wouldn't have recommended her. I had never had the chance to punish Captain Suna for her role in Lieutenant Callum's death due to her negligence. Now, though, it seemed that the royal with the wind power had done my job for me.

"Did you locate the girl?" he asked sharply.

She shook her head. "We engaged in battle with a small group of Children, and amongst them was the girl with the power to control the wind. We were unable to capture her."

Altair didn't look at me, but I was staring at him, both eyebrows raised. "What happened?"

"She raised her hands to the sky, and a series of unnatural cyclones appeared out of nowhere. My eagle and I were flying at a higher altitude and were able to escape, but the others were caught within and smashed to the ground."

"Thank you for your report, Rider," Altair said, and Rhea bowed and left.

"Her ability will change the tide of this war," I said. "The fact that she took down nearly an entire battalion on her own doesn't bode well. We have no hope of capturing her now."

Altair had been watching Ozul quietly, but now he turned his attention back to me. "There may be another way."

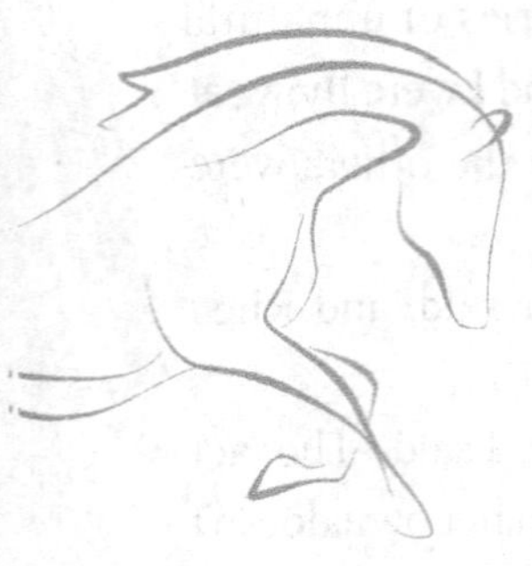

12

ZARA

General Isa interrogated me about my power as we traveled the short distance to the canyon. Naomi had ridden ahead to brief the others on the casualties of the battle and to tell them that General Isa hadn't lifted the order to hide in the canyon's cave system. Not until we could be sure the Zephyrians wouldn't send another wave.

"Can you call upon it at will?" General Isa asked.

"I don't know," I said, my voice thick. I knew what General Isa wanted from me, but I couldn't bear to face it. "I've only used it twice now, and that was when I felt like we would all die if I didn't."

General Isa nodded thoughtfully from astride Kamil. I had already told her about being attacked on my own before, when we had left my home camp. She had reacted with a mixture of horror and intrigue.

"You're at your most powerful when you're defending someone else. That makes sense given your mother's healing abilities. You have a family history of saving others."

I wasn't sure this had anything to do with Ama's abilities, but I nodded to show I was listening.

"If we positioned you strategically, do you think you could call upon enough of the power to take out numerous battalions of Eagle Riders?"

I closed my eyes and took a breath. It was the question I dreaded but, at the same time, understood. She was the leader of our failing army. Of course she would want to use my power as a weapon.

"I don't know," I told her, but I thought of the way the wind felt when I was connected to it. Like there was no end to its vast strength. At the same time, I felt as though it would drain me until there was nothing left. Even now, my heart seemed to beat sluggishly. My breaths came harder, like a horse sat on my chest.

She regarded me with her sharp eyes. "I think you do."

"It hurt my bond with Shazeera. I can't hear her thoughts. I can't communicate with her at all—last time it lasted for an entire day. I don't know what it will do this time." I put my hand on her neck, my voice breaking. "If I channeled the wind's power for longer, to knock that many Eagle Riders out of the sky, it might sever our bond completely. There also seems to be a physical consequence—it feels like it's draining all my energy even when I connect with that magic for just a short time. If I use too much, it may drain me completely. I just don't know." Talking so much had me panting. Shazeera eyed me with concern as I struggled to slow my breathing.

General Isa looked out across the plains as tears streamed from my eyes. "It exacts a terrible price from you, First Daughter," she said finally. "And we will talk with your mother to see what she thinks the risks are." She and Kamil came to a stop, and she turned to look at me as Shazeera halted, too. "But I will tell you this. We are on the verge of being destroyed as a people. At this rate, the Zephyrians will overtake us within mere months.

Although we can't say what this emperor will do, we know historically his father killed the royals of conquered countries and forced the people to give all of their resources to the Zephyrians."

I swayed on Shazeera's back at her blunt words.

"Your gift from the Earth Mother gives us an advantage we never had. We could fight back. Make them afraid of *us* for once. It will even give us bargaining power."

With shaky fingers, I stroked Shazeera's mane, wishing I could hear her thoughts on what the general was saying. *Gift from the Earth Mother.* Mariyah thought the same thing. Could they both be right?

General Isa reached over and took my hand. "There isn't a single one of us who wouldn't understand how soul-crushing it would be to have our bond with our horse broken. But you must also know that I would lay down my life to save our people. As queen, your mother would do the same. Sometimes we are asked to make a sacrifice that will destroy us, but we must do it. For the good of our people." When I still didn't say anything, General Isa asked, "First Daughter, do you love your people?"

"Of course," I said firmly.

"And you want to save them?"

"I have always wanted to save us from this war. I hate that I can't help Ama."

"And now . . . ?"

My hand tightened on Shazeera's mane. "I'll do what I have to, even if it costs me everything."

General Isa nodded with approval and more than a little relief. "You will make a superior queen one day."

When she rode on ahead, I laid my head on the back of Shazeera's neck and cried.

GENERAL ISA, MARIYAH, and I rode down a winding trail into an enormous cave that had been carved deep into the Nazeeran Canyon by Queen Jazela's power. Her purple pavilion had been erected just inside, and she met us at the entrance, dragging Mariyah in for an embrace.

"Are you unharmed?" she asked, her gaze searching her daughter.

"Yes," Mariyah said, returning her hug. "Citrine was injured, but Dani healed her."

"Everything happened too fast," Queen Jazela said. "When General Isa rode to bring you both back, I made sure Queen Rana was safe. But before I could lend all of you aid, you had already defeated the Eagle Riders." She studied each of us in turn, her expression heavy with unspoken questions.

"There are things we must discuss," General Isa said, and with a glance at the interested looks of the many daughters and sons who had taken refuge in the canyon, she added, "in private."

Queen Jazela nodded before turning her attention to me. "Your mother waits inside."

My stomach dropped at the thought of the upcoming discussion, and I placed my hand on Shazeera's strong neck for comfort. Mariyah and Citrine followed Queen Jazela into the pavilion, and we walked into its cool and cavernous space. Like the one I shared with Ama, there were two rooms that led off the entrance, but we continued into the main living area, where we found Ama sitting on a plush rug, propped up by satin pillows. Ama looked pale and drawn, and the moment she saw me, she got heavily to her feet. She hugged me close.

"You're all right?" she asked, pulling back to examine my face. "You look pale." She narrowed her eyes in concentration as she watched my chest rise and fall shallowly. "And are you struggling to breathe?"

"I'm all right," I said, my gaze darting briefly to General Isa. "I just need to sit down."

Ama watched me closely as I flopped ungracefully onto one of the pillows. After a moment, she sat next to me. "Should I call a healer?" she asked, her expression tense, and I knew it pained her to have to ask that. I had never been healed by anyone but her.

"I think we need to talk first," I said, glancing again at General Isa.

"Fine, but as soon as we are done, we'll call Dani to see you." Ama looked up at General Isa. "Any casualties?"

"We lost eleven guards and their horses."

Ama nodded somberly. "They will be given a hero's funeral. It was reported that there were fifteen Eagle Riders, so I have to say, I'm shocked that the losses weren't greater and that the battle concluded so fast."

"Majesty," General Isa said with a brief glance my way, "that's what we wanted to discuss with you. First Daughter Zara has revealed an incredible power from the Earth Mother. One that could completely change the war in our favor."

Queen Jazela and Ama stared at her with rapt attention.

"When the Eagle Riders attacked," General Isa said, "they quickly overwhelmed us. First Daughter Mariyah's life was threatened. That's when Zara seemed to control the wind itself; she summoned a cyclone so powerful that it blew the riders out of the sky into a broken heap on the ground."

Mariyah beamed at me, pride clear on her face. I couldn't help but feel my heart swell just a bit; despite the terrible effect my power had on my bond, it *had* allowed me to save my cousin and the others. For the first time in my life, I felt useful.

I was so busy congratulating myself that I almost missed the shared look of concern Ama and Aunt Jazela gave each other.

"I know it would be an enormous sacrifice to ask that First Daughter Zara join me on the battlefield," General Isa continued, "but I believe that only a few demonstrations of her power will change the tide of the war. We have never been able to fight back at this level. And without their aerial assaults on us, the Zephyrian soldiers would be easily defeated by our riders." Her cheeks were flushed, and her eyes shone.

"I'm willing to risk everything to save our people," I said when neither queen said anything. "I don't know the limits of this power, but I think it's enough to finally gain the upper hand on the Eagle Riders—or, at least, make them think it's enough to defeat them. To maybe even force a treaty. To bring an end to this terrible war."

"What is the cost of this power?" Ama asked, her tone and expression much calmer than I would have thought. Didn't we just tell them we had the key to defeating our enemies?

"It weakens me significantly and hurts my ability to communicate with Shazeera," I admitted. "The first time I used this power—" I faltered in my speech for a moment when Ama gave me a shocked look and then glanced at General Isa accusingly. "It was when an Eagle Rider attacked Shazeera and me on our own when we had fled camp. I should have told you about it, but I was scared of what it could mean. That first time, I couldn't hear her in my mind for a full twenty-four hours. But that was only one rider . . . I don't know what will happen this time."

Shazeera looked at me, and I wished I could hear what she was thinking. Though I didn't have to read her mind to know that she, too, would be willing to risk our bond to save everyone else. Horses always put the good of the herd first.

Ama stood and walked over to Shazeera. I held my breath when she rested her forehead against Shazeera's. They both closed their eyes. After a few painful moments where the silence seemed interminable, she finally said, "The link between you is still there–I feel it. It's only been suppressed, not broken, so I'm confident it will be restored once again." But before I could smile with relief, Ama met my gaze. "But it's weaker than it was, like a fraying rope. Each time you use this new power, you risk breaking your link permanently."

Shazeera's head and tail dropped, and my shoulders slumped. Mariyah scooted closer and linked her arm with mine. It hurt to hear what I had suspected to be true from the moment I first used the power.

Ama turned to General Isa. "And you would ask her to risk her bond with Shazeera?"

To her credit, the general didn't even flinch. "We have all made sacrifices in this war, Majesty. Shielding us with your wards is draining your very life. Soon, your body will give out, and you will die. There have been many of us who have already given up our lives–or the lives of our horses–for the good of our people. I think First Daughter Zara understands what a ruler must do for her people."

"Do not put words in her mouth, General," Ama admonished. "Do you understand that using this power again can destroy your bond with Shazeera permanently? And I cannot predict when that will happen. It could be the next time, or the time after . . . but based on the way the thread between you has already deteriorated, it won't survive many more times."

I could feel the color drain from my face at her words. When my eyes sought out Shazeera, she gave a little bob of her head.

But before I could respond, General Isa interrupted. "As terrible as that would be, comparing the loss of a bond to the annihilation of our people is no contest. Look back at history!" she said, her eyes flashing. "Half of our tribal nations fell to the Zephyrians. There are only three of us left, and we are hanging on by a thread. We will not last a month. The Zephyrians will conquer us, kill those who stood against them, and crush the rest. So forgive me if I don't hesitate to recommend that First Daughter uses this wind magic no matter the price."

The tension in the room was so heavy it felt like a storm had descended upon us. Ama and Queen Jazela had matching murderous looks on their faces.

"Tread carefully, General," Ama warned.

"I'm only asking that you give your daughter the chance to make up her own mind for the good of her people, just as *my* daughter willingly gave up her life in this war."

"Your daughter was a hero," Ama said, her expression somber, "and we will never forget her sacrifice. However, she wasn't First Daughter with the responsibility of carrying on the Sorayan line."

"You're not listening to me, my queen! Soon, there won't be a line to continue. We will all be dead or enslaved."

Ama's eyes flashed. "You overstep, General. How dare you talk down to me."

General Isa closed her eyes and took a deep breath. "Forgive me, it certainly isn't my intention to talk down to you, my queen. I just want First Daughter to be given the chance to choose for herself."

"I will do anything to save our people," I interrupted, forcing my voice to sound strong despite the fact that my hands were shaking, "even risk my bond with Shazeera."

"Surely the Earth Mother wouldn't be that cruel," Mariyah said, her own eyes shining with tears at my distress. "Why would earth magic hurt a bond between a daughter and her horse?"

Ama and Queen Jazela had only to look at each other for me to know the answer, but it still made my chest constrict painfully.

"Because this isn't earth magic," Ama said.

Mariyah's mouth dropped open, and even General Isa recoiled slightly.

"Summoning the strength of the wind has nothing to do with the earth," Ama said. "It is magic of the sky."

Queen Jazela nodded slowly when Mariyah glanced at her for confirmation.

"Where did it come from?" I asked, heartbeat loud in my ears.

"Not from the Earth Mother," Queen Jazela said.

"Earth magic can only be passed from mother to daughter," Ama said with an admonishing glance at her sister. "All the First Daughters have abilities that can be traced back to the Earth Mother. It's part of their royal inheritance."

"I know all that," I said with more than a little frustration leaking into my tone. "What are you trying to say? I'm not really a First Daughter?"

"You are, but using this power jeopardizes your position as future queen," Ama said.

I went still with shock. "Why have you never told me this?"

"In all our recent generations," Ama said, "it has never been a problem. All power and abilities travel along the maternal bloodline, no matter who sired you." She suddenly looked tired. "You may even have weaker abilities you can tap into from your father's side, but they would never be more powerful than the earth magic inherited through our Sorayan line. I never thought it would be an issue."

I leaned toward her. "Then who sired me? Is that where this power comes from?"

"I had many suitors at the time."

It was her standard answer—a step above simply saying, *I don't know.* Not knowing for sure was common, as many daughters, including queens, took many suitors when they were ready to have a baby. Growing up, surrounded by so many loving people and horses, I had never given much thought to who my sire might be. Daughters and sons fell in and out of love all the time without deciding to join themselves together in a life partnership. Queens, especially, typically took countless royal consorts. Queen Jazela was unusual in that she had been with Prince Malik for decades. Ama, with her numerous suitors before I was born, was far more in line with tradition. But I still had this terrible suspicion she wasn't telling me everything. I couldn't help but compare myself to Mariyah again, who had been sired by Prince Malik. There was no mystery surrounding her parentage. The magic may only flow through the maternal line, but obviously in my case, something else was going on.

"Who your sire is doesn't matter," Aunt Jazela said, jumping in. "What's important here is that the Earth Mother won't give you her blessing if you continue to use a power that isn't earth magic. And without her blessing, you won't be able to lead our people." It felt like a knife twisted in my chest. So this is what Ama had meant before by the wind magic being dangerous. Using it could potentially prevent me from ever taking my rightful place as Queen of All Queens.

General Isa's expression mirrored my own stunned disbelief.

This hadn't been how she'd expected this conversation to go. She had no doubt thought that they would both jump at the chance to finally gain the upper hand on our enemy.

"So, if Zara uses this power again, she'll have to give up the throne?" Mariyah asked incredulously. "How has this never been a problem before?"

"Our bloodline has always been strong enough to overcome any weaker abilities being passed on."

Sons often had weaker manifestations of earth magic than daughters. The royal lines were the strongest, and any sons born to queens usually had some form of earth magic. Kai, a distant cousin of Queen Jazela's royal line, was extraordinarily strong, beyond the normal limits of humanity. But none of this explained my ability to call on the wind.

"There's a chance if you stop using this ability, then your earth magic will awaken," Ama said. "We need to discuss it with Samira."

Aunt Jazela nodded emphatically. "Yes, Samira has always been the genealogist of the family."

Ama stopped her pacing. "I'll send word to her immediately."

She strode out of the room without another word to us, presumably to write a letter to Queen Samira.

Mariyah just pulled me in for a tight hug. "I'm sorry, Zara. I had no idea about any of that–I didn't even know that power wasn't earth magic. But maybe this is good, in a way. Now you won't feel pressured to risk your bond with Shazeera."

As I leaned into my cousin's embrace, I glanced at Shazeera, and I knew–even without hearing her thoughts–that we were experiencing the same tumultuous feelings.

My whole body felt heavy, and my shoulders drooped with it like a wilted flower. Ama's and Aunt Jazela's reactions were devastating, but not because my ascension to the throne was in jeopardy.

I had never felt worthy of being First Daughter. I had spent my life dreaming of having healing abilities like Ama. When years went by and I still didn't have any signs of earth magic, I begged the Earth Mother to bless me with the power to save my people. To be useful for once.

For the briefest moment, I thought she had.

Now, emotions crashed over me like relentless waves–relief that I wouldn't have to put my bond with Shazeera at risk, guilt that I felt such relief, and crushing disappointment that I wouldn't be able to save my people from almost certain destruction.

But most of all, the plummeting feeling that I would never be a worthy First Daughter.

13

ZARA

I knew from the moment I woke on the seventh day of not being able to communicate mentally with Shazeera that something potentially devastating was about to happen.

No psychic skills necessary.

Almost an entire week had gone by. With each passing day, I sank deeper into a pit of despair in my mind, terrified I would never escape.

What if it never gets better? What if we can never talk to each other again?

I shoved such thoughts away–I refused to think like that.

Ama had sent Dani in to heal me after the meeting, and though she had taken much of the fatigue away almost instantly, I struggled with my breathing for days. That was to be expected, considering she didn't have the healing capabilities of a royal. Ama would have been able to heal me completely, but she still struggled to heal herself.

Ama had gotten a little stronger each day, looking less pale and more like herself. But she still couldn't raise the wards. Even if she did have the energy to raise the wards again, the Zephyrians had proven they had found a way through them. Because of this, we had to remain in the caverns. With a desperate fervor, she worked with me to find the earth magic she was convinced was locked within.

"The more you focus on a lesser-known magic like the wind," she said, "the deeper inside you the earth magic will sink, until it will be nearly impossible to access."

Despite the enormous power I had released, I hated not being able to communicate with Shazeera, so I did everything Ama asked until we were both exhausted. And still the healing and defensive abilities stayed out of reach.

I tried again to ask Ama about my sire, as it became clearer by the day that my wind power suppressed the Sorayan line's earth magic—despite what Ama said about it being the stronger power.

"What magic did my sire have?" I asked her after a particularly grueling session.

"I don't know," Ama said.

"How could you not know?" I demanded, my tone sharp with frustration.

"I never worried about such things, since I've always known our earth magic is stronger," she said flippantly.

"Then let's find him and ask him."

"That's not possible," Ama said with a shake of her head that had me gritting my teeth.

"Why not?" I asked.

But she had refused to answer no matter how many times I asked. Eventually I groaned and left in an exasperated huff.

I waited to hear from Queen Samira, hoping that perhaps she had come across such a power in one of the ancient lines. Maybe then I would have answers.

Today, though, when I went looking for Ama, I couldn't find her inside the pavilion. The wind tore through the rooms, threatening to uproot the stakes that held it in the ground. It made a terrible howling sound like a wolf through the cavernous space. I got dressed quickly as it tugged and pulled at my clothing and hair.

Expecting a gale storm outside, I stood momentarily dumbstruck at the fact that only my pavilion was affected. We were still evacuated to the canyon cave system, but the pavilions had been erected where we could still see the sky. It hung low above me now, steel gray and ominous, but only a light wind whispered through the camp. Cold fingers raced down my spine. What was the wind trying to tell me then?

Some . . . is . . . the wind whispered, though I caught only snatches of the words.

Something . . .

Something is coming.

The hair on the back of my neck rose as I glanced around warily. Everything seemed as it should. People and horses were carrying on with their daily business without distress. Hoofbeats echoing on rock made me turn around, but it was Shazeera who approached, ears pricked forward.

"Has it been long enough for the bond to recover?" I asked her. "Can we communicate again?"

Her gaze was intent on mine, but after a moment, she shook her head. A flicker of dread stirred in my belly.

"I heard whispers on the wind just now," I said, feeling a bit odd saying it out loud. Usually I just showed her mind-to-mind what I'd seen.

Shazeera lifted her head higher, nostrils flared as though

scenting the wind. She shook her head again, which I supposed meant she didn't sense anything.

Her attention shifted to the top of the canyon, where guards faced toward the east. With a snort, she started toward the path that led up, and I knew her well enough to follow. Together, we made our way up the pathway to the top of the canyon and back onto flat ground.

As soon as we made it past the line of guards, I was surprised to see General Isa, Ama, and Queen Jazela all mounted and waiting. They were pointed toward the east like the guards. When I followed their line of sight, I saw they were watching a retinue of riders coming toward us. In the very center of the long line of riders was Queen Samira, riding her stallion. They were both fully outfitted in our people's most regal dress with the queen wearing her headpiece of horsehair accented with golden tassels. Her bodice was studded with rubies to match her split crimson skirt, where beneath she wore black leather leggings and nothing on her feet but a golden ankle bracelet. Her stallion had a red embroidered halter with golden bangles on his forehead and red-and-gold tassels that hung down both cheeks.

Mariyah came from behind the line of guards, mounted on Citrine. "What is Queen Samira doing here?" I asked her when she was close enough to hear me. I knew Ama had written to her, but I'd assumed she'd respond with a letter.

Mariyah watched the queen's approach. "Ama said they weren't expecting her. She never leaves her wheat fields, so this is strange."

The wind blew in my ears and snatched at my clothing. Since everyone else was mounted, I quickly pulled myself onto Shazeera's back.

Queen Samira and her retinue were close enough now to see the determined look on her face. Again, I was struck by how formally she was dressed—why was she outfitted as though she was about to participate in a royal ceremony?—but then even above the gusts of wind, I heard it.

The *thump, thump, thump* of powerful wings.

The urge to run gripped me powerfully, but Shazeera and I stood rooted in place as we glanced skyward.

There were five Eagle Riders. And they were landing.

14

ZARA

Instantly, the mounted guards who had lined the canyon had moved forward to stand in front of the queens, Mariyah, and me. With arrows drawn, they watched the Eagle Riders in the sky above us.

"Hold," General Isa commanded, and I realized the rider who was in the lead held a white flag in his hand. Were they surrendering? But that didn't make sense . . . Why would they fly here and surrender?

Shazeera shivered beneath me, and I wished I could talk to her. We had never been this close to an Eagle Rider and not been under attack, but that didn't make us any more relaxed. Still, I couldn't help but notice things I'd never had time to see before, like the fact that they all wore a supple type of armor that seemed to be made from leather, only it was a dusky gold in color, and it was accented with eagle feathers on their pauldrons.

On their heads, they wore helms that looked like the head of their eagles, with a curved beak that shielded their eyes and feathers that spread all along the back. Up close, their eagles were terrifyingly large, with wingspans that measured five horses wide, and standing taller than three horses put together. I glanced at Ama, but she was so tense that Nafalla was repeatedly pawing the ground.

"The emperor has received your message," the lead Eagle Rider said.

Was this a trick to draw the queens out of the canyon? I reached out and touched the wind blowing from the west. My gaze shifted to each of the five eagles. Before, I had knocked three times that number out of the sky. If it came down to it, I would call upon the wind power again to defend my people.

Suddenly, the line of our archers parted, and Queen Samira rode forward on her stallion. "Thank you for coming," she said, and the lead Eagle Rider bowed his head in acknowledgment.

I stiffened in shock as, beside me, Ama and Jazela both gasped. So even they hadn't known. I turned to look at Ama, and her face was as dark and ominous as a summer storm.

"Samira, what–" Ama hissed in our native tongue, but the other queen continued speaking to the Eagle Rider.

"I'm glad to see your emperor is willing to talk peace at last, particularly in light of recent events."

I could feel my whole face contort in confusion; I still had no idea what she was talking about. I had to wonder, too, why she had ridden all the way here. If she had truly contacted the Zephyrians–which was unbelievable–then why wouldn't she have arranged to meet them in her own territory?

Queen Samira ignored Ama and turned to Queen Jazela. "We should have a meeting in your pavilion. I'm sure you and Rana will want to hear what they have to say."

Queen Jazela looked like she'd rather tell Queen Samira to go to hell, but in the end, she swallowed her anger and nodded. "Come with me," she said tightly.

The leader with the white flag dismounted by sliding down his eagle's wing in a single graceful movement. He strode toward Queen Jazela while the others stayed mounted on their eagles.

Ama rode over to Samira's side and grabbed her arm. "What is the meaning of this, Samira?" she demanded.

"You'll find out soon enough," she said.

The Eagle Rider removed his helm and tucked it under his arm as I approached on Shazeera. His gaze flicked to me briefly, and without the helm hiding part of his face, I froze in horrified shock. This was the Eagle Rider who had hunted Shazeera and me down near our camp, when I first called upon the power of the wind. Shazeera must have felt my reaction and came to a jarring halt. How had he survived? What was he doing here?

But then Queen Samira was dismounting and showing him the way, and the moment passed. I could only follow them in a cloud of disbelief, Ama at my side, her head high and her back stiff.

As we wound our way down the canyon path toward Queen Jazela's pavilion, people looked out from their tents, their faces twisted in surprise and fear.

When we arrived at Queen Jazela's purple pavilion, the Eagle Rider had to duck slightly to fit through the entry, and his muscular body took up most of the space. He stepped inside without hesitation, as though he had nothing to fear from us. And maybe he didn't. Maybe he was just as skilled a warrior without his giant eagle as he was while riding it.

The rest of us dismounted. With so many horses, they would have to wait outside until the meeting concluded. I ran my hand down Shazeera's soft cheek, desperately wishing I could talk to her.

Before Ama and I could enter, General Isa strode over to us. "I'm coming, too," she said, in a tone that promised she was walking into that pavilion whether Queen Samira wanted her to or not.

But the queen said nothing, only walked through the opening, which I noticed was flanked by two armed guards—a son and a daughter. There were more guards waiting when we entered the throne room, and once we were all inside, it was crowded to the point where all of us were pressed close together. All except the Eagle Rider, who seemed to maintain a personal bubble of space around himself no matter how close the rest of us got.

Queen Jazela and Ama seemed content to force us all to stand awkwardly, but Queen Samira jumped in like she had the right. She held out her hand to the rider. "Please, sit." She indicated one of the wide, plush pillows on the floor, like they belonged to her.

Queen Jazela sucked in her breath in obvious irritation.

When I stole another glance at the rider, his expression didn't reveal much, but I thought I saw a hint of a lip curl before he finally did as she asked. I wondered if it was because he wasn't used to sitting on the floor, or because the pillow closest to him was made of purple and pink satin. Supposedly the Zephyrians were averse to color.

After a moment, she and Ama sank down gracefully onto the wide pillows. Mariyah and I did the same. General Isa remained standing by the door.

"With so many people in the room, you're no doubt wanting introductions," Queen Samira said. "This is Queen Rana, Queen of All Queens, and her daughter, the First Daughter, Zara." She then indicated a silently seething Queen Jazela and worried Mariyah. "Queen Jazela is queen of the Nazeeran Canyon and

Mid-Plains, and Mariyah is First Daughter here. No doubt you've already heard of General Isa."

The Eagle Rider's eyes flicked back and forth amongst us before returning to Queen Samira's face. "In your letter to the emperor, you claimed to be writing on behalf of the alliance of the Children of Earth."

Almost in unison, Queen Jazela and Ama gave Queen Samira furious looks. "How dare you write on our behalf!" Ama said, with barely restrained fury.

"When you see the peace treaty this rider has brought with him, then I'm sure you will understand," Samira told her with a calm tone that set me on edge. Queen Samira had always had a flair for the dramatic, and she loved to stir things up—even amongst allies. But the words *peace treaty* had the effect she wanted. We all now hung on her every word.

"And who are you?" Ama asked when the Zephyrian seemed to have no intention of offering his name.

"I am Commander Talon, cousin to the emperor of Zephyrus, and one of the leaders of the Eagle Rider Aerial Army."

"We are pleased you could come and speak with us peacefully," Queen Samira said, and I could feel the waves of animosity coming from Queen Jazela, who was the most volatile of the three queens. "We have long sought an agreement that would satisfy both our countries."

"Yes, but they have never been able to guarantee that we would be able to keep our ancient lands. Grasslands we need for our horses," Queen Jazela added in a biting tone as she stared at Commander Talon.

For his part, he met her gaze without blinking, without any sign of remorse on that cold face. It was a face wasted on a man from that empire, with striking icy-blue eyes and a sharp jawline that was tempered by full lips. But he ruined it all with that stony expression that never changed.

"However, in light of recent events," Queen Samira said, and the way her gaze shifted so briefly to mine before dancing away made that terrible feeling that I wasn't going to like the outcome of this–that indeed I was mostly likely the *cause* of it–come back with a vengeance.

"Which recent events?" Ama interrupted.

"She is referring, I think," Commander Talon said, and all three of us turned to him with eyebrows raised, "to a release of power that was devastating enough to kill fifteen Eagle Riders." His gaze settled on mine. "That was the second time this power was used. Though Neo and I managed to survive and serve as witnesses to the first."

I flinched. Not only had the bastard lived, but he'd returned to the emperor–his *cousin*–to tell him about it.

When Ama sent word to Queen Samira to ask for her advice, I was sure she didn't expect her to react by demanding a peace treaty from the Zephyrians. Not without broaching the subject with the other queens first, especially Ama, who outranked them all. Samira overstepped her place by not convening with them. So much so, in fact, that I may have called her a traitor had she not arrived with hopes of finally ending the war.

"I sent word describing your devastating abilities as well," Queen Samira said to me, and Ama shot her a look of shocked hurt. "I asked for peace."

"You threatened us," Commander Talon corrected. "You said her power could wipe out numerous battalions."

At that moment, I looked up to find General Isa watching me, and I could almost hear what she was thinking. Threatening the

Zephyrians with my power was exactly what we had planned to do, and a peace treaty was the exact outcome we had desired. My blood pounded in my ears, drowning everything out. I knew it couldn't be that easy. There was more to this.

"Yes, but that's why I asked for peace," Queen Samira was saying. "If First Daughter Zara joins the battle in the north, your battalions will be destroyed in an instant, but we can avoid all of that with a treaty."

I was almost positive that level of power, if I was even capable of it, would not only destroy my bond with Shazeera, but also cause the Earth Mother to forsake me as future heir to the throne. But the Zephyrians didn't know that.

Commander Talon pulled out a scroll from a leather bag slung across his chest and at his hip. "I have a treaty here, signed by Emperor Altair, but it comes with three terms."

"What are they?" Ama asked.

"The first is that we will receive twenty percent of every trade and sale of your exports in the port city of Rhythos. In exchange, your land, including the Northern Plains, Mid-Plains, and Southern Plains, will remain under the rule of the Children of Earth. Additionally, you may migrate across the continent as you see fit, under the protection of the Zephyrian Empire."

Queen Samira paled at that number. Since she grew the vast majority of crops in the south, it would affect her the most. Perhaps she deserved it for keeping my mother in the dark about her plans.

Ama may have argued with a tax of that size, but it appeared she felt as I did and that it was a just punishment for Queen Samira's actions. She merely nodded and said, "Go on."

"The second is that you will engage your daughter, the First Daughter Zara of the Children of Earth, to the emperor of the

Zephyrians, for marriage in a month's time, which is the customary engagement period for Zephyrian royalty. In doing so, our people will become her people, and she will never again be able to use the power of the wind against us."

I half stood—I thought I was about to run from that tent, or perhaps vomit all over Commander Talon, or possibly faint—but Mariyah linked arms with me in solidarity and held me still.

"And the last term?" Ama said, her voice tight.

"The First Daughter will come to stay with the emperor immediately upon signing this treaty, where she will learn the ways of our people, and prepare for her role as empress. She will never use the power of the wind against us, or this treaty will be considered forfeit, and we will retaliate as necessary."

All I could hear was the blood pounding in my ears. They wanted me to come with them . . . to leave my people and become one of them. The thought made my chest constrict so painfully I let out my breath in a pained hitch. Beside me, Mariyah gasped, but a strange calm had descended on me. My family—save Queen Samira, who had probably suggested it in the first place—all sat frozen in shock, but my mind raced ahead. The suddenness of this news hit me like being shot with an arrow. And yet . . .

All my life, I had wanted to be the First Daughter my people could look up to. Someone like Ama, whom everyone came to at the first sign of trouble. When the years crept by, and it became more and more obvious I would never have my mother's abilities, I began to descend into despair that I would ever be useful. And then my own power manifested, one so destructive it had the potential to break the bond I had with Shazeera. For the briefest moment, I thought I would be the one to save my people from their suffering. But then that, too, had been taken away from me.

And now, here was my enemy, offering me another chance to save everyone from this war, doing something only I could do.

Across the room, General Isa and I locked eyes. Out of everyone in the room, I knew she understood.

"May I see the treaty?" Ama asked, pulling me from my thoughts.

Commander Talon handed it to her. We all waited in silence as she spent several minutes poring over the words. The writing on the scroll was precise, neat lettering, all except for the bottom, where the emperor's signature was a bold flourish.

"How do I know this is truly his signature?" she asked.

"It also has the emperor's seal at the bottom, which is illegal to duplicate," Commander Talon said.

And there, down at the bottom, was a golden wax seal with a crowned eagle, its wings spread wide.

"We will need some time to discuss these terms privately," Ama said, and I leaned into Mariyah a little more. She squeezed my arm.

"I will wait outside," Commander Talon said. He stood gracefully despite his tall stature and left the room, flanked on either side by Queen Jazela's guards.

Queen Jazela whirled on Queen Samira as soon as they were gone. "How could you do this? Why didn't you speak to us about it first? This is the worst kind of betrayal–Zara is your cousin!"

Queen Samira looked unrepentant. "I knew Rana wouldn't want to make the sacrifice, so I forced her hand. Before you tear into me, though, you know we need a peace treaty with the Zephyrians. They will wipe us off the face of the continent otherwise."

"But why wouldn't you come to us, Samira?" Ama asked, her

arms wrapped around herself like her insides hurt. "Why go behind our backs?"

"I actually had intended to arrive here before the Eagle Riders—I didn't want to make quite so dramatic an entrance," she added with a little laugh that had me rolling my eyes, "but the crops needed a little extra care before I could leave them."

"Oh, that's wonderful," Queen Jazela said, pacing with balled fists back and forth across the rug. "You let your family be completely blindsided because you wanted to stay home and take care of your plants."

A wrinkle appeared on Queen Samira's forehead. "That reminds me—the export tax on crops seems a little high—" Queen Jazela shot her such a nasty look that she had the sense not to continue.

"As this concerns Zara," Ama said, turning to me, "I think we should hear from her."

I looked around at all the strong women in this room and tried to still my shaking hands and roiling stomach. I couldn't even ask Shazeera's opinion, or how she felt about possibly being shipped off to live in the mountains amongst terrifying eagles and cold, emotionless people. I was First Daughter; I belonged here, with my people. But I thought of the eleven guards and their horses who had been killed, of all the injured and their horses, and all the people and horses still at war, of Eagle Riders with skills superior to ours.

Using this wind power would bring me nothing but pain and suffering . . . could ultimately even destroy my bond with Shazeera. A choice lay before me. I could refuse and join the battle to the north, use my power even though Ama forbade it. I could wipe out the Eagle Riders—maybe, hopefully, assuming I was even that powerful—and never again communicate with

Shazeera or even sense her presence in my mind; she'd be as good as dead. Or I could sacrifice everything I'd ever known and loved, go to live with our enemy, and marry a man I neither knew nor loved.

But all my people would be safe and at peace.

And suddenly, I saw the only answer I could possibly give, even if it cost me my soul. I realized what would finally make me a worthy First Daughter, and it was something only I could do.

General Isa watched me, her expression steady and strong. It comforted me. She trusted me to make the right choice. Mariyah gripped my arm, her face twisted in pained sympathy. Ama, though her eyes still shone, watched me with a calm and peaceful expression, as though she knew I would make the right decision.

"I will do it," I said, my throat thick.

"Oh, Zara, no," Mariyah said, her eyes spilling the tears mine held back. "There must be another way. How will you survive in that cold place? How will you live amongst those evil people? You saw Commander Talon! He has absolutely no expression on his face, and every rider I've ever seen is the same! You don't deserve this."

"Mariyah," Queen Jazela said sharply. "Don't make your cousin feel bad when she is making an enormous sacrifice on all our behalf."

Ama's eyes shone with unshed tears, but her voice was strong when she reached out and touched my cheek. "You told me before that you wanted to prove yourself to be a worthy First Daughter, and you always have been. This is a great sacrifice being asked of you, but it will mean peace for our people at last. No more death and injury and losses of daughters and sons and horses. No more enduring the trauma of eagles preying upon our horses before our eyes. There is a reason you've been given this power, Zara, and as an empress, you will have greater influence than you even would have as Queen of All Queens.

"You are resilient, and you will survive no matter where you are. You will breathe life into a cold people and change them for the better. And you won't be without an ally. Shazeera will be there, and you will never again have to test the bond between you." She squeezed my hand. "There's more, my daughter. The power you have will draw evil things to you—ancient creatures better left alone in their dark caves—and now that there are many who know you have this ability, you would be safer with an empire as powerful as the Zephyrians."

I nodded mutely, not trusting my voice.

Mariyah jumped in. "You can't possibly think she'll be safer there! With our enemy?"

Mariyah had a point, considering our enemy regularly committed war crimes against us. Why should we believe them when they offered peace? They could bring me back to the palace, far away from any of my family and allies, and then remove the threat by killing me. On the other hand, how could we possibly afford to refuse a treaty at this point?

My thoughts raced to find a solution.

"What Her Majesty says is true," General Isa said. "You have seen the strength and abilities of their warriors. As their empress, they will defend Zara with their lives."

"They may be strong, but Mariyah has a point about not being able to trust them completely," I said. "I think there will need to be some sort of fail-safe to make sure they don't try to double-cross us once I'm at the palace."

"Yes, exactly," Mariyah said, and I felt a surge of love for her for defending me so strongly. "What if the emperor doesn't marry Zara and, Earth Mother forbid, they kill her instead?"

General Isa turned to me with a shrewd gaze. "What did you have in mind, First Daughter?"

I thought of how quicky the Zephyrians had reacted to my wind power. We had been at war with them off and on for a hundred and fifty years, but suddenly, they feared this power so much they were willing to offer a treaty almost immediately. "We should use the Zephyrians' ignorance of our people and our magic to our advantage. We can tell them that there are others who have manifested this wind power, and if they don't uphold the terms of the treaty, then we will retaliate with that power."

General Isa silently considered what I had said for a moment before nodding. "I think that will work to keep you safe, First Daughter. But of course you must be vigilant when you are in the enemy's palace. Keep daggers hidden on you at all times."

I touched the hilt of the one currently strapped to my thigh. "I always do."

"Then we will make sure Commander Talon understands what will happen if they try to harm you," Ama said solemnly. "Are you ready to finish this, Daughter?"

I nodded. "I'm ready. You can call him back in now."

Mariyah turned to me and threw her arms around me. "Are you sure?" she whispered. Her voice was raw with emotion. I knew she'd come to the same conclusion I did. This had to be done to save our people.

"I'm sure," I said out loud, forcing my voice to sound strong.

I had made my decision and knew it was the right one, but inside, it felt as though a harsh wind was tearing me apart, piece by piece.

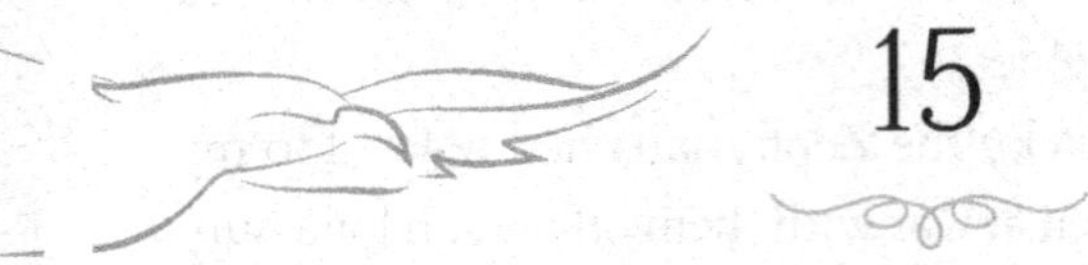

15

TALON

The two guards—a man and a woman—fidgeted at my side as I stood motionlessly outside of the Mid-Plains Queen's pavilion. I kept my body perfectly still, my breathing slow and even, and my face neutral so that I would give away none of my thoughts. In contrast, the guards were in constant motion. Grimacing, gazes darting about, muscles twitching. They were like the horses they loved so much.

The events inside the pavilion had been enlightening. It seemed that the Southern Queen, who had contacted us through a messenger, had done so without the knowledge of the Queen of All Queens, threatening us with her own cousin—not that we didn't already know about her power. I resisted the urge to touch the back of my head where it was still tender from my first encounter with her. Beside me, the guards continued to twitch and shoot me looks from the corners of their eyes. I wouldn't give them the satisfaction of seeing me move.

My mind turned to the First Daughter as I struggled to reconcile that image of a girl with stunning beauty raining down absolute hell upon me, to the same girl with wide eyes looking pale but determined. Before, she had seemed like a goddess of death wielding the elements against me when she nearly killed Neo and me. She had been responsible for the demise of Captain Suna and an entire battalion of Eagle Riders. But now, reeling from the news I brought her, she seemed vulnerable. I didn't want it to, but the situation humanized her.

She was full of contradictions. A Daughter of Earth, but seemingly without any of the earth magic abilities we had documented. She was fierce and terrible in her power, and yet young and—if her accuracy with the bow was any indication—inexperienced in battle. We knew they could split open the earth like an egg, launch a storm of rocks at us, and even cause crippling pain by turning our own bodies against us. But in all our intelligence reports, there was no mention of wind manipulation. Had they succeeded in keeping this secret from us? Only to be betrayed by one of their own—the Southern Queen?

The Southern Queen may have sold out one of her own, but she had the sense at least to do what it took to end this war. I could only commend her for it.

I couldn't imagine what it would be like to be told that you not only have to give up everything you've ever known, but also have to marry your enemy . . . I needed only to look around at the campsite here to know that I couldn't do it. I could never leave the mountains with the cool, crisp air and live either exposed and unprotected on the grasslands or hiding like an animal in a canyon cave.

But I also knew, without a doubt, that as unprepared as the Queen of All Queens was for Queen Samira's betrayal, she would sign the treaty. She had sought peace for so long and suffered too many losses to refuse. Even at the price of her own daughter. Honestly, she should have thought of the idea herself. She clearly was too soft, which was why they were losing this war in the first place. The question was, would the First Daughter come willingly?

There was a contingency plan to this whole treaty, one that was considerably more dangerous. If the First Daughter didn't agree to sign the contract, then I was to take her forcibly. With the sorcerer lurking behind Emperor Altair, my cousin had told me that I must return with the First Daughter—no matter the consequences.

That will be a difficult extraction, I had warned Altair when we discussed the plan. *The limits of her power are unknown, and she will be surrounded by royals with earth magic abilities.*

Behind him the sorcerer shifted, and Altair had tilted his head, listening to something I couldn't hear. A chill breeze whispered along the back of my neck, tensing my muscles. *Do whatever it takes to bring her here,* Altair had said, his eyes devoid of emotion.

More than any of his advisers, this sorcerer clearly wielded enormous influence over the emperor. I suspected that it was not completely in Altair's control, but so far, Altair had rebuffed any attempt to talk about it—and that was before I had wasted all that time healing in a hospital bed.

Altair, I had tried to reason, *she defeated me on her own, and she will have others with power to immediately come to her defense.*

His eyes had flashed. *That's an* order, *Commander.*

I had no other choice but to obey, though instinct told me not to trust any directive coming from that creature. Altair had convinced himself that he and the sorcerer were allies, but I didn't see their arrangement the same way. The creature had its own agenda. So long as its goals aligned with Altair's, they were allies. But I worried about the day when their objectives deviated. Would the sorcerer's goals serve the Zephyrian Empire then?

It was twenty minutes before someone came for me. By that time, each of the guards outside the pavilion had shifted from foot to foot nearly one hundred times each, and my own eye was twitching from having to restrain myself from shouting at them to *be still for skies' sake*!

It was the female warrior who escorted me back to the throne room, the one who looked at me with unbridled hatred on her expressive face. It was almost painful to look at. What would that be like, to have your every little thought and emotion displayed on your face for the world to see? And if this was how the warrior appeared, then how much worse would it be for the First Daughter?

I followed the warrior, never letting my guard down. The moment I saw the First Daughter, though, I knew what decision they'd come to. Relief made my chest lighten considerably. I would avoid a difficult extraction, then, and this whole process would go easier. It would still be a challenge for her, but at least she wouldn't have to watch me kill people she loved to remove her by force.

Surprisingly, her face didn't have the absolute devastation I expected. Her jaw was set with determination and, yes, an undercurrent of fear. She was trying to mask it, but judging from everything I'd seen so far, she had no idea how to be anything other than completely transparent.

Her gaze met mine, and for a moment, my own expression almost slipped, but I regained control. She looked at me like I was the cause of all her pain, and I supposed that was partly true. I thought of what would happen to her next, leaving everything she'd ever known and flying to the palace . . . marrying my cousin. Inevitably facing the creature that hid in the shadows. I was a soldier, not a diplomat, and I had never wanted to leave a place so badly as I did right then.

16

ZARA

Commander Talon had returned, his movements precise, his expression the same as it had been, even though my whole world was crashing down around me. Even though I wanted to leap astride Shazeera and run and run and run until I was far away from here and all these terrible responsibilities. I found myself wishing he were smirking at me, or grinning evilly, or rubbing his hands together in triumph over my fate, if only so I had someone to direct this black mass of grief and misery onto that was building inside me. If anything, though, when his gaze flicked to mine for a moment, the emotion hiding in the depths of his eyes looked more like sympathy. But that only made me feel worse. If an emotionless monster could feel sorry for me, well, my situation must be pretty dismal.

He stood before Ama. "What have you decided?"

Ama turned to me. "Zara?"

I tried to pull myself from the deep swell of self-pity, but it was like an unforgiving sea that kept dragging me under again. "We will sign your treaty," I said tightly, "but we have one condition."

His expression didn't change. "And that is?"

"You should know that First Daughter Zara is not the only one with the power to control the wind," Ama said, so smoothly I almost believed her. "We have prayed to the Earth Mother for the means to end this war once and for all, and she has gifted us with this newly manifested power. We were in the process of gathering all the wind magic users before you arrived with the offer of a treaty."

"There are others with wind magic as strong as the First Daughter's?" Commander Talon asked, his tone both skeptical and concerned.

"Yes," Ama said without blinking.

He was silent for several moments before finally saying, "And you will unleash this wind magic against us if we do not adhere to your condition for the treaty?"

He may have been carved from stone, but he wasn't stupid.

"Yes, if you cannot guarantee First Daughter Zara's health and safety, then we will bring the full force of the wind and raze your palace and cities to the ground."

His gaze shifted to mine, and I startled when he addressed me. "I can guarantee your health and safety, First Daughter," he said.

There was no way I would just take his word for it. I wanted to see it in black and white. "If you add that to the treaty," I said, "then I am willing to go with you."

He nodded once and then accepted the quill and ink General Isa handed him. In bold strokes, we watched him add the condition to the document.

He handed it to me to inspect. "Satisfied?"

He had done everything we asked, but the weight of everything still settled on my chest, making it difficult to draw a breath. "Yes," I managed to say.

"Emperor Altair will be pleased," he said. "I will serve as witness for our people, and it would seem you already have plenty of witnesses of your own."

"We will sign today, but we ask for two days to prepare," Ama said.

Commander Talon shook his head. "I can give you only one, and it's for your own benefit. This treaty, once signed, must be hand delivered by me for the emperor to declare an end to the war. Any delays will cost more lives."

I couldn't argue with such reasoning, because of course I didn't want anyone else to be killed, but the thought of leaving here tomorrow made my hands shake with the need to scream.

"Very well," Ama said.

General Isa and Queen Jazela moved closer to Ama without her having to ask, and then the hated scroll was unrolled and waiting for Ama's signature. She dipped the quill in the ink, and in a matter of moments, my life had been signed away.

"We will have a feast tonight in honor of my daughter," Ama said. "In the interest of this peace treaty, your Eagle Riders will be allowed to attend."

"Though don't expect the most welcoming reception," General Isa added, as though she just couldn't help herself.

"We will consider it," Commander Talon said, easily ignoring General Isa's dig, "and I appreciate the invitation." He turned to me then, that sympathy still lingering far in the depths of his sky-blue eyes. "You won't need to bring much. Everything will be provided for you."

He made to leave, but I spoke before he could. "Wait," I said, and he turned. "What about—I *will* be bringing my mare," I corrected myself. I wouldn't ask for something this important. I was still First Daughter, and if I was soon to be empress, then I would be obeyed. "I won't leave here without her, and I will need guarantees that she will never be in any danger and will also be well provided for."

"We assumed you'd bring your horse. It will be treated well."

"*She* will be treated well," I said, and his eyebrows rose a fraction of a degree. "She is my equal in intelligence—and likely smarter than you. I want her treated as well as I hope I will be amongst your people . . . and your eagles."

For some reason, my words, though they were antagonistic, made that little softness of sympathy in the depths of his eyes shift into something else. His expressions were hard to read. It was difficult to attribute emotion to a statue.

"You have my word she will be treated well," he said.

"Thank you," I said, and I felt a little bubble of relief that I'd managed to do that much at least. My whole world might be coming to an end, but I didn't want to drag Shazeera down with me.

He gave a quick nod of his head, and then he departed, scroll tucked under one arm.

Chaos erupted the moment he was gone. Ama began giving orders to handmaidens for the feast tonight and things I would need to pack. General Isa began barking orders to her guards, starting with finally lifting the canyon evacuation since we weren't under threat of attack anymore. Mariyah and Queen Jazela jumped into the discussion on the feast preparations. Queen Samira sat totally at ease, like she hadn't shown up and completely disrupted our lives. I tried to stand tall and dignified even though my legs had turned to jelly. Over and over, my mind tortured me with one question: *What if I made a terrible mistake?*

Zara, a voice said in my mind, just as I was at the height of my inner panic. *Zara, what has happened? What are the Eagle Riders doing here?*

I let out an explosive breath that was half sob and half relieved whimper. It was Shazeera. At last.

"Ama, I must go to Shazeera," I tossed over my shoulder as I hurried outside.

"Zara," she said as I raced by, but I didn't stop.

Shazeera was waiting right outside the pavilion, her concern for me coming through our renewed bond strongly. She was also dying to know why the Eagle Riders had come.

I sent an image of us going for a run before I hauled myself astride. Shazeera cantered easily to the top of the canyon, her head pointed toward the plains beyond . . . and freedom, if only for a moment. When we were no longer hindered by tents and people and animals, Shazeera lengthened her stride into a full gallop. The wind greeted me with a kiss as it flowed through Shazeera's mane and tugged on my own braided hair.

We ran and ran, and as we did, I fed memories to her of everything that had transpired within the tent. She let out a distressed whinny when I came to the end. The treaty was signed, and we would soon be leaving to live with our enemy, but there was never a moment's hesitation in her mind about coming with me. She was braver than I was.

It's not as though I'm not afraid to go, Shazeera said as her hooves thundered over the grasslands, *because I am, but we'll be together, which is all I care about.*

I put my hand on her sleek neck. *I know. I feel the same.*

This will be hard for you, but it will be easier on you than it would have been for any other daughter. It may be a secret to everyone else, but I know you've always been drawn to the eagles. Perhaps you'll finally figure out why.

I hid my head in her mane. *I feel only shame over that now. Think of everything we've seen the eagles do! How could I possibly be interested in such creatures?*

They are predators, and we are prey, she said with a mental shrug. *It is their nature, as yours is wind and flight. Even my fleetness cannot satisfy that need within you.*

I wrapped my arms around her neck. *Don't say that. You are enough. You are everything.*

You are my *everything, which is why I will gladly follow you up the mountain and into the eagles' nests.*

We had galloped clear to the other side of the lake, and now we stood overlooking its beauty, the canyon in the distance. *You are my heart's sister,* I told her, *and hearing you say that makes me feel better. Though I hope we won't have to live in an eagle's nest. I was hoping for slightly more elegant accommodations.*

Amusement flowed through our bond.

And at least our bond need never be tested again. There will be peace at last.

Yes, she said with a sigh, *at last.*

As the sun dipped lower toward the horizon, I looked out at our land and thought of all the horses who would soon be able to graze freely without fear of eagles swooping down on them. Of sons and daughters who would no longer have to go to war to defend our people. I may never see this land again, but at least I would leave knowing my sacrifice made it safe for my people and horses.

At long last, the war that had raged between our peoples for a hundred and fifty years was now over. Somehow, in spite of not having any earth magic, I had managed to fulfill my duty as First Daughter. The thought brought a sense of calm over me, even knowing that Shazeera and I would soon be walking into the unknown.

I knew my sacrifice would bring peace to my people, but for me, the battle was far from over. I had been born with the respect of my own people, but soon, I would have to earn it as future empress of a culture I knew virtually nothing about.

The true battle, though, would be with the emperor himself. I was under no delusions that he would automatically see me as a royal on the same level he was. For the good of my own people, I would have to fight to rule as his equal.

That was assuming I could bring myself to marry him in the first place.

FOR THE FIRST time since we arrived in Queen Jazela's camp, people seemed happy. At the feast, they talked animatedly, their faces simultaneously joyful and relaxed. The dark cloud of war had been lifted with the announcement of the peace treaty . . . and settled over me instead.

Commander Talon and the other Eagle Riders had remained on the outskirts of our camp, and none of them had shown at the feast, which was a relief. I would rather not watch them force themselves to participate in our revelry.

Mariyah was sitting silently beside me on a rough-hewn bench, her usually cheerful face withdrawn.

We picked at our plates of food half-heartedly, and it was bizarrely comforting that we knew each other well enough not to have to discuss how upset we both were. Besides, there'd be time enough for that tonight.

Suddenly, a quiet fell over the crowd of people around us, and Mariyah and I looked toward its source.

It was Commander Talon and his eagle, its wings tucked close to its sides as they both walked to the outskirts of the camp center where the feast took place. Nearby horses tossed their heads and cantered away, still unwilling to be near a known predator.

"I can't believe he showed up," Mariyah said, folding her arms across her chest.

"I didn't think he would." I imagined if our situations were reversed, and I was the one entering a camp full of his people. A suffocating weight pressed down on me when I realized that very soon, I would be doing just that.

"Does he have any other expressions besides that ice-cold look?" Mariyah demanded. "We may have a peace treaty, but as far as I'm concerned, he's still the enemy. He's commander of an army that killed our people and let their eagles feast on our horses."

When she put it that way, it was hard to imagine him standing here amongst us so casually.

Maybe I was getting used to looking at his expressions after spending a highly emotionally charged period with him in the pavilion, but it seemed he was looking around with interest. His gaze was moving, at least, and his eyebrows were ever so slightly lifted. No one approached him, though, or showed him the way to the food, and I didn't stir from my seat beside Mariyah. This was my last night with my people, and I didn't have room for pitying someone I would probably be forced to see too much of in the coming days. Anyway, he had managed to survive being blown out of the sky by my wind power, so I figured he could take care of himself.

The eagle stood calmly by his side, towering over us all, its golden eyes moving constantly. The eagle wore a large, flat saddle on its back, secured by a leather harness that stretched across its breast and under its wings. As we always rode bareback, I looked at this apparatus with a sneer, until I remembered that Shazeera never flipped over in the air. I supposed a saddle was necessary when you were upside down.

Commander Talon and the eagle seemed content to just stand there and observe, so I forced myself to direct my attention elsewhere. Although I soon found I wasn't entirely successful. My gaze kept slipping away to look at them, and I told myself it was because it was like keeping an eye on a wolf who stood too close to a flock of sheep.

But we are not sheep, Shazeera said. *You'd do well to remember that, Zara. We're about to go live amongst them, and if you are to be their empress, you cannot think of yourself as a sheep amongst wolves.*

I closed my eyes for a moment. *Of course, you're right.*

It was you who defeated him, remember? He's probably terrified to make you angry.

A smile touched my lips. *True. But I can't use that power ever again.*

He doesn't know that.

You're pretty sly for a horse.

I could feel her amusement from somewhere behind me, where she was grazing.

Mariyah hissed in a breath beside me, and I turned to see Commander Talon walking toward us. His eagle remained where it was, but everyone made sure to get out of the commander's way. Mariyah looked like she wanted to bolt, too, but she was too loyal to abandon me, so instead her hazel eyes flashed with warning at him as he approached.

He nodded a greeting at both of us and then said, "Tomorrow, we will need to leave early. Just after sunrise."

"Wow, ever heard of small talk?" Mariyah said as an aside to me, but loudly enough for Commander Talon to hear.

He looked unperturbed. "I didn't want to take up any of your time, so I jumped right to the point."

Mariyah shook her head, but I was slightly more sympathetic. "I can be ready to leave early," I told him.

"Good." He fell silent, watching the bonfire and the people talking and laughing as they ate. The smoky smell of burning wood was in the air, joined by all the spices we used in the many dishes that filled a long table for the feast, and I breathed in deeply, trying to forget my enemy standing right next to us. My people talked joyously and loudly, their faces lit up by the flames. I couldn't remember the last time I had seen everyone look this relaxed. Even General Isa wore a huge smile on her face as she ate and drank with Naomi.

Warmth spread through my chest knowing I had done that for them. At the same time, though, I fought tears at the thought of leaving all of this. Of traveling to enemy territory and marrying an emperor I had never seen, much less met. What were Zephyrian feasts like? Did they eat the same foods we did? I glanced down at my earthenware plate now, sitting mostly untouched. I had filled it to the brim with all my favorite foods—spiced honey squash, seasoned grains, creamy cheese, and soft bread. But all I could do was sip my fermented kir, enjoying the burn of the alcohol on its way down.

I had done such a good job of ignoring Commander Talon beside me that I startled when he spoke. "Whatever you have on your plate smells good," he said.

Mariyah gave me her look that meant, *What's with this guy?*

"Are you hungry?" I asked after a moment's hesitation. "I'm not sure what you're used to eating, but we have plenty."

"We generally have meat and vegetables with bread. Wine."

Mariyah and I shared a look of disgust. A meat eater. I shouldn't have been surprised, but the thought of tearing into flesh that once had a beating heart made my soul quake with horror. "Well, we don't eat innocent creatures, so you'll have to settle for things that can't fight back, like vegetables, grains, and bread."

"Pity," he deadpanned. "It sounds like a boring meal without slabs of bloody meat to feast on."

"Ugh," Mariyah said, turning away dismissively.

I had the sense that he was joking, though. "Sorry to disappoint—no carcasses on the menu tonight."

Something flickered across his face then—just the barest twitch at the corner of his mouth. Not quite a smile, but close.

"Will you show me?" he asked. When Mariyah and I looked at him with surprise, he added, "So I will know what I'm eating?"

It was on the tip of my tongue to refuse him—I wanted to go back to letting the alcohol burn in my belly and not think about this man or the enemy land I was about to venture to tomorrow, but then I noticed everyone stealing glances at Commander Talon. Everyone wore various expressions of hostility. I imagined what it would feel like to go to the table alone and serve himself food while everyone watched with barely concealed hate. I stood, slow and reluctant. "Very well."

"This is so strange," Mariyah interrupted. "Am I the only one who thinks this is awkward? I mean, didn't you try to kill each other last time you met? And now Zara's willing to help you fix a plate?"

I elbowed her and shot her a warning look. Obviously I felt the same way, but I didn't want to spend my last night here fighting with the man who was supposed to deliver me safely to the emperor tomorrow. The faster I helped him fill a plate, the faster he would hopefully eat and leave. And then we could all finally enjoy the feast.

"My orders were to bring her in alive, so actually, First Daughter Zara was the one trying to kill *me*."

Mariyah shot me a surprised look. "You weren't trying to kill her?"

He grinned. "If I were trying to kill her, she'd be dead."

I laughed. "Is that so? And who was it that got knocked out of the sky?"

"Maybe I let you," he said, and I rolled my eyes. "No, the truth is, you defeated me, but I survived. I consider the matter settled." He glanced over at his eagle. "We'd have to ask Neo how he feels, though. He has only just now healed from a broken wing."

We glanced at the eagle, who looked back at us with the reflection of flames flickering in his enormous eyes.

"Hmm, and what about you, Zara?" Mariyah asked. "How do you feel about calmly talking with the rider who tried to hunt you down?"

A flash of that moment, where I realized he was far more skilled than me, when I feared Shazeera really might be killed, went through my mind. How *did* I feel about it? Everything had happened so fast with their arrival and the treaty that I hadn't had the chance to really think about it. An echo of that fear slammed through me now, its reverberations making my blood run cold.

And yet . . .

You are not a sheep, Shazeera had said, and she was right. He had hunted us down, but in the end, I had blasted him from the sky and we had escaped with our lives.

"It was war," I said. "It wasn't personal."

But what if he let his eagle eat horses? What if he personally killed someone I knew?

I tried to ignore those thoughts, but they were like barbs that burrowed under my skin.

"You're lucky Zara is as emotionally intelligent as her mother," Mariyah said. "I would hate you until my dying day."

I couldn't help but laugh at her audacity, and a smile touched Commander Talon's lips, making him seem slightly more human.

"If you had hurt Shazeera, I probably wouldn't be as understanding about it all as I am now. You'd be halfway to the other side of the world in a cyclone right now had you or Neo touched her."

He seemed able to intuit who Shazeera was without my having to tell him, because then he said, "And if you had permanently injured Neo, then I would never be able to let it go."

Mariyah and I glanced at each other. Did the Zephyrians have a bond with their eagles as we did with our horses? We'd always assumed they'd domesticated wild eagles but couldn't communicate with them like we did. I wanted to ask more, but something held me back. Maybe it was because I didn't want to waste my last night with my people talking to my enemy.

"Good thing it didn't end up that way, then." I turned away, Mariyah eyeing my every movement. "I can show you to the food now if you'd like."

"Thank you."

He followed me through the crowds, which parted with wide eyes and whispered asides as we walked to the tables laden with food. There were roasted vegetables, salty cheese, bowls of honey, warm bread, sun-dried fruit, and trays laden with grains tossed with butter and herbs. I handed an earthenware plate to Commander Talon. This close, I could smell the mountains on him: the fir trees and the cool air, the leather from his armor, and something metallic . . . his sword? Shazeera always said I had almost as keen a sense of smell as a horse.

He spent some time looking at each of the dishes of food, but occasionally, his gaze would shift to me, as mine would to him. I didn't expect him to suddenly attack me after everything that had happened, but I couldn't seem to explain that to my heart. He seemed to be suffering the same problem if his glances at me were any indication.

Don't worry, I'm not going to suddenly unleash the power of the wind on you. Though even as I thought that, the wind made an appearance, swirling around me and bringing the scent of the mountains. *As long as you stick to the peace treaty, that is.*

Normally the feel of the wind lifted my spirits, but now it only reminded me of the recent harm to my ability to communicate with Shazeera. In an effort to push all those thoughts away, I said perhaps a little too loudly as I indicated the food before us, "No meat, as I said, but everything is delicious." I pointed to a clay jug. "That holds kir, which is fermented goat's milk and honey."

"Fermented is good," he said, and I glanced at him sideways to see if he was joking. Shockingly, I couldn't tell if he was or not.

"Have as much as you'd like, then," I said and handed him an earthenware cup.

For a barbaric meat eater, he didn't shy away from filling his plate with a little of everything, and I followed him to fill one of the big horse bowls with grains for Shazeera.

"What about your eagle? Will he need to . . . ?" I couldn't bring myself to say *hunt.*

"He'll be fine. He'll hunt later tonight."

"As long as it's far from here," I snapped, with a sharp look.

To my surprise, he smiled. A real smile that actually reached his eyes. It made his face seem much less harsh. "None of your horses or livestock will be in any danger, I promise."

"Never again, right?" I said.

"That's what the treaty says."

And it will be up to me to make sure all of you abide by it, I thought. I held up the bowl full of grains. "I should get this to Shazeera. Enjoy your dinner."

As I made my way back to Mariyah and Shazeera, many watched me go by and reached out to touch a part of my clothing, heads bowed. A smile played at my lips as I tried to absorb this good memory of my people before I left. Of them happy and relieved because the war was finally almost over. Of their never having to watch their horse or sibling or mother slaughtered before them again.

I could do that for them. I could be the First Daughter they needed.

"Finally," Mariyah said, pulling me from my maudlin thoughts as I set the wide bowl of grains down before Shazeera. "It's your last night, and we haven't even danced yet." She turned to Shazeera. "Hurry and eat that and then join us."

Shazeera only sent amusement across our bond as she enjoyed the honeyed grains.

Mariyah's own mare was already at her side, coat glistening like copper in the light of the fire.

"Well?" Mariyah said, holding out her hand to me.

I agreed because I knew this might be the last time I ever got to dance with my people.

17

TALON

The food wasn't bad. It wasn't what I was used to, but all the flavors complemented each other. Salty and sweet, tangy and fresh, savory and herbal. I didn't feel overly full when I finished my food like I usually did at our own feasts, but it made me wonder if I'd be hungry again in an hour.

The food wasn't the only difference between our feasts and this one. Ours were formal affairs with heavily decorated tables, porcelain plates, and silver utensils. We ate quietly, the conversations kept to the person next to us, in a polite murmur. We had music, but it, too, was quiet and reserved. Only the elite nobles were invited by the emperor, in contrast to the massive crowd present here.

All around me, the Children of Earth spoke loudly, boisterously, and it was clear by their smiles and laughter that they were enjoying the food and each other. The music, once it began, was almost primal, with drums that throbbed through my body, the beat swimming in my blood. Many were dancing, and it was nothing like our controlled synchronized movements. Their bodies followed the music, moving in time to it until they shone with sweat and their cheeks were flushed.

Why are they thrashing around like that? Neo asked, his sharp eyes darting rapidly to keep up with them. *Are they convulsing?*

No, I thought back with an inward grin, *they're dancing.*

Dancing, he said, disapproval clear in his thoughts.

I tended to agree with him, but then the First Daughter and her cousin joined the others. Everyone else made room for them, and I soon understood why, as they had their horses dancing with them. Hoofbeats followed the drums, slow at first, the girls weaving through their horses with graceful, almost hypnotic movements. I couldn't look away.

The tempo increased, faster and faster, and the girls and the horses kept pace, until Zara and Mariyah seemed in danger of being trampled by flinty hooves. The girls laughed, joining hands as their feet moved to the beat of the drum, hips swaying, too, in ways that would have made the stiff court ladies of the palace frown darkly. It captivated me, my plate forgotten in my lap.

And then the music swelled, the voices of the singers crying out all at once, and the horses reared. Zara and Mariyah vaulted beneath them, nearly bashing their temples on flashing hooves, and I stood so suddenly my plate fell to the ground. How would I explain the future empress's skull being bashed in on her last night with her people? But Zara twisted easily away, laughing as she did so.

There was a wildness within her that I knew would be tested when we returned to the palace. I thought of the austere ladies, the somber colors, the polite, murmured conversations. I thought of my cousin, with his frequent changes in mood, the times when he was deeply depressive and reclusive, or when he was easily angered. And then I thought of his ally, Ozul, who I had a feeling wouldn't simply vanish to wherever he'd come from now that this treaty was in place. I knew, even if my cousin didn't, that their goals weren't the same.

I almost feel sorry for her, I told Neo. *She doesn't even know what she's walking into.*

She'll just have to toughen up if she isn't already, Neo said, as usual without sympathy. *The palace is uncomfortable for all of us—except maybe the emperor's most favored nobles.*

This was true enough, but still, it seemed sad that the emperor would break her. He broke all his favorite things, and I knew this girl, this First Daughter who was once his enemy, would be impossible for him to resist. Some children destroyed their toys because they were naturally too rough or because they had a mean streak, but Altair was different. He broke them before his father could use them against him.

I remembered a summer when we were still young enough to like each other, when my mother brought him a soft toy eagle she'd made herself from wool and eagle feathers. I'd seen the look on his face when she gave it to him: wonder and disbelief. Not because he didn't have toys of his own—he did. But because she'd made it just for him.

He'd carried that thing around until it was filthy, and then one day, his father saw him clutching it tight to his chest.

You're too old for stuffed toys, he had said, the derision clear even to my young ears.

Aunt Luscinia made it for me, Altair had replied, his voice hesitant even as he gripped the toy harder.

You don't see Talon running around with a stuffed toy like a pathetic excuse for a boy.

I do have one Mama made me, I had said, flinching as my uncle whirled on me. *I sleep with it at night.*

His lip had curled, but he didn't respond to that—he didn't like the narrative that I was presenting: that it was normal for boys our age to have stuffed toys. *Then hand it over, Altair, and I'll put it in your room for you. No one wants to see the future emperor running around the palace clutching a stuffed animal. They'll think something is wrong with your brain, Son.*

To my surprise, Altair had shaken his head. *No.*

What did you say? my uncle had asked in that dangerous tone of voice that made me freeze like a rabbit.

I won't let you have it, Altair said, and before his father could snatch it from him, Altair set his teeth and ripped the stuffed eagle to pieces. Tears were streaming down his face, though it was contorted in anger, and I watched in silent horror as feathers and wool littered the floor.

It wasn't until I was much older that I understood. Altair had ripped his beloved toy apart so that his father couldn't do it. He'd rather it be by his hand than be forced to watch his father do that to something he loved.

I didn't want anyone to suffer the same fate, not even the First Daughter.

And just because Altair's father was no longer alive didn't mean she couldn't be used against him.

I won't stay at the palace long, then, I thought to myself. I wouldn't be able to watch the light go from her eyes, the color from her cheeks—this girl who had bested me as a warrior, whom I couldn't help but respect.

In the morning, though, I would do my duty and bring her back to the palace, to the emperor whose only real concern about her was whether or not she was beautiful. Unfortunately for her, she was—a wild, untamed sort of beauty that was as fierce as a sudden storm on the plains. It would be better for her if she were unremarkable, because then my cousin wouldn't want to keep her close to him for all to see. I knew as soon as she arrived, and he got a look at her, she'd be dressed like a doll, everything that made her who she was stripped away, until she wore the drab but elegant clothing favored by the court. I would go and tell the emperor that there were others here with the power to control the wind, though I had seen no proof of this myself–nor demanded any. Like the Children of Earth, I wanted an end to this war. Bringing the First Daughter back only to have her assassinated by one of Altair's advisers would only plunge us back into war. They were clever to request a safeguard for her, because honestly, the palace court couldn't be trusted.

I hope you would not be so sympathetic to her if she had crippled my wings, Neo said, his tone wry.

I would pity anyone having to spend time in that court. Sometimes, I even pitied the emperor himself. He didn't get to be the way he was by living a happy, carefree life, and in many ways, the court reflected what he'd been through in his childhood. What he was still going through with the memory of his father.

But as I watched Zara throw her arms around her cousin, laughing as the music ended, I could only think, *I'm sorry.*

THE NEXT MORNING, after Neo returned from hunting, I went to the pavilion of the Queen of All Queens. The other riders had gone on ahead, to bring word that the peace treaty had been signed, and I was alone. Outside the tent, the same warrior who had accompanied the queen and First Daughter before waited outside, her eyes narrowed as she looked at me. I kept my expression carefully blank, though I wanted to glare back at her. Everyone here wore every emotion they had on their faces for the world to see. She may as well have said, *I hate you. I hate that the First Daughter will be going with you.*

"I'm here for the future empress," I said, and maybe I was pettier than I thought, because I knew she wouldn't like me calling her that.

She added a slight curl to her lip to accompany her glare. "I'll let the First Daughter know. Wait here."

They made me wait for quite a while, until I had to suppress the urge to shift from one foot to the other. When they finally emerged, Zara carried a heavily tooled leather bag in one hand, as well as her bow and arrows strung across her back. She wore a slim leather breastplate studded with aquamarine gemstones and a flowing skirt that was cut down the middle to reveal leather leggings and boots beneath. Her horse was on her right, and her cousin Mariyah and mother on her left. Zara's and Mariyah's eyes were so red it looked as though they'd stayed up all night crying. Something twisted inside me, but I didn't let it rise to the surface. Pity wouldn't make her feel any better, especially from me.

Zara embraced her cousin first before turning to her mother, who whispered something to her and held her tightly. A black mare came forward then, too, and Zara bent her head to touch foreheads, one hand on the mare's cheek.

"May the Earth Mother keep you and guide you," her mother said, holding her hand out in blessing.

"I love you all," Zara said, her voice wavering. "This isn't goodbye forever."

But I could see it in her face that was too easy to read. She believed it was. I couldn't tell her any differently. Even as empress, she would be subject to the whims of the emperor.

They said their goodbyes one last time, and then she and her horse stepped toward me. "Neo is waiting for us at the edge of camp," I said, and she nodded.

Lines of people waited for her, holding their hands out as she passed by. "Bless you, First Daughter," they said, or, "Thank you for bringing us peace."

She touched everyone who held their hand out to her, sometimes stopping for a few moments to speak with them, and I tried to stay patient, but we had far to travel. I took hold of her arm and guided her away. "We must go now. We have already delayed too long."

She pulled free in the next instant, her eyes flashing at me. "I can see Neo from here. I don't need your guidance."

And then she turned to her horse and was astride in the next breath. She kept her gaze forward after that and wouldn't look at me again, though she continued to stop to speak to the people who had come to see her off.

When we arrived at Neo's side, I waited for her to dismount. After a few breaths, I realized she had no intention of getting off her horse. "We will get there faster if we fly."

Her whole body went tense, and she slowly turned to me. "What about Shazeera?"

I nodded toward Neo. "He's strong enough to carry us all."

"Yes, but how?"

I thought it would have been obvious, so the question took me by surprise. "You will ride on Neo's back with me, and your horse will be carried in his claws."

"His claws," she repeated, her face rapidly losing color.

"Yes."

"No."

I turned to face her fully. "What do you mean, 'no'?"

"I mean, no, I will not subject my horse to such a terrifying thing. How could you even ask us to endure that?"

Did she think Neo would puncture her horse with his talons? She must know that her horse could not travel as swiftly as Neo. Her reaction baffled me. "She won't be injured in any way. It's much faster to fly, and eventually, when we reach the mountains, it's the only way to the palace."

"It doesn't matter if she'll be injured—you don't see how it would be frightening to be held in the claws of a predator? We can figure out what to do then, but for now, I want to leave this camp the way I came into it. On horseback."

I stared at her in silence, hoping she'd see reason, but her stubbornness was powerful to behold. She merely stared back at me, arms crossed over her chest. I could see that we would waste more time arguing than if she were to ride.

"Fine, but the second you can't keep up, you're both being flown the rest of the way."

She nodded, chin tilted up, a picture of stubborn pride as the mare cantered away.

How long do you think they'll last? Neo asked as I leaped onto his back and settled just behind his wing joints.

An hour at most.

His laughter went through my mind. *That's assuming I don't fly as fast as I'm able.*

I almost agreed with him—that after her stubbornness, she deserved to be taught a lesson—but then I remembered where we were going. At the palace, she'd be faced with nothing but lessons.

Just fly your normal traveling speed. Let her hold on to her pride while she can.

It would be broken soon enough.

18

ZARA

The sun was still high in the sky when I knew Shazeera could go no farther that day. I only hoped they'd allow us to make camp and rest, but somehow, I knew that wasn't a possibility. She'd kept pace with the eagle flying just ahead of us, but she had to maintain at least a canter or fast trot the entire time. Now, her nostrils flared so wide I could see red inside, her sides foamed with sweat, and her breaths came in heaves.

"Enough," I said to her and to Commander Talon above us as I flung myself off Shazeera's back. *Keep walking!* I told Shazeera when she threatened to halt. She couldn't just stop now; she risked her muscles seizing and worse things.

She walked in tired circles around me as Neo landed nearby.

Why didn't you slow when I asked you to?

Better to collapse than willingly be carried by that monster, she said, her inner voice sounding as exhausted as she looked.

Commander Talon walked over to me, his boots making soft sounds on the grass. "I don't know much about horses, but she doesn't look like she can go on."

I looked over to Shazeera, where she was stumbling along.

"Can we make camp here for the night? I know it's only afternoon, but–"

"No, the treaty needs to be returned as soon as possible."

I stared at Neo, whose talons were as long as daggers and who looked right back at me with his golden eyes.

"How do you know he won't hurt her?" I asked, arms wrapped around myself with a shudder at the thought of Shazeera being attacked in front of me. "What if he gets hungry?"

"He knows she's important to you. And he ate a big breakfast."

It was obvious now that Commander Talon and his eagle could communicate, possibly on the same level that I did with Shazeera, but still, I felt sick every time I imagined her in the eagle's clutches.

"I still worry she'll be terrified," I admitted.

Commander Talon glanced over right as Shazeera stumbled for what must have been the tenth time. "I don't think she even has the energy to be frightened at this point. Have you considered blindfolding her? It might help with any fear of heights."

I'll do it, Shazeera said suddenly in my mind. *He's right that we need to get the treaty back. I shouldn't have been so selfish.*

You weren't being selfish. You were afraid.

Still, many lives hang in the balance.

I walked over to her and put my hand on her sweaty neck. *Are you sure? Do you want me to blindfold you as Commander Talon suggested?*

Shazeera swung her tired head toward Neo. After a moment's thought, she said, *Yes.*

I went to my bag and pulled a silk scarf free before returning to her, tying it carefully over her eyes, and securing it beneath her throat. *Just rest easy here. I'll talk you through everything so you won't be surprised.*

I followed Commander Talon over to Neo's side, and maybe it was because I was trying to be brave for Shazeera's sake, but I didn't even flinch when Neo turned to look at me with those piercing eyes.

"Would you feel safer riding in front of me or in back?" Commander Talon asked as I tilted my head to look up at Neo's saddle far above us.

My mouth suddenly felt dry. It was slowly sinking in that I would soon be in the air. On the back of an eagle. Part of me was thrilled—flight was something I'd always dreamed about. But the other part of me—the part born on the soft grasses of solid earth—wanted to fling myself onto my belly and refuse to leave the safe and familiar ground. "What would you suggest?"

"Wind currents that high can get pretty strong, and since you're not used to it, if you rode behind me, they might rip you off Neo's back." He said all this matter-of-factly, and I tried to nod as though I were taking it all in calmly. In reality, my heart raced so fast in my chest that I felt a little faint. "Ordinarily, if that happened, Neo could catch you." He pointed to Shazeera. "However, he won't have that ability this time."

"So, in front of you would be best."

"Yes, that way I can catch you if we hit rough air."

"Rough air," I repeated slowly.

"Unless, of course, you can control the wind currents," he said, his gaze holding mine. "Then you can make the flight as easy as you'd like."

Could I do such a thing? I wasn't even sure, but I also knew I couldn't let Commander Talon know that. It was better for all if they thought my control over the wind was complete. "I only call upon the power of the wind in desperate situations," I said, which was the truth.

"It shouldn't be desperate, but Neo can fly low to avoid it."

That wasn't reassuring, but I tried not to let my apprehension show as Commander Talon took my leather bag and secured it to the back of Neo's saddle. When he finished, he held his hand out to me. "I'll give you a leg up."

I looked at the huge expanse of eagle before me, without a mane or withers to help me pull up. "Where do I hold on?"

Commander Talon reached up and grabbed a piece of leather from the saddle and harness secured to Neo. "You can use this to hoist yourself up. When you get up there, kneel and then sit back on your heels so that your legs don't hinder his wings."

Commander Talon joined his hands together in front of him to give me something to jump from, and I put my booted foot in the center of his palms. I gripped the leather strap and sprang from his joined hands, feeling a powerful boost at the same time, as Commander Talon launched me into the air.

I landed on Neo's back much more roughly than I would have done to Shazeera, and without thinking, I put my hand on his feathers to apologize. Neo turned his head slightly to look at me, and I yanked my hand away with a yelp.

His feathers were much tougher than I expected them to be, still smooth, but with a rigidity to them that made them nothing like chicken or goose feathers. I was positioned just behind his head, in between his wings, which rose on either side of me. Neo was bent forward so that his back was level, his wings outstretched to keep his balance.

With one hand on the same strap I used, Commander Talon sprang from the ground and pulled himself up at the same time, settling into the saddle behind me much more lightly than I did. He knelt, too, his powerful thighs on either side of mine. I glanced down at them, heat rushing to my face. I definitely hadn't expected to be sitting this close to him. As soon as he was on Neo's back, the eagle folded in his wings and straightened. In that moment, I realized why he'd been bent forward in the first place. When he stood, Commander Talon and I were nearly vertical, and it was only my strong leg muscles—honed from years of riding bareback—that kept me from falling back against Commander Talon's chest. I gritted my teeth and squeezed, legs pressed into smooth feathers. My hair was tumbling back onto Commander Talon, no doubt directly into his face.

"Neo," Commander Talon said, his voice slightly strange since we were effectively hanging onto the eagle's back like a pair of ticks, "remember that we have someone who has never flown before on your back."

There was a shifting beneath us, and then Neo leveled out again, once again allowing us to remain horizontal on his back.

"Was it because I landed so roughly on his back?" I asked, and I couldn't believe I was worried about an eagle's comfort. But then again, this particular eagle had not just me, but Shazeera at its mercy, and I couldn't afford to offend it. "If so, tell him I'm sorry."

I turned my head just enough that I could see Commander Talon out of the corner of my eye, but he appeared to be smiling. "Believe me, you are so light that you're nothing more than a fly landing on his back. He didn't even notice."

"Good," I said.

"You will need to hold on now, though. He's going to lift off first before taking hold of your horse."

Cold fear trickled through me at that announcement, more on Shazeera's behalf than my own. I glanced over at her where she stood, head hanging in her exhaustion, eyes still blindfolded.

Shazeera, the eagle is flying over to you now. Be ready.

Shazeera lifted her head, her ears twitching this way and that, and I knew despite her fatigue, she was afraid. My stomach churned with a sickly mix of regret and nausea. She was doing this for *me.*

Neo shifted again, and we seemed to be lowering as he crouched. On either side of me, Neo's powerful wings pumped once, then twice, and then we launched into the air, leaving my stomach far behind. Commander Talon was right in that Neo flew like we were no more than flies on his back. He flew high above Shazeera, talons spread.

I barely had time to think to Shazeera, *The eagle is coming now–faster than I thought.*

Neo grabbed hold of her, claws wrapped carefully around her belly. And then, with a weak scream from Shazeera, Neo pumped his wings rapidly until we rose higher in the air. The wind buffeted my ears with every beat of his wings, louder than the roar of thunder.

Are you all right? I asked Shazeera, but all she could convey to me was the sense of weightlessness, and the ever-present wind.

Commander Talon gently touched my shoulder. "Lean forward just a little," he said. The moment I did so, I slipped beneath the airstream, and the wind grew much calmer. He did the same, leaning forward with me slightly. "Better?"

"Yes."

"Your horse didn't die of fright?"

I turned to glare at him–this didn't seem funny to me–but the wind grabbed a lock of my hair that had come free of its braid and threw it into my face.

With a laugh, Commander Talon reached forward and pulled it out of my mouth for me. "That's something else I didn't think about," he said, pointing to his own short hair.

And then Shazeera finally answered me. *I'm not being pierced by talons, so I'm well enough.*

I let out my breath in a powerful sigh. I hadn't realized how tense I was until I knew for sure that Shazeera was okay. But now that I did, I couldn't help but notice my surroundings.

The sky. How long had I stood below, staring up at it in awe? How many times had I wondered what the clouds felt like? Now, we flew through them, and it was like riding through mist on a cold day. The clouds were a brilliant white, made brighter by the sun, and when I glanced down at the earth I knew to be below me, I couldn't see anything anymore. There was nothing but the bluest sky all around–like we were in the middle of the ocean.

The sight was mesmerizing, so much so that I found myself trying to sit up again to take it all in, only to have the wind hit me with so much force I slammed back into Commander Talon's unforgiving chest. His arms came around me, and again, he pushed me forward. The warmth of his body surrounded me.

"Stay down until we hit a calmer patch of air," he said, his voice directly in my ear to be heard above the wind. Warmth crept up my neck. I should have felt incredibly awkward and uncomfortable being shoved against him like this, but there was something about him that put me at ease. Which was weird considering how we'd first met.

I did as he suggested, and even though I couldn't take in the sights as well, the sensation of flying was everything I'd always imagined it to be. It was like galloping full out on Shazeera, and then plunging over a cliff, with a drop that went on forever. Even the wind seemed delighted that I was in the air, as a warm breeze that had no business being this high curled around my neck like a scarf. I knew I shouldn't feel like this. Guilt hung around at the edges of my consciousness, threatening to pull me under, but

I selfishly ignored it. I only wanted to revel in the feeling of soaring through the sky without any of the repercussions. With Shazeera dangling from Neo's talons, though, that was impossible.

Time passed swiftly—the speed we were traveling made it seem fast, perhaps, or maybe the fact that I dreaded the moment of arrival.

Suddenly, I could feel us begin to descend from the clouds. Below, Shazeera let out a worried whinny, and my heart rose to my throat.

Down we went, sinking through the clouds like a stone in deep water, and then the mist cleared. Laid out below us were the plains, endless grasslands, and beyond that, forest. But rising from the earth like jagged pieces of stone were the mountains, gray and snowcapped. There was an alien beauty to them, especially from this vantage point, where I was practically looking down on them.

Commander Talon leaned toward me. "We're almost there."

We had flown over two hundred miles, across the Mid-Plains of Equnox to the Angora Mountains in the east in mere hours. The swiftness of our travel was staggering. And just beyond the trees I could see it, rising from the side of the mountain as though it had grown there.

Golden Eagle Palace.

19

ZARA

As we approached Golden Eagle Palace, which loomed as gray and forbidding as the mountainside, I felt impossibly small. The scale of it took my breath away. The Zephyrians had carved an entire city out of the rock, transforming outcroppings of Crane Mountain into buildings. It was Naharu, the capital city I'd only heard about. The city spread out across three wide mountain peaks, and above it all was the palace. Countless turrets with flags bearing the insignia of the emperor—the golden eagle—flew from the red-tile roofs. A massive waterfall plunged from within the center palace like a yawning mouth, spilling over the side and down far, far below. As we came nearer, the water roared and showered us with a cold mist. No doubt it came from a spring in the heart of the mountain.

Neo banked, and I leaned precariously over the edge for a moment before Commander Talon reached forward and steadied me. The eagle flew toward an enormous opening in the palace, where guards were stationed in regular intervals, carrying spears with golden flags that hung from the base of their sharp tips. When the guards caught sight of Neo and Commander Talon, they saluted with left arms crossed over their chests. They wore elaborate golden armor and serious expressions that made something inside me grow cold.

Neo descended, his wings once again buffeting the air painfully into my ears until I couldn't hear anything at all. But then it became obvious why he was doing so. He was hovering to give Shazeera a chance to gain her footing. I leaned over the side of Neo to see, hand reached out toward Shazeera as if I could help her. She stumbled once or twice as her hooves met the granite floor, but then she was standing on her own.

Neo landed just behind her, keeping his wings stretched wide so that his back would remain level.

"Neo says he hopes you enjoyed your flight," Commander Talon said from behind me, and as I looked at him, something danced in his eyes that was almost like mirth.

"Tell him thank you for getting us here safely," I said, though I couldn't quite bring myself to smile at him. My legs quivered unsteadily, and I didn't think it had to do with the flight as my mind raced with thoughts of what was to come. What would the emperor be like? What did the Zephyrians expect from marriage? The concept of agreeing to marry someone for political reasons was so foreign to me it was incomprehensible.

Neo turned his head so one of his huge bright eyes met mine.

"He heard you," Talon said from behind me. "I'll get down first, and then I'll help you, all right?"

I glanced over Neo's wing. It was a long way to the floor. "Yes, all right."

Commander Talon swung his leg over Neo's back and slid down smoothly, landing with a heavy thump. "If you turn to face outward with both legs on the same side, you can just slide down from there."

Carefully, I did as he said, swinging my left leg over Neo's neck. Talon held out his arms to me and caught me easily as I slid down, his large hands spanning nearly my entire waist. I was glad for his help, as it was a much farther drop than I was used to, and my legs felt like jelly after being folded on Neo's back for so long. I glanced up at Talon when my feet hit the floor, and for just a moment, our eyes met. "Thank you," I murmured.

After another breath, he released me and took a step back with a bow of his head. "Of course, Future Empress."

He turned back to Neo and retrieved the leather bag I had brought with me from the back of Neo's saddle.

On shaky legs, I ran to Shazeera and untied her blindfold. She shook out her mane as she took in our surroundings. We'd flown into a veritable chasm, with a ceiling so far above it could only just be detected. Guards lined either side of a wide expanse. It was clearly to give eagles room to land and spread their wings comfortably, but we were lost in the middle of it, like field mice in the midst of a widespread meadow.

Immediately, a heavily armored guard approached Talon and saluted him with one hand over his chest. "Commander, the emperor has requested that you bring the future empress to the throne room."

I saw Talon's jaw flex once. "Does the future empress have time to change before her first appearance?"

The guard hesitated. "Briefly, sir. The emperor is waiting."

Talon nodded, then turned to me. "Come. I'll show you to your chambers."

I found my voice suddenly didn't work, so with my hand on Shazeera's neck, I followed Commander Talon into the depths of the palace. Neo stayed behind, though I saw him spread his wings again as if he meant to fly away. We passed many more silent guards, servants dressed in gray who never met our eyes or even stopped to stare in curiosity, and people who were dressed in fine clothing who *did* stop and stare, but with guarded expressions that made it impossible to guess how they felt about my arrival.

Finally, we arrived at a suite of rooms carved directly into the mountainside. The guard opened the door for me and stood aside. I hesitated on the threshold, thrown by the sheer opulence: polished stone floors, an enormous bed draped in lace and gold, a wide hearth already burning, and windows that opened to the sky. Everything gleamed with wealth and power—and none of it felt like mine.

"Five minutes," Commander Talon said quietly as I stepped inside.

I glanced back at Shazeera, who stood patiently beside the commander, and just knowing that she was here steadied me. I was miles from home, but I wasn't alone.

I dropped my bag just inside the door, peeled off my travel-worn clothes, and changed into my most formal outfit—something I rarely had occasion to wear at home. I pinned up my hair, secured the headscarf, and fastened the golden diadem in place with trembling fingers. Then I looked into the polished mirror and saw a stranger: regal, composed, and outwardly unshaken. No one would know I'd just flown for hours or left almost everything I loved behind.

With a deep breath, I pulled open the door. Commander Talon didn't say anything when I stepped back into the hall, but his eyes swept over me once, lingering just long enough to make heat rise in my cheeks before he turned away.

"If you would follow me," Commander Talon said. He turned and began walking, and I fell into step beside Shazeera.

Wide halls yawned before us, the walls uncovered. I frowned

at the cold gray granite everywhere I looked, while the only color came from artifacts on display. Enormous jade vases sat on marble pedestals beside paintings with such startling detail I found my steps slowing in wonder, and life-size sculptures of animals made entirely from glass filled the space.

Silence reigned, so much so that every hoofbeat from Shazeera rang like drums, and even my slippered feet echoed. I glanced frequently at Commander Talon, but whatever glimpse of amusement I'd seen in his eyes before was now gone, to be replaced by the guarded expression that seemed to be how everyone's face here looked.

The alienation hit me so hard I nearly whimpered. I hadn't been here five minutes, and I desperately missed color, and smiling, and talking, and laughter.

Are you all right? Shazeera asked.

Just homesick already, and we've been here approximately twenty seconds.

We passed beneath marble columns wider than two horses, and then we arrived at doors so tall and wide a giant eagle could walk through with its wings outstretched.

The first thing I noticed as I walked into the throne room was the silence. It was thick and pressing, like the calm after a violent storm. Emperor Altair sat on a granite stone on a dais facing a cavernous room with regular intervals of columns. Behind him stood an eagle, smaller and more delicate-looking somehow than Neo.

The cavernous room dwarfed everything in it—even the giant eagle. When I looked out at the crowd of people, a sea of black, white, and gray gazed back at me, the style so different from my own. High necklines, long skirts, and wide-cut sleeves covered them in such an austere and modest way that it made me look half naked in contrast. I admired the fabrics, though. The women wore silks and heavy satin with intricately embroidered robes that fell all the way to the floor. Extremely impractical, but beautiful. The men wore black leather armor or high-necked tunics with pants, their boots scrupulously clean and shiny.

I stood out like a peacock amongst crows. Even though I was met with haughty looks, it didn't bother me. I was taught that our bodies were a thing of beauty, and being around mostly women and horses my whole life had made me very unselfconscious.

What *did* bother me was the fact that the men were in the middle of the room facing the throne, while the women were separated from them and off to the side. A glance at the dais where Altair sat showed a smaller throne slightly behind and to the side of his. I supposed that one was for me.

Emperor Altair stood and held out his hand to me, but he didn't smile. Commander Talon continued by my side as we approached the dais. My first real look at the man who was to be my husband, and I felt underwhelmed. Next to his cousin, he seemed much thinner and frailer, like he spent most of his time indoors. They both had similar features, like straight noses, though the emperor's was slightly more curved, reminding me of an eagle's beak, which I supposed was appropriate. They both had strong, angular jaws, though Commander Talon's was shadowed with dark hair and more pronounced, whereas the emperor still had baby-smooth skin. Their mouths, too, were similar, with full lips that seemed to balance out the more masculine features.

Commander Talon handed over the treaty with a bow. After a quick glance at Ama's signature, Emperor Altair passed it over to a servant dressed all in black.

"Commander Talon has returned from the Mid-Plains bearing a signed peace treaty with the Children of Earth," Emperor

Altair announced as I climbed the steps of the dais and turned to face the crowd of people. "The war is officially at an end."

Murmurs ran through the crowd along with shared looks of surprise. No cheers or other expressions of joy, though. You would think everyone would be happy for the end of a war.

Emperor Altair motioned to me. "May I present First Daughter Zara of the Children of Earth," he said to the people. "In a gesture of goodwill for both our peoples, I will be marrying First Daughter Zara in one month."

Silence greeted me. No bows or curtsies or any other sign of respect.

One man with closely cropped hair approached the dais, brought his hands together over his abdomen, and bowed—but only toward Emperor Altair.

"Yes, Lord Heron?" Emperor Altair said, his hooded eyes contributing to the impression that he found this whole process tedious.

"Will the Children of Earth be in attendance?"

"No."

I shouldn't have been surprised, not really. It was impractical to say the least. How would we even get everyone to the palace? There was no way any of them would consent to being carried by eagles—the thought of Mariyah allowing that to happen forced me to suppress a grin. I also didn't want anyone to witness my participation in the humiliating ceremony. But I couldn't ignore the fact that it was insulting, and my lip curled as I glanced from Lord Heron to Emperor Altair. It seemed obvious that the question had only been asked to make sure my people wouldn't be there to foul up the ceremony.

Commander Talon took a step forward to draw the emperor's attention. "With your permission, Lord Emperor, now that the treaty has been safely delivered, I will give the order to recall the Eagle Riders and infantry."

My breath caught in my throat at his words as I pictured our enemy leaving the battlefield at last—something we hadn't even dared dream about for so long.

Emperor Altair nodded once, and Talon saluted him before turning on his heel and striding out of the throne room. I swallowed hard when I glanced around the room now bereft of anyone I knew. At least I still had Shazeera with me. I leaned into her warm side, enjoying the momentary flood of relief that spread through me. No longer would daughters and sons face the horrors of war.

Thanks to you, Shazeera said.

Thanks to manipulative Queen Samira, really, I said, barely able to hide my smile.

Emperor Altair returned to his throne and gestured for me to join him. I left Shazeera at the bottom of the dais, my back prickling at the many unfriendly eyes that watched me walk to the smaller throne beside him.

"Let the zither player come and entertain us," Emperor Altair said.

An older man came forward then, his beard neatly styled and shot with gray. He wore a black tunic with silver embroidery, black pants, and boots trimmed in fur. In his hands was an instrument with many strings, small enough to fit in his lap. As he bowed to Emperor Altair just as Lord Heron did, I could better see the beautifully carved instrument. The reddish-brown wood was polished to a high shine, and beneath the numerous strings were hand-painted images framed in gold: an eagle, the mountains, and little curlicues of blue and silver that I think must have represented the wind.

The man settled the zither carefully in his lap, his posture impeccably straight, only his neck bent gently toward the instrument.

Everyone else in court sat in wooden chairs facing the throne and the zither player. The music came then, tinny and spidery, like an arachnid making its way across its web. The sound increased in intensity until it was a strong, driving rhythm, to the point where the audience could clap along, but they did nothing even close to that. Emotionlessly and without moving, they watched him play. It was so far removed from the music of my people, with its primal drums and vocals that forced my blood to pump faster and compelled my feet to move. This was a lullaby in comparison. A beautiful lullaby.

After a time, some of the women who had been seated off to the side stepped forward, dressed in flowing white robes with subtle embroidery. They moved like swans, elegantly graceful. Slowly, and with arm movements that were as smooth as water cascading over rock, they danced. They moved around one another in time to the music, their feet hidden by the folds of their clothing, which trailed behind them. They kept their faces absolutely still, and I came to realize it was like an art form to them.

Though it was beautiful at first, the zither player continued to play, and the dancers to dance, until my eyes grew heavy. I was tired from the stressful journey, and I hadn't eaten since breakfast. I glanced at Emperor Altair several times, but he always seemed entranced. Who would have thought it possible to be bored to tears in the palace of my people's enemy?

Beside me, Emperor Altair shifted so that he was leaning closer. "Do you like music?"

"I do, but ours is very different. This is beautiful, though."

He looked at me with interest. "What is yours like?"

"Much faster, with drums. We dance with our horses."

He raised his eyebrows. "I would like to see that."

We could dance now, if you'd like, Shazeera said, amusement filling her tone.

I barely restrained letting out a laugh. *Can you imagine what they'd do?*

Already, the crowd kept stealing glances at Shazeera with varying degrees of disdain. I thought of their jaws dropping with horror at Shazeera's and my fast-paced dancing and had to bite my lip to keep from laughing out loud.

To Emperor Altair, I said teasingly, "That could be arranged." When he smiled back at me, I added, "Though I have to admit, I'm surprised you're even interested."

Even before our peoples had been at war, the Zephyrians had never made any attempt to travel to our lands and learn about our culture. Even in the common port cities, they treated our people with contempt. To my knowledge, Commander Talon had been the first to ever attend one of our feasts.

He didn't say anything to that, so I decided to ask him what I really wanted to know. "What made you sign the treaty with us?"

"This was my ancestors' war—not mine. In truth, it's been a colossal drain on our resources. I want to rebuild my empire's coffers."

"So you decided to tax my people to do that."

He gave a small shrug. "It's better than being at war, right?"

Queen Samira certainly wouldn't agree, but I tended to think he had a point. Maybe in time I could change his mind on the percentage. The Zephyrians controlled so much of our continent already—how many more resources could they need?

I glanced at the man who was supposed to become my husband. In this unfamiliar place, I didn't know what to expect. We treated relationships so differently on the plains. "Can you tell me more about royal marriages here? What are the expectations?"

He looked momentarily stunned. "You agreed to this without knowing what would be expected of you?"

"I would have agreed to almost anything to save my people."

"That's very brave," he said, and when I searched his face, he looked sincere. "Usually, the goal is to produce an heir as soon as possible."

Now it was my turn to be blindsided. Somehow, I hadn't thought that far ahead. I had only imagined how difficult it would be to leave my people and live here amongst my enemy, but my imaginings had never gone so far as to think of what it would be like to have a *baby* here. A baby without Ama or any of the other daughters, who wouldn't be there to help. We never raised children alone. Everyone helped. Everyone shared the knowledge of their mothers. I knew in this cold place that none of that would be the same.

Never mind that I didn't want to have a baby for many more years. And certainly not here.

The horror must have been apparent on my face, because he said, "I can see that wasn't what you had in mind. Things are different amongst your people?"

"Yes," I managed to say.

"You will have a month to get used to the idea, then," he said before returning his attention to the zither player.

My breaths were coming too fast, and my vision narrowed. Every instinct inside me told me to run. But even if I was willing to throw the treaty away for my own happiness, I would never make it off the mountain alone.

I was trapped.

Just breathe, Shazeera said, her voice a soothing balm in my mind.

I closed my eyes for a moment. *There's no way I could ever do that–have a baby here without any of my family.*

You will have time to figure out a solution.

I repeated her words like a mantra until my breathing slowed.

After the performance, servants came and removed the chairs to allow us room to mingle and speak to one another. Emperor Altair remained on the throne, so I did the same. We watched as the people kept stealing glances at me before talking behind their sleeves. "They're looking at your outfit," he said.

I looked down at the outfit in question, one of my most elaborate ones that I only wore on the rare occasions Ama held court. This one was the pink of a sunset, which set off the golden tones of my skin beautifully. The bodice was cut low and trimmed in braided gold with rubies that glinted along the neckline. The skirt was separate, though the bodice covered most of my torso, and it was of a voluminous silk chiffon, split down the middle for ease of movement. A golden belt with bangles was secured around my waist, and there was a matching golden collar that fanned out in the same dangling rubies that fit flush around my neck. My dark hair was secured with a silken headscarf in the same sunset pink. A golden diadem had both rubies and diamonds that hung in delicate chains along my forehead. This was as regal and elegant as I could muster, especially after having just ridden on an eagle for hours. "Why?"

"The color, for starters. All that skin," he said, glancing away. "Black and white are the shades of choice here. Maybe gray. I can have tailors sent to your room, fit you for a new wardrobe."

"That's kind of you, but no thank you. I prefer my own clothing."

"They will judge you harshly for it."

"I cannot be anything other than what I am," I said unapologetically, and he watched me closely for a moment, as though turning my words over in his mind.

"That is . . . a radical way of thinking here," he said finally. "I can't say you'll be rewarded for it, though. And you may end up regretting it."

"I would think it would be even stranger if I came here and immediately started dressing and behaving as though I were a Zephyrian when it's obvious to everyone that I'm not."

He let out a small laugh. "That's true, though that's exactly what they expect of you."

"Well, I can't control other people's expectations of me," I said, and he looked at me again like I was speaking an unfamiliar language. When he was quiet again and seemed like he would remain that way indefinitely, I said, "What do we do now that you've made your announcement to the court, and we've listened to the zither player? Shouldn't we go talk to the nobles?"

He leaned back in his throne. "If anyone wants to speak to me, then they must approach me here."

I looked at the dais, raised high enough that anyone who wanted to approach the emperor would have to crane their neck to look him in the eye. I didn't see that happening. "I'm going to go and see if I can speak to any of them." Surely not everyone was cold and removed.

"Be my guest," he said dismissively.

When I climbed down the steps of the dais, Shazeera came over to me. Each echo of her hooves across the cavernous room made the nobles look at us like she was a rodent who had scurried into their midst. It made my blood boil.

I'll wait here, she said with a little shake of her mane. *I have a feeling they'll never talk to you if I'm by your side.*

Absolutely not, I said. *We are a bonded pair, and where I go, you go. If I show weakness now, they'll never accept us.*

She swished her tail, which was what she always did when she disagreed with me, but when I walked away, she stayed by my side.

We moved toward a group of women who were talking, at least. That seemed like a good sign considering that most of the room held a heavy silence. Although the emperor had spoken in a common tongue—no doubt for my own benefit—the other nobles were speaking in their own language, of which I had only a cursory knowledge. As monstrous as they'd always seemed, I was surprised by how innocuous their language sounded. It was smooth, even monotonous, without emphasis on any of the syllables.

I tried not to think of my own people, how any of us would have turned and welcomed a newcomer—even an enemy. Hadn't I even shown Commander Talon to the food table myself? But though the women behaved politely, bowing when they saw me walk close to them, they kept their shoulders turned in such a way that I couldn't join their circle. I noticed their gazes dart toward Shazeera many times, too, but instead of it being a potential opening for conversation, they refused to speak to me at all—much less about the horse in the room.

Here, though I was surrounded by people, I had never felt more alone.

We wandered throughout the room, but it was the same treatment no matter which group we came close to. So when Lord Heron approached us of his own accord, I watched him warily.

"We haven't formally met. I am Lord Heron," he said with a stiff bow, "one of the emperor's oldest advisers."

His expression was deliberately even, so it was hard to tell what his intentions were, but I doubted he was trying to make friends. "Pleased to meet you, and I'm sure you already know my name, but allow me to introduce my bonded sister, Shazeera," I said, and she bobbed her head at Lord Heron.

He looked at us both how you might regard manure on the bottom of your shoe. "I'll refrain from introducing myself to a horse."

"Then I have no use for you," I said, turning away from him dismissively, while a red rage flushed my cheeks. "I don't know how you became adviser to the emperor since you obviously know nothing."

"I know that somehow the riders have convinced the emperor that you have an undefeatable power," he said in a low voice. "But no one is invincible."

I turned back toward him. He didn't have a sneer on his face, and his tone was even, but I knew a threat when I heard one. Even though the hair on the back of my neck stood on end, I couldn't let him see my true reaction.

"Are you sure of that, Lord Heron?" I asked with a careful smile.

His expression darkened like a cloud suddenly blocking the face of the sun. "Our emperor is known to be eccentric, but even so, none of us will accept this." He leaned closer and lowered his voice so that he could fully unleash the venom of his tone. "We won't accept a filthy-blooded horse girl to be our empress."

Shazeera let out an affronted whinny, ears pinned back against her head. *How dare he speak to you that way!*

I smirked at Lord Heron, taking advantage of the fact that my face could make the normal range of expressions. "I don't need your or anyone else's approval. I signed the treaty to save my people, and no pathetic attempt at intimidation can dissuade me from that goal."

Did he think I wanted to be here in this cold place? To chain myself to the emperor in marriage? Energy crackled over my skin as anger took hold.

Lord Heron opened his mouth to say something else equally provoking, but suddenly, Commander Talon stood beside him. There was a tightness around his jaw that made me wonder if he'd heard what Lord Heron had said. I hadn't even seen him return to the throne room.

Lord Heron's eyes widened just enough that I thought he might be wondering the same. "Commander Talon," he said with a little bow of his head.

"Be careful, Lord Heron," Commander Talon said. "Like it or not, First Daughter Zara will be your empress . . . with the power to strip anyone of their noble title, no matter how old their family line."

This got his attention. I was rewarded by seeing his face pale at Commander Talon's threat.

"May the wind carry you far, Future Empress Zara," he said with a bow before moving stiffly away to the other side of the throne room.

Commander Talon turned back to me. "The nobles may attempt to intimidate you with their words, but as you can see, they are easily reminded of their place."

"I can stand up for myself, but I haven't forgotten I'm an outsider here. It will be hard for them, I think," I said as I put my hand on Shazeera's neck.

But Shazeera was no longer listening. I could tell by the way her ears were pricked toward a far corner of the room that her attention had been captured elsewhere.

"What is it?" I asked.

I sense something strange, she said.

As if it felt us looking, something shifted just behind the thrones. Though I couldn't make out the details, what I saw was enough to freeze me in place. A shadowy figure lurked, half man and half beast. A malevolent miasma surrounded him, like smoke wafting from a fire.

Shazeera, whose senses were much stronger than mine, snorted violently and half reared. *What is that thing?*

Through our connection, I saw the creature through Shazeera's eyes. The humanlike form it had taken was nothing like its true self. It radiated darkness and wasn't just standing *in* the shadows but *was* the shadows. It peered back at us with hungry red eyes.

Shazeera let out a scream that caused the eagle on the dais to raise his wings and shriek in answer. Powerful talons scraped across the marble, the sound so loud and piercing it made me cover my ears. Something snapped in that moment in Shazeera's mind. The fact that a giant eagle, mere feet from her, had made such a threatening noise, along with whatever demonic creature cloaked itself in shadow, was too much. She reared and plunged, tossing her head as she pranced. Everything in her demanded that she run. Fear had pushed her over the edge, and now her natural instincts were taking over.

Her mind was nothing but a red wall of terror.

Shazeera, you have to get control of yourself!

And though I tried many times to calm her, she ignored my pleas. I reached out for her, my hand brushing her neck futilely as she reared.

I was jerked back, away from her flinty hooves, and Commander Talon pulled me into his body.

"She won't hurt me," I told him, trying to pull away and go to her, but he held me fast.

"I'd rather not test it," he said, his arm tightening around me.

People had to jump out of her way to keep from being trampled. Guards marched forward to corral her away from the nobles. Panic spread through my veins like ice water when I saw one guard race out of the room only to return with chains.

Shazeera, please, I begged.

"My Lord Emperor, you must remove this creature from the throne room!" Lord Heron shouted to be heard above the screams of the people, my frantic horse, and the occasional shrieks of the eagle.

Emperor Altair signaled his guards, and they came at her with chains.

"No!" I shouted, pulling free from Talon and jumping between Shazeera and the guards. There was no wind here in this open space, but I called for it anyway. It came, buffeting around Shazeera and me powerfully, a force strong enough to form a barrier around us. I turned to face Shazeera and threw my arms around her neck. Finally, she shuddered to a halt, trembling all over and breathing hard.

She was still too terrified to answer me, but I could sense her still—I hadn't released anywhere near the power I did when I fought the Eagle Riders. Perhaps this was why our bond hadn't been affected this time. In fact, the wind I had called hadn't even chased away Shazeera's fear. The only reason she had stopped was that her body was so exhausted she could barely stand.

A pregnant silence filled the room as nobles watched us with horrified expressions.

Lord Heron looked at us with naked disgust before quickly

climbing the dais to the emperor. After a quick bow, he spoke to Emperor Altair in low tones.

Talon came close to my side. "I'll do what I can for you," he murmured, "but this is bad."

"First Daughter Zara has broken the treaty by using the wind power against us," Lord Heron announced.

"I didn't use it against you! I was only trying to calm my horse. The eagle frightened her . . . and that creature—" I felt Talon subtly take hold of my wrist and squeeze what felt like a warning. That was when I realized that the shadow being had disappeared. If not for the way Shazeera had reacted, I would have thought I had hallucinated it in a fog of exhaustion and stress.

"Lord Emperor," Talon said, "I have been on the receiving end of First Daughter's power, as you know, and I can assure you this was nothing but a cool breeze in comparison. She meant no harm."

The emperor was quiet for a moment, as though considering Talon's words, but Lord Heron spoke to him again. I strained to hear, my hands curled into fists, but they were too far away. Altair looked like he didn't know whom to listen to—he kept glancing from Talon to Lord Heron.

"First Daughter Zara should have restricted access to her horse until we can be sure we can trust her," Lord Heron said. He glared at me from close to the emperor's throne. "Your horse will only be safe if you keep that power under control."

I swayed on my feet at his words. How had this gone so horribly so quickly? I had never wanted to turn back time so badly.

"Please," I said, my hand tangled in Shazeera's mane, "you have my word I'll never use that power again." Emperor Altair looked unmoved, so I cast my gaze around to anyone who would defend me. Only Talon appeared remotely sympathetic.

"Lord Emperor," Talon said again, "the Children of Earth are bonded to their horses the same as we riders are to our eagles. It will hurt the future empress to be separated from her horse."

Lord Heron stepped forward with a sneer. "Then she should have thought of that before she let it go wild in the throne room and threatened us with a strange power."

After a moment, Emperor Altair gestured toward Shazeera. "Guards, take her to the upper pastures."

Every muscle in my body burned with the desperate need to take Shazeera and flee, and I broke out in a cold sweat as I fought down the rising panic. "Then I'll go with her. I'll sleep outside. I'm sure it'll be more comfortable."

All around me, there were gasps and expressions of contempt. I caught the loudly whispered barbs that the nobles were too cowardly to say to my face.

So ungrateful.

Disgraceful.

Barbaric animal.

Emperor Altair looked like he'd rather just shrug and let me go on my way, but then Lord Heron spoke. "Your place is here, beside the emperor. It would be humiliating for our people for a future empress to sleep outside with the livestock."

A fiery anger burned through me. "Shazeera is my bonded sister. That is deeply insulting."

Lord Heron merely stared back at me with his cold eyes.

Another woman, dressed in a belted floor-length dress of dove gray, said loudly enough for us all to hear, "Well, there's always the lower pasture."

I didn't need to be familiar with the palace to know that whatever the lower pasture meant wasn't good, especially when Lord Heron smirked.

"That's true," he said. "We can always send your horse to the feeding pasture instead. The eagles are always looking for fresh meat."

The blood drained from my face in an instant. My choices flashed through my mind. I could try to fight all these guards, but I would be easily overpowered. I didn't want to risk the full power of the wind and damage the bond I had with Shazeera. I would have to let them take Shazeera—the only true ally I had here—and bide my time and get her back. Emperor Altair didn't seem like he'd be difficult to persuade—if I could get him away from his horrible adviser.

"That won't be necessary," Talon said, stepping forward and gently tugging me away from Shazeera. "I will accompany the future empress's horse to the upper pasture."

"She'll be safe," Talon said near my ear. "You have my word."

I'm sorry, Shazeera said. *I don't want to leave you. Especially with that creature.*

It's not your fault. I'll come see you as soon as I can.

She touched my arm with her velvety-soft nose. *Don't ever let your guard down. I'm afraid you're in very real danger here—not just from that thing, but also Lord Heron and all the others in this room. They give off nothing but a sense of hostility.*

Her warning made my knees weak, but I nodded. *I'll stay safe. You do the same.*

Talon led her from the room, and she followed with lowered head and tail, obviously exhausted. It killed me to watch her walk away, to not know how long we would be separated.

The emperor returned to his throne, leaving me with Lord Heron. Tears threatened, but I refused to let him see how badly this affected me.

"Shall I escort First Daughter Zara to her room, Lord Emperor?" he called out to Altair.

Altair nodded once, his expression conflicted.

Lord Heron tried to take my arm, but I jerked it away from him. I wouldn't be dragged off to my room like a naughty child.

"Lead on, then," I told him tightly.

With everyone watching, I held my head high as we left the massive throne room. In the dimly lit hallway, wall sconces made shadows dance ominously as we walked, two guards trailing behind us at a distance.

"You're off to a bad start here," Lord Heron said. "Now the members of this court will have even more reason to kill you."

My hands strayed close to the dagger I had strapped to my thigh, no doubt in my mind that Lord Heron was a threat. I hid my reaction behind a bored expression. "Wouldn't that be a breach of the treaty you defended so strongly just a moment ago?"

"Not if it's done in a way that could easily be accidental. We are on the side of a mountain, after all."

"Who are you to threaten me?" I snapped, tired of his constant antagonism.

He widened his eyes in faux innocence. "I would never threaten you. I'm merely the adviser to the emperor. No, the ones you should be on guard against are the ladies of the court," he said, and I immediately thought of the elegantly dressed women who had watched me with thinly veiled hate. "You see, you—a barbarian no less—have stolen their opportunity to marry the emperor and become the most powerful woman in the empire."

I started to tell him that they could have him—I didn't even want to be empress—but then I thought of my people. My marriage to the emperor was what would unite our people and keep us safe.

We arrived in front of a set of wide double doors, and Lord Heron waited for the two guards to open them. My whole body tensed as we stood before the threshold. Lord Heron leaned toward me. "A parting piece of advice: I would watch myself in the dark corners of the palace. Some shadows have teeth."

With those words, he shoved me through the opening, and before I could spin around, pulled the door shut with an ominous *thunk*. I grabbed hold of the handle, but I found it locked.

"Just a safety measure," he said with a chuckle through the thick wood.

I leaned against the door and closed my eyes, swallowing down the panic that threatened to crash over me like a flash flood. Too late, I realized the treaty assured my health and safety, but it never said I should be treated like the future empress I was. There was nothing to stop them from leaving me in here forever.

With my heart set on Shazeera, I reached out to her. *Shazeera?* I thought through our connection, but there was only silence. When I dug deeper inside myself where the shimmering bond lay, I could tell she was too far away to hear me.

I glanced at the opulent multichambered room behind me. A large mahogany bed with a lace canopy and white and gold bedding dominated the space, while across from it was an enormous fireplace, already burning. There were windows that took up one entire wall, with a view of the sky, the clouds floating by lazily. From here, I could see there were two other rooms, a bathing area and a sitting room.

It was no dungeon. But even amongst all this space and fine furnishings, the locked door beneath my hand made my throat tighten with dread.

Was I a prisoner here?

20

TALON

Before escorting the First Daughter's horse to the pasture, I summoned three of my most trustworthy Eagle Riders: Baz, Zamir, and Kestrel. They came quickly, shooting Shazeera curious looks but holding their tongues until they heard from me first. The three of them lined up in front of me and saluted.

Baz and I had known each other since childhood, as our fathers had flown together in the aerial army. He dwarfed the others with his hulking frame. Beside him, Zamir flashed me a ghost of a smile, her dark eyes unreadable. Petite already, she looked even smaller next to Baz, but if it came down to a competition, she could probably best him with her daggers. Kestrel stood on the other side of Zamir, arms crossed and a characteristic smirk on his face. He was an ass, but I trusted him with my life. He had saved me more than once.

"I want the three of you to rotate shifts watching over the First Daughter's horse in the upper pasture," I said, meeting each of their eyes in turn.

"You don't trust the emperor's guards," Baz said knowingly.

"No, I don't," I said.

"This horse is that important?" Kestrel asked with a nod toward Shazeera, whose head drooped with fatigue. "Looks like a nag to me."

At that, her nostrils flared, and she tossed her head in what was obviously a gesture of affront.

"She is bonded to the First Daughter as we are to our eagles," I said, with an edge to my voice so they would understand how serious this was. "I need this horse kept safe. If anything happens to her, the First Daughter could refuse to marry the emperor and wreck the treaty I worked so hard to secure."

"We understand, Commander," Baz and Zamir said together.

When Kestrel remained silent, I narrowed my eyes at him. "Is guard duty beneath you, Sergeant?"

"No, Commander," he answered quickly.

I stepped closer so I invaded his space. "Then perhaps you would like to risk this peace treaty and go back to war?"

"No, Commander," he said again, gaze straight ahead without meeting mine.

"Then you will guard this horse like you would any other precious thing?"

This time, they all responded with a loud, simultaneous, "Yes, Commander."

I relaxed my stance and took a step back. "Who will take first watch?"

"I will, Commander," Zamir said, walking over to Shazeera and touching her neck. "I am Zamir," she said with a short bow of her head, which Shazeera returned.

"Let's start with twelve-hour rotations," I said. "You can decide amongst yourselves who guards when, so long as she's never without one of you present. Remember, the peace treaty depends on the health and safety of this horse."

The three of them saluted again, and then I went with Zamir and Shazeera to the pasture.

After making sure Shazeera would be well cared for, I headed toward the aerie to talk to Neo. Seeing the Devourer again had shaken me more than I liked to admit.

The first meeting between the First Daughter and Altair couldn't have gone worse, but I knew it wasn't entirely her fault. It was that creature's. After that first horrible moment I had seen the Devourer beside my cousin, it seemed to have disappeared. I had almost been able to convince myself that it had gone back to whatever hole it crawled out of. But now the First Daughter had seen it, which seemed to make the situation all the more real. Part of me had hoped it was all a pain-induced nightmare I had after my crash.

I could hardly blame the First Daughter's horse for reacting like that when even Neo had been disturbed. It was unfortunate that Zara had found it necessary to use her wind power like that in the middle of court. Lord Heron would make it his personal mission to do everything he could to control her and possibly even dissolve the treaty. My muscles tensed involuntarily at the thought of him. He was a warmonger just like Lamir, Altair's father.

Before that, though, the First Daughter had surprised me. From her kindness to me on her last night with her people, to the way she looked around her while flying on Neo, eyes open wide like she wanted to take it all in. If I'd expected a sobbing, emotional mess, she had proven me wrong at every opportunity. Even the Zephyrian nobility, who viewed dignity and poise to be an art form, would have found it hard not to be impressed, save for one thing. She lacked their cold detachment. There was too much expression in her face, too much *life* in her eyes. And for this, she would undoubtedly always face difficulty in getting the nobles to accept her.

I couldn't shake the feeling that I had delivered her to a pit of vipers.

That's because you did, Neo said as I strode into the aerie. The twenty-two other eagles glanced at me the moment I crossed the threshold and dismissed me just as quickly. I wasn't a servant to bring them food, so I wasn't worth any interest. Neo was perched high on a branch of a fir, his weight bowing the tree. A small copse of trees had been planted here long ago, and their canopy served as the roof, allowing the eagles to come and go as they pleased.

Who invited you into my head? I asked as I stood beneath his branch.

Neo stared down at me with a little gleam in his eyes as I reached his side. *I wanted to see what happened when that girl met the emperor.*

And? Did you see?

Yes, he said, his feathers ruffled in agitation. *I see the creature has made itself known again. The emperor has attached himself to a dangerous being. It's only a matter of time before it reveals its true power.*

That's what I'm afraid of.

The eagles turned as one toward the entrance to the aerie, their attention attracted by a servant entering.

"Commander Talon?" he said, hurrying to my side with a bow. I recognized him as Bran, the emperor's steward and head of the palace staff.

"Yes?"

"The emperor is requesting your presence in his private quarters."

"Of course he is," I muttered under my breath.

"Commander?"

"Yes, I'm coming. One moment."

Bran nodded once and took a step back.

I rubbed the back of my neck, where the muscles were already beginning to ache. *I think it might be another long night,* I said to Neo. *You should go on without me.*

Neo's feathers ruffled. *What else is there to talk about?*

The wedding. The peace treaty. First Daughter Zara. My muscles continued to tense as I thought of just how long my cousin could potentially keep me when all I wanted to do was eat and go to sleep.

Then refuse.

I can't. It's the only way I can be useful. The war's over now, but as you've already seen, that creature is still lurking in the shadows, and even if it isn't the Devourer of legend, it's still a powerful sorcerer. There's no way the treaty will appease a creature like that, and if I were to abandon Altair now, then I'm afraid there wouldn't be a palace–or even an empire–to return to.

I didn't know how we'd ever disentangle the creature from Altair or banish it from our empire.

Still, I would do what I could. For the empire.

Go and rest, I told Neo. *I will find you later.*

My offer to fly us both far over the ocean still stands.

All hope isn't lost yet.

Neo shook his head once before spreading his wings wide and taking off. I knew he didn't agree. He thought we should escape now while we had the chance, but I would never abandon my people—even the nobles at court that I couldn't stand to be around.

"Let's go," I said to Bran.

When we reached the doorway to the aerie, Bran bowed low. "Commander, there is something I must ask you before I take you to see the emperor."

"What is it?"

"I have tried to bring this to the attention of the emperor, but he has been . . . distracted by other things." Bran looked uncomfortable. "Recently, several men and women have turned up missing, and after investigating, we found their families haven't heard from them, either."

A whisper of warning made my muscles tense. Still, this was what I hated about life at the palace—there was always some crisis to deal with. "Although I'm sympathetic to your dilemma, I'm a soldier and wouldn't even know where to begin such an investigation. What is it you want from me?"

"I understand that, Commander, I do, but you're also the emperor's cousin, and he listens to you. I would like guards to comb the palace and Naharu for the missing staff. The emperor has said that I am overreacting, and that this is a situation of delinquent staff, one he doesn't want to waste resources on."

"But you don't think so?"

He shook his head. "Maybe if it was only one or two, but seven are now missing."

Much as I hated to admit it, seven was a lot of people to not report to their posts. "I can't guarantee that the emperor will listen to me." It depended on his mood, which was ever-changing. "But I will try."

He closed his eyes once. "Thank you, Commander."

We continued to the emperor's rooms, and I spared a brief glance at the chambers that now belonged to the future empress. I wondered what she had thought of her rooms, and if she'd already eaten, but then we arrived in front of the emperor's door, and I had to push away all other thoughts.

Bran opened it for me, and I strode in without preamble. I found the room dimly lit—not unusual for Altair—but as my gaze swept over the space, I didn't see any sign of him. There was, however, someone else inside.

Bran marched past me to confront the man, looking like a dog with its hackles raised. "What are you doing in His Majesty's private chambers?"

The man, who by his ashen robes was a lower-ranking servant than the steward, bowed quickly and offered a stuttered explanation. "His Majesty sent me to find something for him—his journal," the servant added when Bran glowered at him. He held up the book in question, finely made but garishly appointed with gemstones.

Bran held out his hand, and the servant relinquished it without hesitation. "I oversee such matters. A servant of your station should have come to me immediately."

"Yes, head steward," he said with another bow, and where the light hit his hair, it shone peculiarly. It had a red tint to it, like a ruby. This was notable, as the only hair colors any Zephyrian had were either a brown so dark it was nearly black, or inky black.

"Where are you from?" I asked the servant.

"From the Spine," he said, which was a mountain chain on the eastern coast. Although part of the Zephyrian Empire, the people there spent most of their time tending goats. Very few traveled beyond their territory, and even fewer could be found at the palace.

"You're a long way from home," I said.

"Yes, my family is very proud that I have the honor of serving the emperor as a servant in his palace," he said with a bow.

Bran narrowed his eyes. "How lovely for you all, but they'd be prouder if you did your job and remembered your place."

"Yes, head steward," he said with another bow.

"Be gone with you," Bran said, and he hurried away.

"I'm sorry for the delay, Commander," he said to me.

I shook my head dismissively before continuing to Altair's study. I knocked once at the wide door, the steward just behind me.

"Talon," Altair said when he saw me standing in the doorway. "Come in." He caught sight of the head steward behind me and sighed. "What is it?"

"Majesty, I have your journal that you requested."

Altair held out his hand, and Bran hurried over to place it in his palm. Altair looked at the steward's face for a moment. "Didn't I send someone else?"

Bran laughed nervously. "Yes, Majesty, but I . . . I was accompanying Commander Talon here anyway, so I told him I would bring it."

Altair waved his hand. "I didn't need that long of an explanation. Please leave us. I have something I must discuss with Talon."

Bran looked like he wanted to say more, and he shot me a pleading glance once more before bowing and doing what the emperor ordered.

"He keeps irritating me with stories about missing servants," Altair said with a roll of his eyes. "I've told him that it's his problem to deal with people not showing up to their posts."

"Majesty," I said, "it does sound strange that seven are missing. I could see one or two, but—"

"Oh, not you, too," Altair said with a groan, leaning back in his chair and throwing his head back dramatically. "Why should I care where they've gone?"

"These are the people who serve you. It's your duty to care."

"I'm far too busy. Why don't you figure out where they've gone?"

"I will if you'd like," I said. "The head steward would like your permission to search for them in Naharu and the palace."

"Fine," the emperor said with another dismissive wave of his hand.

I gestured toward one of the servants waiting nearby. "Go and tell the head steward that the emperor has given his permission to search for the missing servants."

The man bowed and hurried out the door.

"I have a more pressing assignment for you," Altair said, leaning forward and resting his hands on his desk. "I want you to guard the future empress."

I was afraid he'd ask this of me. Despite what we'd gone through together during our childhood with his father always comparing the two of us, Altair took comfort in having me around. I was familiar, I suppose. A remnant of a time when Altair hadn't been emperor. "Guard her from . . . ?"

"It's more that I want you to keep an eye on her. After she so readily called that wind power in the middle of my throne room, I'm not sure she can be trusted."

"She wanted to gain control of her horse."

"Yes, well, now we will use her horse to control *her.* You will need to report any future instances of her using that power. I can't have her using it against us here."

"I don't think she will—they seemed ready to give anything for peace," I said. "This concern doesn't seem like one of your own. It seems like something Lord Heron would worry about." I glanced around the room to be sure he wasn't slinking around in the dark corners somewhere. "Where is he anyway?"

"Last I saw him, he was leading Zara to her rooms," he said dismissively.

"What?" I said sharply. "How am I supposed to guard her if you let that snake be alone with her?"

"He was my father's most loyal adviser."

I didn't respond to that since there were too many problems with trusting that man, namely, that he always put his own interests first, and they very rarely benefited the rest of the empire.

"You should also know that the Children of Earth informed me that there are more with the power to control the wind, and if anything should happen to the First Daughter in violation of the treaty, they will retaliate against us."

He looked taken aback by that, but he didn't question it further, thankfully. "Lord Heron merely escorted her to her room."

I wanted to immediately go to her, but Altair was in a talkative mood. Better to question him about Ozul while I could.

"And what does he think of that creature you've allied with? Do you even need its help now that the war is over?"

"Lord Heron thinks the same as I do. Ozul is key to helping me expand this empire beyond our continent."

I stared at him as his words slowly penetrated. Expanding the empire meant more fighting, more war. Just when I thought it was all over. "Forgive me, Majesty, but haven't you said before that our resources would soon be depleted by the war with the Children of Earth? Wouldn't continued expansion drain them further?"

He looked disgusted with me for asking. "Ozul has promised to lend me his power to conquer other lands."

"Then Ozul must be incredibly strong if it can make up for a lack of resources for an entire army," I said with a pointed look. "I think it's time you told me how you even came across such a sorcerer. Neo and I were away fighting this endless war, and when we returned, you had already allied yourself with Ozul."

He looked introspective for a moment before finally responding. "I'd heard whispers of a powerful sorcerer deep within the mountains, so I sent men to see if the rumors held any merit. They saw signs–scrying bowls and animal bones–so I went myself and persuaded him to ally with us. Ozul agreed."

I doubted it was that easy. I knew Altair hid the full truth from me. "Yes, but *how* did you persuade it?"

"I can be persuasive when I want to be," Altair answered flippantly, and I crossed my arms over my chest.

"Whatever the price of an alliance, it's too high," I said, worried for not only my cousin's soul, but for everyone here. We could all be in danger.

Every instinct in my body said we should throw that thing out of the palace and back into whatever dark depths it crawled from.

"We both know that thing is known by a different name," I said, wondering if I pushed Altair hard enough, would he admit what he was still keeping from me?

Altair just glared at me, but I stared calmly back. It could call itself whatever it wanted, but I knew it for what it was. The Devourer. It was why we lived in the mountains but never ventured too far into their depths; why we stayed safe in the skies and never below. It was a creature from the Old World, one that had seemed to follow us here. As far as I knew from the stories passed down, there was no other like it in the world.

"He has only ever said to call him Ozul," Altair said.

"And where does Ozul stay when it's not terrifying horses in the throne room?"

Altair's gaze shifted to his father's portrait for just a moment. "The west wing."

My eyebrows lifted. "Your father's chambers?" I didn't like the sound of that–this creature holed up in the former emperor's rooms.

Altair seemed to retreat into himself, and I knew I didn't have much longer before he refused to speak about this at all.

"Ozul is more comfortable there where he isn't disturbed."

"Altair, it sounds like it's setting itself up to be emperor. You must know that. Break ties with this creature–before it's too late."

His expression hardened, and just for a moment, he looked like his father. "I don't remember asking for your opinion. Go and do the job I assigned you."

"What's to stop it from taking over?" I pushed.

He pointed to the door. "That was an order, Commander."

Irritation flashed through me as I stiffly saluted him and left.

There was no way I could let this go. This being threatened the empire, and my cousin was too blind to see it. Clearly, he wouldn't listen to me, so I would have to find another way to free Altair from its influence.

21

ZARA

I could already tell it wasn't Lord Heron at the door, since whoever it was knocked before unbolting it. I had no doubt Lord Heron would have just barged in.

"Future Empress?" Talon called as he pulled open one of the double doors. "May I enter?"

"You can do whatever you want, as you can see," I said with a nod to the heavy wooden plank that had sealed me in.

He frowned and brought the plank inside the room. "Now you'll have the option to lock yourself in if you choose," he said, pointing to another set of brackets that enabled me to barricade the doors from this side. "I recommend that you do."

"So, I'm not a prisoner?"

"Did you expect to be?"

"Honestly? When I first came here, I naively thought I would be treated like a future empress. Not locked in my room and separated from my horse. But then, how could I expect anything more from people who committed war crimes against us?"

The smallest crease appeared between his eyebrows. "What do you mean?"

I shot him what I hoped was a withering glare. "You're really going to play dumb? I thought you were a commanding officer."

"I am, but I don't know what war crimes you're referring to."

"Because there are so many?" He just looked at me, so I plunged ahead. "I'm talking about the fact that not only did your eagles attack and *eat* our bonded horses, they did so off the battlefields. And worse still, there were innocent civilians and horses who were attacked days away from the nearest battlefield, who were hunted down and killed for sport."

He had the decency to look floored. "These are serious accusations. You know this? For sure?"

I searched his face for a moment. He could be faking his surprise, but I simply didn't know him well enough to be able to tell at this point.

"Commander, I was witness to it," I said, my jaw clenching at the memory of not only the attacks on myself, but of the carnage I had watched Ama struggle to heal.

"I wasn't made aware of this," he said slowly, like his mind was racing. "The Eagle Riders abide by a strict code of honor—"

I scoffed. "Well, obviously not all of them follow this code. I had hoped the treaty would put an end to it, but now that I have been shoved into my room like a political prisoner, I don't know what to think. Are my people safe?"

"I will personally investigate these war crimes, First Daughter, but the Eagle Riders have been returning steadily. The message that the war is over has spread quickly."

I nodded once, the adrenaline still pumping through my veins at confronting him about these atrocities. I didn't know if I could trust him to do something about it, but at least I could investigate it myself if he didn't.

"That's a relief to hear."

"You must be starving," he said, and it triggered my stomach into tightening painfully. "Shall I send for a servant to bring you something to eat?"

"I am hungry, but I'd rather go check on Shazeera first."

"You can't ask her through your bond if she's all right?"

I narrowed my eyes at him. "She's too far away. I would rather see for myself that she's comfortable."

He looked for a moment like he wanted to argue, but he wisely reconsidered it. "I will take you to her."

The sleeping palace was quiet as I followed Commander Talon through the halls, which were pointlessly labyrinthine. We went down when I thought we should go up, left when I thought we should go right, until I was so thoroughly confused that a little tremor of unease ran through me. It would be difficult to navigate this place without a guide and far too easy to get lost.

"That thing I saw in the throne room—the reason Shazeera panicked—what was it? I know it wasn't human. I could tell from Shazeera's perception of it."

He closed his eyes for a moment, like this was the last thing he wanted to talk about. "The emperor calls it Ozul."

"That doesn't tell me what it is, though."

He glanced at me from the corner of his eye. "My people have folklore about a creature called the Devourer. A being that moves in the shadows and devours souls, leaving only walking corpses behind."

My eyes darted to the thick shadows of the halls around us as a cold chill crept over me. I remembered Ama's strange warning to me about dark creatures. But then, she thought I would be safe here. It seemed like the opposite was true.

"And that's what Ozul is? This creature from folklore?"

"It's what I suspect but haven't confirmed," he said.

I thought about how Mariyah had said that Ama and Queen Jazela had told her someone had used magic to scry our exact location. How we had to flee, and then almost immediately, we were attacked by Commander Talon. I stopped, and Talon turned to me questioningly. "This Ozul is the reason you found us? He used magic to find our camp once the wards were down."

"Yes, it was the first time we were able to successfully find the Queen of All Queens' location. Emperor Altair believed her capture would force a one-sided agreement entirely in our favor."

I let out a soft snort. I was pretty sure that's exactly what they got from the current treaty.

We continued down yet another hall, and I asked, "So Ozul has the power to scry, and he may eat souls and leave behind walking corpses—but you have no proof of that, right?" When he hesitated, I glanced at him sharply.

"I don't know yet."

"Yet?"

"There are some disappearances that I intend to look into."

The earlier chill deepened, sinking beneath my skin. I wrapped my arms around my body while I turned his words over in my head. The shadowy being that I had seen through Shazeera's eyes had the power to overcome Ama's earth magic. Consuming souls for energy was obviously a very dark magic, one that my people were unfamiliar with, though we had stories, too, warning us of the danger of delving into things better left alone. Just what kind of monster had the emperor brought into the palace?

When at last we made it out into fresh air, I had to stand for a moment and bask in it, letting the wind tug playfully at my hair to cleanse away the fear that clung to me like oil. Somehow, the path we'd followed out of the palace had led directly out into the valley, though I could have sworn we'd spent the last ten minutes climbing to the very top of the mountain. The mountains surrounded us, looming darkly in the moonlight, their tops just seeming to brush the sky. Before us was a wide expanse of pasture, and though it was too dark to see properly, I could tell by the fresh smell that the grass was thick and verdant. Sheep bleated in the distance, and the sound relaxed something inside me. The scene was far more picturesque than I'd expected to find.

Commander Talon continued out into the pasture, and I let out my breath in relief when a familiar blood bay mare immediately came toward us. Beside her was a slip of a woman with shiny black hair and a guarded expression. She wore the dusky gold leather armor that I had come to recognize as belonging to the Eagle Riders. First Talon had been assigned to guard me, and now another Eagle Rider watched over Shazeera. Were the emperor's guards not to be trusted?

I heard you coming, Shazeera said, still sounding exhausted.

I just had to see for myself that you were all right, I told her. *I'm not sure who I can trust here, but I'm glad Talon kept his word to me, at least.*

"First Daughter Zara," Talon said, "this is Lieutenant Zamir, who volunteered for the first watch of guard duty for Shazeera."

The lieutenant bowed deeply. "At your service, Majesty."

"Thank you," I replied with a smile before turning to Talon. "Did you arrange for an Eagle Rider to guard Shazeera?"

"Yes, I wanted to be sure she was well taken care of."

I furrowed my brows at him. "Because you don't trust the emperor's guards?"

"Because I trust my own Eagle Riders more," he said smoothly.

I don't trust any of them, Shazeera said, *but at least she's quiet and hasn't brought her eagle to the pasture. Are you staying safe? No other encounters with demonic shadows?*

Safe enough, I suppose, I told her, *but Lord Heron might be just as dangerous as that creature.*

I caught her up on everything that had happened since we were separated, and she tossed her head in dismay.

How can Talon not be sure if there are walking corpses shambling around the palace?

I inwardly laughed at her skeptical tone. *I can believe it. This place is a labyrinth, cut into the mountain.*

Maybe you should come stay out here with me.

With a glance at Commander Talon and Lieutenant Zamir, who were both still standing like silent sentinels, I lowered myself to the grassy hill and tucked my legs under me. The wind made the grass dance like waves, and I watched its hypnotic movement in the pale light of the moon. *I'm tempted to. I didn't like the palace* before *I learned about the soul-sucking sorcerer and potential walking corpses.*

She snorted. *You will need to be constantly on guard. I know you're not going to like hearing this, but I think you should practice summoning the wind.*

I jerked my head toward her. *And risk our bond here? Away from everyone who cares about us?*

You've always been drawn to the wind, but maybe it's time you tried speaking to it. What if there's a way to control it better?

I wouldn't even know where to begin, I argued, but already I felt myself wavering. Shazeera could be annoyingly persuasive when she wanted to.

That creature was pure malevolence, she said with a shudder. *Whatever you can do to protect yourself–and possibly others–you need to do it.*

They won't like me practicing that here.

How would they even know? You can start by just opening yourself to the wind. Listening to it.

"We should get back," Talon said, his deep voice startling after my silent conversation with Shazeera.

I would have argued for more time, but my stomach chose that instant to growl loudly.

You haven't eaten yet? Shazeera said in an utterly horrified tone. Missing a meal was unthinkable to a horse.

I wanted to check on you first.

She tossed her head in irritation at me but allowed me to hug her neck.

I'll come back as soon as I can. Don't eat so much of this grass that you founder, I warned her. *This isn't like the grass on the plains. It's thick and rich.*

She mentally rolled her eyes at me. *I've been a horse longer than you. I can keep myself from getting sick.*

I smiled to myself as I followed Talon out of the pasture. I thought of what Shazeera had said about communicating with the wind. It was true that I had only called upon that power during desperate times, and this last instance, I had managed not to release too much power. When Ama first signed the treaty, I had thought I would never have to call upon the wind again. And I still hoped I wouldn't have to. After all, Talon admitted he didn't have proof of the shadowy creature doing anything but scrying. Hardly life-threatening, especially now that my people had no reason to hide. But I also wasn't foolish enough to shrug my shoulders and just hope for the best.

I stole a glance at Talon. What would he think of my future attempts to control the wind? Would he consider that a breach of the treaty? I thought of the way he defended my actions in the throne room, and how he thought I could ask the wind to give us a calm flight. He would certainly be more understanding about it than Lord Heron, but for now, I would play it safe. Talon wasn't actively hostile toward me like others I had met, but that didn't mean he wanted to be friends. He still served the emperor and couldn't be trusted.

When we arrived in front of the double doors of my room, I tensed, half expecting to be shoved inside and locked in again. But instead, he opened the door and went in by himself, striding around purposefully and disappearing into all the connected rooms before coming back out. "It's safe," he said, holding the door open for me. "I'll get your maidservant to bring you something to eat and anything else you require."

"Thank you," I said, grateful that he had checked my room already so I wouldn't have to worry that the dark corners hid assassins. At least for tonight.

"Bolt the door behind me and only open it when I return," he said, turning to leave.

"I'm in that much danger? Why is the palace security so lax?"

He surprised me when a grin touched the corners of his mouth. "As I've been assigned by the emperor to guard you, I will try not to slack off in my duties."

"You'll be my guard?" I asked incredulously. "Isn't that beneath your station as an Eagle Rider, Commander?"

"There's nothing more important than your safety," he said, holding my gaze.

I hated the sense of peace that settled over me at the thought of Talon being on guard. I didn't want to trust him—it was dangerous to let myself without proof of his trustworthiness. Most likely, the emperor had asked him to do it in order to spy on me.

And if I followed Shazeera's advice and tried to get a better handle on my wind power, that could be problematic. Still, in spite of what I told myself, I felt better knowing that he would be watching my back.

"I can't argue with you there," I said, "especially now that Shazeera has her own Eagle Rider guard. Thank you for that, by the way."

He bowed in response. "You needn't thank me for doing my duty. I'll leave you now, First Daughter, so that you can finally rest."

The moment he mentioned feeling tired, all the stress and exhaustion of the day hit me at once. My mind raced through everything that had happened in the past twelve hours, though it felt like a week's worth of activities crammed into one day. I thought of the flight here, meeting the emperor for the first time, the horrible reception in the Great Hall, Shazeera and me being separated, being locked in my room, the shadowy thing that had terrified my brave horse, and I nearly swayed on my feet.

I nodded weakly to Talon, since he seemed to be waiting for a response.

His gaze swept over me, and he hesitated before finally walking toward the door. "I'll be just outside if you need anything," he said.

When he left, I dutifully bolted the door behind him. But as I eyed the deep shadows in my room, I wondered if locked doors would be enough to keep me safe in this place.

MY MAIDSERVANT TURNED out to be a girl around my age named Raven. She had an open, friendly face, stick-straight black hair that she kept in a braided bun at the nape of her neck, and a cheerful demeanor that I instantly liked. Best of all, she brought me an entire cart full of food.

"Commander Talon informed me that you do not eat meat, so I brought you a little of everything else," she said with a smile, "so I could be sure you found something you liked."

There were steaming bowls of broth of some kind, colorful vegetables that had been cooked in what looked to be a savory sauce, and plenty of warm bread and butter.

"This all looks delicious," I said, suddenly feeling like I hadn't eaten in days. The smell alone—a savory and aromatic combination of garlic, onions, and peppers—made my mouth water.

"I hope you enjoy it," Raven said, still smiling wide at my praise. "If you would like to bathe before bed, just let me know, and I can prepare everything for you. You can call for me anytime by pulling that rope there." She indicated a gold velvet rope hanging close to my bed.

After I thanked her, she left, and I ate almost all the food she brought. When I finished, I glanced over at the plush bed, exhaustion hitting me hard.

Even with a full stomach and the knowledge that Talon guarded my door, I slept fitfully. I missed the sounds of the plains. Every night I fell asleep to the rustling grass blowing in the wind, the crickets' loud nighttime chirping, even the occasional howls of the coyotes. Here, all nature sounds were muffled by the thick stone walls. I didn't dare open a window for fear of freezing to death. The fire crackled, but it was a quiet, intermittent sound. And after seeing that creature, I watched the lengthening shadows warily by the light of the dancing flames.

The next morning, after Raven had brought me breakfast and I'd eaten in lonely silence, a knock came at the door.

"The emperor is here to see you, Future Empress," the guard

who had replaced Talon while he presumably went and rested called out through the door.

I removed the plank and opened it to find Altair dressed much more casually than he had been the first time I saw him. Today he wore warm-looking pants and boots with a thickly brocaded jacket lined with fur. "May I come in?"

In answer, I moved to the side to let him in. He walked over to the sitting room, and I let him stand awkwardly there without asking him to sit, which I knew was petty. But I still didn't know if Lord Heron had decided it would be fun to lock me in my room last night, or if the emperor had ordered it. I wouldn't play nice until I knew what kind of man I was dealing with.

"Have you found your accommodations comfortable?" Altair asked.

"Mostly," I said, "though I didn't appreciate you ordering Lord Heron to lock me in my room last night." My insides quivered because I knew what I was about to say could cause trouble for me that I wasn't ready for, but it had to be said. "Honestly, I don't know how I can marry someone who treated me like that—former enemies or not."

He watched me quietly for a moment. "Are you saying you no longer wish to uphold your end of the treaty?"

My mouth went dry. "No, I'm saying I refuse to be treated like a prisoner."

"I see," he said, leaning back on his heels slightly. "Then perhaps you shouldn't have displayed such power in the middle of my throne room."

"I meant no harm. I was only trying to calm my mare, and now, she's been separated from me."

"There are many here who fear earth magic, especially your ability to call the wind." I didn't bother to correct him—that I didn't even have earth magic. "They want to see that you have incentive not to use that power against them. Had I done nothing, the people would have turned on you."

I felt a sickening lack of control over my own life. "Does this mean I will continue to be separated from her?"

"Your mare can stay in the upper pasture, and Talon or another guard can escort you to her anytime you desire," he said, without quite answering the question. "You have to admit it's the best place for her." He waved his arm around my room, which was large, but admittedly not as easily accessible to the outdoors as our pavilions. But that didn't mean I liked him telling me what was best for her. "I don't think she would be as comfortable surrounded by stone instead of grass and sky."

When I remained suspicious of his intentions, he sighed and ran his hand through his hair. "You have my word that she will have the best care. Complete freedom of the pastures, access to a stable if she chooses, and fresh grain to supplement the grass."

"That does sound like she'd be well cared for," I admitted. Shazeera would always prefer the open sky and grass to being trapped inside. But the separation made me ache for her. "The guards know I can go to her anytime I want?"

"Yes. You need only tell them."

Tell, not *ask*. Relief spread through me, and I glanced over at the chairs in front of the fire. "Would you like to sit?"

He sat in a plush wingback chair, and I took the one across from him. "What do you think of the palace?"

"It's beautiful," I told him truthfully, "if a little cold." I glanced toward the window. "The heights take some getting used to, too."

"You've lived on the plains your whole life?" When I nodded, he said, "The flight here must have been intimidating."

"It was a little frightening at first, I suppose, especially for

Shazeera—my horse," I added quickly when I caught the flicker of confusion in his expression. "But then I'd always wondered what it was like to soar through the clouds."

I was a little surprised I had told him that—it was something I never would have admitted to my own people. But I supposed I would be spending a lot of time with this man in the future, so I may as well be honest.

"I'm glad you weren't afraid. That's impressive, actually, because even I hate to fly. It's my dirty little secret, you could say, although I don't think it's much of a secret. My father used to have his eagle carry me in his talons as a child—dangling from whatever clothes I was wearing at the time, not holding me securely—to help me overcome my unnatural fear of heights."

I grimaced at that small glimpse into what his childhood must have been like. "Did it help?"

"No. I hated it more than ever." Before I could say, *Your childhood sounded miserable*, he added, "I asked you that about flying because I thought maybe you, as a Daughter of Earth, would have understood, but I guess I really am the only one—just like my father always said."

"Well, I'm not a typical Daughter of Earth in that regard, so I wouldn't beat yourself up over it. I could easily name about fifty other people who would have been terrified to fly."

He didn't look convinced as he stared into the flames of the cheerfully burning fire. When the conversation threatened to fall into awkward silence, I changed the subject. "What will my duties be as empress?"

"Duties?" he repeated, brow furrowed.

"Yes, I can't just sit around and do nothing."

He looked like he had never given it a second's thought how I would spend my time here. "I suppose you can be in charge of any matters pertaining to your own people—but only after we are married."

"Then I will be able to change the tax percentage as I see fit?"

He shrugged. "Provided you get Lord Heron's approval first. He oversees such matters."

"Lord Heron has say over my people and what I choose to do as empress?" I asked, unable to keep the incredulousness from my tone. Considering he was the one who had locked me in my room, this wasn't a good thing.

"He oversees many things for the empire on behalf of my father," Altair said, and my brows knitted at the way he put it. Did he feel like he still had to live up to his father's expectations even though he was dead? Either way, Lord Heron seemed like he had far too much power here.

"What is expected of me before we are married?" I asked.

He met my gaze. "I hope you can get acclimated to the palace. I know it's very different from your life on the plains." I must have looked perturbed at the prospect, because he added, "The nobles may expect you to conform to the way things are done here, but I won't ask that of you. I hope you can make this your home."

I hadn't expected that. "That's kind of you."

He gave a quiet laugh. "You sound surprised."

"I just didn't know what to expect," I said, a small smile tugging at my lips. "I'm assuming this means I will be able to move freely around the palace, too."

"As long as you take a guard with you and stay away from the west wing."

"What's in the west wing?"

He looked troubled. "It was my father's quarters."

I wondered if it had anything to do with the shadow creature

I had seen, but where I was perfectly willing to ask Talon, I found myself hesitating when it came to Altair.

A silence descended on us then, and I kept stealing glances at him as we both watched the fire. I could see how many would find Altair attractive, but I found myself continually expecting to see Talon when I looked at him. Was that because I had met Talon first? Because I reluctantly trusted him?

Or is it because you find him sexier?

I squashed that line of thinking immediately. It would do me no good.

I pulled my chair closer to the fire and wrapped my arms around my body.

"Are you cold?" Altair asked, concern in his eyes as he leaned toward me.

"I'm always cold now that I'm here in the mountains."

He stood. "Why didn't you say so? I will have a seamstress brought in immediately to outfit you properly."

I thought of the way everyone in the palace wore drab colors, and held out my hand to him. "Wait, do you think she could just make me a warm cloak or something? I would like to still wear my own clothes." I had brought very little with me, but they were still mine.

"Of course. Whatever you would like. For now, here," he said and began unbuttoning the fur-lined coat he wore, leaving him in a thinner shirt that hugged the lean muscles of his arms and chest. He shrugged out of it and draped it over my shoulders. The warmth from his body still clung to the material, and I immediately stopped shivering.

"Thank you," I said as he opened my door and called for Raven.

"Yes, Majesty?" she said with a little bow, looking wide-eyed at being addressed by the emperor.

"Summon the seamstress for the future empress. She's in need of warm clothes."

"Right away," she said and hurried off.

To me, he said, "I will have to take my leave of you now, but do not hesitate to ask me for anything else you need–or want."

I started to take off his coat to give it back, but he touched my hand. "Keep it. I have many, and it will keep you warm until the seamstress can make you something."

"Thank you," I said, keeping my tone neutral. Who would have thought the enemy of my people would care about my comfort?

He bowed toward me and left, leaving me still wrapped in the warmth of his coat that smelled like allspice.

22

ZARA

Days went by, and I saw no sign of either Talon or Altair. A new guard named Baz stood outside my room, leanly muscular with dark, closely cropped hair. He said very little, other than he would be temporarily taking over Talon's guard duties. Despite what Altair had said, Baz seemed reluctant to accompany me anywhere other than the pasture.

As promised, though, the seamstress came and took my measurements for a warm cloak. An older lady in her sixties, she dressed in a simple gray dress with clean lines. Her movements were quick and efficient as she worked, writing each measurement down in a small notebook. She eyed my richly colored clothing with suspicion, her nose wrinkling ever so slightly.

"The cloak will be charcoal-gray wool with fur trim," she said when she finished. "I will have your maidservant bring it to you as soon as it's finished."

"Thank you," I said, and she bowed and immediately gathered up her things to leave.

I couldn't help but think of what it was like when our own seamstresses measured us for clothing. Of laughing and talking, of choosing an array of colors, of consulting us with the styles and fabrics we would like. Here, there had been none of that. She had seemed like she wanted to spend as little time with me as possible.

Alone again, my thoughts turned to Ama. On my last night on the plains, Ama had told me that I must continue to try to access the earth magic inside me.

You will need the ability to shield yourself in the palace of our former enemies, she had said, taking my hands in hers. *And healing is always a useful power.*

I had promised I would continue our training while I was here. But every time I entered that place in my mind where power lay dormant, all I found was the connection to the wind. It waited closer to the surface of my mind than ever before. If anything, it grew stronger.

I thought about Ama now. Had she recovered? At least the treaty meant that she would no longer have to worry about the wards. Maybe her body could finally regain its strength.

In a desk in my room, there was thick, creamy paper. I decided to sit down and write to her, but as I stared at the blank page, my hand began to tremble. The shadowy creature in the throne room, the separation from Shazeera, the hostility from the nobles here all flashed through my mind. But then I remembered what Altair had said—that I would be expected to produce an heir—and I tore the letter into tiny pieces.

I couldn't bring myself to tell her any of these concerns yet. To begin with, I had no way of knowing whether the Zephyrians would even deliver my letter. More importantly, I didn't want to burden Ama with things she had no control over. How could she help me from two hundred miles away?

I started to write a new letter asking how Ama was recovering, but then I thought better of it. What if the Zephyrians—specifically Lord Heron—read my correspondence? I didn't want anyone to know she was in a weakened state. That seemed like dangerous knowledge, treaty or no treaty.

Without Shazeera by my side to talk to, I felt more isolated than I ever had.

After nearly a week of little to no contact with anyone, Raven became my only outlet.

"You seem sad today, Future Empress," she said one morning after bringing me tea and helping me try on my new cloak.

"Just homesick," I said, taking the cup from her gratefully. It warmed my hands while she draped the cloak around my shoulders and fastened it with an eagle-winged brooch at my throat. Though the colors were much duller than I was used to, it was still beautifully made, and the fur immediately warmed my neck.

"That happens to me, too," Raven said as she met my gaze in the mirror, "but mostly at night. I miss my sisters."

I turned to look at her. "How many do you have?"

"Two, but they're younger than I am. Being promoted to serving you has been a huge blessing from the Lord of the Skies because now my sisters will have better prospects for marriage."

I was dumbfounded for a moment, completely out of my depth at this small glimpse into Zephyrian society. "I'm sure your family is extremely proud of you."

"It's certainly worth the homesickness to know I'm helping them," she said with a kind smile.

"I can relate."

Her eyes widened. "Yes, of course. I'm sure your people are so thankful that you agreed to the terms of the treaty. It must have been really hard leaving your family."

She was the first one who had said this to me, and it had the immediate effect of causing my eyes to well up. Embarrassed by the sudden flood of emotion, I swallowed hard and nodded. "Anything for peace," I managed to croak out.

"We owe you our gratitude for that, too." She handed me a soft cotton cloth to dab at my eyes. "I'm sorry! I think I've only made you sadder."

"No, it's been so nice feeling understood for a moment."

She still looked at me with concerned sympathy, but then she sucked in her breath. "I know what will help. Have you been to the hot springs yet?"

"No, I didn't realize there were any near here."

"They're in the palace, on the lower level. The water is green and as big as a lake. It feels amazing."

My new cloak would keep me warm, but I loved the idea of soaking in hot water. "I would love to go."

She walked briskly out of the sitting room and pulled open the door to the hallway. "The future empress would like to go to the hot springs now," she told Baz, who stood guard.

He hesitated. "I'm not sure—"

"The emperor told me he hoped I would get acclimated to palace life," I interrupted. "Surely a visit to the hot springs is nothing out of the ordinary?"

He looked from me to Raven before finally nodding. "Of course, mistress."

"There are plenty of thick robes for you to use to dry off with," Raven said. "Baz will take you to the private area for royalty only so you will have the space to yourself."

After thanking her for the suggestion, I followed Baz down the long hallway and into the labyrinth that was the palace. We walked in silence for a few minutes, until we turned a corner and suddenly heard voices. Lord Heron and two noblewomen looked up at our approach, and immediately, a sudden chill raced down my spine.

Their expressions were pure disdain.

"Future Empress Zara," Lord Heron said with a mean smile, "how nice to see you out of your room."

I just arched an eyebrow at him in answer, refusing to rise to the bait.

"Allow me to introduce Lady Corvina and Lady Starling," he said, and each woman did a quick bow.

They were both dressed in heavy fur-trimmed brocade gowns, one a dove gray and the other a winter white. Both wore their shiny, jet-black hair in low chignons. That was where the similarity between the two of them ended, though. Lady Corvina watched me with small, narrowed eyes, her mouth pursed in what looked like a permanent pout. Lady Starling wore a smile that could have just as easily been a grimace.

"These are prominent ladies from noble houses," Lord Heron continued. "Either of them would have been considered a good match for the emperor."

I didn't know how I was supposed to respond to that, so I just stared at him until he shifted uncomfortably.

"I tell you this because they can be invaluable at helping you to learn Zephyrian etiquette—if you're open to that, of course."

"I'm sure I could use the instruction," I said, trying to keep the sarcasm from my voice. "I was just heading to the hot springs, though—"

"We would be happy to accompany you," Lady Starling said.

"Yes," Lady Corvina said, though she looked like she'd rather do anything else.

"Fine by me," I said, just ready to get into the warm water at this point.

"I will leave you to it, then," Lord Heron said with a bow and a shared look with Lady Starling. A skitter of warning went up my spine. I hadn't forgotten what he had said to me in the throne room, and from the looks of these ladies, neither had any real interest in helping me.

"Ready, mistress?" Baz asked.

"Yes," I said, and then gestured for the two noblewomen to go ahead of me. I would rather not be stabbed in the back on the way there.

With tight smiles, they did as I asked.

Baz led us deep into the palace, down many hallways and twisting staircases, until all at once I could smell the change in the air. It took on an almost herbal scent, and the temperature rose until it was nearly as warm as it had been on the plains.

Baz stopped before an open doorway cut into the rock, where beyond I could feel the steamy warmth. Once I walked into the cavernous space, I just stood there and stared. The water was as green as jade, bubbling gently and emitting a fresh scent into the air. But it was its size that had me standing still with my eyes wide. The springs fed into countless pools, each separated by stalagmites rising to a cavernous ceiling, and the entire space was farther across than I could see. I heard the echo of voices, but nowhere nearby, and as the whole place was so large, there was no concern for it being overcrowded. Dimly lit and quiet save for the bubbling of the water, it was like we had the springs to ourselves.

"This way to the royal alcove," Lady Starling said, waving one slender hand at me.

I hesitated for a moment, watching to see what Baz would do, but he merely waited for me.

They led me to a pool that had outcroppings that served as

underwater benches. Hung on hooks from the stalagmites were heavy brocade robes in creamy white. Baz stood guard with his back to the pool, which I found both prudish and potentially dangerous considering I might be bathing with women who wished me harm.

For the moment, though, they weren't paying attention to me. They kept their gazes averted as they carefully took off their clothes and hung them on one of the empty hooks. I stripped out of my own clothing unselfconsciously and then did the same.

When I stepped into the water, though, I immediately let out an appreciative groan. It was the perfect temperature—hot enough to soothe muscles, curls of steam coming off the surface. They both shot me looks like I had just done something unforgivably crass. With eyes still averted from each other's naked bodies, they slipped silently into the water.

They made no effort to talk to me, so I tried to pretend they weren't there and enjoyed the warm water instead.

After a few minutes of peace, Lady Corvina deigned to speak to me. "Has the emperor taken you into Naharu yet?" she asked, her voice barely above a whisper.

"No, but I would love to see it."

They both winced like I had shouted my response to them. "You mustn't speak so loud, First Daughter," Lady Starling said, her tone soft but reproachful.

"This is my normal speaking voice."

"It's best to speak quietly so that everyone is forced to listen closely," Lady Starling said, in a way that suggested this was a well-known proverb.

I didn't really want to go around whispering, so I just nodded and barely lowered my voice. "Do you live in Naharu?"

"Yes, we both do—in the royal district," Lady Corvina added with unmistakable pride.

"That's the area closest to the palace," Lady Starling said.

"How many districts are there?" I asked, fascinated despite myself. I did like learning about other cultures, and there was so little that we knew about the Zephyrians.

"Four," Lady Corvina said. "Royal, Merchant, Artisan, and Tradesman."

"So each area is divided by family occupation?"

"Yes," Lady Corvina said in her strange whisper.

"I would love to go visit Naharu. Or anywhere, really. I would like to travel the continent now that the war is over."

They shared a look. "An empress doesn't travel."

"What do you mean?"

"The empress must never leave the palace or its immediate vicinity, like Naharu," Lady Starling said in a tone that suggested it was offensive for me to say otherwise.

"I'm afraid that's a rule I won't be able to follow. For one thing, my entire family lives on the plains."

"This is why you'll make a disgraceful empress," Lady Starling said with a sneer. "You have no regard for the rules and customs of our people."

"Not when they're completely isolating and barbaric."

Lady Corvina let out a barking laugh that got her a nasty look from Lady Starling. "This from someone who lives in primitive tents and barely clothes herself."

"We shouldn't have even bothered to help you learn about the Zephyrian ways. You're obviously incapable of it," Lady Starling said, still in that ridiculous half whisper.

I wasn't sure how they thought they were helping me learn the Zephyrian ways after such a short conversation, but I also knew they were just a couple of mean, petty women who would never like and accept me. I thought of Lord Heron's warnings about the dangers of the nobility, and I almost snorted out loud. These women were pitiable, not dangerous.

"Then leave," I said with a shrug of indifference that I knew by Lady Starling's narrowed eyes got to her more than if I had reacted badly, like she expected. "I never wanted the two of you here with me anyway."

"Do you know who we are?" Lady Corvina hissed at me. "We are from the noble houses of–"

"Do you know who *I* am?" I interrupted. "I am the First Daughter Zara of the Children of Earth and the future empress of the Zephyrians. *Your* future empress. You'd do well to remember that when you speak to me."

Lady Corvina opened and closed her mouth several times, which was satisfying until I caught the dark look on Lady Starling's face. She looked like she wished she had a dagger to stab me with. If I hadn't glanced at her, I wouldn't have noticed the growing shadows behind her.

The shadows coalesced into a dark, writhing mass. I felt the color drain from my face as it moved like smoke toward us. The shadows reached Lady Starling first and poured into her until her eyes were black.

I flung myself to the water's edge just as the shadow streamed into Lady Corvina in the same way.

Before I could make it out of the water, each woman latched onto my arm and pulled me under. I didn't even have time to scream for Baz. I fought wildly, but they held me down with inhuman strength. I could see their distorted faces through the green water. They were eerily calm as they tried to drown me.

I was young and strong, but I couldn't hold my breath forever.

A renewed surge of panicky adrenaline flooded my veins. I kicked out while trying to wrench my body away from them. They held tight, having the advantage of height since they were both standing on the outcropping and using their combined body weight to hold me under. My lungs burned, desperate for air.

I have to have air, I thought. Would the wind respond underwater? I imagined the way a strong wind could toss waves and churn the deep waters of the ocean.

I sank deep inside myself to where that power rested, and pulled it to the surface of my mind. All I could think about was how I needed to get out of the water. And then suddenly, a million effervescent bubbles surrounded me. They swirled around my body faster and faster until finally, I felt an incredible force beneath me. It lifted me so powerfully that both Lady Corvina and Lady Starling were blown back. I landed hard on the edge of the water, coughing violently and gagging.

Baz finally heard the struggle and came to my rescue, but Lady Corvina and Lady Starling threw themselves upon him. They clawed him like wild animals, screaming and fighting. He struggled to subdue them.

Before I could get to my feet, a warm robe was thrown over my body, and I was pulled against a rock-hard chest.

"Haul them before the emperor," Talon shouted to Baz as he and the other guards finally managed to subdue Lady Corvina and Lady Starling. "I will take care of the First Daughter since obviously you cannot."

"I'm sorry, Commander," Baz said, his expression twisted with regret. "It happened so fast. I never would have thought—"

"Enough!" Talon cut him off.

Talon's face was twisted with a mixture of fury and concern as he helped me turn to my side and then pounded my back. "Get it all out," he told me gently. I coughed some more until finally all the water had come up. I fell back against him, breathing hard.

"I've got you, just breathe," he said near my ear, his arms warm around me.

I had never wanted Ama or Mariyah or any of my family so much in my life. I thought of Shazeera, not even at my side. Had this brief blast of wind power damaged our connection again? Another blow to our bond that I hadn't even meant to do.

After a moment, I leaned away, partially covered with the robe. I turned to look at Talon, and he gazed down at me, eyes wide with concern. I didn't even think about it first; I threw my arms around him and held on tight. He froze for a moment, but then he returned the embrace.

"You're safe now," he said into my neck.

His own distinctive smell—leather and mountain air—surrounded me.

I thought of the shadows that entered the two women before they tried to drown me. I was definitely not safe here, and I wasn't sure I ever would be.

I got shakily to my feet, and the robe he had thrown over me pooled on the ground. Talon's eyes darkened for a moment before he averted them.

We weren't afraid of nakedness, so to watch the Zephyrians take such pains to avoid looking at the human form was disconcerting. I struggled with the robe for a moment, my whole body still shaky and difficult to control.

He must have still been watching out of the corner of his eye, because he came behind me and held the robe up. "Let me help you."

I was finally able to slide each arm into the holes and belt it. When I turned to face him, I saw his throat move like he was swallowing hard. He was wearing a robe, too, though his was black and open to reveal a muscular chest.

"I'll escort you back to your room," he said, and I nodded.

As we walked, he kept close enough for me to feel the heat from his skin. "What happened? How did you end up with Lady Corvina and Lady Starling?"

"I came across Lord Heron and the two of them on my way to the hot springs, and he all but forced them to accompany me."

His voice dropped into a low, dangerous tone. "He is behind this assassination attempt?"

I thought of how the shadows poured into Lady Corvina and Lady Starling, turning their eyes black. "I think they were there to put me in my place. Before they tried to drown me, they were entertaining themselves by attempting to belittle me. I didn't get the sense they had murderous intentions."

"Until they held you under?"

I shivered. "Until then." I opened my mouth to say more, but then I considered the deep shadows on either side of us in the dimly lit hallway. "I'll tell you the rest when we get inside my room."

We walked quietly down more hallways and upstairs, passing a few guards who saluted Commander Talon. Finally, we arrived in my room.

Raven was inside waiting, and the minute she saw us both, she left to get us hot tea. I went and sat on one of the wingback chairs, but Talon remained standing.

"Why do you think they tried to assassinate you?" he asked as soon as we were alone.

"This sounds far-fetched, but I saw shadows pour like smoke into them, turning their eyes black. They held me under right after that."

Some of the color had drained from his face. "Shadows? You're sure?"

I nodded. "They reminded me of the creature we saw in the throne room."

"If the Devourer is targeting you," he said, his tone gruff, "then you're in danger. Where was your guard?"

"He was there but behind one of the stalagmites. Your people have some sort of aversion to nakedness, so he wasn't willing to be within view of me. He couldn't hear me drowning."

He muttered something under his breath. "He could have stood where he could watch but kept his eyes averted. Regardless, I'm going to up the number of guards outside your door." He ran his hand through his thick hair and met my gaze. "I'm sorry I had to leave you for a couple days."

"Where did you go?"

"I had some things to look into."

I thought back to the other conversation we had about the shadowy creature. "Did you find out what happened to the missing staff members?"

"All I know is they've completely disappeared—no family members have seen them, and they haven't reported to their stations in many days. But I haven't gathered more information than that. I was on another mission."

"What mission was this?"

He hesitated for only a moment. "I discovered that both my riders and their eagles were known to be attacking your people and horses off the battlefield."

"Yes. Including innocent civilians."

"Yes."

I took a deep breath. "And who was it that confirmed this for you—since my word was apparently not good enough?"

"I encountered several scouts who witnessed the war crimes firsthand."

I shook my head. "So it had to be your own people telling you before you'd believe. Well, at least you know now. What will you do about it?"

"The offenders are to be exiled immediately," he said. "Though the few who participated in these crimes the most are already dead."

He caught me by surprise with that. "What do you mean?"

"You killed them, First Daughter. With your wind power."

Emotions flitted through me: surprise, the remnants of fear from that day, cold satisfaction.

"I have to admit, Commander, I'm surprised you did anything at all about what I told you," I said, and I couldn't hide the admiration in my voice.

"We have a strict code of honor we're supposed to uphold at all costs," he said. "Killing off the battlefield is a breach of that honor."

"Even the horses?"

Something like regret flashed across his face. "We didn't know about your horses being intelligent until you yourself told me, so the greater crime in our eyes was the killing of innocent civilians."

I winced at the callousness of that statement. "I can't fault you for that when I didn't know about your eagles, either."

"Maybe now that the war is at an end, we can find out more about each other," he said. When I glanced quickly at him, he amended, "About each other's people, I mean."

"Yes, of course," I said, lowering my gaze to my hands. "Thank you, Commander. For telling me."

Raven returned with steaming cups of lightly spiced tea,

which I took gratefully. When she offered it to Talon, though, he shook his head.

"Have additional guards arrived outside the First Daughter's room?"

"Yes, Commander," she said.

"Then I should go change and report the attack to the emperor," he said to me with a bow. "I will return soon."

I nodded, but my stomach twisted into knots, bringing on a wave of nausea as I watched him walk out the door. Of all the people I had met, Talon seemed to be the most honorable–if I could trust that everything he had told me was true. The longer I stayed here, though, the more I realized there was not only great evil, but it could evidently infect anyone.

A sudden chill spread throughout my body despite finally being warm in front of the fire as another thought grabbed hold of my mind. Whatever goal this creature had, this most recent attack proved that it had set its sights on me.

But hell if I was going to come this far only to be assassinated.

23

ZARA

That night, Emperor Altair came to my door looking haunted. His eyes were shadowed, his eyebrows drawn low, and his mouth was a tight line.

"Future Empress," he said. "Baz and Talon informed me of the attack on you. Are you all right? Do you need me to send for the healer?"

I shook my head. "That won't be necessary. There wasn't any lasting damage."

"I'm relieved to hear it. Then, if you're up for it, will you come with me? I'd like to speak with you."

I glanced at the unfamiliar guard outside my room, frowning. I didn't have any reason to be wary of going somewhere alone with Altair, but it was hard not to feel a little uneasy after nearly being killed earlier that day. Still, I couldn't hide in my room forever.

"Of course," I said, hiding my apprehension behind a smile.

He led me down the hallway, lined with enormous portraits of regally dressed men and women. Flames flickered in sconces over each painting, making it seem like their eyes followed us as we walked.

We continued in silence that was growing more awkward by the second, until Altair glanced at me and said, "I wanted to show you a part of the palace that has always been my refuge. I used to spend as much time as possible here as a child."

The tension in me relaxed just a tad. "Did you grow up in the palace? You've never lived anywhere else?"

"I've been here my whole life," he said with a little backward glance at me, "except for the time a year ago that my eagle, Sky, and I visited Talon and his mother in the foothills."

"Talon didn't grow up here, then?"

He shook his head. "No. He was lucky. He only came for brief visits–a few weeks here and there–but he never had to live here."

I stole a glance at his expression, but he kept it masked. I thought of what he had said before about his father letting him dangle from an eagle's talons despite his fear of heights. No wonder he said Talon was lucky. Why did his mother allow him to be treated that way?

"What about your mother? Did she enjoy palace life?"

He glanced back at me once. "My mother died giving birth to me," he said.

I froze midstep. To be raised without a mother was unimaginable for our people. To us, our mothers were everything, the heart of our people.

"I'm so sorry to hear that," I said.

"You sound like you actually are," he commented with some surprise.

"I really am. I can't imagine being raised without a mother, especially when your father was . . ." I trailed off as he came to a stop in front of an open archway.

"My father was what?" he asked, eyebrows raised.

A tyrant. A murderer. Cruel. Sadistic. "He didn't seem to be the most loving man."

Altair laughed, but it was without humor. "That's an understatement. What was your father like?"

"I've never met him," I said, and he gave me a look that was equal parts disbelief and envy. "Queens may take any number of suitors, and I'm not sure my mother knows exactly who sired me."

I thought of the conversation I had with Ama before I left. How she refused to tell me more about my sire or even entertain the idea of finding him. Talon had arrived soon after with the peace treaty, and we hadn't had time to talk about it again.

"I can't even imagine what my life would have been like without my father," he said, interrupting my disturbing thoughts, but it wasn't with a sweet, nostalgic tone. He seemed to ponder it with longing. "But here we are. The place I wanted to show you."

He held out his arm for me to go through the archway. The moment I entered, I stood motionless as I took in the beauty surrounding me. We must have been at the center of the palace, for there was no ceiling, only open sky. There were enormous trees, and flowers with a riot of color–pinks, purples, even blues. A white bridge crossed over a mountain stream, and there were banks of green grass. The wind came and greeted me like a friend as a warm breeze enveloped me.

"This is incredible," I said. "You can almost pretend we aren't at the palace anymore."

Altair smiled, and this time, the expression reached his eyes. "That's why it has always been my favorite place."

Our gazes caught and held for a moment—he was truly beautiful when he smiled. He turned back to the stream. "The palace can be a dangerous place, especially for outsiders, but I honestly thought you would be well protected by the guards. Lady Corvina and Lady Starling are being stripped of their titles and exiled from the palace."

I widened my eyes at him. For the two of them, as much as they spoke of their high status, that would likely be a fate worse than death.

"I didn't think they were capable of such violence," he added. "But I will not tolerate any attacks on my future wife."

Talon most likely already told him what I had witnessed, but I still wanted to see his reaction. "I'm not sure it was entirely their fault. Before they tried to drown me, I saw shadows pour into them."

He glanced at me, expression unreadable. "And what do you think the shadows were from?"

"I think it had something to do with that creature I saw the first day in your throne room. The one Talon calls the Devourer."

"That's impossible," he said dismissively. "Ozul never leaves the west wing. No, though it embarrasses me to admit it, those women wanted to kill you just to try and take your place."

"Then how do you explain the shadows I saw? The way their eyes turned black?"

His expression softened with sympathy. "By all accounts, you had a near-death experience. It's hard to trust your memory after such a traumatic event."

He delivered this line so smoothly I almost believed him. But I knew better. I knew what I had seen.

He had obviously decided to deny the Devourer's role in the

attack on me, but I wanted answers about the creature. "Emperor Altair, in only three weeks, we will marry. I think I deserve the truth from my future husband. Who–or what–is Ozul?" I pressed.

After searching my face for a moment, he said, "A powerful sorcerer. Your people were gifted with magic, but mine have none. The war would have stretched on forever had I not evened the field."

I gaped at him. "Evened the field? Your Eagle Riders massacred our warriors easily. We were only successful with magic against your infantry."

"Yes, but our resources aren't infinite. It costs a fortune to maintain an army. Now your people's land and resources fall under Zephyrian rule."

I gave him a sharp look. "I thought it was just a tax."

"For now. Until we have need of more. The Children of Earth are now part of the Zephyrian Empire, and we rule the entire continent of Zephyrus."

"The treaty never said–"

"The queens understand this, believe me. It's better to be with us than against us."

I felt like we had been outmaneuvered on a chessboard we couldn't see. "It sounds like you've got everything you wanted, then. Why not send the sorcerer away?"

He looked at me, and his eyes burned with ambition. "My father was never able to expand the empire beyond this continent, but I will."

I froze, barely able to get the words out to form a response. "And you need the sorcerer to do that?"

"It takes untold power and resources to expand an empire," he said, not quite answering my question.

His goals made my blood run cold. In my mind, I saw years of war in front of me. What would it mean for my people? Would they be forced to fight alongside the Zephyrians now that we belonged to their empire? Altair spoke of traveling to distant countries and conquering them as he had done here. This was the man I was supposed to marry and produce an heir with, but the thought sickened me. How could I stand beside him and watch that happen?

"And what does the sorcerer want in return for helping you expand your empire?"

He seemed to retreat into himself. "That's none of your concern." Before I could say anything else, he changed the subject. "I should have brought you here sooner. I know more than anyone else how the palace can seem like a prison."

His words made me think of what Lady Corvina and Lady Starling had said about an empress not being able to travel. "Are you required to remain in the palace at all times?" Would we be forbidden to travel because of some rigid Zephyrian law?

He shook his head. "I can leave for short periods of time, though it's like any other throne. It shouldn't be left unattended for long."

I turned that over in my mind. I wondered if that included traveling to distant countries to conquer them—or would he just send his Eagle Riders and remain safely hidden away in the palace? "I was told that the empress couldn't leave the palace or surrounding area," I said, "but I can promise you I won't do well under lock and key. If it came to that, the treaty between us would be null and void."

He watched me for a moment before nodding. "I remember what it was like to be kept here against my will. I wouldn't wish that on anyone else. You may travel by my side when I venture beyond this continent."

I wasn't sure I wanted any part of that, but at least he wasn't saying I would be locked away in the palace. Maybe I could get closer to him and change his mind about the need for conquering other countries. I nearly scoffed out loud at myself. If I had even half of Ama's abilities, then I might have a chance of influencing the emperor. As it was, I'd be lucky if Lord Heron didn't convince him to lock me in my room.

"Have you ever been to the Equnox Plains?" I asked in an effort to engage with him again. Ama would know exactly what to say to draw him out, but I was a poor substitute.

"Not in a very long time."

"We could go together. My family would like to meet you," I said, and his eyes widened a bit, like he couldn't believe someone would want to meet him.

"I would like that," he said after a moment's hesitation. "My father always said I was too cowardly to travel much farther than Naharu, so I had tried to make peace with the thought of only seeing these far-off places on a map. Everything changed when he died, though."

I was still reeling from how casually he spoke of his father's cruel words and for a moment I only stared at him. "I've never traveled beyond my homeland, but I would like to see the other continents one day. I've never considered people who don't like to travel cowards! I understand, actually, because the idea of traveling by ship makes me nervous."

"And I've never wanted to fly, but perhaps one day we can do both."

I gave him a gentle smile, a natural response to the sorrow that radiated from his eyes. "Your father was wrong about you, you know. It takes more courage to form a treaty than it does to continue a war."

A veil fell over his face, and he retreated into himself.

My smile slipped from my face. What had I said to upset him?

"My father is never wrong."

He shifted from foot to foot and then took a few steps before stopping again, as though barely restraining himself from pacing in agitation.

"I must go," he said, and I looked at him in surprise. Before I could reply, he added, "You can stay here as long as you'd like."

He strode away, shadows on his face.

I sat down in the grass, the energy draining from me all at once. I'd never missed Ama so much in my life.

24

TALON

Finding Zara nearly drowned kept replaying through my mind, making it impossible to sleep. I was tortured with remembered images of her lying naked beside the hot springs, dripping wet and struggling to breathe. I could still feel her body pressed against mine, arms wrapped around me. It had set off a war within me. One part wanted to hold her close while the other wanted to hunt Lord Heron down and slit his throat. He may not have directly attacked the First Daughter, but it was no coincidence that he had sent Lady Corvina and Lady Starling to the hot springs with Zara. Somehow, it connected to Ozul. And if the creature could possess someone with shadow magic, then no one was safe from its malevolent powers. The only question was why it had thus far not staged a bigger attack. What kept it in the west wing?

I never should have left. If I had still been here, I would have kept them from even getting close to her. But after hearing the First Daughter's accusation that my own Eagle Riders had been preying on civilians and allowing their eagles to eat the horses, I had to investigate. What I found out finally made everything that happened with Captain Suna make sense. Captain Suna and the others hadn't abandoned their post to go hunting that day. They were terrorizing civilians and their horses, deep in enemy territory—for sport.

Those loyal to Lieutenant Callum were the ones who showed me the documents he had been collecting, including eyewitness statements. He had planned to present it all to me, but then his outpost was ambushed, and he was killed.

First Daughter Zara, though, unknowingly avenged those fallen civilians and horses when her wind power destroyed Captain Suna and her squad.

Still, my mission was badly timed. Although Baz had come to Zara's rescue as soon as he realized she had been attacked, it was still almost too late. I wouldn't have allowed Lady Corvina and Lady Starling to join her—not when they were so closely aligned with Lord Heron.

The morning after the attack, I went to see Altair. There was a time when he would have told me everything, but he had withdrawn so much this past year that it felt like I barely knew him anymore. I found him sitting before a roaring fire, dark circles beneath his eyes.

"Majesty," I said with a bow, "you exiled Lady Corvina and Lady Starling in response to the attack on the First Daughter, but I have reason to believe Lord Heron was involved, too. I would like your permission to interrogate him and reprimand him as I see fit." And maybe if I went a little too strong on the interrogation and removed him from the equation, then it would be one less threat to the First Daughter and this empire.

"Lord Heron is my father's oldest adviser," Altair said. "His knowledge of the empire is invaluable."

"He has threatened your future wife."

"Lord Heron didn't attack Zara. Lady Corvina and Lady Starling did, and they have been dealt with."

My hands tightened into fists at my sides as anger rippled through me. "He locked Zara away in her room the first night she was here."

Altair waved his hand flippantly. "That was in response to her use of wind power in my throne room."

"I believe he is in league with that creature," I said, and a silence fell over us both.

"I'm only going to say this once," Altair said quietly. "Ozul is bound to me, not Lord Heron."

It felt like a cold blade had touched the skin of my back. "Are you saying that you ordered the attack on Zara?"

"No," he protested so vehemently that I relaxed—marginally. "Ozul often has . . . requests . . . that I refuse. But unless he accompanies me, he stays in the west wing. That was part of our agreement."

I scrutinized his face, looking for any telltale signs of lying. It seemed unlikely that such a creature would obey my cousin and remain in the west wing until called forth like a dog. "Are you sure he never leaves his area of the palace without your knowledge?"

"Talon, this was an instance of extreme jealousy on the part of those women leading to an attack on the future empress. They have been dealt with accordingly. As for the shadows Future Empress Zara claims to have seen, I believe it to be due to her brush with death."

"Right," I said skeptically, "I, too, have hallucinated shadows when I nearly died in battle."

He looked unperturbed. "You are a seasoned veteran of war. Even brushes with death wouldn't terrify you like they would someone like the future empress."

"You don't even know her!" I snapped. "How would you know what would scare her or not? And there are shadows in this palace, Altair, I've seen them."

Altair stilled, something unreadable flashing across his face. "You overstep, Commander Talon."

I let out a frustrated breath. "You asked me to guard First Daughter Zara, and then she was attacked. I just want to know how much danger she's in. As your cousin, I'm asking for the truth. Is she in danger from that creature?"

"No," he said, but I watched his throat spasm as he swallowed hard.

"Altair, please. I can't help if I don't know what's going on. What keeps Ozul in the west wing?"

Altair let out a sharp breath and ran his hand through his hair. "He is starved for souls right now and physically weak. He was drawn to Zara's power when he first saw her, but I won't let him have it."

I stared at him in disbelief. Souls. It truly was the Devourer of souls. And the creature wanted Zara. I thought again of her clinging to me, naked and vulnerable. "Why First Daughter Zara? Why her power?"

Altair shifted uncomfortably, and for a moment, he seemed like he would refuse to answer me. Finally, he said, "Souls with magic are more powerful and thus give him more strength. First Daughter Zara's wind magic is superior to any other earth magic we've encountered."

My whole body went rigid as I fought off the rising need to take immediate action against the enemy Altair allowed in our midst. I unclenched my teeth and tried to reason with my cousin. "From the very beginning, Ozul has posed a threat to us all. You are tempting fate by keeping such a monster locked up. It's only a matter of time before it escapes. Tell me how to remove it from the palace, and I will respond with force."

"I cannot give that order. I will need Ozul's magic to expand this empire."

"The entire continent of Zephyrus is under your rule now. Four nations: the Semalians of the coast, the Nazcas of the Black Forest, the Angorans of the mountains, and now, the Children of Earth. What more is there?"

A glint appeared in Altair's eyes. "The world beyond Zephyrus."

I'd hoped his talk of conquest was bluster, but the glint in his eyes told me he meant every word. "We just ended a war, and you seek another? Besides, conquering other countries takes a tremendous amount of resources, which have been depleted by the last war. We'd have to travel by ship. The number of infantries it would take would be enormous."

"I need only bring Ozul to their shores," he said darkly.

My knuckles turned white from clenching my fists so hard. Not just because we had all thought the war was over and we could finally have peace, but because the thought of unleashing that creature on an unsuspecting country chilled my blood.

"You risk not only your future empress's life with this creature," I said firmly, "but also the peace treaty that finally freed us all from this never-ending war. Did you consider, too, that if that creature has no care for the woman you are supposed to marry, that it may not care for you, either? What's to keep it from killing us all?" I demanded.

"I told you before that the future empress is not in danger, and that Ozul wasn't responsible for the attack. That's all you need to know."

"Altair," I began, but he held up his hand.

"You're dismissed, Commander."

My fingers twitched at my sides as I struggled against the desire to slam my hand on his desk, to *make* him listen. He wasn't telling me the truth, and I had the sense that he was playing with things beyond his control.

I looked at my cousin's face, so gaunt and shadowed now, and I thought of the way he was as a child, fat cheeked and bright-eyed. His eyes had lost their brightness over time, the result of constant abuse and belittling by his father. But ever since his father's death and the discovery of Ozul, Altair had looked haunted, slowly wasting away with the desperate need to prove he was a better emperor than his dead father.

As I left Altair's rooms, I reached out to Neo mentally, who had quietly eavesdropped on our conversation. *Did you catch all of that?*

Yes, Neo said with a somber tone. *Just when we thought the war was finally over.*

I don't think these are truly Altair's goals. I think they are Ozul's and Lord Heron's. He is being manipulated into giving up this time of peace.

It's dangerous to abide by a demon's goals, Neo said. *Ozul doesn't care about Altair or this empire–only itself.*

And we'll be caught in the middle, I said, clenching my teeth at the thought of flying to distant lands to conquer them.

If he will not listen to you, then perhaps he'll listen to his future mate, Neo said thoughtfully.

I bristled at the thought of that. *Altair already admitted that Ozul desires Zara's power. I don't want her anywhere near that creature.*

You care for her, Neo said, searching through my mind. *You wish she were your mate,* he added, surprise in his tone.

I couldn't deny any of it, because he could see my true thoughts and feelings before I blocked him out. *It doesn't matter how I feel for her. She is promised to the emperor.*

An emperor who is rapidly losing his way–and is taking us all with him.

I will do all I can to protect her, I promised myself and Neo. But already I could feel the distance between Altair and me growing like a chasm.

I wished I could save Altair from himself.

DAYS WENT BY after the attack, and I made sure to have Zara guarded at all times by either myself or trusted Eagle Riders. The Devourer had always felt like a threat, but now it seemed somehow like we were running out of time. In only two weeks, she and Altair would be married, and by law, she would be completely under his power. What would he and the Devourer do then? Use her? Sacrifice her? A dangerous thought took root in my mind. If either of them hurt her, if she so much as looked at me with a silent plea for help, I would not hesitate to betray blood. Something had to be done before it came to that–before it was too late. I needed to seek out the old tomes in the library that held our oldest stories. The oral traditions the scribes had recorded centuries before. Maybe there was something about how to destroy the creature.

At the same time, though, I wanted to stay as close to Zara as possible. I figured getting her out of the gods-forsaken palace for a time and away from what lurked in the shadows was a good way to do that. Baz and Zamir, both stationed outside her room, saluted me, and I returned their greeting with a nod before knocking quietly on the First Daughter's door. After a few moments, she answered, dressed in a turquoise-studded bodice that revealed a slim section of her abdomen, and that same split skirt over leggings that she always wore. She was barefoot, with her hair still damp and hanging in waves down her back. My mouth went dry, and against my will, I remembered what her body had looked like when she was gleaming wet and naked—all fascinating curves and long legs.

"Commander Talon," she said, bruising on her arms darkening against the bronze of her skin. A flicker of shame lit inside me that I had been remembering her naked when she'd nearly been killed.

I cleared my throat to chase away the thoughts. "Would you like to accompany me to Naharu? We could go and get Shazeera from the pasture first if you'd like."

Her smile was blinding. "I would love that. Just a moment, and I'll get my shoes. You're welcome to come in and wait."

I stepped into the entry of her room, noticing the warm cinnamon-vanilla smell that seemed to follow her. She disappeared into one of the antechambers that held her clothing.

"I'd offer you something to drink," she said from the other room, "but Raven hasn't returned this morning from the kitchen."

"It's no problem," I said.

She reappeared, wearing knee-high boots and a warm-looking cloak. "You have truly saved me today. I thought I would lose my mind if I had to stay in this room any longer."

When we walked out into the hallway, Baz and Zamir saluted again. "I'll need you both to accompany us to Naharu," I said.

"Yes, Commander," they responded.

Zara gave me a curious look, so I said, "I want to make sure you have a full guard when we go to the city."

"All right, though it can't be any more dangerous than it is here," she said with a scoff.

We made our way to the pasture, where Sergeant Kestrel stood guard while Shazeera grazed. She looked up at us, eyes bright.

Sergeant Kestrel saluted us before relaxing into an easy grin. "Are we going on a trip, or what?"

"We are, actually," Zara said.

"To Naharu," I clarified when he looked surprised. "After the recent attack on the First Daughter, we can't be too careful. I'd like you to accompany us, too."

"Be happy to," Kestrel said. "It'll be a lot more fun than standing around this pasture all day." Shazeera turned her head toward him at that. "Not that I don't enjoy the peace and quiet," he added hastily.

Ignoring his commentary, I turned to Zara. "Are you ready now, First Daughter?"

"Yes, let's go," she said, grinning at Shazeera prancing in place beside her. "Shazeera is just as eager to leave this boring pasture as you are, Sergeant," she tossed over her shoulder at Kestrel, who immediately looked chagrined.

Baz, Zamir, and Kestrel fell into a V-shaped formation behind Zara and Shazeera, while I stayed by their side as we walked to Naharu.

The city was as it ever was, loud, crowded, and overstimulating in every way. But seeing it through Zara's eyes was like experiencing it for the first time. When we first set foot in the city, in the market district, she came to a stop, one hand on her mare's neck and eyes wide. Her silken outfit and fur-trimmed cloak that had so captivated me when I first saw it fluttered gently in the breeze that seemed to be ever present with her, billowing out her hair and making her look like some regal ancient goddess. I felt no such breeze, but only the cold and the permanent state of fatigue I always felt while staying at the palace. I looked again at the city, trying to see it from her perspective. In contrast to the somber shades of the palace, the marketplace was an explosion of color. Brightly colored tents provided shelter for the merchants' wares. There were bolts of silk from Rhythos, fur from Angora Mountain trappers, feather headdresses and coats, jewels and precious metals mined from deep within the rock, leather goods, and farther down, tents containing a variety of food, hot and steaming. These were from only a few of the closest tents; there were at least one hundred altogether, wrapping around the broad face of the mountain.

"What do you think?" I asked.

"It's so much more colorful than the palace," she said, her eyes darting from one shop to another. "Less intimidating."

As I looked around, I could see what she meant. Everyone had stopped to stare, but it wasn't with that undertone of hostility like it had been in the palace. For one thing, she'd covered her beautiful outfit—the one that had revealed more skin than the court had ever seen—with a finely knit wool cloak. And for another, these were people who were used to seeing other cultures and customs in their travels for goods. Word had spread of the peace treaty and the emperor's intent to marry a Daughter of Earth, so people here were naturally curious and eager to get a glimpse of the future empress. Still, I couldn't be too careful. With a subtle nod at my three Eagle Riders, I beckoned them a little closer.

"I've always been more comfortable here, too," I told her. "The palace can be cold and austere, which makes sense considering the nobles compete with each other for who can emulate the Holy Austerity of the Lord of the Skies the most."

Her eyebrows drew together. "The Holy . . . what?"

"It's a book. A tome, really, of how to achieve godliness like the Lord of the Skies."

"A dead boring book," Kestrel said. "Puts you to sleep in an instant."

Zamir elbowed him in the side and shook her head at him, but she also hid a smile. He wasn't wrong, after all.

"Hmm," Zara said. "And austerity is godliness to you?"

"I am not a noble, but we Eagle Riders do believe in mastery over our emotions."

"That explains a lot," she said with a grin. "My cousin and I said all of you look like statues walking around with no expressions on your faces."

Behind us, Baz snorted a laugh.

"Better that than to have every thought revealed on your face for the world to see," I said.

"Oh really?" she said, hand on her hip. "And what is my face saying to you now?"

I searched her face, but I was like a moth to a flame. I couldn't look away. Her eyes drew me in first, the color like amber. But then the smile playing on her lips made me stare at her mouth and imagine it on mine, plush and hot. I'd better get control of myself fast. "Honestly? It wouldn't be polite to repeat it," I said, and she let out a peal of surprised laughter.

"Wow, was that a joke?" she asked, her tone still full of laughter. "I didn't know you did that."

I glanced down at her briefly. "I joke. I even laugh on occasion."

She and her horse snorted at the same time. "I didn't think you were capable of laughter, either," she said cavalierly. "I learned something today."

"We call him Commander Jokester because he's constantly joking," Kestrel said, and Zamir let out a groan.

"Don't listen to a word he says," Zamir told Zara. "He isn't happy unless he's saying something disrespectful."

"I'm not sure the commander is capable of laughter," Baz deadpanned.

"I laugh," I said, "but only if something is amusing enough to warrant it."

"No pity laughs from you, huh?" Zara asked, that same shine of mirth in her eyes.

"Not unless a scoff counts," I said, and she laughed again, the sound light and infectious. Many turned their heads toward her and smiled, though they couldn't have known what she was laughing at.

I felt a strange buoying in my chest, which I belatedly realized was pride. It felt good to make someone laugh, to make *her* laugh. The war had cast a dark cloud over everything for so long, it felt like years since I'd found anything amusing.

She pointed to one of the market stalls covered with a bright red and yellow tent. "That smells incredible—what is it?"

I knew exactly the smell she was talking about, like honey and yeast. "It's trifala bread, made from mountain bees' honey."

"Shazeera would like that, too," she said as we made our way through the market.

"So would I," Kestrel called out, while Baz and Zamir gave him matching exasperated looks.

Beside me, Zara and her mare froze when they caught sight of a trader and his mount. The animal's snowy gray back was heavily laden with trade goods. Its rider, with only his beard showing out of his snow leopard cloak that covered him from his head to mid-calf, held on to his mount's curved horns wearily. "Is that a . . . goat?"

"A Zephyrian mountain goat," I said.

The citizens of Naharu rode a type of mountain goat, nearly as big as a horse, with cloven hooves and powerful legs that could easily handle the steep incline.

She watched the goat with wide eyes. "What would Mariyah say?" she asked, but she had turned to Shazeera, who snorted in what sounded like amusement.

"Is Mariyah your cousin who was with you at the bonfire?" I asked, and instantly my mind brought up images of the two of them dancing with their horses, firelight flickering on Zara's golden skin.

"Yes," she said, still smiling as she turned back to me. "Mariyah is like my sister. She also really loves goats. I try not to hold it against her."

A shadow passed over Zara's face, and I knew she was thinking of her cousin and probably everyone else she left behind. I didn't comment on it or ask her whether she missed her friends and family; it was obvious she did. Instead, I did what any of us ever did when faced with difficult emotions. I turned to a distraction.

I pointed to the many stalls lined up. "People from all over the Zephyrian Empire come to sell their wares here. Gemstones and jewelry from the Angorans, Semalian glass, and Nazca woodcraft."

The corners of her mouth turned down, and she shared a look with Shazeera. "So this is where all the great tribes that once made up my people have ended up–hawking their wares. I wonder when the Sorayans will take their place here. Unfortunately, all we've done for the past century and a half is survive a war, so we aren't known for our goods."

Her tone had a bite to it, and I silently regarded her, thoughts turning in my head. I had never looked at the market in that way. Those tribes had been part of our empire for so long that I had not given much thought to how they felt about being conquered. But obviously, for Zara, her experience was much different.

"As future empress, it will be different for your people," I said, trying to ignore the sharp pain in my chest at the thought of her future position—and marriage to the emperor.

Her eyes flashed. "These *are* my people. We are all descended from the First Daughters who were given earth magic from the Earth Mother herself."

"You're right," I said, "these are your people. Both from your ancestry, and as the future empress. And thanks to the peace treaty and your upcoming marriage to the emperor, you will be able to advocate for them."

She grumbled something that sounded suspiciously like "You make a good point," but I decided not to push.

We came to the baker's stall then, and Zara's eyes lit up. The bread was lined up on clean white cotton cloth, each loaf still steaming. The merchant was a robust woman with gray hair pulled back in a neat bun on top of her head. She watched us with eyes almost hidden by deep folds, and a smile that revealed several missing teeth.

"Will you have some trifala, lady?" she asked Zara, who had drifted closer to the loaves than I was. Kestrel moved forward, too, until he was nearly breathing down Zara's neck. I shot him a quelling glance, but he only shrugged.

Zara suddenly glanced at me, a blush touching her cheeks. "How will we pay for the food? I didn't even think of bringing coins with me."

I took out a golden pendant I wore on a chain around my

neck. It had the symbol of the emperor raised in the center, a crown uplifted by two eagle wings. The baker grinned when she saw it. "This will buy us anything we'd like."

Zara let out a breath in relief. "That's handy. In that case, since you're buying," she added to me with a teasing grin, "I'll have a loaf for myself and one for my mare." She turned to the rest of us, arching a brow in question. "One for each of you?"

"Yes," I said after Baz and Zamir each gave me a polite nod. "So that's four more, please," I told the baker.

"Two for me," Kestrel said, rubbing his hands together. "With butter," he added as the baker's plump hands reached for the bread.

"That's the only way to eat it," the baker said with approval. She handed each of us our loaves wrapped in cloth and dripping in butter. I took my own, savoring the warmth of the bread in my hands.

Zara immediately began feeding pieces to her mare before she took a bite herself, and I was once again grudgingly impressed. It's what I would have done for Neo, too.

"This is delicious, thank you," she said to the baker when she finally ate a piece.

"My pleasure, lady," she said with a polite bow.

We started to walk away, but Zara's horse bumped her arm, and she turned back to the merchant with a sheepish expression. "May I have two more loaves, please?"

"Of course. There you are," the baker said as she handed over the bread. "Anything else?"

The mare bobbed her head, but Zara shot her a look that clearly said, *Enough*. "No, thank you."

"We have more in common than I thought," Kestrel told Shazeera as he finished wolfing down his second loaf.

"Disgusting," Zamir commented, taking a dainty bite of her own.

"Shazeera wanted a sack of grain," Zara said to us with a grin as we turned away from the stall.

"The palace clearly isn't feeding her enough," I said, and she laughed.

"Don't forget the race today," the baker called from behind us.

Zara whirled around with eyebrows raised. "Race? What race would this be?"

"The Naharu Cup," the baker said, with a nod toward another Zephyrian goat walking past us, this one led instead of ridden.

I had forgotten all about the race today—not that I cared much for it—but Zara's eyes were lit up even brighter than they were when she first tried the trifala bread.

"And the goats will be racing?" she asked.

"I'd give you a strange look for such a question," the baker said with a smile, "but it's obvious you aren't from around here. Yes, they race Zephyrian goats."

"Thank you," Zara said before turning to me. "We have to go watch. Will it be soon?"

"If you hurry, you can still get a good spot," the baker said.

"Thank you," Zara said again, starting in the direction the goat had gone without even waiting for me.

"I take it you like races," I said, and she glanced back at me with a grin.

"You should have told me there'd be one today." She slowed her steps for a breath until I was beside her once again. "Where is there room for a track? We're on top of a mountain."

"You'll see," I said, and I found myself eagerly anticipating her reaction when she saw it.

Shazeera, Zara, and I walked abreast while Baz, Zamir, and

Kestrel followed until the crowd grew so thick we were forced to walk in a single-file line. In that fluidly graceful way of hers, Zara pulled herself onto her mare's back, and the two followed me so closely that I could feel the horse's breath on my neck.

"Shazeera said you may ride, too, if you'd like," Zara said after a few moments, her tone slightly surprised.

"Thank you for the offer," I said, meeting the mare's steady gaze, "but I wouldn't burden you with my weight."

"She says she was only being polite, so her back thanks you."

I let out a scoff, but the corners of my mouth were curving up. So, the horse had a sense of humor as much as Zara did. Interesting.

"You speak to Neo like I do Shazeera," she said after a moment of quiet walking. "But are you close to Neo—closer than fellow soldiers, I mean?"

"He is like my brother—that's the best word I can think of in the common tongue—but he is much more than that. We've been together since he was a fledgling, and I was a child."

"I understand," she said, reaching out to touch her mare's neck. "It's the same with Shazeera. She is my heart's sister. We grew up together, too. Each of us is bonded to a horse from nearly the moment we can walk . . . and ride. Before that, we're kept with our mother's horse."

"Heart's sister," I repeated. "Yes, I think I know what you mean."

"And does everyone have one—an eagle?"

"No. Only those who can trace our lineage to the first Eagle Riders—the ten original men and women."

Her lips parted in a little O of surprise, and I was momentarily captivated. "We have a similar story with our earth magic. Those of us who are direct descendants of the first six who were given earth magic from the Earth Mother herself carry on those bloodlines."

"It is similar, though, of course, we weren't given the ability to use magic."

"True, but flying on eagles seems to be working out for you despite not having magic," she said with a wry smile.

"There is nothing like flying," I said with a glance up at the clouds. "The vastness of the sky, the freedom of being so far above the earth that it's only you, your eagle, and the wind." I gave her a knowing look when I saw her hanging on my every word. "You enjoyed flying, too, I think."

A tinge of pink filled her cheeks, and she shot a sheepish look at her horse. "I think it's safe to say it was one of the most exciting things I've ever done in my life. The emperor was surprised I felt that way."

"He asked you about it?" Some unidentifiable emotion flitted through me then, making my shoulders tense. I didn't realize Altair had spent time with her, enough to talk about things together. And immediately, I admonished myself for the thoughts. Soon, my cousin would *marry* the First Daughter. Of course they should talk to each other.

She glanced back to check on where the others were, and when she saw they had fallen back out of earshot, she said quietly, "The emperor has told me of his fears of flying—and the horrible way his father treated him because of it."

I shouldn't have been surprised that Altair confessed this to her. There was something about Zara that was calm and trustworthy, like you could tell her anything—any dark secret—and she wouldn't judge you for it. But the fact that he had grated on me more than I expected. "The previous emperor was a very hard man, and his treatment of Altair took its toll on him. It made him desperate to surpass him as emperor."

"I can understand the need to live up to a parent's expectations," she said. "Though my mother was always supportive and kind. She always thought I would inherit her healing abilities. No one expected me to have the power to call the wind."

"It's not an ability that's passed down in your family?"

She hesitated. "No—not on my mother's side at least."

I turned what she said over in my mind, examining it. I had assumed her father was one of the Children of Earth, but this suggested otherwise. "And what of the others who have manifested this power? The ones you warned us would retaliate should anything happen to you?"

She shifted from foot to foot. "We're not sure of this power's origin. As we told you before at the peace treaty signing, it manifested in response to the war."

She looked uncomfortable, which I found curious. What secrets were they hiding about this wind power? Besides the fact that I didn't quite believe there were many with the same power—despite their efforts to convince me. But before I could decide if I should question her further or not, the noise of the crowd increased tenfold.

We had finally arrived at the race, even though the press of people was still so thick I couldn't see. Instead of following the people down closer to the start of the track, I led Zara and her mare higher—not just for a better view, but to be in a stronger position to protect her.

"I don't understand," Zara said as she dismounted so her horse could haul herself up the steep incline. "Where's the track?"

"Down there," I said, with a nod toward the screaming crowd.

She walked to the very edge of the ledge we'd claimed, and

looked down. I stepped next to her so that my body would prevent her from falling. "I don't see anything."

I followed her gaze. I could see the shifting, colorful crowd down below, and the riders mounting their goats. The beasts pranced and tossed their heads, some even butting heads, the sound echoing like a crack of thunder before the riders could pull them apart. They all stood on a natural outcropping that was relatively flat, but below them was the rocky mountainside and the tops of the evergreen trees.

I leaned closer to her. "The mountain is the track."

Her eyes widened as she glanced up at me. "Seriously? They're going to race down the mountain?"

She'd reacted exactly like I expected, and I arched a brow at her teasingly. "Where else would mountain goats race?"

"That's a good point," she said, moving to sit on the edge, swinging her legs while her horse watched from behind her. I sat beside her, at a respectful distance, though my body kept leaning closer to her without my permission. Baz, Kestrel, and Zamir spread out behind us, eyes constantly roving for potential threats. "How will we see who wins?"

"We won't be able to see that, but we'll see the beginning, which is what everyone is here for. It's when they all plunge over the edge."

Zara shared a long look with her horse. "That brings up memories."

"It's a good way to break a leg," I said.

Zara let out a quiet laugh. "That's what I told Shazeera when we galloped down the mountainside."

I looked at her in surprise. "Why were you galloping down a mountain?"

She glanced at her horse again, like she was sorry she'd said anything, but I was far too curious to let it go. "It was in the Ridgeline Foothills, nothing as steep as this," she said, and even this raised my eyebrows. The foothills were outside of the Children's territory. "We were being chased by a giant eagle—a mother defending her nest—and the only way we could escape was by going over the edge. Shazeera never faltered, but still, I wasn't sure we'd make it."

There were so many things in what she said that raised questions in me that I didn't know where to start. So I went with the most unbelievable. "You saw a wild eagle?"

"You seem surprised."

"I am, considering how dangerous wild eagles are, especially when defending their nests. I thought the Children of Earth did anything they could to avoid them." Imagining this scenario had my muscles tensing again. It could have been disastrous—why would she risk such a thing?

She and her mare shared a look. "We do. It was a chance encounter—I didn't go looking for it."

"Still pretty reckless."

She looked introspective for a moment and then seemed to decide to tell me more. "Sometimes I would go where the wind called me," she admitted. "And at least the wild eagles tend to not eat our horses—unlike your aerial cavalry."

Far below us, the crowd had quieted, waiting for the horn to sound and signal the beginning of the race.

"Neo would never do that. He doesn't like the taste of horseflesh."

"That's wonderful," she said with a nod and more than a little sarcasm. "That's what keeps me from eating Zephyrians, too, you know. I know I won't like the taste of your flesh. That's the only thing stopping me from killing and eating you."

I barely suppressed a laugh at her sardonic tone. "I'm thankful you're not a meat eater, because you seem to be bloodthirsty," I deadpanned.

She shot me a baleful glance before returning her attention to the race. The master of the race held a curved ram's horn to his mouth, and as everyone leaned forward as one, he blew into it, the sound deep and long, echoing over the mountain.

Beside me, Zara gasped as the racers leaped down the mountain, the goats in free fall, their strong legs connecting with the rock for only a moment before launching into the air again, moving continuously downward.

We wouldn't be able to watch for long, as they were racing beneath the cover of trees, but the riders and their mounts jockeyed each other for the best position. One goat leaped high to avoid the hooves of another and ended up tangled in the branches of a tree.

All too soon they'd disappeared beneath the cover of the forest, where even from our lofty position we couldn't see them.

"That was incredible," Zara said, a little breathlessly. There were high spots of color on her cheeks, and her eyes danced. For a moment, her beauty captivated me into a stupor.

"I haven't watched a race in years," I said as I watched the crowd still craning their necks for a glimpse at the racers.

"Too busy?" she asked, the question clearly loaded by the look in her eyes.

"Neo isn't a fan of land races," I said.

"Shazeera and I love to race. There's none faster."

"On land, maybe," I said with a grin. I wondered if she loved thrilling things as much as I did. Maybe that was why she'd seemed so fearless when Neo and I had flown her to the palace for the first time.

"She was faster than that wild eagle."

"That reminds me," I said, and the teasingly smug look on her face disappeared. "Why were you in the foothills in the first place?"

There was a heavy pause, and then she said, much too flippantly, "I like to explore."

I was sure that wasn't the whole truth, and my instincts were telling me that the reason she had been trespassing was important to know. But I could also tell by the stiff set of her shoulders that she wasn't going to tell me.

But that was fine with me. I could be patient.

AFTER THE RACE, we took a leisurely walk back to the upper pasture. Zara was quiet until we had returned, and I quickly realized it was because she didn't want to be overheard. After a quick glance over her shoulder at Baz, Zamir, and Kestrel, she said in a low voice, "Your Eagle Riders you've chosen as guards—you trust them, right?"

"With my life," I told her sincerely.

She nodded like she expected me to say that, and then said, "I didn't want to bring this up when we were in Naharu because I wanted the chance to escape it for a little while, but I spoke to the emperor about that shadowy creature."

My muscles coiled with tension as I imagined how that conversation went. Altair had become increasingly sensitive when I brought up Ozul, quickly shutting down and refusing to communicate about it. I forced my breathing to come in slow, measured inhales, though my instincts told me that she had been in very real danger.

"What did you say to him?" I asked carefully.

"I told him about the shadows I saw, and that I think they possessed Lady Corvina and Lady Starling. I asked him what Ozul was." She kept one hand on Shazeera's neck, as if needing comfort. I wanted to reach out and touch her, but I kept my hands to myself. "He said only that he was a sorcerer."

"A demonic sorcerer," I said, my tone coming out in a growl.

"He spoke of wanting to expand the empire beyond this continent–to conquer other nations," she said tightly, and her beautiful face looked anguished. "Just when I thought we were at peace, now he's talking of more war. Will my own people be forced to take up arms when we have only just now found peace? It would mean my own sacrifice for this peace treaty was useless. How can I stand aside while he brings death and destruction to another nation?"

The fact that she trusted me enough to tell me these things made my chest feel heavy. "Altair expressed the same ambitions to me. He isn't satisfied with the conquering of this continent."

"I asked him what Ozul would want in exchange for his help, but he wouldn't answer." Her amber eyes met mine. "I'm afraid whatever it is, the price is too high."

I steeled myself to tell her the terrible truth of what Altair and the creature planned to do, but we were interrupted by the sudden approach of Sergeant Falcon, one of the youngest officers in the aerial cavalry.

"Commander," he said after saluting me, "I have been asked to pass on a message to you by the head steward. He would like to meet with you as soon as possible; he says he has important information on the disappearances of the staff."

I hesitated, glancing at Zara.

"We will guard the First Daughter, Commander," Baz said.

"Go," she said, as if she could sense my reluctance to leave her under the protection of anyone else. "I'm going back to my room anyway."

I nodded, but before I could walk away, she reached out and touched my arm. "Thank you for showing me Naharu."

I took hold of her warm hand and bowed over it. "It was my pleasure," I said, meeting her gaze. Her pupils widened before I finally dragged myself away.

This growing attraction to Zara was a dangerous thing. In only two weeks, she would marry the emperor. I was assigned to protect her as my future empress. Letting myself imagine her in any other way was borderline suicidal.

But when I thought about the threat on her life—a blind rage filled me. And I knew. I knew this was more than a passing attraction. I cared too much already.

She was in more danger here than she'd ever been on the plains, even during wartime.

25

ZARA

When I walked into my room later that day, I bit my lip, unease churning within me when I saw that Raven still hadn't returned. In her place, a new handmaiden waited. "I'm filling in for her, Highness," she said, her plain face betraying no emotion.

"Do you know where she is?"

She shook her head. "I was asked to bring you your evening meal and tea." After she put down the silver tray, she turned to me. "Will there be anything else you require? A bath, perhaps?"

My mind was still on thoughts of Raven, so I nodded absently. She left the room to prepare the bath, and all I could think about was what Talon had told me about the missing servants. They had never been found. Was Raven yet another victim? What was happening to them? Something to do with that horrible creature?

I almost went into the hall to ask Talon about it, but then I remembered that he had been replaced for the night by another guard. I picked at my food and drank my tea. When the other handmaiden finished preparing the bath, I barely registered the soothing hot water.

"Shall I help you bathe?" she asked.

"That won't be necessary."

She left as quietly as she came, and I sank low in the water. As I washed my hair with the perfumed oils, I swore to myself that in the morning, I would investigate Raven's disappearance. She had mentioned a family—maybe she had been called away suddenly. There could be a perfectly innocent reason for her not being here.

After washing myself, I lay back in the water and closed my eyes. The heat felt so good now that I was constantly cold.

As I lay in the bath, my thoughts drifted to Talon. It was hard to believe I had once feared him, that I had called the power of the wind down on him and nearly killed him. Now I couldn't imagine how I would endure the palace without him.

I had seen another side of him in Naharu—relaxed and at ease. The way his eyes crinkled at the edges when he smiled kept playing through my mind, making my own lips curl in response. I thought of the way he had held my gaze before leaving the pasture, and a warmth spread through my chest, slow at first, then consuming, like sunlight breaking through the clouds.

Shazeera's words to me in Naharu drifted through my mind. *It's a shame he isn't the emperor.*

Heat snuck up my neck as I remembered my response, only half in jest. *I would have married him already.*

But that was the problem—how could I let myself be attracted to Talon when I was supposed to marry his cousin? The thought made a cold pit form in my stomach, like I had swallowed a stone.

The muffled sound of a man's voice suddenly filled my quiet bathing room, and I sat up to hear better. I thought at first it was coming from the hallway, but then I realized it was coming from the other side of the wall.

Emperor Altair's room.

There was something about the tone that even though I couldn't hear it clearly, I could still tell it was distressed. I grabbed a silken robe and got out of the bath. Wrapping it around me, I quietly stepped toward our shared wall.

More murmurs came through, and this time, I heard another voice. Shamelessly, I pressed my ear against the stone wall.

"This has gone too far," Altair said.

"There's no going back," the other voice said, and I thought it sounded like Lord Heron. He said something else, but I couldn't quite make it out.

I pressed my ear harder against the wall, bracing against the cold stone with my hands. As I did so, some mechanism inside clicked, and a door cracked open. Stunned, I held my breath, sure I would be discovered. But they continued their conversation without pause. I peered through the slight opening, wondering distantly if it was a lovers' door for the emperor and his empress.

Altair stood before a roaring fire, almost unnatural in its intensity. It burned so high and bright that it looked like it would escape the hearth. Lord Heron stood to his right, and both had their backs to me.

"Every day he grows in strength, and soon he won't stay confined to the shadows," Lord Heron said.

"Bring me the girl," a new voice said. It seemed to come from the fire itself, the deep and gravelly sound covering my skin in goose bumps.

"I can't do that," Altair said. "The treaty—"

"I need her power," the voice interrupted, and I thought I would be sick. They were talking about me—I was sure of it.

"Now that we have her here, you won't even need the treaty with her people," Lord Heron said, and I clutched the wall tighter.

My breaths came faster, but I tried to suppress them. If I was caught now, I had no doubt they would hand me over to that shadowy creature immediately–just to shut me up. "Ozul will consume her power and be unstoppable. You will conquer not only this continent, but the entire known world."

Altair shook his head. "She entered into this agreement in good faith, thinking she was saving her people."

"And what about your own people? She doesn't matter. She's not one of us."

My hands clenched at my sides, and a desperation rose within me. Should I make a run for it now? Get Shazeera and try to escape? I thought of the impossibly steep mountains, and the goats they used to traverse them. I thought of Neo flying through the clouds to get us here. We would never make it out on our own.

Talon, then? Would he even help me? And what would happen to my people and the treaty?

"Harming her goes against the treaty," Altair added weakly. "The Children promised that others with that same power will rise against us if anything happens to her."

"If Ozul consumes the wind power, it won't matter," Lord Heron said confidently.

I could feel the blood drain from my face, and I had to brace myself on the doorway to keep from falling.

Altair seemed to draw himself up straighter. "I won't do it."

For a moment, Lord Heron was quiet, and only the roaring of the fire could be heard. But then he said, "Maybe your father was always right about you. Or have you forgotten what he used to say?"

The flames flickered and flared brighter, and then suddenly, images appeared in the midst of them. The man from the paintings that hung throughout the palace–Emperor Lamir–glared out from within the fire. His hair was darker, without as much silver as it had even in the painting. He was holding what looked like a broken-off leg of a chair. Near the base of the flames, bloodied and crying, was a very young Altair. He couldn't have been older than seven.

"Please, Father," young Altair cried, holding up his hands to ward off the blows. "I'll do better with the spear. Please stop hitting me."

"Stop crying," the emperor roared, beating him again, but never in the face. "Your cousin Talon has already mastered the spear, and he's only a few months older than you!"

The beating continued, Altair's wails having no effect on his father.

"Why was I cursed with a worthless son like you? I wish you had died with your mother."

I flinched away from the savage words, the cruel blows, but I could see that this beating was not a unique event. It had happened before, and it would happen again, many, many times until his father finally died.

Altair now stood before the phantom images in the fire, shoulders hunched as if to ward off the blows.

"Worthless and better off dead," Lord Heron said.

Altair shook his head roughly. "Stop it!"

"And then, of course, there's the truth I helped you hide. The truth about what you did to him—your own father."

The images changed to reveal an opulent bedroom. Altair quietly entered under cover of darkness, gripping a dagger in his right hand. His father slept quietly, bare-chested despite the cold. Altair walked over to his father's bed, dagger raised, and in that moment of hesitation, his father opened his eyes.

"You wouldn't dare," he said and closed his eyes again.

The sound of the dagger hitting his chest was as loud as a punch, and when his father opened his mouth in shock, blood bubbled out.

"Finally you grew a pair," he said, and promptly died.

He killed his father. He killed the emperor. It seemed impossible, and yet, I'd watched him do it, and I knew the emperor was dead. Obviously, the palace had covered it up and spread the word that Altair's father was killed in battle.

The weight of it–seeing the truth of what happened to the previous emperor–felt like being suddenly doused with ice-cold water. I couldn't move. I could only watch helplessly as Lord Heron and the creature continued their torture.

Tears streamed out of Altair's eyes as he stood over his father's body, and he shook so violently, I thought he was seizing.

"I freed myself of the monster that had abused me every day of my life, but I didn't know what the consequences would be," Altair said.

"It led you to Ozul, so that was well worth it," Lord Heron said.

The flames told the story of how Altair had been tortured by the memory of taking his father's life. He relived it almost constantly, until in the dark of night, he fled the palace on his eagle, Sky.

They landed in the mountains, and Altair had fallen to his knees, gripping his hair like he would tear it out. Sky tried in vain to comfort him, but Altair was deaf to all his attempts. Night had fallen by then, the moon hidden by clouds.

From the shadows a creature crept toward them. It hid amongst the flames in the fireplace, and I couldn't see it with any clarity. Like they did in the hot springs, shadows coalesced into one writhing mass, which flowed toward Altair. And he had brought that thing back to this palace, where it now hid itself, slowly growing in strength.

"Bring me the girl," the gravelly voice repeated.

Altair groaned and shook his head. "Send another servant," he told Lord Heron, and with a sick twist in my gut, I thought of the disappearances. Talon had said people were vanishing. Could this be why? I didn't want to believe it—but the thought took root and wouldn't leave.

And Raven.

"You can only put this off for so long," Lord Heron said.

"Just do it!" Altair snapped.

Reluctantly, Lord Heron bowed. I backed away slowly from the crack in the door before he could turn around, feeling for the mechanism with my hand. I held my breath as my fingers brushed over the indentation again.

As it slowly swung back into place, I heard Lord Heron say to Altair, "The time will come when you have to make a choice. The girl. Or you."

I suppressed a whimper as my heart slammed painfully into my ribs. The emperor barely knew me, so it wasn't hard to guess what he would choose.

But that didn't mean I was going to wait around for the ax to fall.

THAT NIGHT, I barricaded the bathing room with heavy furniture, knowing it was likely not going to keep the emperor out of my room if he decided he wanted to sacrifice me. But with the door to my room locked and the bathing chamber sealed off, I felt marginally more in control.

I lit every candle I could find until my room blazed with light. Outside, the wind howled. I threw open my window despite the freezing cold. As the wind surrounded me, it chased away some of my fear. I remembered what Shazeera had told me before we came here—that I wasn't a sheep. I could defend myself.

Calling upon the wind had saved me from the assassination attempt in the hot springs, which I now knew must have been not only ordered by Lord Heron but also likely demanded by that creature.

I paced around my room, my thoughts racing through my head. Should I attempt an escape with Shazeera? Perhaps we could go to Naharu to see if the paths leading there were more accessible. I thought again of the mountain goats and the conspicuous lack of horses. It seemed the city and the palace were inaccessible to anything but eagles and goats.

Would Talon be willing to help? Shazeera trusted him. He had always acted honorably, even when I told him his people had been slaughtering my own outside of battle. But I would be asking him to go against the wishes of not only his cousin, but the emperor. How could I trust that he would choose to help me—a virtual stranger—over his own flesh and blood?

Assuming I did escape, then where did that leave my people? The treaty would be void, and the emperor would not only resume the war, but likely destroy us this time.

Lord Heron had said that every day, Ozul grew in strength and wouldn't always remain in the shadows. What happened when he was freed?

The wind seemed to wrap itself around me, gently rustling my hair as if trying to bring comfort. Shazeera had said I should try to communicate with it, and despite my trepidation, I was running out of options.

Somewhere inside my mind, I sensed Shazeera. And although the short burst of wind power in the hot springs hadn't hurt our connection, the distance made it feel muffled. Maybe it was because of this that I suddenly became aware of another presence in my mind.

It felt completely different than Shazeera. Where her presence was as familiar to me as my own heartbeat, this felt alien and immensely powerful. It wasn't a natural part of my mind like Shazeera. No, this was another being reaching out and making a temporary connection with me.

So many questions raced through my mind, things I had always wanted to know, but I got the sense that this being wouldn't stay with me long. Even now, I could feel the strain of our connection weighing me down.

Who are you? I asked.

The long pause made me almost give up when suddenly I heard a whisper drift through my mind.

I am Mistral, the spirit of the wind.

Mistral. The name tugged at my subconscious, like maybe I had heard it before in a different context.

How am I able to speak with you? Hearing the spirit's voice in my mind so clearly after years of sensing the wind's power but never being able to communicate made my stomach flutter with excitement.

Your blood calls to me, through a bond formed with your family long ago, Mistral said.

I stilled. *My sire's family?* I thought of all the times I had asked Ama about my sire, and of her complete avoidance of the subject.

Yes.

Eagerly, I asked, *Who is my sire?*

A wind caller like you.

Wind caller. I repeated the unfamiliar words to myself. This didn't really give me much to go on, and yet, it was so much more than I had been told. So my ability *did* come from my father's bloodline. Who was he? How did he possess magic more powerful than my mother's?

A wave of fatigue hit me, and I closed my eyes.

You don't have the strength and training to maintain a connection with me.

There was so much more I needed to know, but my mind felt muddled. This whole experience had me awestruck, and I didn't want to lose my connection to Mistral. *That creature. What do I do?*

Ride the tempest, tame the wind.

Tempest–like a storm? I thought back, at a total loss.

You can channel my power, but only for brief periods. It drains your energy too fast, and without proper training, you could burn yourself out like a dying star.

I struggled to make sense of what the wind spirit was telling me, but I couldn't hold on to any one thought for long.

The connection is draining you too much even now. I must leave you.

"Please don't leave," I mumbled.

I'm never far.

The moment the wind spirit left my mind, my tensed muscles gave out, and I dropped to my knees. I stayed there, dragging in breath after breath, too drained to move. Eventually, I forced myself to bed.

I didn't have the strength to be afraid of the shadows anymore, but I still slept with one hand wrapped around my dagger.

26

ZARA

The next morning, Raven still hadn't returned. I watched the other handmaiden with a lump in my throat. I knew she had been sacrificed to that creature—maybe even in my place. The thought made my eyes burn as a heavy weight settled on my shoulders, pulling me down. I prayed I was wrong.

After the horrible things I had seen and overheard last night, I was desperate to talk to Shazeera. I refused breakfast and dressed quickly. When I opened the door, I found my night guard had been replaced by Talon. I nearly groaned with relief. Surely after everything he had told me about his concerns about the Devourer, he would be sympathetic when I told him what I overheard.

"First Daughter," he said with a bow. And then he must have gotten a good look at my face, because he took a step toward me protectively. "Is something wrong?"

I nearly broke down then. Nearly pulled him into my room and unburdened myself of all the terrible things I had witnessed last night. But I stopped myself. Instead, I glanced down the hallway, toward Altair's rooms. "I need to see Shazeera," I said, trying but failing to keep the desperation out of my voice.

His dark eyebrows furrowed, but he didn't say anything. He stayed by my side as we walked, close enough that I could feel the warmth from his body. Still, I cast nervous glances toward the shadowy places in the hallway. We wouldn't be safe to speak until we were in the fresh air of the pasture.

After a tense walk through the palace, we finally emerged into bright sunshine and clear blue skies. Shazeera galloped over to me immediately.

I could feel how upset you were once you got close enough–even behind the stone walls, she thought to me with a snort. *I had just asked Kestrel to send word to check on you.*

Her words distracted me for a moment. *What do you mean you asked Kestrel?*

My guards have come up with a simple communication system–things like pawing the ground or nodding–to convey my needs.

That's genius, I said, surprised and touched that they cared enough about Shazeera to let her communicate what she needed.

Yes, but never mind that, Shazeera said. *What happened to you?*

I wrapped my arms around her neck and just rested my forehead on her mane, the stress of the past few days hitting me hard. Shazeera dipped her head, hugging me back as the wind blew gently around us. Kestrel guarded her today, and he came and joined Talon. They stood quietly near us, not interrupting our reunion. After a few moments, I took a shuddering breath and filled her in on the horror show that was my night.

She whinnied in distress when I came to the part about Altair barely resisting Lord Heron wanting to sacrifice me to Ozul.

You cannot possibly marry the emperor now, she said. *We must escape. There has to be some way off this mountain.* She looked at Talon. *Surely he will help us. If anything, he wouldn't want that creature feeding on your power.*

I'm not so sure we should immediately try and leave, I thought, and then I showed her how I was able to connect with Mistral, the spirit of the wind.

Tempest? Shazeera repeated, her tone confused. *What does that mean?*

I don't know. I could barely maintain the connection with Mistral—it was taking everything out of me, so I couldn't push for an explanation. But I thought maybe it means I'll have to face down a storm—learn to tame the wind?

She shook her head. *Ama may know more, and maybe she'll finally tell you the truth about your sire. You are in real danger here—this proves it. The treaty will be useless anyway if you're killed.*

We both looked over at Talon, and a rush of emotion hit me as we caught each other's eye. Ever since the day he brought the treaty, Talon had treated me with kindness and respect. When I told him about the war crimes against my people and our horses, he hadn't ignored me—he had physically gone and investigated it. I only wish I had known at the time that I was meting out justice to those who had committed such atrocities against my people. It would have made the victory so much sweeter.

He moved closer to me, and the now-familiar scent of fresh mountain air and leather enveloped me. When I met his searching gaze, heat crept up my neck. Every time he came near me, my body had a physical reaction to him—from the very first time we flew together. I tried to ignore those feelings at first; I didn't want to be attracted to my enemy. But after getting to know him, I couldn't deny that he was a man of honor and integrity, even though he fought for the other side. This man had been there for me after I had been attacked and seemed to understand how dangerous the sorcerer was, but I still had to ask myself if he was just doing his job. I was afraid to trust him completely, but the prospect of having no one here to trust was so much worse. Before I could say anything, a sound came over the quiet valley, and Shazeera's ears flicked back and forth nervously.

The steady *thump* of wings.

I knew I was in the mountains, with eagles everywhere, but it was still hard to ignore the cold douse of fear that flooded my senses at that sound. We had been conditioned from a young age that the sound meant almost certain death.

"It's Neo," Talon said, his voice low and soothing, and my cheeks flushed that he had noticed I had reacted nervously.

Neo appeared over the mountain, wings spread wide to catch the current. As he came closer, the wind created by his powerful wings buffeted us, stirring our hair, and making Shazeera's mane and tail stream behind her. She had moved closer to me; it was hard to erase all instinct of fight or flight the moment we heard an eagle approaching.

At last Neo landed beside us, tucking his wings close to his sides. I was once again struck by the sheer size of him; he was three times as tall as Shazeera, and I expected a shot of fear to take over as I looked up at him, but mostly I was filled with a sense of awe. Suddenly his golden eye was on me.

"Neo hopes he didn't frighten you," Commander Talon said. "He wants you both to know that he already ate a full meal and isn't the least bit hungry."

I glanced back at the eagle as my lips twitched in surprise. "I take it he has a sense of humor."

"He thinks he's hilarious, yes," Commander Talon said, and the feathers on Neo's neck ruffled until they were all sticking up straight.

A murder machine with a sense of humor, Shazeera said loftily, *how quaint.*

I snorted a laugh, and when Neo and Talon both looked at me questioningly, I gestured toward Shazeera. "She said she was glad to hear Neo isn't hungry."

If you're not even going to translate me correctly, then I'm just going to go back to grazing, she said, turning her back on me with a swish of her tail.

Neo made a sound, and I looked up to find him watching me. Talon said, "Neo wants to take you on another flight–where we can't be overheard."

I glanced at Shazeera. *What do you think?*

I think you'd love to go, and there's no one here to judge you. More importantly, he's right about the inability to eavesdrop while you're in the air.

Neo must have anticipated my response, because he spread his wings and lowered his body so that he was no longer vertical. I grabbed hold of Neo's saddle leathers and pulled myself up. It was a long way to his back, but at least I did it with a minimal amount of flailing this time.

"Does Shazeera want to go?" Talon asked.

Goddess, no, Shazeera said with a distressed whinny.

"I think that's a no," I told him.

"I didn't want her to feel left out if I didn't offer," he said with a smile playing on his lips.

I knelt and then sat back on my heels the way Talon showed me the first time. The second I was settled, Talon vaulted up behind me. His muscular thighs were on either side of mine, and as his arm slid around my middle, a low fire burned inside me. I glanced back at him, and his eyes held mine. Our faces were separated by mere inches, and only one small movement from either of us would close the distance. Butterflies erupted inside my abdomen as I imagined what it would be like to press my lips to his.

"You can hold on to the pommel there," Talon said, his voice a little gruff as he pointed to a rolled piece of leather that provided a handhold when in flight. "Ready?"

I did as he asked and then nodded. In the next instant, Neo gave a few pumps of his powerful wings and launched himself into the air. I had a death grip on the pommel, but then I found it wasn't necessary. Talon held me close to his chest, where I could feel his taut muscles flex.

Neo caught an air current that carried us high above almost instantly, and with his wings spread wide, we glided above the pasture. In no time at all, Shazeera looked like she was the size of a sheep from our lofty height.

But it wasn't the earth I was looking at; it was the sky, the blue above and around us seeming to stretch on forever. The wind didn't tear at my eyes and hair this time. With nowhere pressing to be, Neo rode the currents, making small adjustments with the feathers of his wings, but rarely having to flap them. We were gliding through the air, between craggy mountains, and as I looked down at the world below, it made me lightheaded. I knew I should be afraid to be so high up, but all I felt was this immense sense of freedom. Which was ridiculous considering whom I was flying with. This man was once my worst enemy, but now, somehow, he had become a confidant, and ally, and hopefully, a co-conspirator.

"Are you all right?" Talon asked, leaning forward so I could hear him. The air around us was frigid, but he radiated warmth.

"The view just makes it a little hard to breathe. It's all so beautiful."

"That's not just the view," he said and made a gesture with his hand, catching Neo's eye. "The mountain air is thin. I'm going to have Neo fly lower because you aren't used to it."

"Is that why I feel so dizzy?" I asked with a laugh that was lost on the breeze.

Neo dropped altitude then, and it felt like I left my stomach behind somewhere in the sky above us. Immediately afterward, though, I could take a deeper breath than I had before, and as the oxygen reached my brain, I realized just how much I'd been lacking in air.

"Better?" Talon whispered in my ear, his lips brushing my skin. His deep voice sent a thrill through me, and all I could do was nod.

I turned to glance up at him, and his gaze met mine, and the way those bright blue eyes reflected the sky around us captivated me. They dropped to my lips, and heat rose in my cheeks. I could feel his heart beating strongly through my back. I had to tear my gaze away.

Why did I feel so safe with this man? He was cousin to the emperor who had allied himself with a monster, and yet, even in this cold environment, warmth flooded me any time his gaze met mine.

The mountains loomed higher above us now, and we were even with the heavily wooded forests. I let go of the pommel and stretched out my arms, letting the wind dance over them. If I closed my eyes, it was like that primal dream of flying that everyone had, though we'd never once been creatures with wings. I was weightless and freer than I'd ever been, even at a full gallop.

The wind whispered in my ear, and I found it hard to ignore. *You belong here,* it said.

I shouldn't have loved it. But I couldn't help the way my soul soared along with the eagle's wings, even as my mind tried to remind me that I was born a Child of Earth. Was it my sire's blood, then, that reveled in this? The longer I stayed here, the more I wondered if it was less because of my resiliency that I was able to acclimate and more because of my secret heritage. The wind spirit had said my sire was a wind caller like me, and it would seem none of the Zephyrians knew of such a power.

Unfortunately, the only one who could give me the answers I really wanted was miles away, and I had to immediately push away the thought of her before my eyes teared up.

Talon was quiet behind me, and for once, I didn't find his silence uncomfortable or strange. There was something about soaring high above the trees, between craggy mountains, and through a bright blue sky that demanded a hushed reverence.

I didn't want to break it with talk of Altair and that demonic creature I had heard–not yet. I pushed those thoughts aside for now and drank in the awe-inspiring sight of flying so far above the earth.

It made me think of the Earth Mother, and the origins of our people. I wondered if the Zephyrians had their own beliefs, their own origin stories. Before I could think about it, I'd opened my mouth to ask Talon. "Where do you believe your people come from?"

I turned my head to look back at him and found his gaze upward, toward the clouds. "Are you asking about our gods?"

"I am. I'm curious to see if it's anything like ours."

"I can still remember my mother teaching me about it when I was young," he said, his voice a deep rumble behind me. The wind didn't snatch at his words, as though it, too, was listening. "She tells it much better than I do."

"That's okay. I still want to hear it if you're willing to tell it."

"In the beginning, there was no earth, but only sky. The Lord of the Skies created us to live amongst the clouds, to fly without wings. But of course, we weren't satisfied with that. So, he created the mountains, the forests, and the grasslands. He sent us to live amongst them, but then we longed for the skies. The Lord of the Skies took the sunlight as it pierced the clouds and wrought it into the first giant eagle. He wanted us to have the ability to soar amongst the stars once again."

Sunlight and clouds. When I looked at Neo's wings, blindingly golden in the rays of the sun, I could see why they thought that. "And were the people finally satisfied?" I glanced back at Talon.

The corners of his lips tipped up. "Are we ever?"

My people are, I thought. *We didn't start this war.*

"There's more to the story, but that's the best I can do," he said. "Now it's only fair if you tell me yours."

"Ours is more earth-centric, which I'm sure comes as no surprise," I said with a wry smile. "We believe the Earth Mother brought forth the first Children by pouring her blood out upon the earth. She could have made us from her blood alone, but she wanted her children to be a part of the earth that would shelter and feed them. She gave the Children of Earth horses by forming them out of the wind—taking handfuls of earth of all colors and pouring it into the shape of a fleet-footed beast with the breath of the wind. They are our connection to the divine, meant to be our sisters in life, to lead us back to the Mother in the end."

"Horses and earth instead of eagles and sky," he said after a moment. "Makes sense."

"But no dissatisfied people," I said over my shoulder. "Just people thankful for the earth and their lives and their horses."

"I can't argue with that, though haven't you ever wondered what it would be like to explore beyond the grasslands? The mountains? The sky?"

I looked out across the sky now, reveling in the feeling of weightlessness as the wind danced through my hair.

"Of course not," I lied.

Neo made a sound beneath us then, a high-pitched warble that sounded suspiciously like he was scoffing at me.

"Neo doesn't believe you," Talon said. "He knows you love flying too much."

After a few more minutes of enjoying the wind in our faces, Talon leaned closer and said, "Are you ready to tell me why you were so upset earlier?"

My jaw tightened, and I closed my eyes for a moment against the flood of thoughts from the horrible night before. "I overheard Altair and Lord Heron speaking through the wall, and I found a hidden door that connects our rooms. I spied on them."

His arm tightened around me. "That was incredibly dangerous," he said tightly.

I turned to look at him, and I found his expression laid bare for once. Jaw clenched, and the promise of murder in his eyes.

"So you admit it's dangerous to eavesdrop on the man I'm supposed to marry?" I asked

"I think it's no secret that Lord Heron is a potential threat to you," Talon said carefully.

"I needed to know the truth, especially now that my handmaiden is missing. It wasn't long before the emperor told Lord Heron to send more servants to that creature."

"The head steward told me that all of the missing servants had been summoned by Lord Heron before disappearing," he said heavily. "I assumed it had to do with Ozul, but this confirms it."

"And what do you think the creature does to them?"

He hesitated for a moment, and all I could hear was the whistling wind. "The old stories have always warned that the creature feeds on the souls of the living, leaving walking corpses behind."

My vision narrowed to a single feather on Neo's head as every muscle tensed. From the moment I saw that creature in the throne room, I knew it was dangerous. But this was a living nightmare. "Lord Heron demanded that the emperor hand me over to the creature, but he refused. For now."

"He what?" Talon said, his voice dangerously quiet. Gently, his hand touched my cheek and turned my head toward him. His expression was murderous. "That snake threatened you? I should have killed him when he tried to have those possessed women assassinate you."

"He wants the emperor to give in to the creature's demands. Ozul was asking for me. At least, I think it was. It kept saying, 'Bring me the girl.' It said it wanted my power."

"I won't let it have you," he said, his body tightening around mine. Our gazes caught and held. My breaths came quicker as though we suddenly flew through thin air again. "I should have never brought you here."

My eyes widened. "It wasn't your decision. You couldn't have known–"

"I should have put it all together faster," he said, breaking eye contact with me and plunging one hand into his hair in frustration. "Altair asked Ozul to scry for the queen, but the coordinates led me straight to you. I think it has wanted your power all along. Altair has been resisting handing you over to it because he knows if he does so, he'll lose what little control over the creature he has. I think it's physically weak right now–starved for souls. That's what has kept it hidden away in the west wing this whole time."

Again, a desperate need to escape this place filled me. I wanted to beg Talon and Neo to fly Shazeera and me back to the plains, to the dubious safety of my own people. At least there I wouldn't face constant threats of assassination. But then what would the creature do? Consume all the souls in the palace until it was strong enough to leave? And then what? It had to be stopped.

"How can we kill it?" I asked Talon.

"I combed through all the old stories. Most of them are fragments, and none ever tell how to destroy the Devourer—but there must be a way."

I thought about it as the wind rushed past my ears. When the shadows possessed Lady Corvina and Lady Starling, the wind chased away that dark power. What if I had the ability to destroy the Devourer, at least when it was in a weakened state? I asked Talon, but his arms immediately tensed around me.

"The risks to you are far too great," he said.

"You said it was starved for souls and unable to even leave the west wing. Surely the time to do something about it is now?" I glanced back to look at him, and his jaw was clenched like he'd rather not even consider any of this.

"Yes, but what if I'm correct and its main goal has always been to consume your power? Even if you are willing to risk your life, then there's the possibility that it may use your power to fuel its strength and become unstoppable."

There was always the risk, too, that using the wind to defeat such a creature might finally sever the bond between Shazeera and me. I wondered, then, if I could reconnect with Mistral. Would he even tell me what I needed to know? I thought of how fast communicating with him drained my energy last night.

"If I try and contact the wind spirit again," I said to Talon, "will you hold on to me? Last time I spoke to it, I could barely stand afterward."

His eyes widened at that. "You can communicate with a wind spirit?"

"Not very well–and only one other time. But I thought he could at least tell us if the Devourer can be defeated."

He nodded solemnly. "I will keep you safe."

With his strong arms around me, I closed my eyes and focused on the steady current as Neo flew.

Mistral? I thought, and the noise faded, like I had entered a bubble of quiet. I could feel the wind listening.

After a moment, I heard a voice directly in my ear, but it was little more than a whisper. *You have summoned me, wind caller, but you still lack the strength to maintain a connection.*

His words brought awareness to my body, where even after only a moment's conversation, my breaths came harder.

There is something I need to know, I said.

Ask.

Can the Devourer be defeated?

Yes, it replied, the words a struggle to hear. My muscles burned, and I felt Talon's strong arms hold me up.

If I use the wind's full power against it . . . will it sever my bond with Shazeera?

In the Devourer's final form, the force you call upon will be too great for your earthly bond to survive. One more question, he warned. *Your body is weakening.*

I hesitated, chest heaving. *What if I strike before the creature reaches full strength?*

Then you may yet keep her, he whispered. The ache in my chest loosened, just a little.

Mistral pulled away then, and all at once, the wind came rushing back in my ears. I leaned back against Talon, struggling to catch my breath.

"I've got you," he said in my ear.

When I finally could catch my breath, I turned to look at him. "Thanks for keeping me from falling."

"Neo and I would never let you fall," he said, his gaze holding mine.

"The wind spirit said the Devourer can be defeated, but the risks will be too great when it's at full power. We need to act now."

Mistral had confirmed that using my power against the Devourer now wouldn't sever my bond with Shazeera, which was all I cared about.

Talon's expression hardened. "I still don't like this. It goes against everything in me to let you risk yourself. It would be cataclysmic, too, should your power fall into the creature's hands."

"But the alternative is this creature will be released on other nations, and who's to say it won't turn on Altair once it grows in power?"

He looked down at Neo like he was listening to the eagle.

"What does Neo think?" I asked, and Talon let out his breath in a frustrated sigh.

"He says it's far easier to hunt weak prey than strong."

"Very wise." When Talon still didn't agree, I said, "If I have a power that can defeat this thing, then I must at least try. I can't sit around and hope it goes away. It seems like it'll eventually find a way to kill me if I don't destroy it first."

He closed his eyes like he hated hearing every one of my arguments because he knew they were true. Finally, he said, "This may not even work."

"I still have to try."

He was silent for a moment, and I turned to find him looking resolute. "We don't have to try this alone. There are a few riders who are loyal to me. I'll be asking them to go against their emperor, but the stakes are too high to do nothing."

"I'm sure they'll see stopping a demonic sorcerer is more important than obeying the emperor. We'd be protecting Altair and all Zephyrians by destroying Ozul."

If what Altair said about Ozul being able to take over entire lands on his own was true, we would be protecting the world from its evil.

"Then we should act while it's still weak. During the day, when there are fewer shadows."

I tried to ignore the hair-raising dread that held me in its grip. "Tomorrow, then?"

The beating of another eagle's wings prevented him from answering. Neo slowed his pace, and a dusty gold eagle pulled up next to us in midair, carrying Baz.

"Commander," Baz said, saluting Talon.

"Lieutenant," Talon said, with a slight incline of his head. "What is it?"

"The emperor is asking for you."

"Now?"

"Yes, Commander. A letter has arrived from the country of Mistral."

I froze. Mistral? I *knew* the wind spirit's name sounded familiar. If I were more skilled at geography, then I would have recognized it instantly. Mistral was a small country far to the east, across the Modavian Sea, that I knew little about. It was located on the continent of Darkhan, where the Zephyrians originated from.

Talon sighed, but only I could hear it. The wind and the eagles' wingbeats were too loud.

"I'll be there directly," he said.

Baz saluted again, and then his eagle banked and flew back toward the palace.

"I'm sorry to end the flight early," he said. "Should I bring you back to the pasture?"

"No, I'm going with you."

To his credit, he didn't even hesitate in his agreement.

As Neo flew back over the pasture, I could see Shazeera, far below.

"Can you fly a bit lower—just for a moment?" I asked Talon and Neo. "I want to tell Shazeera where we're going."

Neo heard me and did as I asked, changing altitude in a gentle descent.

I'm going back to the palace with Talon, I told Shazeera. *Altair summoned him because of a letter, and I want to find out what's in it.*

I'll be here. Just let me know if we need to make a run for it.

Only if that grass gives you magical wings. I sent her an image of us plunging over the mountainside like the Zephyrian goats, and she rolled her eyes.

I'm more sure-footed than some goat.

I felt for the bond between us, relieved that the wind spirit had said it could survive an attack on the Devourer when it was in its weakened state. The stakes were higher than ever to defeat it now, while we could. I never asked the wind spirit if it could even be defeated when it reached its final form.

We would just have to destroy it before it got to that point.

27

TALON

My muscles ached from being so tense—not only from what Zara had told me, but also from having to constantly hold myself back from kissing her every time she turned to look at me. The way she looked at the sky while flying, her eyes shining with wonder, made me wish I could stay in this moment forever. With Zara safely above the earth and everything that threatened her. But when she told me she had eavesdropped on such a dangerous conversation, I had fantasies of destroying anyone who threatened her—starting with Lord Heron. I knew it was only a matter of time before Altair gave in to Lord Heron and the Devourer's demands for Zara's power. My need to keep her safe overwhelmed me. Only the possibility that her power might save us from my cousin's horrible mistake restrained me. I kept thinking of the way Zara had looked after she nearly drowned. Could I really ask her to face such a monstrous evil? But then I remembered the powerful cyclone that had torn us from the sky. As powerful as Neo was, the wind had ripped through him like he was as insubstantial as a songbird. What could that kind of power do against the Devourer? Still, my thoughts warred with each other. I wanted to save my empire from this terrible threat, but I also didn't want Zara to risk herself.

Zara stayed close to my side as we made our way to Altair's room, a determined look on her face. The latter was to dissuade me from telling her she couldn't come with me, but I had no intention of doing that. I knew it was a waste of breath.

When we arrived in front of Altair's door, I knocked, but there was no answer. *Not a good sign,* I thought.

The moment we entered the room, I made sure to keep Zara behind me. An ominous atmosphere hovered in that room like vultures circling above a kill.

Altair sat at his desk in almost total darkness. I could only just make out the whites of his eyes. I couldn't imagine what Zara thought about it, but it was clear to anyone with sense that Altair wasn't well.

Lord Heron hovered behind Altair's desk, arms crossed over his chest. I thought again of how Zara nearly drowned because of this man, and my hand twitched near the dagger I kept hidden. It would be so easy to lunge toward him now and slit his throat. He wouldn't even see it coming.

"My Lord Emperor?" I asked carefully. "What happened?"

He didn't answer, so I moved closer until I could see him more clearly in the dim light. Without answering, he slid a letter over to me across his desk.

"This is the letter from the messenger?" He nodded. Whatever the letter contained, it couldn't be good.

"I sent servants to find you," he said.

Lord Heron sent an accusatory glance at both Zara and me that made me bristle. "Yes, it took quite a long time."

"Well, I wasn't far from the palace." I picked up the letter, and I immediately noticed the seal at the top, like a swirling gust of wind. The only country that had an emblem like that was Mistral. And though it was located on the same continent the Zephyrians had once called home, it may as well have been a mythical kingdom for as much as we knew about it. Rumors and legends; that was all.

Zara moved closer to read the letter over my shoulder, and Altair didn't object.

After the seal was a greeting and all of Altair's various titles, which I skipped over to get to the meat of the letter:

It is with great apprehension and dismay that I, the King of Mistral, write to you. I have been informed that you have made an alliance with a creature of such evil that it would be the greatest sin for me to stand by and do nothing. I must ask you to sever your alliance with the creature known as Ozul. You have forgotten the old stories, and you do not realize what you have awakened. It will destroy you, your country, and everyone else on Zephyrus. It has only one goal: power. And the means with which it gets it is the most disturbing of all. I dare not even write about it.

If you do not sever your alliance with Ozul immediately and turn it away from your nation now before it has a chance to grow in power, then Mistral will have no choice but to declare war on you. Ozul will only grow more unstoppable over time, and if I should refuse to act now, it will finish destroying Zephyrus, only to turn to the sea and the nations beyond. Not even Mistral will be able to face it then.

I will expect your prompt reply. I hope you understand that I will do whatever it takes to protect my people, even if it means declaring war before an even more devastating one can come to fruition.

It was signed by the king of Mistral, with all his titles, a king I knew very little about. And even though he was essentially declaring war on us, I could understand why.

Somehow, the king of Mistral had discovered the unholy alliance Altair had forged with this demonic creature, which meant there was a spy in our midst.

I let out a frustrated breath. "I warned you that Ozul should have been banished the minute we successfully forged a treaty and no longer needed its dark magic—if we ever did," I said to Altair.

Lord Heron stepped forward. "The sorcerer is what enabled us to counter the Children's magic and scry even the Queen of All Queens' location," he said smugly, and Zara looked up with a frown. "How dare you attempt to scold His Majesty for allying himself with such a powerful being. It was because of this that we were able to draw up the peace treaty."

Zara looked deeply disturbed, which worried me. If she spoke now, Altair might turn his anger on her—and that was a risk I couldn't let her take.

"Cousin, this threat from Mistral is bad." I appealed to Altair rather than Lord Heron. "The treaty saved the lives of many, but we still lost riders and countless infantry, and our resources are depleted. We won't be able to sustain another war."

He looked up, the flame of the lantern flickering in his eyes. "Even more reason to keep Ozul on our side. We will need his power."

"That is foolish. We know little about Mistral or its allies and resources. Give the order, and I will lead all the riders to the west wing to destroy this creature." I didn't want to tell him about my hopes about Zara's power–I didn't want Lord Heron to be able to warn the Devourer before we descended on it. But if Altair at least gave an order for my riders, then I could have hundreds at my back instead of the few who would follow me and not the emperor.

Altair let out a dark laugh. "You make it sound so easy."

"I don't think it'll be easy, but we have to at least make the attempt. This alliance with such a demonic creature could destroy this empire," I said, and Lord Heron puffed out his chest like he thought he could take me on. I didn't even glance his way. "Now we'll have to do what we can to break free."

"It's always my fault, isn't it?" Altair said, his voice taking on a dangerous edge. "I'm always the one making idiotic mistakes. You sound just like my father."

"We all make mistakes," I said, in an attempt to be soothing, but honestly, I lacked that skill. I preferred to stick to the truth. "When you are emperor, those mistakes just have bigger consequences."

"I'm finished discussing this," Altair said, his head in his hands.

"I have seen this so-called sorcerer from my horse's eyes," Zara said, stepping forward to be noticed. My muscles tensed at the risk she was taking. "And there is nothing inside but darkness. Once it gets whatever it wants from you, it will turn on you and devour your soul along with everyone else's. The commander of your aerial army wants to stop it before it's too powerful to be killed. Perhaps you should listen to him."

Altair's jaw hardened. "You're turning on me, too?"

"I'm trying to get you to listen to reason."

Lord Heron narrowed his eyes at Zara, and I shifted instinctively, ready to put myself between them. "How dare you speak to the emperor in such a way, especially when you've done nothing but comport yourself in a disgraceful manner since the moment you arrived. Where were you? Why did it take the servants so long to locate you both?"

The question took us both by surprise, but it was Zara who answered. "I have the freedom to go where I please. We were flying above the upper pasture. As my guard, Talon accompanied me."

"Oh, I'm sure," Lord Heron said with a knowing look. "He was all too willing to accompany you to a lonely pasture."

A muscle twitched in Altair's jaw, and I didn't like how the conversation was rapidly turning against us.

"Is he or is he not my guard?" Zara demanded. "Should he have let me go alone?"

"He shouldn't have let you go at all," Lord Heron said.

Her eyes flashed a warning, and her spine went rigid. "I will not be told where I can and cannot go. And there are more important things to discuss, Lord Heron. Like the threat of war from a powerful country." She moved toward Altair. "I know this letter must have been threatening to receive, but the best thing to do is to take action quickly."

Altair shook his head once, and then he was gripping both sides of his head with his hands. A wave of unease hit me hard, tightening my chest like a vise.

Zara moved even closer, reaching out to touch his shoulder. Altair glanced at her, and as he did, his eyes seemed like a shadow passed over them, turning them black. Zara had said that the women's eyes turned black when they were possessed by the Devourer. Was Altair losing control? I stepped toward her, wanting to pull her away from him. Her hand made the briefest contact, and then Altair jerked himself out of her reach. "Don't touch me," he said in a growl, while Lord Heron shot us both satisfied looks.

It began with silence, and I knew Altair was listening—to what, I could never be sure. I turned and took Zara by the arm. "We'll give you time to think about what we've said," I told him. Zara resisted when I tried to guide her to the exit, and I tugged more insistently. I would pick her up and carry her if I had to. Skies forbid, but there was still the real possibility that one day, she would be married to Altair. The thought was so abhorrent, my body went rigid, as though preparing for battle. I wouldn't be able to shield her from the dark thoughts that overtook him, but for now, I would do what I could.

It felt like an arrow in the back when he spoke. *Too late,* I thought.

"I've already thought about what you said, and I think you're right, Zara," he said, deceptively lucid. She had turned at the sound of his voice, and my hand fell away from her arm. "It's important to never show fear. My father would never have shown fear, and he just reminded me that, when my authority as emperor is questioned, a show of force is the correct response."

"The First Daughter wasn't challenging your authority, Majesty," I cut in, "and neither was I."

"Weren't you?" Lord Heron said, and suddenly, all the former provocations I had suffered from this man triggered the violent side of me. I took several strides forward until he was backed against the wall, and I glared down at him. His eyes widened like a trapped animal.

"Do not dare contradict the First Daughter," I told him, and he flinched at the growl in my voice.

"Enough, Talon!" Altair shouted. "Father does not like you to threaten his adviser."

Reluctantly, I backed off. I kept my eyes on Altair, who seemed to be listening again to something none of us could hear. A glance at Zara showed her brows furrowed in a look of concern, but she wisely kept silent.

"Better that we all sleep on this," I said, though the thought of the letter from the king of Mistral had every muscle tense. Still, I knew Altair was in no mood for logic.

He was quiet again, listening with his eyes closed. I tried to tell myself he was listening to the crackle of the fire, but I knew it wasn't true.

"We know what we heard," he finally said. "But go." He waved his hand at us. "Maybe we will talk more in the morning."

He didn't have to tell me twice. I wanted Zara out of there from almost the moment we set foot in the room, and I knew I wouldn't be able to relax until she was safely behind a locked and guarded door. "After you, First Daughter," I said, gesturing for her to go ahead of me so I could guard her back.

She looked at Altair, and I could see that she wanted to reach out to him, to connect with him in some way, but he had already disappeared within himself. Reluctantly, she turned and walked out into the hallway.

Once we had passed Altair's guards and found an alcove to speak alone, she leaned toward me. "He won't do anything about the letter or the sorcerer Ozul," she said quietly.

"No."

She turned to me. "Then we must continue with our own plan."

I nodded. "I will speak to my riders tonight, and we will make for the west wing in the morning. But first, I need to find the spy—that's the only way the king of Mistral could have known about the alliance."

She looked at me sharply. "A spy?" She thought for a moment. "That does make sense, though. How else could a king far across the sea know of an alliance formed with a sorcerer?"

I nodded. "It could be anyone, though it would be unlikely for it to be an Eagle Rider. A guard, though, or someone who could get close to the emperor without being noticed, like–"

"A servant," she said. "You and the others speak in front of the servants like they aren't even there. There was a servant in the room just now, and none of you even glanced his way."

I struggled to recall the man she referred to, but not even a single facial feature came to mind. All I had was a vague image of someone with brown hair and average height. That was the point, I was sure. To be of non-notable looks, making it difficult to recall what he even looked like.

"I'll speak with the head steward, see who the servants closest to Altair are," I said, and she nodded.

She looked pensive for a moment and then said, "There's one thing I should tell you about my conversation with the wind spirit that was especially puzzling–now that we've had a letter from the country of Mistral. The wind spirit told me his name was Mistral."

My brows furrowed. "What does that mean? This wind spirit has something to do with that country?"

She shrugged one shoulder. "Or some past king decided to name the country in honor of the wind spirit. I don't know, but I thought I should tell you since it's an odd detail."

I turned it over in my mind. I doubted it was coincidental. There was some meaning to it, but I didn't know what it could be. Or if it would turn out to be a good thing . . . or a bad thing. "Mistral, as you may already know, is a relatively new country–it came into existence after my people had already left the continent of Darkhan." I'd heard whispers before in one of the ports that the people of Mistral had an impressive power that made them formidable enemies, but no one knew anything about it.

We had assumed they were lies spread as a deterrent for future attacks since the country was so small, but as far as we knew, Mistral didn't produce any goods worth fighting over.

She nodded, looking thoughtful. "Yes, I knew of its geographical location, but it's not a country we spoke a lot about—we've been too concerned with what's happening on our own continent. Do you think they have any connection to your people?"

"It's possible—it could explain why they were spying on us to begin with. Before the Zephyrians left the continent, there was a civil war, and our people split apart. Our countrymen wanted the Eagle Riders to stay, but King Taos—the Eagle Rider leader at the time—wanted to go and conquer other lands. To become an empire."

"So these people in Mistral could have been related to Zephyrians centuries ago when you both lived on the same continent." When I nodded, she continued. "And it's interesting that they know of the sorcerer—they even mention old stories about it that the Zephyrians have supposedly forgotten. It's almost like the creature *came* from Darkhan."

I looked at her in surprise. "It does seem like that, though I don't know what that means, exactly. Other than this evil has been unleashed here on this continent now."

"Too many strange pieces to this puzzle, and I'm not sure how they fit," she said, looking suddenly drained. Her shoulders slumped with fatigue, and her eyes were heavy.

I started to reach out and touch her cheek, but I checked myself at the last second and touched her arm instead. "You should rest up for tomorrow."

"I'll try," she said with a tired smile.

When we got to her room and she saw Baz and three of the

emperor's guards outside, she turned to me, a crease of worry between her brows. "Will you not stand guard tonight?"

The fact that she wanted me there made my chest swell. She trusted me. She wanted me to guard her. "I'll be back later tonight, but for now, I'll go and speak with the head steward."

She nodded, closing her eyes in relief. "I understand."

After checking that her room was safe, I left her under the protection of Baz and the other guards, with her room securely bolted from the inside. It was hard to leave her. Lord Heron hadn't been wrong to suggest I wanted to be alone with the First Daughter. She was all I thought about. But I was a soldier. I had to put that all aside and focus on the task at hand. Destroying the Devourer.

Even with the promise of the help of Zara, a woman with intuition and power enough to knock even Neo and me from the sky, I had a feeling this would end badly. My cousin, in his quest to live up to his father's ghost, had let in darkness itself.

I didn't think it would leave easily.

There was something about the look that came over Altair right before we left that made me think of the cold-burning rage my uncle used to succumb to. When provoked too far by Altair, which was usually over something as trivial as Altair failing to seem enthusiastic enough about his Eagle Rider training, he would take him away from all the eyes of the palace and beat him. It was always in places that no one would see—chest, stomach, legs, arms—but I saw the aftermath. I tried to stand up for him, to beg leniency or try to distract my uncle, but that would only make him angrier.

"See how your cousin has to speak for you? Pathetic!" he would shout, and he beat him harder for it.

So I held my tongue. I held it when we were young, and I held it even after my uncle's death.

I thought Altair would be free once the emperor was dead, but he wasn't. He was still struggling to fulfill his father's impossible expectations of him, and I knew it had grown into an entity of madness in his mind.

And this was darkness I knew both the Devourer and Lord Heron would take advantage of.

Had I spoken up sooner, none of this would have even reached the point of another potential war. Maybe then I could have saved Altair from Ozul, and himself.

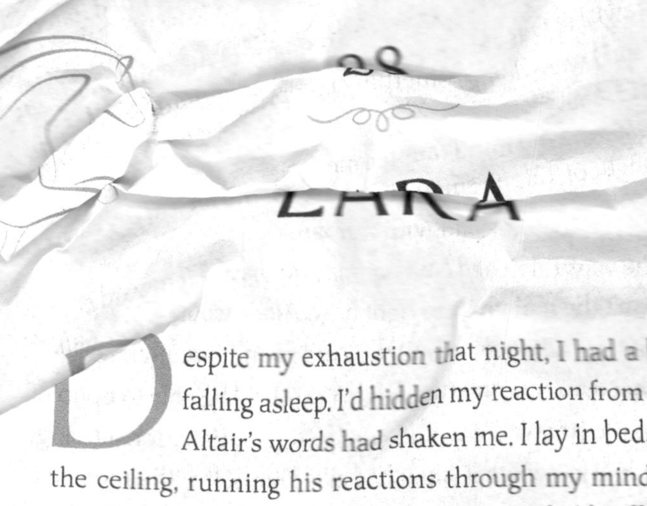

28

ZARA

Despite my exhaustion that night, I had a hard time falling asleep. I'd hidden my reaction from Talon, but Altair's words had shaken me. I lay in bed, staring at the ceiling, running his reactions through my mind over and over. I could think of only one other person who'd suffered something like that, but I'd never forget the signs. A daughter in our camp had a twin sister who had died, and afterward, she'd lost all sense of reality in her grief. She continued to see and speak to her sister as though she were alive, which had taken some getting used to, but was relatively harmless. But she wasn't an emperor of an entire people, and one who hadn't lost a beloved sister, but instead, a sadistic father. What might this ghost of the past emperor be telling his son?

It made me think of when Altair had brought me to that inner sanctuary, and he'd said his father was never wrong. I'd thought at the time that it was strange to speak of his father in the present tense, but that maybe it was just a slip of the tongue. Now, though, it seemed that he believed he could still see and speak to his father. Not good considering how much his father had hated my people.

And Lord Heron . . . even the thought of his name made my skin crawl. He was clearly manip[illegible] into thinking that Talon and I were doing [illegible] which was ridiculous.

Is it though? my mind taunted [illegible]

I thought of Talon's [illegible] through his dark hair, the sunlight on his skin. I covered my face in my hands.

"I hate this place," I said with a groan.

But the way Talon and I may or may not have felt toward each other wasn't the real problem right now. Altair would never willingly break his alliance with Ozul. And even if we managed to destroy that demonic creature, I didn't think I'd be able to uphold my end of the treaty. We would need to renegotiate, considering none of us had known that Altair had allied himself with a monster.

More than anything, though, I desperately wanted to see Ama. I craved her wisdom and guidance, but at the same time, I knew she would never sanction this plan to confront the Devourer. Not when I wanted to use the power of the wind against it.

First chance I got, I was going to see Ama in person. She needed to know what was really happening here. And she owed me answers about my sire. Answers that I realized now she'd long kept a secret.

Assuming I lived through the battle with the Devourer, that is.

With that comforting thought in mind, I finally drifted off to sleep.

I AWOKE TO a dark room, the fire having burned low, and clouds blocking most of the three-quarter-full moon. Waking in the middle of the night had become my new normal here, but I immediately knew this night was different. My heart slammed repeatedly against my chest as though I had awoken in the midst of a nightmare. I had this terrible sense that something watched me from the darkness. My eyes scanned the room, landing repeatedly on the deep shadows.

"Future Empress?" a voice called, familiar and yet slightly distorted, like the speaker had something caught in their throat. It came from the shadows.

I sat up in bed. "Raven?"

Shuffling footsteps, and then Raven moved into what little light came from the window. I let out a low groan of horror and threw myself out of bed. I immediately saw why her voice sounded strange. Her throat had a gaping, jagged wound where the blood had blackened over time. She looked at me with black-rimmed eyes, her scraggly, blood-soaked hair hanging in her face.

The legends were true. The Devourer could turn people into walking corpses, and somehow she had gotten into my locked room. Fear paralyzed me. I couldn't even cry out.

She shambled to me, her clothes covered in that black blood and hanging from her in tatters. She kept her hands out, fingers curled into claws. I held my dagger at the ready, slowly backing away from her.

"Please don't do this, Raven," I said.

She didn't answer, only continued in that unnatural gait.

I dashed past Raven, but she lunged faster than I expected and latched onto my arm. Her clawed fingers dug deep, past skin and into muscle. I screamed as she tore a gash into my forearm. With the other, I brought my dagger down, driving it deep into her chest with a terrible crunching sound. It did nothing to stop her.

With tremendous strength, she grabbed me and threw me to the ground. Before I could gain my footing again, she was on me like a rabid animal. Her yellowed teeth snapped inches from my face as I struggled to keep her from biting me. Her clawed hands tore my skin, and I screamed in pain. From my door, I heard a repeated slamming sound, and it rattled on its hinges. *Talon,* I thought and remembered that the door was still barred shut. Before I could call out to him for help, Raven opened her mouth again, and black shadows poured out. They engulfed me, thick as fog.

The wind.

It was there, just outside my window. It would burst through the glass and come to my aid. Agony ripped through me again as she clawed me, and my panic blinded me. She came at me again, grabbing hold of my arms, her dirty nails digging into my flesh. I cried out. I couldn't think–couldn't focus enough to call the wind.

"I need your strength," Raven said in a voice that sounded like her own but deeper. Her fetid breath blew in my face as I struggled to free myself.

And then suddenly, Raven flew through the air. Her body crashed against the wall. The shadows receded rapidly, and Talon was there, his face murderous. He stood above me like a vengeful god.

"Zara, are you hurt?" he asked, his face twisted with worry as his eyes scanned my body for injuries.

While he focused on me, Raven got to her feet again.

"Behind you!"

Talon turned with his sword raised. Raven launched herself at him. In one clean motion, he severed her head from her body.

My former maidservant fell to the floor in a heap, finally still.

"Can you stand?" Talon asked, and when I nodded, he bent down and carefully helped me to my feet. I stood there shaking so hard my teeth chattered, and Talon instantly pulled me against his warm chest. He wrapped strong arms around me and gently rubbed my back.

"Skies, Zara," Talon said, letting out a sharp breath. "How did that thing get in here?"

"She came out of the shadows while I was sleeping," I said shakily, my skin breaking out in goose bumps as I remembered my sudden nightmarish awakening. "She was my missing maidservant–Raven."

He tensed around me. "Then the legends are true. The Devourer did this." He pulled back, sweeping his gaze over my body. "Are you hurt?"

"Just my arms," I said. My arms were shredded where Raven had dug her sharp nails into them, and blood poured from the wounds. I thought of the shadows that came from inside her. It could have been so much worse.

"Do you want me to send for a healer? These wounds need treatment to prevent festering."

When he moved like he was about to leave, I grabbed hold of his wrist. "No, please stay. I can clean it myself."

It may have been child-afraid-of-the-dark level of fear, but I couldn't stand the thought of being left alone right now.

"You sure you're not hurt anywhere else?"

"Just here," I confirmed.

"Thank the skies," he said, closing his eyes in obvious relief. Gently, he guided me over to one of the chairs in the sitting room. "I'm sorry I didn't get here sooner–the door was boarded from the inside, and I had to break it down." His jaw tightened. "I was terrified I wouldn't make it in time."

"You did, though," I said with a shudder as I looked at poor Raven.

If he was as disturbed as I felt, he hid it well. "Did she say anything?"

"She called my name, and then she said, 'I need your strength.'"

He nodded thoughtfully. "When I broke through the door, you looked like you were shrouded in shadows. I could barely see you."

"It wanted my power," I said with another shudder.

"It's getting more desperate," Talon said with another glance at Raven's broken body. She didn't so much as twitch.

"I think it was trying to use Raven to catch me unawares, and admittedly, I didn't want to hurt her. Even when she looked like . . . that."

"You hesitated, and she hurt you," he said, and for a moment, he sounded like General Isa scolding me for not firing my bow fast enough. "But I should have been here to stop her," he added with a frown. "Next time I won't make the same mistake."

"What are you supposed to do? Sleep in here with me?"

He gave me a look that said that was *exactly* what he planned to do. Despite everything, heat bloomed across my cheeks.

"I'll get something to clean and bandage your wounds," he said before disappearing into my bathing area and coming back with a pile of clean cloths, fresh water, wraps for bandaging, and some sort of strong-smelling ointment.

"This may sting a bit," he warned before proceeding to gently clean out the gouges in my left arm, where it was the worst.

Pain burned through me like being clawed all over again, but I refused to make a sound when he was trying so hard not to hurt me. His calloused fingers brushed over my skin so softly, and as I looked down at the prominent tendons on his strong hands, I was struck by the way this skilled warrior could still be so gentle. I watched his face as he concentrated, my eyes tracing the line of his jaw. He was heart-stoppingly handsome, but it was more than that. Even though we had once been enemies, he was always there when I needed him. I sucked in my breath when my eyes dropped to his plush lips.

His gaze flicked to mine. "I'm sorry," he murmured, thinking he had hurt me. "I'm trained in field dressing, but I'm not the best healer."

"I've actually never been doctored in the normal way before," I admitted quietly. "Ama–my mother–always healed any wounds I had. She used to tell me one day I would be able to do the same."

He rinsed my left arm again before drying it and carefully applying the pungent ointment. "But that day never came?"

I held my other injured arm up in answer. "I got wind power instead." I just didn't go on to tell him that my abilities had nothing to do with my mother's earth magic.

"You should have used that power tonight," he said, his crystal blue eyes holding mine. "If it meant keeping you safe."

"Somehow I don't think the emperor or Lord Heron would agree with you."

He reached out and touched my cheek, his hand warm and strong. It was meant to be comforting, but it sent shock waves of awareness through me. I couldn't stop staring at first his arresting eyes and then his full lips. "I don't want anything to happen to you," he said, his gaze dropping to my mouth before sweeping over my thin white nightgown. Heat flared in his eyes for a moment before he turned his attention to treating my other wound.

When he finished, he added more wood to the fire until it blazed, setting the whole room aglow and banishing all the shadows. He walked over the remains of Raven, brow furrowed.

"I'm going to have my men take care of this," Talon said quietly. "You shouldn't have to see it."

He crossed to the door and summoned Baz and Kestrel to

remove the corpse of Raven—and her head. I watched grimly as the three of them cleaned up the mess in my room.

"Be sure to burn the remains," Talon said to them.

"Yes, Commander," they replied, carrying what was left of her wrapped in extra linens.

When they left, he came to my side. "You can rest now," he said. "I'll stand guard."

I looked at my bed, the covers halfway on the floor from when I had scrambled to my feet not even half an hour ago. Even with Talon staying in here with me, I didn't know how I would ever feel safe enough to close my eyes again. Surely only nightmares awaited me.

When I didn't move, Talon held out his hand. I took it, and he led me over to the bed.

"What if—" He interrupted himself with a pause and deep breath. "What if I held you? Just until you fell asleep?"

My breath hitched, and I could only manage a nod. Somewhere along the line, my heart had decided he was trustworthy. I thought of the honorable way he actually did something about the war crimes the Eagle Riders had committed against my people, and the way he was just as disturbed as I was about the Devourer. He was a commander of the aerial cavalry, but he didn't seem to want to go along with the emperor's plans.

We both got into bed, and he pulled me against his firm chest, careful not to touch my injuries. I leaned back against him, and he wrapped his arms around me, the smell of mountains and sky, leather and spice, enveloping me. His touch electrified me, and I knew sleep would not come easily now—for an entirely different reason.

After a moment, I glanced up at him, and his eyes darkened

when our gazes met. "Don't look at me like that if you want to get any sleep," he warned, his voice a deep caress.

"Maybe I need a distraction," I said, and he sucked in a breath.

Gently, he reached out and cupped my cheek. My lips parted, and his gaze zeroed in on my mouth. After the slightest hesitation, he lowered his mouth to mine, the kiss achingly gentle. Warmth exploded through me, and I parted my lips more. He immediately deepened the kiss with a groan, plunging both hands into my hair. His tongue slid over mine, and it ignited something within me. Injured arms forgotten, I practically crawled into his lap, tugging him closer to me. He kept one hand in my hair, cupping the back of my head, while the other traced down my spine. His body was all hard lines against my soft curves, and the feel of him under my hands made me desperate for bare skin.

Distantly, my mind warned that this was a bad idea. That this could only lead to heartbreak—or worse. My life here was on a razor-thin wire to begin with, and if anyone discovered I kissed my bodyguard, much less that I was falling for him, Altair would gladly hand me over to the Devourer on a platter.

Am I falling for him? I asked myself, shocked that those words had even flitted through my mind.

But then he trailed kisses down my neck, his lips leaving a trail of burning desire in their wake, and I couldn't form words, much less think. Our mouths met in a tangle of tongues and teeth. He kissed me just as desperately, his hands roaming over my body, as though he couldn't get enough.

I let out a whimper of desire, and he suddenly pulled back, eyes searching mine.

"You must forgive me," he said, looking pained. "I shouldn't have taken advantage of you like that when you're hurt."

I touched his cheek. "I'm fine," I reassured him. "You weren't doing anything I didn't want you to do."

He searched my face. "Then I must honestly tell you I have dreamed of nothing else since the moment you came back to the palace with me." Hope bloomed inside me at his words, fragile and heady, and I gave in to the thought of actually being with him. "It may be wrong of me to want the woman who is meant to marry my cousin, but skies help me, I can't bring myself to care."

The frantic buzzing in my mind—the warning that being with him here was the most dangerous thing I could do—instantly quieted. My body took over as I silenced whatever he was going to say next with my mouth. He responded just as intensely, his tongue stroking over mine. His wide hands spread over my back, pressing me closer to him. I melted against him. His fingers danced up my spine before skimming my ribs on either side. Warmth from his hands penetrated my thin nightgown, and my breasts ached for his touch. I groaned with pleasure when he cupped them in his hands, his thumbs grazing over my nipples through the sheer fabric.

I ran my hands up his arms, the muscles hard under my fingertips, all the way to his dark hair. It was so much softer than I imagined.

"Skies, you're beautiful," he murmured, his hooded gaze touching every part of me, leaving fire in its wake. He looked intoxicated with desire, and it made my body pulse with need.

He kissed me until all I could feel or taste was him. I lost track of time. His hands roved all over my body, but he was careful to avoid my arms. Beneath me was evidence of his arousal, yet he made no move to take it further. All I could think was, *More.* I wanted more of him. All of him.

When we came up for air again, I reached down and tried to

pull my nightgown over my head, but the movement caused my hands to brush my bandaged wounds. Stabbing pain instantly spread over my arms, and I winced.

Talon reached out and stilled my hand. "As much as I desperately want to see what's under this maddening excuse for a nightgown, I wouldn't dream of doing anything else tonight. Not after you were so badly attacked and injured." His hand cupped my cheek as he gently ran a thumb across my lips. "I'm not totally chivalrous, though—I can't resist kissing you. Even though I'm supposed to be guarding you."

"You are guarding me," I said, still a little breathless, "just while kissing me."

He let out a soft laugh at that before shaking his head. "I'm not sure that's what the emperor had in mind when he commanded me to be your guard."

"Do you regret it?" I asked, tensing as I waited for his response.

His eyebrow arched. "Regret what? Guarding you? Or kissing you?"

I flushed. "Both."

"Neither," he said, his voice a deep rumble. "The only regret I have is that I never should have left you. I won't make that mistake again."

Imagining Talon standing guard in my room every night made warmth pool low in my abdomen. "How will I ever sleep?"

He let out a groan before gently picking me up and shifting me so that I was tucked next to him. "Lie next to me so I'm not as tempted. I can't look at your beautiful lips and not want to taste you."

I closed my eyes as his words washed over me, igniting my body with desire. By the way his heart was pounding beside me, he struggled, too. The thought was little comfort. I tried to focus on the steady rise and fall of his chest. We lay there beside each other in the quiet, flames from the fireplace and a few candles providing the only light.

I glanced at him once, only to find his eyes wide open. "Sleep," he said, his voice a caress, as he pulled me closer. With a sigh, I laid my head down on his chest. "I'll keep you safe."

As exciting as it was to have him in my bed, it was also comforting. Warmth spread from his body to mine, making me feel safe. Protected. It chased away the thoughts and fears from my mind. Somehow, despite everything that had happened, exhaustion crept in.

Knowing he would protect me from the shadows in this place, I slept.

29

ZARA

The morning dawned far too quickly. Groggily, I awoke, feeling like I had only slept twenty minutes. Every part of me ached like I'd been beaten—thanks to being knocked down on the hard floor and nearly mauled to death by the undead corpse of Raven. Thank the Earth Mother Talon had come when he did.

With a jolt, I realized Talon was no longer in bed with me. I sat up and groaned in pain—several of my ribs felt bruised.

He appeared by my side immediately. "Are you all right? Don't move too fast." He put his hand on my shoulder, steadying me.

"I'm fine," I said, brushing my thick hair away from my face. "I just feel like I've been trampled."

He put my hair behind my ear for me. "I can't stand seeing you in pain. Can I bring you something to eat?"

"No," I said quickly, grabbing hold of his arm at the thought of staying in this horrible room alone, "please don't leave. I can get something to eat later."

"Of course I won't leave, then," he said, his gaze intent on mine. "Whatever you need. I do need to speak with the emperor soon, though. I want to try one more time to get through to him about Ozul."

At the mention of Emperor Altair, I bit my lip, remembering what I had seen and overheard. The truth about Altair and his father. "Talon," I said, my breath hitching at the prospect of telling him, "there's something you should know. About Altair."

His brows furrowed. "What do you mean?"

I took a deep breath to try to steady myself, but the shaky feeling remained. I wasn't sure if it was from what I was about to tell him, or from the giddy sensation left over from kissing him the night before. "The night I overheard Altair and Lord Heron talking, the Devourer showed horrible things from Altair's life to torture him. I witnessed a terrible beating from his father, and I could only imagine the misery and trauma he went through, so it almost made sense that he would . . ." I paused, suddenly afraid to go on.

Talon touched my cheek, his hand warm. "It's all right. You can tell me."

"Altair had been through so much with his father—he'd nearly been whipped to death. His back was like raw meat. I really think it was only a matter of time before the emperor did kill Altair. But one night," I said, my voice barely above a whisper, "Altair went to his father's room, and he stabbed him to death with a dagger."

The muscles in Talon's neck and arms became rigid, and his eyes widened as he seemed to slowly digest my words. Pain flashed over his face. He shook his head before finally saying, "I should have known he hadn't been killed in battle. The nobles—Lord Heron in particular—must have seen the value in having a young, malleable emperor on the throne. One they could control. One who wanted to expand trade rather than endlessly warmonger. They had to have helped him cover it up."

"Do you blame Altair?" I asked. "The things I saw . . ."

"No, I understand why he was pushed to that point. But taking a life like that, especially your own father . . . it has consequences."

I thought of the way Altair still spoke to his father as though he were alive. No wonder he was so tortured by the ghost of his memory.

"So this is how he let in such a creature," Talon said thoughtfully, his tone somber.

"It's truly evil," I agreed, glancing down at my injured arms. "We need to destroy it as soon as possible." I threw the covers off and got out of bed. "I should get dressed."

His gaze swept over me as I stood beside the bed, still in my nightgown. Flames of desire lit in his eyes, making my stomach flip.

I stared at his beautiful face, my gaze dropping to his lips, as warmth spread through my body. I very much wanted to get back in bed and continue what we had been doing, but I also knew it wasn't the time. By the way he kept zeroing in on my mouth, I knew he was thinking the same thing. After last night's attack, though, we needed to do whatever it took to destroy Ozul—before it killed me first.

I broke eye contact and took a shuddering breath. It seemed to break whatever spell I had over Talon, because he cleared his throat and said, "Before I came to your room last night, I spoke with Baz, Zamir, and Kestrel. They have agreed to help us in our mission to destroy Ozul."

I tried to hide my dismay, but . . . only three? Though they were absolutely the most trustworthy—even Shazeera had said so. "How many servants have gone missing? How many more walking corpses does the Devourer have to send as assassins?"

"At least thirty," he said grimly.

My jaw dropped. *Thirty?* This was so much more than the seven I had expected. I felt suddenly lightheaded. So that meant five against thirty, plus the Devourer's unknown abilities. This was beginning to sound like a suicide mission, but then again, what choice did we have?

"We have to find the spy today," I said. "They could have critical information about the Devourer that we should know before confronting it."

"That's easier said than done, I'm afraid. There's a reason this spy has gone undetected for so long. For one thing, the emperor is always surrounded by servants." Something he said must have triggered a memory, because he suddenly looked thoughtful.

"What is it?"

"It could be nothing, but in thinking about the servants attending the emperor, I remember an instance of someone acting strangely. Shortly after the head steward told me about the missing, we entered the emperor's rooms and found a servant carrying Altair's journal. The head steward confronted the man about it, of course, and it turned out that Altair had asked him to retrieve it, but the whole thing seemed a little strange.

"For one thing, the head steward said the servant had only been there a month and shouldn't have been retrieving such important things, and for another, I remember now that his hair was an unusual color. It had a reddish tint to it."

I thought of all the many people of this continent, and while there were many different shades of brown and black, red was certainly an oddity. "Then surely this servant isn't our spy if he stands out so much."

Talon shook his head. "It was very subtle–I only could tell because of the way the light hit his hair."

"It's the best lead we have, so we should go seek him out," I said.

"Let's start with the servants' quarters. The easiest thing to do would be to speak to Bran, the head steward, and ask him where we can find the man I remember."

I nodded. "I'll get dressed, then."

But when I moved toward my dressing room, it suddenly felt like the room was spinning, and I swayed a bit.

Talon looked at me sharply before moving toward me like he was afraid I'd faint. "Are you in pain?"

I shook my head. "I'm fine. I just got a little lightheaded."

"We can put this off," he said. "Wait until you're fully recovered. You were attacked only last night."

"We both know we can't wait any longer," I said. "I'm not injured enough to delay this."

He looked like he wanted to argue with me more about it, but he knew I had a point.

But once I was alone inside my dressing room, my ribs protested my every movement with a stabbing pain. The scratches on my arms burned beneath their wrappings, and I was thankful we wouldn't be immediately going into battle. Still, I wanted to dress in a way that made me prepared for anything. My hands shook as I hurriedly pulled on clothing that was both tight-fitting—and therefore easier to fight in—and warm. Soon, we would face many more attackers alongside the shadowy sorcerer, with no guarantee that my wind power would be enough to defeat it.

I came out of the dressing room, only to find Talon waiting right outside—as if he was afraid I might have fainted or something inside. Knowing he would guard me against whatever was to come made me feel safe somehow despite just having been attacked in my own room.

We both moved toward the door, and my mind raced ahead. Maybe if I had the power to completely control the wind, I would be able to destroy Ozul and keep it from killing again. As terrifying as the attack from Raven had been, though, it had shown me that I would do anything to keep more innocent people from falling prey to that demon.

Even if it meant facing more walking corpses.

30

TALON

Knowing the Devourer left behind walking corpses and seeing one nearly tear Zara's throat out had turned out to be two very different things. The thought of what could have happened if I hadn't gotten there when I did tormented me. I would never let her sleep alone in her room again, even if I had to torture myself by standing guard and not touching her.

I stole another glance at her, now thankfully changed out of that sheer nightgown. She was too damned beautiful.

Even now, when I should have been focused on finding the spy, I wanted to kiss her again. The way her soft lips felt under mine, the little breathy sounds she made, and the way her cinnamon smell had enveloped me made me burn with desire. As soon as she fell asleep, I had to disentangle myself from her warmth and scent to keep myself from falling upon her again like a starving man. I had stood beside the bed, guarding her while she slept. My thoughts had tortured me.

But last night didn't change the fact that she was promised to the emperor. I gritted my teeth at the thought of having to watch her marry Altair–how could I endure it now that I had finally acted on the fantasy that had tormented me since we first flew back to the palace together, of finally touching her, kissing her? I couldn't stand aside and let her tie herself to Altair, not only because I wanted her for myself, but also because I couldn't stand to watch her suffer at his hands. But her looming marriage to Altair was a problem for another time.

We made our way quietly through the plain and cold servants' quarters. Here, the same stony walls of the mountain continued, but there were no tapestries or art to break up the monotony. As we walked, I noted how few servants we came across. The palace had a staff of over two hundred people, not including guards, so we should have seen someone by now. But the halls were empty.

We passed many doors that led to individual servants' rooms. Finally, we arrived at a set of double doors near the kitchen. The head steward position came with a larger set of rooms that included a small sitting area, bathing room, and bedroom. "This is Bran's room," I told Zara.

"I hope we're not disturbing him," she said, a line of worry creasing her brow. "It's still so early."

A smile pulled at the corner of my lips. Altair wouldn't have given a single thought to disturbing a servant in the middle of the night, much less dawn, but Zara thought of others, no matter their social status.

I knocked on the door lightly. After a moment, we heard footsteps. Bran answered, looking disheveled with rumpled clothing and mussed hair, but he was still wearing his steward attire of a dove-gray tunic and pants.

He paled when he saw us. "Future Empress Zara, Commander Talon," he said with a bow, "how may I serve you?"

I glanced behind us at the empty hallway. Still, someone could be around the corner listening, and I didn't want the potential spy to get spooked if he heard we were seeking him out. "May we come in? Just for a moment," I added when his eyebrows shot into his hairline.

"Of–of course," he said, stepping aside so we could enter.

I held out my hand for Zara to go first. "We hope we didn't wake you," she told Bran as she passed by him.

"Not at all, Future Empress," he said.

Once inside his sitting room, he had us come sit before the fire on hard-backed chairs, worry etched on his face.

"You must forgive me for not having more comfortable seating," he said with another bow toward Zara. "I don't entertain many people here."

"It's perfectly comfortable," Zara said, which seemed to ease some of his concern.

"We won't keep you, so I'll jump right to the point," I said, and he nodded. "We are looking for a servant, and I hope you remember him. When you first came to speak to me about the missing staff, we encountered a man with a reddish tint to his hair." Bran looked thoughtful but not as if he knew whom I was talking about. "You were upset when he retrieved the emperor's journal," I prompted, and his face lit up.

"Yes, yes, I know exactly who you mean. His name is Caelen."

"Where can we find Caelen?" Zara asked eagerly.

"He works during the night, so he should be asleep in his room," Bran said. "Shall I show you the way, Commander?"

"That won't be necessary," I said.

Bran nodded. "Then you'll find his room in the east wing of the servants' quarters. It's the fourth door on the left."

I stood. "Thank you for your help, Bran."

"Of course, Commander," he said, bowing again to us both. Before we could leave, he cleared his throat. "Has Caelen done something wrong, Future Empress?"

She hesitated. "We just need to speak to him about an important matter. We're so sorry to disturb your privacy so early in the morning, but thank you for helping us."

Bran didn't ask anything else, but I could see he very badly wanted to.

We hurried quietly toward the east wing of the servants' quarters, still passing no one else. When we arrived at the fourth door, I didn't knock this time. I pushed on it, only to find it barred from the inside.

None of the servants were allowed to keep their doors locked. With a signal to Zara with my eyes to stand back, I rammed the door with my shoulder. It took several tries, but the weak wood finally splintered under my assault, and I burst through it.

A man I recognized as Caelen stood in front of his cot, face pale as new-fallen snow, with a death grip on a dagger. He was dressed like any other servant, in a somber gray tunic and pants with quiet cloth shoes. His facial features were even and unremarkable, with brown eyes to match his brown hair. In this dim light, it was hard to discern whether his hair held the reddish tint I remembered.

"Possession of a weapon by a servant is forbidden in the palace," I said with a meaningful glance at his dagger. "I suggest you drop it."

He did so warily, never taking his eyes off me, even when Zara came into the room behind me. Caelen's eyes widened when he saw her, and he bowed.

"Future Empress," he said, "to what do I owe this visit?"

I remained in front of the door, blocking the only exit. "Tell me your name," I said gruffly before Zara could respond to him. She would be too kind, and Caelen needed to know I would do whatever was necessary to get the answers I needed.

"Caelen, sir," he replied.

"Caelen—if that's your real name—I know you're not a servant."

Caelen stayed silent, as though appraising the situation. "What makes you say that?"

"I'm more observant than people give me credit for, and I've spent a lot of time with a sharp-eyed eagle." Caelen didn't answer, while I turned the full weight of my stare on him. "If you feel like holding your tongue, I could always take you to stay in the west wing for a night or two. I think we'll find you to be more forthcoming after that."

Caelen paled even more, his face taking on the faint sheen of nervous sweat.

"This is how I know you're not a simple servant. Not even the guards know what dwells in the west wing, but I think you do. Whatever skills you may have, I guarantee you can't win in a fight against the two of us."

I took a threatening step toward him.

"If you know about the dark sorcerer," Zara said, and Caelen's gaze instantly jumped to hers, "then I think you're in need of allies. We"—she paused to gesture toward herself and me—"want the same thing you do: to get rid of it."

"But if you're unwilling to do it the easy way, I won't hesitate to lock you in there with it," I added.

"I'm sure that won't be necessary," Zara cut in. "Maybe there's a way we can all help each other?"

Caelen was silent, and I knew even that wouldn't be enough to convince him. "In order for the king of Mistral to know that creature is here, there must have been a spy, because word hasn't spread beyond the mountain. I tend not to notice servants, like everyone else, which makes your position here perfect for gathering intel." I leaned toward him. "I may not be very observant of servants, but I remember seeing you. You were the one who retrieved the emperor's journal. I'm sure you read it before the head steward and I came upon you. You positioned yourself close to the emperor this whole time. You wanted to be close by when your king sent word."

Caelen's gaze shifted to Zara's and back to mine. "I am a servant, as you see, Commander. If I were a spy, then I'd be put to death by the emperor the moment I revealed myself."

I didn't let his words sway me. There could be other servants who had features similar to his, but then I remembered his reaction to what was in the west wing, and I knew I was right. I pushed on. "You have my word as an Eagle Rider you won't be executed. We will need your help if the emperor is to accomplish the impossible task your king has given him."

Caelen looked at Zara again, and she nodded in encouragement. "You have my word as First Daughter–however helpful that may be," she said, "for your protection."

At last, Caelen said, "I have been here six months now. I was sent originally to assess the war between the empire and the Children of Earth, and I was there in the throne room the day Emperor Altair brought the Devourer to the palace. It was clear the emperor had no idea what devastating evil he'd unleashed."

I held very still. He'd used the same name we did. So the people of Mistral still remembered–the knowledge lived on. Perhaps that was why they still feared it. "Your people call it the Devourer."

"Yes, for that is what the creature does. It is drawn to the darkness in a person's heart, and when it finds someone who has succumbed to the shadows, someone who has given in to despair, then it grows in power alongside that person."

Zara was watching me closely, but I couldn't spare her a glance. I had suspected from the moment I first saw the creature that it was the one from legend, but hearing Caelen call it this made it real. Real enough to make the hair on the back of my neck stand on end. Zara and I shared a look. I knew she thought of the conversation we had just had about Altair murdering his father. "It goes by Ozul to the emperor."

"It goes by many names," Caelen said, "but none know its true name."

"But even as far as Mistral you know it by the Devourer?" Zara asked, her face pale and worried. "Has the creature ventured so far abroad?"

Caelen was quiet before saying, "Our king knows many things about this land, and the Devourer is one of many he is versed in."

"Then he should know that freeing ourselves of the creature now is nearly impossible," I said.

Caelen shrugged as though it wasn't his problem. "Rest assured the king meant every word of his letter."

"Your king seems to know a lot about the Devourer," Zara said. "Do you have the same knowledge?"

"I am well versed in everything having to do with that creature, yes, in order to know what signs to look for."

"All right," Zara said in more patient a tone than I could have managed, "then why don't you tell us what we can do to weaken it?"

"I would take away its food source, for one thing," Caelen said, a hint of a scoff to his tone, lighting a spark of irritation through me like a match.

"It's a little late for that–many have already been sacrificed to this creature," I said with an edge to my voice. "How does the sorcerer devour souls?"

"It feeds off the energy from a soul, but in its current form, that's barely enough to sustain it. Make no mistake, though, it's building its power. Eventually it will have enough energy to build an army of walking corpses. It is the Devourer. Of souls. Of armies. Of whole civilizations."

"How can we stop it?" Talon asked.

"The creature was at its weakest when your future emperor first sought him out," Caelen said. "Now is your last chance. If it should gain the soul of someone more powerful than a servant—like the First Daughter," he said with a glance my way, "then your chances of defeating it shrink to nil. The emperor, too, has made sure it has a steady diet of souls by sending servants down to the dungeon regularly."

Zara and I exchanged a grim look. After Raven's attack, we didn't need Caelen's confirmation—we already knew it was true. "Those orders may not have come from the emperor himself," I said, though the words felt thinner each time I repeated them. "Lord Heron is involved in this, too."

"Regardless of who's giving the orders, many servants have been sacrificed already," Caelen said grimly.

"Those poor people," Zara whispered. Her voice trembled, thick with unshed tears, and she pressed a hand to her mouth as if trying to hold in the weight of it.

"What are its weaknesses?" I asked.

"Before it amasses its army, it can be killed like a mortal man. Once it becomes powerful enough to form its army of the walking dead, it can only be destroyed after each soul it consumed is released."

"Are you saying that however many souls it has consumed is how many times we have to deliver a killing blow?"

"Correct. When it's at full strength."

"This thing has extra lives?" Zara asked, her tone incredulous.

"Essentially, yes. Every day it grows stronger, and then it will take an entire army to stop it."

We had to stop it now. It was our only chance. Zara caught my eye and nodded once, so I knew she had come to the same conclusion.

"Your king threatened the emperor with war if he didn't break his alliance with Ozul," Talon said, "but would he be willing to aid us in destroying the creature?" Maybe with this king's army, Zara wouldn't have to risk herself.

"It would take my king and his army at least a month to arrive," Caelen said. "By then, Ozul will be far too powerful, and the battle against him will claim countless lives."

Not to mention, we would have run out of time before the looming wedding date. I gritted my teeth in frustration, but Zara's face looked resigned.

"Then tell your king we are seeking a solution to the problem," Zara said.

"Yes, Future Empress," Caelen said with a bow.

"We will leave you now," I told him, my mind already racing to the monumental problem ahead.

Caelen hesitated. "You aren't going to throw me in the west wing?"

"Not when you've done so much to help us." I stared him down for a moment. "I expect to be informed when you hear from your king."

"Yes, sir," Caelen said, and he seemed relieved. Probably

because I wasn't going to sacrifice him to the Devourer like the other servants.

Zara and I walked to the door.

"I must speak with Shazeera before we do anything else," Zara said, her expression determined. "She needs to know what we plan to do."

"Of course," I said. "I'll go there with you now."

We made our way through the quiet hallways. Zara stayed close to me, and I could feel the warmth of her body while every breath brought the sweet scent of cinnamon. Now, more than ever, I wished I could take her away from here. But instead, soon I would take her to the pits of hell. A cold weight settled in my chest, pressing down harder with every breath.

In that moment, I hated my cousin for putting us in this position. For Zara having to risk her life. And for my having to let her.

31

ZARA

Shazeera, as it turned out, had been desperate to see me since last night. She had sensed the attack through our bond and was terrified for me. But anytime she asked Zamir to seek me out through the communication system her guards had created for her, Zamir wouldn't leave her post.

The moment I stepped out of the palace and into the pasture, she galloped toward me, blowing hard, her sides lathered with sweat. Zamir immediately went over to Talon and saluted him, and then they began to talk in hushed tones. Talon was no doubt briefing her on everything that had happened and what was still to come, but I could only focus on Shazeera.

Thank the Earth Mother, Shazeera said, closing her eyes and lowering her head over my shoulder in a hug. *I could feel that you were in terrible danger and being hurt, but I couldn't do anything. I couldn't even talk to you!*

The guilt that crashed down over me was like being crushed under an avalanche. *I'm so sorry,* I told her, hugging her around the neck tightly. *I didn't realize you would be able to sense the attack at such a distance. I would have come here immediately afterward to tell you I was okay if I'd known.*

Yes, you should have, Shazeera said, bumping me angrily with her nose. *When I feared you were unconscious and bleeding on the floor. What happened?*

I told her about Raven's attack in the night and how she was no longer the girl I knew, but a walking corpse. Shazeera's eyes rolled in terror, revealing the whites around the normally dark brown irises.

Earth Mother, save us, Shazeera said, her entire body quivering with her instincts telling her to run.

I told her of the Mistral king's letter and finding the spy, and then I took a deep breath and launched into our plan to destroy the Devourer while it was still weak.

And when were you going to tell me this plan? she demanded, eyes flashing and ears pinned back as she stomped her hoof.

I'm telling you now, I said sheepishly and then winced when she let out an angry squeal of rage.

So I'm just supposed to wait here, safe in the pasture, while you take on this threat without me? Wondering if you made it out alive?

A sudden lump in my throat made it hard to swallow. *It would be too dangerous for you to be there–you saw in my memories what Raven was like when she was transformed. The west wing is now full of at least thirty of these walking corpses.*

She tossed her head and looked over to where Talon stood with Zamir. *He will take you far from here if you ask him to. I've seen the way he looks at you.*

I couldn't deny the way that it made my stomach flutter to think he might care for me enough to defy the emperor and help us escape, but even if he was willing, I couldn't do it. *Even if we run now, the Devourer will continue to grow in strength until it's unstoppable–*

that's what the Mistral king said, as well as his spy. It will consume the souls of everyone here, and then it will come for the rest of us.

Then let this Mistral king deal with it if he knows so much about it, Shazeera said angrily. *Why must it always be you who makes the sacrifice?*

I'm not willing to take the risk that Mistral will be able to stop it, I said firmly. *Ozul has made it clear that it will stop at nothing to devour my soul. I could argue that it already attacked me through Lady Corvina and Lady Starling, so I'm merely going on the defensive. The Mistral spy also told us the souls of magic users give it even more power, so it will certainly go on to threaten our people. How can I risk the lives of so many others when I might have a chance at helping destroy the Devourer?*

I don't want you to risk yourself for a chance. The wind spirit told you before that there was a way to harness the wind, so I think you should do everything possible to be prepared to fight that demon.

Ride the tempest, tame the storm? I repeated Mistral's words. I had been so set on facing the Devourer, ready to throw myself into battle at the nearest opportunity. But Shazeera's words pulled me up short, like sliding to a halt mid-gallop. I dragged in a breath, the rush of urgency that had been pumping through my veins now suddenly at war with the nagging feeling I was missing something. *But I still don't understand exactly what was meant by that,* I told Shazeera.

A tempest is a windstorm, so perhaps taming a storm, learning to control it? she ventured. *Talon and his eagle spend all their time navigating the wind—I'm sure they can help you prepare.*

I gave her a searching look. *Are you just trying to delay my facing the Devourer?*

She snorted. *Of course. But you also know I'm right. If there's a way to strengthen your wind power, you must do it.*

I heaved a sigh and nodded. Shazeera's instincts were always right, and I trusted her advice. If she said I must seek out a way to gain more control over my power, then I would do it—even if it meant delaying an attack on the Devourer.

Talon wasn't far from us, and it was easy to catch his eye. He came to my side immediately, making my pulse quicken.

"Talon," I said, "may I ask for a favor?"

"Of course," he said. "Anything."

"When I spoke to the wind spirit, he told me that to be able to 'tame the wind,' I would have to 'ride the tempest.' Shazeera and I believe it has something to do with facing a storm—like a windstorm—and learning to control it." He listened carefully without comment, and I drew a deep breath before asking, "I don't know how to find a storm, either, but I remember you telling me about turbulent wind when I flew with you for the first time. Do you think Neo would know where to find something like that?"

He flashed a grin at me. "Actually, if you're looking for windstorms, you've come to the right place. The wind above the mountains is extremely turbulent."

"Is it dangerous, though—for Neo?"

He shrugged. "Flying through mountain waves—wind that rolls down the mountains—can be dangerous, sure, but Neo has flown here all his life. There's no better flier. And dangerous for us or not—I would never let you go alone."

I threw my arms around him, even though it made the wounds burn. He returned the embrace, his strong hands pressing me closer to him. "Thank you so much."

"Of course," he said and slowly pulled away to look at me again. "When do you want to go?"

I glanced at Shazeera, who bobbed her head meaningfully.

"Now would be good."

"I'll summon Neo."

Not long after, we heard the steady beating of wings, and Neo came into view. He soared gracefully over to us and landed about fifty feet away. With one last caress on Shazeera's soft neck, I followed Talon to Neo's side.

"Thank you for agreeing to this, Neo," I told the eagle, and he fixed one enormous eye on me.

"He said it's an honor," Talon said, "and it is. We want to do everything we can to help you–you've agreed to fight a great evil that my cousin unleashed upon us."

My cheeks warmed at their sincere words. "I pray I don't let you down."

"You could never let me down," he said close to my ear as he held his hands out to give me a leg up onto Neo's back.

As soon as I got into a kneeling position, Talon followed. Now that we had kissed so intimately, the feel of his strong thighs straddling my body made heat flood my cheeks instantly. His biceps flexed as he wrapped his arms around me and pulled me close to his chest.

With a few powerful pumps of his wings, Neo lifted off easily, gaining altitude fast.

"The windstorms are the worst at the top of the mountains, so we'll have to fly high," Talon said, leaning forward so I could hear him.

We climbed higher and higher until the palace and the city of Naharu were beneath us. The Angora Mountains spread before us, with peaks still higher than we currently flew.

Talon's voice was in my ear. "Are you all right? Not lightheaded?"

"I'm fine." I did feel a little dizzy, but I didn't want to hold Neo back.

The wind streamed over us like a river, rippling Neo's feathers and tugging at my hair. At times, it was so strong it felt like it would rip me from his back. But Talon kept me safe, warmth pouring into me from everywhere his body touched mine.

We flew until the palace was a distant speck behind us. In the sky, with Talon and Neo, I felt free for the first time in a long time. Amongst the clouds, there was no fear of undead creatures coming out of the shadows, or assassins sent by palace nobles. On the back of an eagle I once feared, I felt my chest lighten. I hadn't realized how much I was living under the weight of oppressive fear until it was temporarily lifted—even though I knew it would come back the second I touched the ground. My worries hovered at the back of my mind, waiting for the opportunity to come to the forefront again, but flying amongst the clouds kept them at bay.

After another twenty minutes of flying, Talon told me, "Neo says we're approaching a windstorm on the northern peak. Ordinarily we'd fly higher to avoid it, but today we'll fly straight into it—if that's what you want us to do."

I turned and met his gaze. I was about to tell him not to risk Neo and himself by flying directly into the storm, but then I stopped myself. The wind spirit had said to ride the tempest, not look down on it from a place of safety. "Yes, if it won't put Neo in too much danger."

Neo let out a warble beneath me, and Talon grinned. "He says he'll pretend you didn't just insult him right now."

I shot Talon a sheepish look and touched Neo's feathers. "Forgive me, Neo! I know you're an amazing flier. Yes, let's do it."

He pumped his wings hard, flying straight toward a snow-capped mountain peak. Below us were other mountains, studded with trees and shrouded by wispy clouds.

Soon the wind became so strong that Talon pushed me down

almost flat against Neo's back as he leaned over me protectively. He said something near my ear, but the gusts snatched his words away as soon as he uttered them. The feathers on the edges of Neo's wings rippled as he made constant adjustments.

The farther we flew into the storm, the more vicious the wind became, until I could feel it tugging at me from beneath Talon's heavy body covering mine. It poured over our bodies like endless waves. Neo didn't flap his wings or try to fight it; he kept them spread wide, letting the currents carry him.

I closed my eyes and focused on the wind streaming over us. At first, it was like a roaring beast, the sound deafening. But I concentrated on the way it streamed past me, and how I could feel it all around me. Within the roaring, I could detect something else, something like music. I focused on the sound, trying to block out all other sensation. The more I listened, the more I could hear it. It sounded like the way we sang—primal ululations that conveyed everything from deep mourning to joy and celebration. The music made it seem like the wind was a living, breathing creature. And maybe it was.

I thought about how I connected with Mistral, of that powerful windstorm inside me that seemed to hover on the edge of my consciousness. I had only called out to him, and he had answered me. Would this storm be the same?

Focusing on the way the roaring wind had turned to music in my mind, I sang back to it—quietly at first. There was no reaction or response. So I made my voice louder and louder still, until I could almost hear my song over the wind. And suddenly, silence hit me like being struck deaf. All around me, the wind still raged, though I could no longer hear it.

I reached deep inside me where the power lay in wait. And instead of calling forth any wind, I focused on the storm in front of us. When I closed my eyes and listened to the roaring gusts, I could see the wind. Neo flew in a rushing river in the sky, full of white-capped currents prepared to sweep us away at any moment. All the other times I had used my power to destroy my enemies, I had released a burst of power. Now, though, I called the feral windstorm before me, picturing it as nothing more than a light breeze. It fought like a fish caught on a hook, bucking and thrashing against my mind. I maintained my concentration, beads of sweat tracking down my forehead despite the cold. We struggled against each other, but I had only to think of how desperate I was for the power to defeat the Devourer. I refused to give in.

Little by little, the storm stopped fighting and allowed its strength to pour into me. Deep inside my subconscious mind, where the cliffs overlooked the bottomless ocean, the windstorm's strength fueled the power within. Usually, any attempt to call the wind drained me, but this had the opposite effect. I felt like I had just woken up from the perfect amount of sleep and had cold water splashed on my face, invigorating me. My heart beat strong, and even the aches in my ribs and muscles from Raven's attack faded.

Neo straightened out as the wind calmed, gliding high above the mountains. Slowly, Talon sat up, and I did the same. I released my death grip on the pommel and looked around me in awe. When Talon had first suggested that I could control the wind around us for a more comfortable flight, I didn't believe it was possible. Now, there was proof.

"You're incredible," Talon said in my ear, and I glanced back to find him grinning proudly at me.

"I'm still in shock," I admitted. "But this must have been what Mistral meant, because I've never felt stronger." Power coursed through my body, making me feel like I could take on the world. I pictured unleashing all this massive power onto the Devourer. Surely nothing could stand against it.

"Were you able to call the wind?" Talon asked.

"In a way. It wasn't like when I summon a cyclone and release it in a massive burst of power. Instead, I grabbed hold of the windstorm and absorbed its energy."

"And, in doing so, calmed the storm," Talon said with encugh awe in his tone to make me blush.

Neo glided easily through the air, back toward the palace, with only a light breeze ruffling his feathers. Somehow I had done that–controlled the very weather around us. I could only hope it wouldn't have the effect it usually did on Shazeera and me.

"Yes, and maybe this time it won't–" I cut myself off abruptly before voicing my thoughts on Shazeera. I had never told Talon the repercussions of my power, and I was suddenly afraid to trust him that much. He watched me with a curious gaze but didn't pry. Honestly, if he had asked me to continue, I might have shut down. I had only to think of everything we had been through in our short time together to realize he was worthy of knowing my biggest secret. I hesitated for another moment before finally saying, "Summoning the wind usually harms my bond with Shazeera, and I'm unable to communicate with her afterward."

When he stayed silent for a moment, I glanced back at him again. His eyebrows were lifted in shock. "Why would using your power harm your bond with your horse?"

"It's complicated," I said, looking down at Neo's golden feathers. "We still don't understand all of it."

The commander of an aerial army came out in him then, and I could practically hear his brain examining my nonanswer. "The other times, when you've released wind power, you've been unable to communicate with Shazeera?" When I nodded, he continued, "And this time you're hoping that because you absorbed the energy instead, it won't have the same effect?"

"Yes, but I'm too far away to test it right now."

"I didn't realize your power had such consequences," he said, tone somber. "This upcoming battle–it's a lot to ask of you."

I put my hand over his as warmth spread through my chest. "Risking our lives in battle with Ozul is a lot to ask of you, too–and the other Eagle Riders. But we could possibly be the only things standing in the way of this creature becoming insanely powerful."

Talon pulled me even closer and spoke beside my ear. "All of that may be true, but that doesn't stop me from hating the thought of you in danger."

I shivered at the vibrations of his deep voice so close to the sensitive skin of my ear and neck. "If it makes you feel any better, I don't want you to have to face this thing, either."

"It does make me feel better," he said and kissed my neck.

My eyes fluttered closed as I let out a sigh of pleasure and leaned back into him. Behind me, his chest rumbled with a chuckle, and I turned to look at him wide-eyed. "What are you laughing about?"

"Neo," he said, running his hand over my hair. "He's warning me I better not take this any further while we're riding on his back."

"I'm sorry, Neo, we'll behave," I promised, heat from a blush creeping over my skin even as I had to stifle a laugh.

But when I tried to lean forward to put a little distance between us and hopefully cool things off a bit, Talon gently tightened his hold. I gave in, leaning back against his wide chest.

Tomorrow, we would walk through the gates of hell, facing all the horrors within. Despite the countless very real and pressing worries on my mind, being so close to Talon on the back of his eagle, nothing but wind and sky around us, silenced every thought in my head.

All too soon, though, the pasture where we'd left Shazeera and Zamir came into view. Even from this great height, I knew Shazeera raised her head, ears pricked to watch us approach. A shiver of worry whispered through me at the thought that I might not be able to talk to her now, especially when I was about to face the Devourer.

But before I could make the attempt, a familiar voice pushed its way into my mind.

There you are. I was beginning to worry the wind carried you away.

And I'm so thankful to hear your voice, I told her, tension immediately melting from my shoulders. *Even though you clearly didn't have a lot of faith in my abilities,* I added teasingly.

I turned to Talon with a relieved smile. "I heard Shazeera just now."

She snorted. *It wasn't you I was worried about. That eagle could have been simply exaggerating his prowess in a windstorm.*

"Good," Talon said close to my ear. "You were right about the difference in energy distribution this time. It didn't drain you or hurt your bond. Let's hope tomorrow goes the same way."

Neo landed, and Talon dismounted first before catching me as I launched myself off Neo's back. Shazeera waited for us, tossing her head in impatience as Zamir remained statuesque beside her.

I went straight to Shazeera's side and put my hand on her warm neck.

I'm glad you're back safe, she said. *So tell me truthfully: Do you feel fully prepared for the battle ahead?*

Yes, I was able to absorb the windstorm's power until it increased my own. I'm ready, I promised her, though I couldn't ignore the little tremor of apprehension that ran through me.

She couldn't, either, by the way her ears swiveled suspiciously at me. But Zamir drew our attention.

Zamir saluted Talon and bowed her head to me. "Commander, I contacted Falcon as you requested, and he needs to know when he should be here to guard Shazeera."

"Tell him tomorrow at dawn," Talon said.

"Understood," she said and strode away toward the palace, presumably to send word to Falcon.

To me, Talon said, "I've asked Falcon to guard Shazeera since Baz, Kestrel, and Zamir will be with us. He is trustworthy."

I nodded, grateful for Talon's foresight. I didn't want to leave Shazeera unguarded while we faced unknown horrors in the west wing. I stroked Shazeera's silky coat. "I'm worried for Shazeera if anything should happen to us," I said.

She snorted and shook her head. *Do not even speak of such a possibility.*

It would be foolish not to, I told her.

"I've already prepared for that," Talon said, and when my eyebrows shot up, he added, "not that I expect us all to go in there and die, but you should always make plans in case of death during battle. Falcon will fly Shazeera back to your people if we are killed."

"And you trust him?" I asked, anxiety still twisting my insides. I wished it were Baz, Zamir, or even Kestrel—Eagle Riders I had come to know and trust to look out for Shazeera.

"Yes. He's young, but he will carry out my orders. Even if I'm dead."

"Please don't say that," I said, my voice sounding strangled.

"Believe me, I don't intend to die tomorrow. I will guard you with my life," he said. "I only wanted you to know that Shazeera will be taken care of in any scenario."

I nodded. "Thank you for doing that," I managed to get out, glancing at Shazeera.

Tell him I appreciate his concern–for both of us, Shazeera said.

I relayed that to Talon, and he bowed his head toward Shazeera before turning back to me. "I want to speak to Emperor Altair before we carry out this mission. I want to gauge his mental state and make sure he hasn't completely succumbed to Lord Heron's influence."

"Or the Devourer's," I added with a grimace.

"I'll escort you back to your room, and I'll have Zamir stand guard inside."

His words only reminded me that I needed a constant guard now. And even if we succeeded in the morning, likely the threats against me would only increase. I doubted Lord Heron would accept defeat.

I turned back to Shazeera and placed both hands on her cheeks. Our foreheads touched as both of us closed our eyes. She smelled like grass and earth and home. *I love you. As soon as I can, I'll come back here.*

I love you more than life–just come back to me alive. Everything else we can deal with as it comes.

Be ready for anything, I told her. *Even if we manage to defeat the Devourer, Emperor Altair likely won't take it well. It's a very real possibility we'll have to break the treaty and flee.*

She dipped her head in acknowledgment. I hugged her once more before finally forcing myself to walk away. My heart felt like lead in my chest.

Talon stayed close to my side as we walked out of the pasture, and I glanced back at Shazeera, praying it wasn't the last time.

32

ZARA

I awoke to a still-dark room, my head on Talon's firm chest. At some point in the night, he had returned and relieved Zamir of guard duty. I vaguely remembered inviting him into bed with me, but I had slept like the dead we would soon face.

"I'm sorry to wake you," Talon said quietly, his voice a pleasant rumble beneath my ear. "It's just before dawn."

I stretched my legs out where they had been tucked close to him for warmth, and when I looked at him again, his gaze was full of heat. He turned to his side, propping himself up on one arm, bicep bulging. With his other arm, he pulled me closer so I was practically underneath him. I let out a sigh of desire as he captured my mouth with his, his tongue stroking over mine expertly. He ran his hand from my hip to my thigh with gentle pressure, building a fire within me.

I tilted my head back to give him access to my neck and throat, and he rewarded me by trailing kisses on the sensitive skin, his thumb brushing over my nipple. I let out a groan and pulled him closer to me, kissing him again until we were both becoming increasingly desperate.

A knock sounded at the door, and we broke apart, panting.

"Who is it?" Talon called.

"Zamir, Commander," she said quietly from the other side of the thick door. "It's nearly dawn."

"We will join you in a moment," he said.

I looked around in surprise. While we had become distracted by each other, the sun began its ascent, lightening the room. Reality hit me hard. Soon, we would face the Devourer.

Talon seemed to be thinking the same. "As much as I would like to keep doing that–and more–we must go now," he said, his expression pained. "The others are waiting."

Reluctantly, we both got out of bed, and I hurried to my dressing room to change. I chose the same clothing as yesterday because it was easy to move in: leather leggings and boots, a formfitting leather bodice, and my wool cloak for warmth. Fingers moving quickly, I braided my hair out of my face and kept the rest long. Last, I fastened my sword around my waist.

Talon gave me an appreciative look when I came back into the room. "You look far too sexy to be going into battle. Maybe you should stay here."

"Nice try," I said with a scoff.

He shot me a shameless grin before nodding toward the blade at my hip. "How is your swordplay?"

"I'm better with a bow," I admitted.

"I will stay close," he said with a worried frown.

"Just keep the undead off me when we find the Devourer so I can concentrate on summoning the wind."

"I will guard you with my life," he said, moving closer to me. His gaze never left mine.

It lit a fire in my lower abdomen again, and I couldn't help but grab hold of his shoulders and press my lips to his. He deepened the kiss immediately, holding me against him like he never wanted to let me go. I held on just as tightly.

When we finally managed to break apart, I remembered why he had come to my room late last night. "Did you speak with Emperor Altair?"

"Yes," he said, mouth tightening. "He remained much the same as when we last saw him."

"Does he suspect anything–like that we're about to defy him and attack this creature he formed a dangerous alliance with?"

"He is too lost within himself to notice right now–he could barely answer me, and he remained in bed. I don't foresee him searching for us this early in the morning. Also I noted that Lord Heron, for once, was absent from his side."

"I suppose that's good for us in this case, but what about . . ." I swallowed hard, my mouth suddenly dry. "What about the wedding?"

Talon's face may have remained the impassive soldier's mask he had honed through years of discipline, but behind those captivating blue eyes, a storm raged. "He still expects it to take place soon."

I pushed down the clawing desperation within–I knew very soon I would have to make a terrible choice, and the fate of my people hung in the balance. That was if I made it out of this battle with the Devourer alive.

"Ready to go?" he asked, when it was clear that I couldn't bring myself to respond about the wedding.

When I nodded, he pulled open the door, where Zamir waited on the other side.

She saluted us both. "Falcon arrived in the pasture to guard Shazeera as you ordered, Commander," she said. "Baz and Kestrel are waiting for us in the armory."

"Good," Talon said. "Lead the way."

The hallways were quiet as we headed toward the armory, located just off the aerie. It became obvious why Talon had chosen dawn, as most of the palace still slept soundly in their beds.

While I stood guard, Talon and the others changed quickly into leather armor. But instead of the dusky gold outfitted with eagle-feather pauldrons, they all wore black leather. Despite the imminent danger, when Talon walked toward me with his sword at his hip and black armor setting off his dark hair and blue eyes, I froze, lips parted as I drank him in. The armor accentuated his leanly muscular body and broad shoulders.

He walked over to me and leaned close to my ear. "Don't look at me like that," he murmured as he handed me a light sword with ornate filigree on the hilt. My gaze flicked up and met his, only to find them burning with desire.

I was the first to tear my eyes away, a blush sneaking up my neck.

"Everyone said their goodbyes?" Kestrel said, destroying the mood in an instant as only he could.

Talon gave him a withering look. "Let's go."

We snuck through the back passageways that servants usually took, and just like the day before when we went to find Caelen, we encountered very few servants. Clearly, they were keeping themselves hidden.

As we moved steadily to the west, we crossed an interior bridge with a mountain stream running beneath it. It seemed to separate the eastern side of the palace, where we stayed, with the west wing, which now housed a monster.

It was as if I could sense it, though I knew I lacked such skill. I could almost hear something on the other side, like the slow thumping of a heart, the scrape of a claw, the eerie whisper of a voice in the dark. Every hair on my body was standing on end.

Our death waited there beyond the door, lingering in the darkness.

The sound of metal sliding against metal rang out as Talon and the others drew their swords, while Zamir kept her daggers drawn. I gripped my sword as Talon kept me behind him. With a nod, he signaled for Baz and Kestrel to pull open the heavy door.

Walking through that doorway was like wandering in a shadowy wood, knowing something watched from the darkness.

It was a long, dark hallway with only every other wall sconce lit. The shadows were deep and impenetrable. Enormous windows were covered with tapestries, so only weak light shone through from the bottom. A sickly-sweet smell wafted from farther down the hallway, so rotten I covered my nose with my hand. The scent of decay.

Of death.

Talon stepped toward the windows and tore down the tapestries. Light flooded the space, drawing our attention to the rust-colored stains all over the floor. Grim-faced, we all looked at each other as we wordlessly acknowledged what the substance was.

Old blood.

As we moved deeper into the room, the smell grew stronger. And then, in the light of a single sconce, I saw the pale, unmoving flesh of an arm on the ground. My organs felt like they were twisting in knots inside me, like every part of me was trying to flee this place.

We continued, and the eerie silence was worse than constant screaming. But then I heard something.

My whole body froze like a deer that has scented a hunter.

The others stopped, too, weapons at the ready. Beside me, Talon moved closer, his warmth radiating against my side.

And then something stepped forward out of the darkness.

A waif of a girl, dressed in servant's gray, moved toward us, shambling like a puppet on a string. She kept to the shadows, the dim lamps barely illuminating her. My arms broke out in goose bumps as we waited for her to move closer. She lurched into the light, and Talon flinched beside me. Her clothing was rumpled and torn and covered with dark stains. Her eyes stared back at us, black as night, and she was missing her arm. She grinned a terrible smile, unhinged and grotesque on her ashen face.

I froze as my heart hammered against my ribs, each beat sharp and punishing. A walking corpse, just like Raven. My grip on my own sword turned painful. The hair on my arms rose as a heavy feeling pressed on us from all sides, like it came from the shadows.

Before we could make an offensive move, another sound drew our attention, though I never took my eyes completely off the servant girl. That same shambling movement, and then there were five more, all dressed as servants, and as they drew closer, I took in a shuddering breath. They, too, were dead.

In an explosion of violence, the three Eagle Riders leaped forward and cut them down. Zamir was a whirlwind of speed with her daggers, cutting through the walking corpses faster than I would have thought possible. Baz swung his heavy sword and cleaved into two corpses at once. Kestrel took on one after another with his sword. When the dead servants fell to the floor, hope bloomed inside me. Maybe we would get out of here easier than we thought.

The riders stepped away from the fallen servants, turning their attention to farther down the hallway. Somewhere down this passage were the former emperor's quarters, which was where we expected to find Ozul.

"Let's move," Talon said, and we all moved forward, skirting around the macabre pile of rotting corpses.

But as I passed the girl with one arm, she lashed out and grabbed hold of my ankle. Her hand was surprisingly strong, her clawed fingernails digging into my flesh. I stifled a scream, horror chilling me to the bone as I swung my sword. It connected with the girl's neck with a sickening thud. The blade only made it through halfway. Her head hung to one side on her partially severed neck, but her hand tightened on my ankle. I cried out in pain. Talon whirled around to help me. Before he could intercede, I brought the sword down again and decapitated the girl.

Her body slumped to the floor while her hand still clung to my ankle. Whimpering, I kicked it free.

"Their heads!" Talon shouted to the others as the servants began to slowly rise again. "Cut off their heads."

The two riders with swords obeyed, cutting off one head after another until six headless corpses remained. Finally, there was no longer any movement.

"Skies, that was terrifying," Kestrel said with a shudder.

"At least we know what works now," Baz said, though even he looked a bit pale.

Talon bent down to examine my ankle, which was already turning color with a nasty bruise. But at least she hadn't punctured the skin. "Are you okay?"

"I'm fine," I said. Only terrified out of my mind, but there was no going back now.

We continued down the hall, all of us keeping an eye on every shadow. Finally, we came to a massive set of double doors with handles shaped like eagle wings.

"This is the entrance to Emperor Lamir's private chambers," Talon said. "There will likely be other walking corpses. Are you ready?"

We nodded, weapons at our sides.

Talon pushed the door open, and the three riders rushed inside. The room was massive, with several antechambers that branched off from the main entryway. Huge floor-to-ceiling windows covered one wall, but like the ones in the hallway, they were partially hidden by tapestries. Talon ripped them down, letting in the sun. The light revealed ornate marble floors, dusty with disuse. No servants waiting for us. Only the sound of a crackling fire. We followed the sound through an archway that led into another dark room. At one end was a fireplace big enough for a horse to stand inside comfortably.

Two figures sat in front of the fire, their backs to us. The man on the right turned, and when I saw his face, a deep simmering hatred bubbled rapidly to the surface, burning through my veins.

Lord Heron.

He grinned at us, the flickering light of the fire making his smile stretch and distort. The man beside him turned his head, too, and I took a step back.

"Skies," Zamir said in horrified disbelief, "is that . . . ?"

I had only seen paintings of him, and now part of his face had rotted off to the point that only white bone shone through, but I still recognized him.

"Emperor Lamir," Talon said. "How is this possible?"

Lord Heron stood, and Talon tightened his grip on his sword. "I was just telling His Majesty that perhaps his worthless son had finally done something right and convinced all of you to come here and sacrifice yourselves to Ozul."

"How is Altair's father here?" Talon demanded, ignoring Lord Heron's attempts to rile him.

"It turns out mostly dead is a completely different situation than entirely dead," Lord Heron said with an infuriating shrug. "Emperor Lamir's soul still lingered close to his body; even in death, he refused to give up his crown. He has the honor of being the first soul harvested by Ozul."

Talon's expression betrayed no emotion, though my jaw hung open. "Does Altair know?"

"No, he's haunted enough by the ghost that lives on in his mind, much less the walking corpse still wandering around the west wing," Lord Heron said. "But I am here to serve the true emperor."

"Lamir is still dead," Talon said.

Lord Heron laughed. "I didn't mean Lamir. I meant Ozul, who will soon gain all the power he needs to become the ruler the Zephyrians have always needed. Earlier now, thanks to all of you."

"You're mad if you think that demon will rule anything," Talon said. "It only destroys."

"Yes, and when it takes what it wants from this continent, it will move on to another. And I will be here to pick up the pieces."

He wanted to rule in Altair's place, and the emperor had been too easily manipulated to notice. "There won't be anyone left to rule," I said with disgust.

"Ozul has assured me there will be. Just enough survivors that they will be eternally grateful that I have saved them from the darkness." His thin lips curled into a malicious grin. "Pity none of you will live long enough to see my ascension to the throne."

As if they had been waiting for some kind of signal from him, twenty-five dead servants walked menacingly toward us.

Without hesitating, Baz, Zamir, and Kestrel moved into a loose V in front of us and began cutting down the walking corpses. But there were so many that even with their slow, awkward gait, they began swarming over the riders. Fear sat in a cold pit in my belly at the thought that they would overpower them. The plan was to wait until Ozul made an appearance before calling the wind. I had no way of knowing how much power it would require or how long I could even sustain it.

Talon and I fought back-to-back. Used to a bow and arrow, I struggled to remember my sword training. The blade Talon had chosen for me was light and well-balanced, but I still swung much slower than he did. I felt awkward fighting from the ground instead of Shazeera's back.

There were so many that we couldn't focus on beheading them. We had to cut through them like a machete through underbrush. Talon cut through faster and more powerfully than the rest of us. But even with his superior sword skills, he was in danger of being overtaken. The walking corpses fell, but soon they staggered upright again, until it was like fighting many times the number of enemies.

An old man with claw marks on his chest threw himself at me, and I hastily blocked with my sword. But he leaned into it until the blade cut into his chest, drawing old blood the color of rust. He snapped at me like a wild animal, reaching out with gnarled hands to scratch at me. I cried out, muscles straining.

"Hold on, Zara!" Talon yelled, trying to throw off the three servants who had latched onto his armor.

At the same time, Kestrel fell. Once he was on the floor, the dead servants swarmed him. I cried out in horror as they ripped him apart, limbs flying everywhere as he screamed.

It happened so fast, no one had been able to even move toward him, much less come to his aid. With a furious yell, Talon threw off the servants restraining him and cut into them almost wildly—as if they had been the ones responsible for Kestrel's gruesome death.

But I couldn't even mourn his loss. The old manservant pushed harder on my blade, his brown teeth snapping closer to my throat. Talon grabbed hold of him from behind and hurled him against the window. It cracked the glass but didn't shatter it. A terrified scream filled the room as Zamir was pulled to the floor.

"No! Zamir!" I shouted as Talon and I ran to her aid, but we were quickly intercepted by more walking corpses.

Baz was closer to her. He wielded his heavy sword powerfully, trying to cut down as many as he could to help Zamir get back to her feet, but soon many gray hands reached for him, too. Talon moved back so that he was shielding me with his body, slashing powerfully against any of the servants who moved toward us. The wind—I had to call it now. I couldn't stand aside and watch everyone be killed. I reached deep inside myself, and the power surged up like a tidal wave. An explosive shatter filled the small space, and suddenly, the wind streamed into the room. A cyclone swirled around us so powerfully it threw me back into Talon, who caught me, before we were blasted backward.

The wind spun outward toward Baz and Zamir, slamming into the walking corpses. The wind violently pushed the former servants until they collided with the back wall, where they collapsed on each other in a heap. Because Baz and Zamir were already on the floor, they weren't thrown as far. Baz got unsteadily to his feet, pouring blood from multiple wounds, but Zamir didn't move. Talon and I ran to assist them.

It was at that moment that two corpses wrapped arms like

bands of iron around each of our waists, while four more grabbed hold of our arms. They even overpowered Talon, and it seemed like they had all just been biding their time until this moment.

I struggled against the gray hands holding me, their flesh dry and cool as stone, but there was no yield. When I glanced at Talon, I could see that the tendons in his neck were protruding, as though he was fighting to free himself, too.

The servants held us without saying a word, as if they were statues. Their silence was eerie enough to fill me with dread. It was almost as if they were restraining us *for* someone.

I jerked as my body became aware of a new sensation.

A whisper went through my mind. It felt like Mistral. *Something is coming.*

Fear poured over me like being plunged into an icy river. Suddenly, I couldn't draw a deep breath.

The Devourer stepped into the dim light, and though parts of it appeared human, it was so readily apparent by the aura of power radiating from it that it was anything but. Its entire face and head were hidden by a coyote mask made from the pelt of the animal, the creature's gaping eye sockets as dark and impenetrable as a night without stars. It had the torso and limbs of a man, but the skin not covered by leather was gray and mottled, like something long dead.

The Devourer said nothing, just stared at us eerily from within its mask, no eyes or facial expressions to give a clue as to what it was thinking. Fear held me so tightly in its grip I couldn't move.

In the next instant, the creature was so close the fur from the coyote mask tickled my neck. I fought the urge to vomit. I hadn't even seen the Devourer move.

"Get away from her," Talon growled as the walking corpses held him and Baz immobile. Zamir lay motionless, and I watched her chest, willing it to rise. I bit back a cry of anguish when it didn't.

"Did you bring this First Daughter to me as an offering?" the creature asked Talon, its voice deep and muffled from the mask it wore.

So many things happened at once I could barely track them. The dead servant holding me let go, and the Devourer grabbed hold instead. The creature's gray hands, strong as steel and dry as ash, were clamped around my upper arms. A primal fear caught hold of me, every instinct in my body assuring me I stared death in the face.

Talon wrenched his arm free, blood pouring from where the dead servant had restrained him. He brought his sword down in a powerful arc, but the Devourer turned its head toward him, and Talon went flying backward. He slammed into the wall with a brutal *crack*.

"Talon!" The scream tore out of me.

The wind built around me, swirling like a tornado, but the Devourer was caught in the calm center of it just as I was. The missing eyes of the coyote mask stared down at me, swallowing me in their depths as I struggled. And then, the mask did something so strange and horrific, I stilled in the midst of my attempts to escape.

Where before the coyote skin was clearly a mask, it began to stretch and grow, until it covered not only the top half of the Devourer's face, but his whole head. No longer did he have the shadowed chin and lower jaw of something resembling a human. Now, it was the gaping maw of a coyote, with a long snout, yellow teeth, and black gums. The eyes glowed with a smoky-red light, as though a fire burned beneath them. And as the jaw opened wide, saliva glistening, I opened my mouth and screamed.

The wind stole the sound from me as it ripped at my hair and clothes and made the coyote abomination's gray fur bristle. I kicked powerfully with my legs, using the wind to propel me forward with each thrust. From the corner of my eye, I saw Talon rise.

Baz moved to help Talon. Before he could get to him, the walking corpses who had been thrown against the wall by the wind had recovered, their limbs now at broken angles as they swarmed over Baz. He screamed and screamed as they dragged him down, their broken limbs raking and clawing, pulling flesh from bone.

"No!" I shouted, my cry echoed by Talon, who tried to shake off the effect of his head wound.

No matter how hard I kicked, the Devourer didn't release its hold.

With its mouth opened wide, the Devourer leaned even closer, until I choked on its fetid breath. The wind grew stronger, and I could see it—a shimmering silver power blasting at the Devourer's dark aura—but to my horror, I saw it disappearing into the Devourer's open mouth.

Though I continued to struggle, each movement felt strained, as though I were underwater.

The Devourer is draining you, the wind whispered in my ear. *You will have one chance.*

Talon lifted his sword, blood running down his cheek from a wound near his right temple.

With every passing breath, I grew weaker. Agony lanced through me. My head felt like it would burst, and my chest tightened so hard I could scarcely draw breath. I didn't know what the Devourer was doing exactly. Draining my power? My life? But I knew that I didn't have much time left to free myself. Even now,

I might not have enough strength. But it was clear that Talon would attack again, and together, we might be able to push the Devourer back enough to escape.

I just needed to time it right.

I reached for the wind that was being siphoned into the Devourer's gaping maw. Pain cracked through me like lightning, and my heart slowed. I couldn't see blood pouring out of me, but it felt like my strength, my energy—my *soul*—was slipping away. Spots appeared in my eyes, distorting my vision. I didn't have long. I reached deep inside myself and called the wind to me with the desperation of the dying. At the same time, I tracked Talon's movements, waiting until he gathered himself for a thrust of his sword.

One chance, the wind reminded.

I didn't even have enough strength to form a response. The Devourer pulled harder—like it was unraveling me from the inside—and the room spun. But Talon made his move, and the Devourer's attention shifted—just for a moment.

I concentrated all the power of the wind that swirled around me like a cyclone and directed it toward the Devourer. It hit the creature with the force of a hurricane. Its blunt fingernails clawed my arms as it was wrenched back, and black blood spilled from its side where Talon's sword bit into its flesh.

The wind ripped through the remaining walking corpses and Lord Heron, smashing them against the wall. The Devourer, too, was lifted and thrown through the air like a rag doll.

And then I was falling, my energy gone with the wind.

Strong arms wrapped around me and lifted me off my feet. Talon held me against his chest.

"I'm getting you out of here," he said, running toward the broken window with me cradled in his arms.

With the chaos at our backs and nothing but empty sky beyond the window, I suddenly realized what he meant to do.

"Talon, no! We can't leave Shazeera!" I cried weakly, but he continued unheedingly.

He launched us through the gaping hole. We plummeted.

Wind rushed past my ears, deafening in its intensity. Somehow, Talon's arms kept hold of me.

And then, powerful claws wrapped around us and snatched us out of the air like we weighed no more than mice. Talon kept his body wrapped around mine as Neo carried us from the palace.

My head spun, and a terrible sensation pressed against my chest, making it difficult to draw breath. The edges of my vision faded. It felt a lot like I was dying.

I could hear Talon calling my name, but I was beyond answering now.

Shazeera, I thought one last time.

33

TALON

I cradled Zara's limp body close to me as every wingbeat seemed to echo the same thought: *Don't die on me.*

How could I have been so spectacularly stupid? I never should have let her risk her life. I should have gone with my first instinct—to get her the hell out of here and damn the consequences. Every time I glanced down at her pale face against my chest, desperation burned through me. The whole mission had been a mistake. Baz, Zamir, and Kestrel—all dead. The suffocating weight of grief pressed down on me, threatening to pull me under. I didn't even have time to mourn them because Zara so desperately needed my help, but I knew it would hit me powerfully later. I had led three riders—trustworthy and loyal friends—to their deaths. Had I thought because Zara had blown our asses out of the sky that she could take on that demon? Even I hadn't been prepared for that level of evil.

Did you bring this First Daughter to me as an offering?

The worst of it was that we hadn't even succeeded. Just before I grabbed Zara and made a run for it, I had seen the Devourer's bloodred eyes staring back at us menacingly—and still very much alive.

I tried to shake free of the memories as I watched Zara for signs of movement. Her eyes fluttered like she was still struggling to stay conscious, and I wrapped my arm around her tighter to keep her warm. My jaw flexed as I clenched my teeth. I wasn't sure exactly what the Devourer had done to her, but seeing that silvery-white substance being pulled from her destroyed me. It reminded me of the king of Mistral's letter: *It has only one goal: power. And the means with which it gets it is the most disturbing of all. I dare not even write about it.*

Was that what the Devourer had done to Zara? Consumed her power?

I cradled her closer to my body, trying to keep this all-consuming fear at bay.

Before I could think about it more, Zara began to shake violently, her lips turning bluish. The wind roared by, unrepentantly frigid.

Neo, it's too cold for her! She'll freeze to death.

There's a plateau in the distance with some trees—that will provide shelter from the wind.

Go there, then. And quickly.

Neo banked, and I held Zara as tightly against my chest as I could, hoping to impart some warmth. But I could feel the wind snatch it away, weakening her even as she fought whatever the Devourer had done to her.

Hurry, I thought, my jaw clenched so hard my teeth creaked in protest.

I am, Neo thought back, with more than a little irritation in his tone. I hadn't meant to think it across our bond, but now that I had, I couldn't stop thinking it.

Every beat of my heart urged me to hurry.

By the skies, if you don't stop saying that, Neo said, pumping his wings even harder. *What can you even do? You're not a medic.*

I only know she can't endure this cold much longer.

Suddenly, a tremor ran through Neo, and he tightened his grip on us. He let out a deafening shriek—a sound of challenge.

What's going on?

There's a wild eagle flanking us.

My blood ran cold. Where had it come from? They were so rare that this was colossally bad luck. Wild eagles could pose a threat, even to a war eagle like Neo. Our eagles were hatched in the palace aerie and so had been at our sides since the moment they emerged from an egg. Livestock were kept solely to feed them so that they didn't have to hunt to eat or feed their young. They were trained in the art of war and flying with a rider. The wild eagles spoke their own language, were indifferent to the lives and fates of humans, and grew large and powerful thanks to having many different bloodlines to choose from.

They were also extremely aggressive, attacking and killing anyone who flew too close, and asking questions later.

I'm going to need one of my claws, Neo said. *Hold on tight to her, and I'll shift you both to my right one.*

I wrapped my arms even tighter around Zara, hauling her against my chest as I tried to make us as small as possible. Zara didn't even stir. Dread coiled in my gut. Had the Devourer taken too much from her? Was she dying?

Neo barely had time to carefully shift us to his other claw before a screech pierced the air above us.

This is going to be bad, Neo said in the obvious tone of someone remarking on the fact that it was currently raining. *Hold on.*

The wild eagle dove and collided with Neo in midair as they

met each other talon to talon with Neo's one free claw. I gritted my teeth against the pressure of Neo tightening his grip on my ribs. As I'd feared, the other eagle was bigger than Neo, his wingspan so much wider that every beat of his wings pushed Neo back from sheer force. And with their talons locked together, their backs were nearly vertical.

My muscles strained to hold Zara against me as gravity tried inexorably to pull her back down to earth. We spun round and round in a deadly dance, the other eagle holding tight to Neo's claw. The world tilted and twisted around us as the mountains rose fast below. Pressure filled my head, like it would soon burst. My vision narrowed, until it was like I was peering through a tunnel. I couldn't imagine what it was doing to Zara's already drained body.

And then suddenly the eagle released Neo. We somersaulted through the air, so violently that Neo lost control of his flight. My arms were on fire as I fought against the wind to keep hold of Zara. Neo's hold around us weakened. Just as Neo leveled out again, the wild eagle dove, talons spread. At the last moment, Neo met the bigger eagle's talons with his own, spinning us wildly around again. This time we flew only five hundred feet above the rocky ground.

The other eagle used his free claw to tear at Neo's chest, his talons as long as swords. Neo's strong feathers repelled the attack at first, but eventually, the other eagle made contact, puncturing his chest and tearing a scream from Neo.

I shouted his name helplessly as blood stained his golden feathers.

Neo's grip on us loosened.

The other eagle took advantage of his weakened state by lunging toward Neo's neck with his enormous beak. Neo thrashed and tried to avoid having his throat ripped out in midair. At the same time, his claw loosened enough that we dangled in the air.

I'm losing her! I shouted mentally and verbally as the wind tried to tear Zara from my arms.

The only thing that came through our link was desperation as Neo tried to defend himself from the bigger eagle. Finally, Neo wrenched himself free, but the force from the wind and the other eagle was so strong that it ripped Zara from my arms.

I watched her plummet past us, horror choking me as I watched the other eagle dive after Zara.

He'll kill her! I shouted to Neo, and he, too, dove to catch her.

Just before she crashed into the rock, the other eagle snatched hold of her, cradling her in his claws. He turned and shot back through the sky, his speed even greater than Neo's, until he was like a golden blur through the clouds. We pursued him, the blood pounding in my ears along with the screaming wind. The eagle was without a doubt taking her back to his nest, where he would kill and eat her. Now that my hands were free, I gripped the hilt of my sword; I didn't care if it was an eagle or not, I would pierce his heart before I let Zara be killed in such a brutal way.

The wild eagles had no regard for humans and saw them as just another food source, though they tended to avoid us since we put up too much of a fight. Apparently, Zara falling through the sky right in front of him was impossible to resist. And I'd made it all possible by losing my hold on her in the first place. The thought made me desperately want to turn back time and not be so damned weak. Why couldn't I hold on to her?

We'll get her back, Neo said, but he didn't sound like he meant it.

We will, I tried to assure us both. *That thing will land, and then he'll have to contend with both of us instead of just you in the air.*

A plateau loomed in the distance. I didn't think I'd ever wished for an arrow so badly. I pictured firing it now, piercing the eagle's wings enough to force the bird to land. His nest could be anywhere—the top of a tree, the edge of a cliff, or even somewhere that would leave us little room to maneuver.

Do you think you can get above him? I asked Neo, quickly sending him my concerns about the nest locations. *Force him to land on that stretch of land?*

He's too fast for me.

But it was the mountains that ended up helping us, slowing the wild eagle down enough while he maneuvered past craggy rocks and outcroppings, while a strong headwind made it difficult to push forward.

Neo soared higher and higher, until the clouds pressed thick around us. There was no headwind now, nothing to hold him back. He beat his wings harder, shooting forward until the wind was stealing the moisture from my eyes.

Without warning, Neo dove, forcing me forward against his claws. I couldn't see—my eyes were too blurry from the wind—but I could see from Neo's mind that he was now directly above the other eagle. Neo and I dropped from the sky like a stone. I soon saw that Neo had planned it so perfectly that it was a thing of beauty. His talons slammed into the other eagle's back just as we flew over the plateau, forcing the wild eagle to land because of the sheer weight and momentum from above.

Pull up before he lands on top of Zara, I shouted, every muscle straining at the thought that the eagle would crush her.

Neo did so at the last second, and I watched with my heart in my throat as the other eagle laid Zara down gently before landing. Why would he do that if he considered her nothing but meat?

When we landed seconds later, he stepped in front of her with his wings spread and screamed so loudly my ears rang.

I froze. He was clearly protecting her, but was he doing so because he thought Neo wanted to steal his meal? The way he was acting didn't seem to just be aggression over food.

Can you talk to him? I asked Neo.

He doesn't speak Zephyrian, he said. *I'll have to resort to half-remembered screeches and peeps.*

Neo made a soft sound in his throat, almost a warble, and the other eagle answered with another deafening screech. It didn't take a psychic to know he wasn't responding well to whatever Neo had asked.

Translation please, I prompted.

I said the girl is someone important to us and we'd like her back. He answered rather aggressively that she was his and he wouldn't let us have her.

His what? Meal? Tell him over my dead body. I held my sword in front of me as I tried to peer around the eagle to see Zara, but all I could tell was she was still unconscious on the ground.

Neo made another series of sounds, ranging from those mild-sounding warbles to high-pitched screeches, and the wild eagle responded.

He says she is the one he's been waiting for, Neo said, and I could hear the confusion in his tone. *He says we had injured her, and that you were letting her fall to her death.*

"That's not even true," I shouted. "If you hadn't attacked us, I wouldn't have dropped her."

Neo shot me a look as if to say, *Who are you even arguing with?*

Neo said more in that strange eagle language, but before the wild eagle could respond, Zara awoke.

The other eagle turned toward her as she came unsteadily to her feet, and I took a step toward her but had to jump back again when the wild eagle snapped his beak in warning. I watched, speechless, as the eagle helped her walk forward, supporting her with his wing.

"Zara," I said, "are you all right? This eagle won't let us get close to you."

She nodded, but she looked pale.

"Have you ever seen this eagle before?" I knew it had to be impossible, but I still asked.

"No," she said as she took careful steps toward me. I squeezed the hilt of my sword; I was barely restraining myself from rushing toward her. I wanted to see for myself that she was uninjured.

When she got close enough to reach out to me, the wild eagle wrapped its wing around her, effectively cutting her off from us.

"Let her through," I said, holding my sword in a way that required no translator.

The eagle screeched in my face.

"I can understand him," Zara said, her eyes full of awe. "He doesn't want me to go to you."

"Tell him no one asked his opinion," I growled.

She laid her hand on the eagle's wing. "This man and eagle are my friends." She tilted her head, quiet for a moment as she listened to the eagle's response. "He says he could sense that I was in danger, and he thought it was from you and Neo. He came to find me." Her voice dropped, soft and disbelieving. "Talon, I think . . . I think we may have bonded."

34

ZARA

An eagle. Somehow, I'd bonded with an eagle, and I didn't even really know how it happened. I'd just woken up on the ground, the giant creature in front of me, his voice in my head. I thought of the moment I heard the eagle, when the threads of bonding snapped into place. The part of me raised on the plains amongst horses, my feet fully grounded, rebelled at the idea, but the one born of the wind, who dreamed of flying, felt the bond and knew it was right. All those times I'd snuck into the mountains, willingly braving eagle territory, had I subconsciously been seeking out this eagle? I looked at the massive bird of prey now, easily three or four times bigger than Neo. His feathers were a brighter gold around his head, becoming darker through his wings and body. I could see my entire reflection in his huge eye, the color like topaz.

One thing was clear. If there was a small chance before, now I was absolutely certain that my father was not a Child of Earth. I thought again of Ama's evasiveness on the subject. Had it not been for the fact that the wind spirit had called my father a wind caller, I would have thought he was an Eagle Rider. But nothing ever explained being able to use the power of the wind. The wind spirit had told me that I needed to find my destiny to be able to fully harness the wind, and I hadn't understood at the time. As I gazed into the amber eyes of the eagle before me, I thought I knew exactly what Mistral meant.

This is what I've been waiting for all my life, that part of me whispered. But at the same time, guilt crashed over me like an avalanche. Shazeera. What if Emperor Altair had realized we had gone against his orders to not attack the Devourer and took it out on Shazeera? We had to go back immediately. We were much too far away to communicate, so I had no way of knowing if she was okay.

And then another horrible thought occurred to me that made me feel lightheaded with the sheer weight of it. I had never in my life heard of anyone bonding with more than one horse, even after the untimely death of a horse, much less bonding with an eagle, too. Worse, I couldn't communicate with her to make sure the bond was still in place. Whenever I sank within myself to test the bonds, all I could feel was the eagle's blindingly strong connection. It could be that the wind had weakened it yet again, and combined with distance, I couldn't sense it.

There was no way to know for sure, though, until I saw Shazeera again.

But before we did anything, I would have to first convince this enormous wild eagle that Talon and Neo were our friends.

"Tell him that we won't hurt you," Talon said, his attention trained on the eagle towering above me. "I want to be able to speak to you from less than twenty feet away."

I reached up and put my hand on the feathers of the eagle's

chest, stroking them gently. *They really were just trying to save me,* I thought to the eagle.

He looked down at me with those enormous eyes. *I sensed that you were in danger. That you were dying. I came to find you, and when I did, that one had you clutched in his talons.* His gaze shifted to Neo as he snapped his beak threateningly.

I was in danger, but they rescued me from the situation. We were escaping. I took a deep breath and thought of the way Shazeera and I shared experiences. I thought reluctantly of Ozul–of all the people he had turned into walking corpses. I thought of the way he had latched onto me and drained away my energy, my life force, until it felt like I was on the brink of death.

You were, the eagle said, the tone in my head somber. *But once we bonded, I lent you my strength.*

So that's how I recovered, I said, still reeling with quiet amazement. I still felt a bone-deep weariness and like I desperately needed to eat and sleep, but no longer did it feel like my heart struggled to beat in my chest. *How can I ever thank you enough for saving me?*

We are bonded now, he said. *I will protect you with my life.*

The moment he said that, I realized that not only did I know deep in my heart that he spoke the truth, but that somehow, I felt the same way. Even though I had only just met him, I had been waiting for him all my life.

What should I call you? It feels impersonal to keep referring to you as "the eagle" in my mind.

I could feel his amusement. *I have a name, but it's one given to me by the wild eagle clan and may not translate well into your language.*

I considered this for a moment. The way we were communicating now–it wasn't a language I'd ever spoken. The eagle sent his thoughts to me, and my brain somehow translated them. Yet the words seemed familiar to me, like I'd heard them in a dream. If I stopped to think about it too long, I got a headache.

Tell me anyway, I told him. It wasn't like any of this mental communication made sense in the first place.

He thought for a moment before saying, *It's something like "violent wind."*

Like a storm? I asked. He responded back with the mental equivalent of a human wrinkling his nose. And suddenly, I remembered the conversation I'd had with the wind spirit. He had said, *Ride the tempest, tame the wind. Tempest* was another word for a violent, windy storm, and when Mistral first told me, I thought I would have to go out and face down a storm and try to harness its power.

But now . . .

My breath caught in my throat before I tentatively asked, *Tempest?*

The eagle made a little warble sound out loud. *"Tempest" is an acceptable translation.*

Suddenly it all made sense. *Ride the tempest* referred to our bond. I smiled up at him, still stroking the smooth feathers. Did this mean that my bond with Tempest would allow me to fully control the power of the wind?

I prayed with all my heart that it did because I knew my people would need that power now more than ever. By confronting the Devourer, I had broken the treaty by using wind magic against it. Even if I hadn't, though, there was no way I would go through with the marriage now.

I'm still not sure how any of this happened, I thought to him. *Do wild eagles bond with humans?* Much less humans who weren't Zephyrians.

Never.

A shocked silence descended over me. *I don't understand,* I finally said.

I'm not sure I can explain because I'm not familiar with the bonding process. I only know that I was drawn to you, and when I thought you were in danger, I came to your rescue. But the moment I was close enough to hear your mind–even when you were unconscious–I knew I could never be apart from you.

Despite the impossibility of it, we had bonded, but the reason for it was apparently beyond both of us.

The wind spoke of you once, he said.

Surprise shot through me. *You heard the wind?*

Yes, though I didn't know it meant a human until now. It said I was destined to be united in power with the wind caller.

The wind spirit told me the same thing, though I didn't understand at the time what he meant, I said, as the memory clicked into meaning.

I knew the moment I saw you that you were the one. You're the human I've seen since I was just a chick.

Time seemed to stretch and slow, the sheer magnitude of his words reverberating through me. Suddenly, my mind dredged up an image of that day two years ago, when I stumbled upon an eagle's nest.

You mean, you've seen me in your dreams?

Well, yes, but I also saw you once. When I was only two weeks old.

The memory played through my mind. The chick that had come close enough for me to touch . . . before its mother returned and tried to kill Shazeera and me.

You remember, he said, pleased.

How could I forget?

He made a little happy warble.

Have you always been able to understand the wind? I knew it wasn't something any of the eagles in the palace could do, otherwise, none of the Zephyrians would have been so surprised by my ability. Was this eagle unique in his ability as I was in mine?

Yes, it's something all wild eagles learn soon after hatching.

I don't think any of the palace eagles can do that.

Being domesticated will do that to you, he thought wryly.

I, too, have been able to hear the wind. Ever since I was little. I never knew why, though.

It's in your blood, he thought, and I glanced up at him.

How do you know that?

He mentally shrugged. *Same way I knew you were the one. I can just sense it. Can't you?*

In my blood. It was what Mistral had said, too. This was an ability I was born with, even though I was a Child of Earth.

I glanced at Talon, whose face was a mask of concern.

Then, Tempest, will you let my friend approach me unharmed?

Tempest made a grumbling sound deep in his throat, but then he relaxed his protective stance. The moment he took a step back, Talon strode toward me and pulled me into his arms.

I melted into him, the weight of everything that had happened hitting me at once. He lowered his head so that his face was buried in my neck. "Thank the Lord of the Skies you're safe."

I reached up and touched the spot above his temple, my brow furrowing. "What about you? The blow to your head . . ."

"It's fine—head wounds bleed a lot," he said when I gave him a pointed look, my eyes drifting to the dried blood on his cheek.

He took a small step back to look at me. "You're sure you're okay?"

I nodded. "It felt like the Devourer drained the life from me, like all the energy inside me had been sucked away. But the moment we bonded, I felt this surge in power return. I think this is what the wind spirit meant when he said I had to find my destiny."

"I'm at a loss," he said with a slight shake of his head. "I don't understand how any of this is possible." He touched my cheek. "But if bonding with a wild eagle brought you back from the brink, then you won't hear me complain."

I leaned into his touch. When I met his gaze, his eyes immediately dropped to my mouth. Warmth blazed inside me. I parted my lips. It was all the invitation he needed as he pulled me close, and his mouth met mine in a searing kiss. Behind us, Tempest fanned out his wings in disapproval, but we kept on heedlessly. I pressed myself against Talon, my hands plunging into his thick hair, but careful to avoid his wound. He groaned as the kiss deepened. His tongue stroked over mine as he held me against the hard length of him.

We kissed each other like it was the last time. And maybe it was. His hands were simultaneously firm and gentle as they roved over my back. When he reached the sensitive skin of my neck, I let out a soft moan.

He pulled away with a shuddering breath, and my insides shook. "I was so terrified I would lose you."

I felt the loss of him already. My body craved the feel of him against me, but I knew we didn't have much time. "I'm here and alive thanks to you. But as much as I want to keep doing . . . that . . . we have to go back, Talon." I took hold of his hand, the calluses rough against the skin of my palm. "I can't leave Shazeera behind. Who knows what the emperor will do to her the moment he realizes I'm gone?" My eyes filled with tears. "I'm terrified for her."

He shook his head obstinately. "I was an idiot for allowing you to face that thing in the first place. I nearly got you killed. Baz,

Zamir, and Kestrel died because I didn't take the threat seriously enough, and if it had succeeded in taking your power . . ." He trailed off, his face full of self-reproach. The moment he said their names, the pain of grief hit me hard, making my tears come faster as a lump welled in my throat. I thought of going to Naharu with them, only a few days ago. Guilt nipped quickly at the heels of my grief when I knew I wouldn't even be able to think about their deaths right now—not when Shazeera needed me. "I refuse to risk your life again," Talon continued.

"It's my decision—"

"Then I will go with Neo to rescue her," Talon interrupted, "and you will stay here, where it's safe."

I pushed my hair off my shoulder, suddenly irritated by the weight of it. "You expect me to just sit here and wait to see if you can save her? When I'm too far to communicate with her? You won't even know what you're walking into, and you will need my help."

When he remained silent, Tempest suddenly took a step toward him, his talons scraping against the ground with a menacing sound. Talon watched him warily.

Tell him you don't need his permission, Tempest said, eyes locked onto Talon. *I will fly you wherever you want to go.*

"I think you already know that I can go wherever I want at this point," I told Talon. "But it would be better if we make a plan together."

Talon looked back at Neo for a moment before nodding reluctantly. "Then we will return, though I can't imagine anything worse than taking you back to the place that nearly got you killed. You're right, though; we'll have to come up with a plan first. We can't just fly into this blind. The Devourer is almost certainly still alive."

The color drained from my face. "You don't think the wind power I unleashed was enough to kill him?"

Talon shot me a sympathetic glance. "He looked me in the eyes just before I grabbed you, and I doubt he would have the decency to die from his wounds."

"So that . . . thing . . . is still alive, and I just left Shazeera there? Alone?" Before, I had been afraid the emperor might do something to Shazeera in retaliation for my leaving the palace. But the idea that the Devourer might leave the west wing and threaten my heart's sister was enough to steal the breath from my lungs. "Whatever we do, we need to do it fast. I can't communicate with Shazeera from this far away, so I have no idea what we're walking into. They could already have hurt her." My voice broke on the last word, and a knife twisted in my heart. Tempest made a sad sound of sympathy.

"Then we should fly straight for the pasture to rescue her," Talon said. "If both your eagle—"

"Tempest," I interrupted with a glance up at the eagle, who was closely following our conversation. "He said his name is Tempest."

I was wondering when you would finally introduce me, Tempest said, ruffling the feathers of his neck.

I shook my head. *You'll have to excuse my lack of manners.*

"Tempest," Talon repeated. He bowed toward the eagle. "Forgive me for not using your name. I am Commander Talon."

Tempest inclined his head slightly in acknowledgment.

"Then if both Tempest and Shazeera consent," Talon continued, "Tempest can carry both of you back to your people."

Easily, Tempest said.

I'm so thankful to have your help. Out loud to Talon, I said, "I don't think Shazeera will mind flying again if it means we get to go home. What about you and Neo? Will you come with us?"

He shook his head, and my stomach sank. "Neo and I will fly to Mistral to tell them everything we've learned about the Devourer. I will convince them to join forces with your people."

I nodded slowly, heart pounding. Mistral was far, and its people had every reason to be wary of a Zephyrian. But I trusted Talon. If anyone could convince them, it was him. Still, a quiet fear settled over me. If they didn't want to ally with my people–if they refused to fight–then who would stand against the Devourer?

Suddenly, the wind changed.

Where it had blown gently across my face before, now it surged, fierce and cold, like I stood atop a mountain peak with nothing to hold me back from the edge. And then, as if summoned by the very mention of Mistral, the wind spirit filled my mind. Where Mistral's power had threatened to overtake me once before, draining the strength from my body, now Tempest was here–his energy surging through our bond, anchoring me.

Wind caller, Mistral said, his voice curling through my mind like smoke. *You found your Tempest.*

I never imagined you meant that I would bond with an eagle. I tried to suppress my reaction, but it was hard when I was mentally connected and sending thoughts already. *You could have been clearer.*

The ways of wind spirits are not your ways, Mistral said. *You were destined to find each other at the right moment.*

I supposed I couldn't expect a wind spirit to speak like I did. Still, I had to ask my next question. *Will the king of Mistral listen to Talon? Will he be willing to ally with my people?*

Whether he listens is not the question, Mistral said, *but whether the truth reaches him in time.*

I held on to those words, trying to draw comfort from them.

But even as they settled in my mind, another fear rose—sharper, more immediate.

What about Shazeera? I asked, panic rising like a wave. *Is she in danger?*

Time is running short, he said, and my breath caught in my throat.

Then I must go to her immediately, I said, my thoughts spinning into desperation.

I will answer your call, Mistral said, but I barely registered it. My mind reeled, and a terrible desperation held me in a vise.

"Talon," I said, my voice breaking, and he took a step toward me protectively, "Mistral said Shazeera needs us."

"Then we fly." He took hold of my hand and gently tugged me toward Neo. "Let's go."

Tempest let out an angry screech that caused us both to whip around.

No one carries you but me.

To Talon, I said, "He wants to carry me himself."

Talon looked up at Tempest towering over us with a frown. "With no saddle or flight training? She could easily fall."

Tempest's feathers on his neck ruffled in obvious irritation. *Tell him I would never let you fall.*

"He says I won't fall," I told Talon, one hand on the hard muscles of his arm, "and I trust him."

Talon let out a frustrated breath but nodded. "Fine. We'll stick to the original plan—we go and save Shazeera, and Tempest flies both of you back to your people. Neo and I will go seek out the Mistral army and then come find you again. Did the wind spirit say where to find them?"

"He said they are to the northwest. He was vague on how they were traveling or exactly where they were," I said, biting my bottom lip anxiously. "He didn't even guarantee they won't attack you on sight."

"I'll hold up a white flag and hope for the best," Talon said with a flash of a grin. "We'll be fine. The important thing is to get you and Shazeera to safety." He reached out and cupped my cheek again, his gaze holding mine. "Zara, if something happens to us, I want you to take Shazeera and fly. Don't try and save us." When I opened my mouth to argue, he jumped in. "Think of what's at stake. We can't allow them to hand you over to Ozul. If we have any chance at beating that thing, you and your people need to ally with Mistral. You are the key—not me."

I had to swallow around a lump in my throat. This man used to be my enemy, and now, I didn't want to part from him, much less abandon him like he was commanding me to do.

He leaned down and kissed me again, his lips plush and hot against mine. He cradled my face with his hands like I was some precious thing. The kiss was gentle until our tongues met, and then searing.

When we finally broke apart, he said, "If anything happens, don't stop. Keep flying. The Devourer can't capture you, or else we're all doomed."

I hesitated. "Talon," I said.

"You know I'm right," he said firmly.

Reluctantly, I nodded. "Fine," I said, and when he arched a brow at me, I added, "agreed." I knew my role as First Daughter. I would do anything to save my people.

With one last quick kiss, he said, "Now let's go rescue your heart's sister."

I turned to Tempest, who had lowered himself so that he was almost lying on the ground. I leaped astride his back before settling myself in a kneeling stance like Talon had taught me, just between Tempest's wings. Talon waited until I was in position before leaping onto Neo's back.

Tempest stood, and suddenly, I was looking down on Talon and Neo. Tempest was at least ten feet taller than Neo, and when he spread his massive wings, I realized just how much bigger he truly was. While Neo had an impressive thirty-five-foot wingspan, Tempest's wings were at least fifty feet from tip to tip.

With only a few powerful pumps of his wings, we shot into the air. A thrill made my heart soar as my connection to Tempest allowed me to feel what he was feeling–the weightlessness as the air lifted us, the wind running over his feathers, and the powerful flaps of his wings as we soared through the sky. Guilt came biting at the heels of my joy, though, when I thought of Shazeera.

I still didn't know how Shazeera would react to all of this. Using wind power and being fascinated by eagles was one thing; being bonded to one was another.

That was if she was unharmed. Anxiety made my blood pound, and Tempest responded by flying even faster, the wind forcing me down even lower on his back.

I'm coming, Shazeera, I thought.

35

ZARA

Terror for Shazeera spread through my body with every beat of my heart. Tempest flew so fast I had to lie flat against his feathers to keep from being torn off by the wind. It still wasn't enough. We were only minutes away, but I gripped his strong feathers with an urgent desperation that turned my knuckles white. And then, at last, I could see the green of the pasture in the distance. I didn't even have to point it out to Tempest; our connection allowed him to see it from my memories.

Shazeera! I called the second I thought I might be in range of our connection.

Zara, Shazeera said, even her mental voice strained, but I sagged at the relief of hearing it. For a moment, I didn't understand how we could communicate so quickly after my using the wind power, but then I thought of the way my energy had flooded back into me when I bonded with Tempest. He had given me some of his strength somehow, and apparently it had also given me the ability to communicate with Shazeera again despite calling the wind.

We're coming to get you, I told her.

Don't come! she mentally yelled at me. *They've set a trap.*

Are you hurt? I demanded. I wanted to urge Tempest on, but Talon needed to know we were flying into a trap.

We need to circle here, I told Tempest. *There are men waiting to attack us when we land. I need to tell Talon and Neo.*

Tempest immediately did as I asked, without hesitation. Neo and Talon quickly caught up, and Talon shot me a questioning look.

"Shazeera said there's a trap," I told him when he flew close enough to hear me, the eagles' wings slicing through the air as we hovered high above the earth.

His expression tightened. "Find out all the details you can."

I relayed this to Shazeera.

They have me chained, Shazeera admitted. *I tried to break free, but the stake's been driven into rock. Fifty of the emperor's guards are stationed around me.*

I let out my breath in a rush. Fifty! So many.

Talon's eyes turned flinty when I told him. "Ask if there are any Eagle Riders."

I looked at him in stunned silence. Surely they wouldn't turn against their own commander, but then again, if the emperor himself had ordered it . . .

Shazeera was quiet for so long, I was afraid something had happened to her.

Falcon tried to stop them, she said haltingly, and the sorrow in her voice made my eyes fill with tears before she even finished.

No, I whispered, recoiling from the thought.

They killed him and his eagle. To my knowledge, there are no other Eagle Riders here.

I met Talon's gaze through blurry eyes, my throat thick. He

must have known what I would say, because he swallowed hard and bowed his head. "She said there are no other Eagle Riders, but the guards killed Falcon and his eagle when he tried to defend her." My voice broke on the last word. Falcon had been so young–only a year or two older than me. And he had died trying to save my heart's sister. It only made me think of Baz, Zamir, and Kestrel dying such horrible, agonizing deaths, and my vision blurred with unshed tears. I let the wind dry them from my eyes before they could fall.

"That's four I have sent to their deaths now," Talon said, expression anguished.

I couldn't even say anything to comfort him, because now I felt the same. I had defied the emperor and the treaty by confronting the Devourer and using my wind power, and it had already had very real consequences.

It would destroy me if Shazeera was one of those consequences.

We're coming–

Don't! Just leave me. They'll overpower you, Talon, and Neo.

Just the thought of leaving her to her fate was so abhorrent I recoiled mentally. *I will never leave you, and you should know . . . it's not just the three of us.*

A flutter of nerves filled me. I hadn't given much thought to how Shazeera would react to this news. I closed my eyes tight as I opened my mind to her, allowing her to see everything that had transpired since we last parted.

The moment Shazeera watched my memories of bonding with Tempest, a stunned silence descended upon her. A deep, pervasive hurt followed rapidly on the heels of her shock, and though she tried to hide it from me, I still felt it reverberate through my heart.

So, you're an Eagle Rider now, she said, and the tears burned in my throat.

No, I'm a Daughter of Earth, bonded to my horse sister, and now that part of me that has always known the wind has somehow bonded with a wild eagle, too.

I understand now, why it felt different when you came into range and we could talk again, she said. *I sensed another presence, and I wondered if it was the wind.*

I take that as a compliment, Tempest said, barging in on our conversation. Before I could even respond, he added, *But we must focus on the task at hand–introductions and feelings can come later.*

Talon must have been of the same mind because he said, "Neo and I will fly in first, draw them away, and then you can rescue Shazeera."

I nodded. "We'll give you a head start."

Neo took off then like an arrow, wings in an M shape to cut through the wind like knives. I watched them go, an ill feeling of dread gripping me.

Moments later, I watched him dive toward a swarm of guards, talons extended. Shazeera transferred everything she saw to Tempest and me through our bond. Ten guards circled Shazeera, spears pointed outward. The others engaged in battle with Talon and Neo, being led slowly away from Shazeera. Talon and Neo seemed reluctant to kill the guards, only swooping down on them threateningly and drawing them away from Shazeera as promised.

Let's go, I told Tempest when I saw they had moved all the way across the pasture and away from Shazeera.

I'll grab hold of her and break the chains, Tempest said.

How will you avoid all the spears?

I'll kill the guards holding them, he said matter-of-factly.

No! We should avoid killing if possible. These men and women are just following orders.

That complicates things, Tempest said, *but I'll do my best.*

He took off like a lightning bolt, the wind forcing me flat against his feathers again. We arrived in less than a minute.

Tempest's enormous wings blotted out the sun, casting a shadow over the entirety of the guards attacking Neo and Talon. The guards looked up in stunned silence. But as we soared past them to rescue Shazeera, they quickly regrouped. Half split away from the battle with Neo and Talon, launching spears at Tempest as he shot toward Shazeera.

Tempest knocked them aside with his powerful claws like they were toothpicks.

Shazeera reared, lashing out with her hooves at the guards surrounding her. At the same time, she pulled powerfully at the chains wrapped around the base of her neck and staked into the ground. A red rage ignited through my body at the sight of her abused in such a way. I almost told Tempest he could kill them all.

You may get your wish if they keep launching spears at me, he said darkly.

A screech echoed across the pasture, followed by the thunderous beating of wings. I jerked my head toward Talon and Neo, but they still hovered above the other guards.

And then Tempest shrieked a warning, the sound so painfully high-pitched that I covered my ears.

Twenty Eagle Riders flew above the pasture, fully dressed for battle with burnished gold armor, spears, and bows and arrows. I couldn't see Talon's face from this distance, but I could only imagine how he felt now that his own aerial cavalry threatened us.

Talon and Neo flew to our side. Talon didn't say a word, but his actions made it clear. He had sided with us.

Lead them away from Shazeera, I told Tempest, an edge of fear to my voice. I was terrified she would be hurt in the cross fire.

Tempest banked left, and Neo followed. With a shout, the Eagle Riders pursued until we were clear across the pasture. They shot a torrent of arrows at us, but Tempest flew like he had eyes in the back of his head, easily avoiding them. Out of the corner of my eye, I saw Neo perform the same maneuvers he had used when I tried to fire arrows at him all those weeks ago. He spiraled through the air, feathers knocking the arrows aside.

The line of Eagle Riders split, half surrounding Neo and Talon, and the other half attempting to do the same with Tempest. He outmaneuvered them easily.

Am I allowed to kill these eagles and their riders? Tempest asked.

No, I said quickly. *I don't want anyone else to die.*

Then if you won't let me fight back, what is the plan? Get Shazeera and fly out of here?

That would be ideal, I said.

A female Eagle Rider launched a spear at us, but Tempest caught it and snapped it in half like a twig. *Would you be open to maiming them?* he asked, irritation making his tone sharp.

Another Eagle Rider caught my attention as he hauled a metal cylinder up until it rested on his shoulder. He attempted to point it right at Tempest, but my bonded eagle was too fast. Ice-cold fear ran through my veins at the sight of it. I didn't know what kind of weapon it was, but neither did I want to find out.

I reached inside me for the power that waited like a vast ocean just beneath my subconscious. Just before calling it forth, I hesitated. The shimmering bond with Shazeera, like a chain of light connecting us, glowed brightly. Beside it, Tempest's was just as strong. Mistral had said that I needed to find Tempest to be able to truly control my wind power. But more importantly, bonding with Tempest had made it so I could communicate with Shazeera again right away—even after calling the wind in the west wing.

I will lend you whatever strength you need, Tempest promised.

With a deep breath and a prayer sent to the Earth Mother, I grabbed hold of the power inside me, and it surged instantly to my command.

I pictured a cyclone just strong enough to force the eagles to the ground, but not so powerful it tore them apart. I just wanted to incapacitate, not injure.

With my hands lifted skyward, I released the wind power within me. An enormous cyclone manifested, terrible in its intensity. Tempest was blown back, and I had to scramble to hold on. The Eagle Riders in front of us slammed into each other with screams and screeches, wings and talons tearing at the air uselessly. They were ripped out of the sky like flies in a storm.

Mouth agape, I watched as they crashed violently to the earth. Grass and dirt sprayed up where they hit, each eagle and rider slamming into the ground so hard they made a booming sound on impact.

When the wind died down, they were motionless, weapons thrown free, wings and limbs at terrible angles.

All dead.

You should have told me you wanted to take care of them yourself, Tempest said with a little huff, *I would have prepared myself for the onslaught of wind.*

I didn't—I tried—

I couldn't even form the words. My breaths came quickly. I had intended the wind to merely push them to the ground—not violently assault and kill them. Could I even still communicate with Shazeera?

I'm here, she said. *Our bond is unharmed.*

I closed my eyes and let my breath out in a rush. Thank the Mother for that, at least. I could call the wind, and I could unleash its power without harming our bond, but I couldn't control it.

With shaky hands, I glanced over at Talon, unsure how he might react to the fact that I had blasted the men he used to command from the sky. But he was still engaged in battle with his own soldiers. Neo and another eagle had locked claws and were spinning through the air in a deadly dance.

Movement from the palace drew our attention. A sinking sensation overtook me as I watched Emperor Altair stride onto the field, accompanied by fifty more guards. The moment she saw him, Shazeera reared, nostrils flared, as she trumpeted a warning. But I didn't need her superior senses to see for myself what had happened.

A dark aura surrounded Altair now, and even from here, I could see his eyes had turned entirely black, no whites to be seen.

We need to get Shazeera now, I told Tempest. *Before he orders the guards to harm her.*

Agreed, Tempest said, flying back toward her.

The emperor and his guards tracked our flight, but Tempest was too fast for them to mount an attack.

Tempest hovered over Shazeera, his wings beating hard enough to make the guards stumble and to rip their spears from their hands. Even Shazeera swayed against the strong wind he created. Then he wrapped his claws around her sides and lifted her as easily as he had me. The chains snapped like threads.

Are you all right? I asked her. *I'm so sorry you have to be carried again.*

Anything to get off this mountain.

We'll be home soon, I said.

I turned to signal Talon and Neo, but at the same time, an Eagle Rider closest to Talon had brought out that same cylindrical weapon I had seen before. The rider aimed it at Neo and fired.

I shouted a warning as an enormous net ejected from the weapon, but it sped through the air like lightning. It landed over Talon and Neo, and they plummeted in a snarl of ropes and wings.

"Talon!" I screamed, and the wind surged up in answer to my fear.

Neo thrashed to try to free himself from the net, while Talon's blade hacked at the net's strong ropes. I nearly collapsed with relief when I saw they were alive.

Emperor Altair's guards surged toward them, while some of the other Eagle Riders landed.

Use your wind power, Tempest said.

I could feel it, hovering just beneath the surface of my skin, waiting. *I can't,* I cried out to him mentally. *I have no control. I could easily kill Talon and Neo.*

Before Talon could even cut through one of the ropes, the guards surrounded them. Talon's gaze met mine. "Go!" he shouted from across the pasture.

Tears sprang to my eyes. I shook my head.

"Zara, go!" he shouted again as they pulled him away from Neo.

I must get you to safety, Tempest said.

I thought of Shazeera, who dangled from his claws. Tempest couldn't fight back now, and I couldn't trust my control over the wind. I might just as easily kill Talon and Neo. My breaths came in a panicked rush. I couldn't save him.

Don't make his sacrifice be in vain, Tempest urged.

I choked on a sob. "Talon," I cried. "I'm so sorry."

And then with a few powerful pumps of his wings, Tempest shot away, faster than an arrow.

The other Eagle Riders flew toward us, but I knew they would be too slow.

"Zara!" Altair's roar chased after us.

I looked back once, but not at him.

At Talon, whose expression was laid bare. He looked as gutted as I felt.

With effort, I turned away, pointing myself resolutely toward home.

36

TALON

Even with Altair howling in the background, and knowing he'd soon turn that rage on me, I couldn't tear my eyes from the place where Zara had disappeared. Even still trapped in a net with Neo, I let my breath out in a rush of relief that she had escaped. No matter what happened to me now, Tempest would get her to her people. They could ally themselves with Mistral, and they could mount a defense against the Devourer.

At the same time, darkness swallowed me whole. I would likely never see her again. It felt like my heart had been ripped out of my chest.

A guard cut the netting off me and jerked me roughly to my feet. He grabbed hold of my right arm, while another grabbed my left.

His wings still bound, Neo shrieked a warning as guards approached him.

The second you can, fly out of here, I told him.

I won't abandon you to your fate, Neo said.

There's nothing you can do for me now, I said. *One of us needs to be free.* I knew what would happen now. Altair would unleash all that fury on me, and I would likely be executed for treason.

Altair stalked over to me, and I had to restrain myself from recoiling at the sight of him. His tunic was ripped from the collar to his chest, as though he'd taken hold of it and pulled, and his hair was standing in several different directions. "You knew about the eagle and kept it from me."

"It happened after we tried to confront Ozul," I said in as calm a tone as I could. He was listening to something I couldn't see, and the thought of that made my flesh crawl.

"You wanted her to escape," Altair said, his eyes narrowing at me while he pointed aggressively. It took all my discipline and training to stand impassively in the face of his increasing hostility. "You want her for yourself."

I hesitated, disturbed by how much he had figured out. I made the mistake of looking him in the eyes, and something shifted there. What looked back at me wasn't my cousin. I jerked back.

"You always wanted what was mine," Altair said in a snarl. "Father was all too happy to give it to you, too. He wished you were his son and not me. He tried to have me killed." His last word ended in a strangled sob, and I held out my hand to him instinctually, reacting to my cousin's pain. Maybe there was some way I could reach him, pull him back from the brink.

He slapped my hand away, his face shadowed again. "Your father is gone now, Altair," I said. "He can't hurt you anymore." Something swam in the depths of his eyes, something dark and unfathomable.

"Altair—"

"Guards," Altair said, and instantly, the guards holding me stood at attention. "Take Talon to the dungeon."

Before they could, I let my body go slack, and then while they were off their center of balance, I spun out of their hold with a jerk and ran to Neo. The guards came after me, but I grabbed hold of the net and pulled.

Five guards tackled me, knocking me to the ground with a gut punch that pushed all the air out of my lungs. I fought wildly, gasping for breath.

Neo spread his wings as guards threatened him with spears.

Go, I told Neo.

Talon, he pleaded.

Go–they'll kill us both! If you're alive, there's a chance I can escape.

He wavered. He didn't want to abandon me. He would rather stay and fight, die beside me as my brother, but he knew I had a point. If there was any chance at all that I could escape, I would need him alive and free to do it.

I'll come back for you, he promised.

Someone slammed the hilt of his sword into my head as another kicked my ribs. Ears ringing, I could still make out a beautiful sound. The heavy beat of wings.

Altair stood over me as they hauled me to my feet. "You had designs on the future empress. You committed treason against your emperor by helping her to escape."

I spat out blood. "You allowed Lord Heron to have free rein of the palace and try to have her killed–*twice.*"

"I will make an example of you, Talon," Altair said, his expression calm but his eyes full of darkness. "Anyone who dares betray the throne will be punished–kin or not. Throw him in the dungeon to await his sentence," he told my guards.

"You need me," I said to Altair, trying one last time to secure my freedom. "There's a war coming. Who will lead your army?"

"I have a new army commander," Altair said, and then, from out of the shadows, it emerged.

Ozul. The Devourer.

And as it made its way to stand beside my cousin the emperor, I knew that all hope was lost.

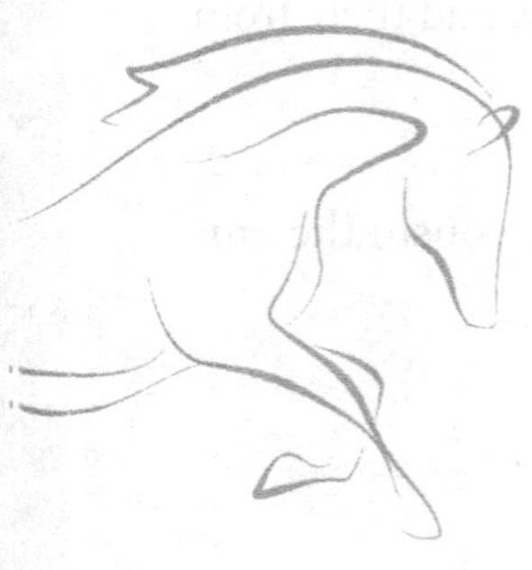

37

ZARA

We flew to the Nazeeran Canyon, where I knew we'd find Ama. She wouldn't have left Queen Jazela, and with our people supposedly at peace, there shouldn't have been a reason for Ama to hide anymore. My mind continually tormented me with the look on Talon's face when we abandoned him to his fate.

Flew to safety, Tempest corrected.

Did exactly as he asked us to do, Shazeera said at the same time.

They had both tried their best to comfort me during the flight, but I couldn't stop crying. I clutched my abdomen and sobbed until I couldn't breathe.

He'll kill him, I kept telling them. *The Devourer had completely taken Altair over, and he'll want revenge on Talon for letting me go.*

I thought of all the times Talon had been there for me when I had been attacked, and now no one would be there for him.

Your power in the hands of that creature would have sentenced this entire continent to death, Shazeera reminded me—repeatedly.

That's the only thing that's keeping me from begging Tempest to fly me back as soon as I get you to safety, I told her.

That's not happening, Tempest said firmly.

I could still feel Talon's lips on mine, his hands on my back and in my hair. We hadn't even had time to explore our feelings for each other. But I knew without a doubt I was falling for him.

And I had left him behind to his fate.

Amidst a bright orange setting sun, the sky a dazzling array of pinks and purples, we made our descent over the Nazeeran Canyon. In my desperation to return to my people and grief over leaving Talon and Neo, I hadn't thought about the potential reaction to a giant eagle swooping down in the middle of the encampment.

We were greeted with shouts and screams, as Tempest's wings buffeted the tents and pavilions.

Should I take off again? Tempest asked, his concern pressing at my mind. *These people seem hostile.*

They're my *people. They won't attack.*

A line of archers marched to the forefront of the crowd, drawing their bows.

"Don't shoot!" I shouted as Tempest lowered Shazeera carefully to the ground. I leaped down from Tempest's back and spread my arms wide in front of him, Shazeera by my side.

There was a terrible moment where we stared each other down, and Tempest kept sending me images of him scooping me up and flying me to safety, but at last, a voice cried out.

"It's First Daughter Zara, you fools!" Mariyah said, shoving herself to the front of the crowd. She didn't even blink at the giant eagle behind me but instead strode directly to me and threw her arms around me.

And then we were both crying and laughing, while the archers slowly lowered their bows with bewildered looks on their faces. It only made me laugh harder, in that slightly unhinged way of someone who is exhausted and relieved and just really glad to be home.

"What did you do? Steal one of their eagles and escape?" Mariyah asked when we'd had enough crying and hugging.

I glanced back at Tempest, who still eyed the archers threateningly. "It's a really long story."

"Will you have the time to tell it?" she asked, her tone turning serious.

I knew what she meant. Was I back for good? "Yes," I said. "Well, until war breaks out."

Her face paled. "I never agreed with you sacrificing yourself for a peace treaty. There has to be another way—even if it means war again."

"Although I admire your loyalty, I wasn't the one who breached the peace treaty, and it's another war I'm talking about. But let's find Ama and hopefully General Isa, and I'll explain everything."

"I won't have to wait long then," she said with a nod toward the crowd. "Here they come"

Ama rode Nafalla beside Queen Jazela and her mare with General Isa following on Kamil. The crowd parted without resistance, their gaze darting from their queen to Tempest.

"My daughter has returned bearing important news," Ama announced to the murmuring crowd, and I recognized her strategy. She wanted to quickly assure them that my coming wasn't a shirking of my duty to the peace treaty, but rather something that was necessary and possibly even sanctioned by the Zephyrians. "Prepare a feast to celebrate."

The effect was instantaneous, changing the overall mood

from one of suspicion to one of joyful anticipation. Everyone loved a chance to dance and feast. They dispersed quickly after that, rushing off to make preparations.

Ama swung down from Nafalla's back, and I hurried to meet her. When she embraced me, I was enveloped by her familiar smell of cloves and sage. "Oh, Zara," she whispered into my hair. "I don't know why you've returned, but I am so happy to see you."

"I missed you so much," I said, my voice thick. "You have no idea. There's a lot to tell—a lot that happened after I arrived at the palace."

Ama looked over my head at Tempest. "I can see that. Come, we'll go to the pavilion and talk." Her gaze shifted to Mariyah, who waited behind me. "You're welcome to come, too, Mariyah."

"I would have hung around outside the pavilion and listened in if you hadn't invited me," she said, and Ama grinned.

"I know. That's why I'm telling you to come along."

I started to follow Ama, but then I remembered that I would have to tell Tempest where he could go. I was used to Shazeera knowing her way around the camp; she had already gone to graze with Citrine.

I'm with my family now, I told Tempest. *I'll be safe, but I want to be sure you are, too. The Twin Plateaus aren't far from here, and there are trees where you can roost.*

I doubt that the emperor will give in so easily, he said. *I will fly perimeter checks. I'd rather stay nearby—close enough to hear if you need me.*

Relief filled me so swiftly, I realized I had been afraid to be separated from him. How quickly the bond had brought us together.

Be safe, I said as he took flight.

I returned to the others who had waited for me before

proceeding to Ama's pavilion. Mariyah leaned in close. "That's the biggest eagle I've ever seen. I peed myself a little when I saw it looming behind you, even though I knew logically that it must have brought you and Shazeera here."

"He would never hurt me, so you needn't worry, but you're right. He's enormous. Talon said–" I felt my face flush even as a deep pain struck me in the chest. *Talon.* I swallowed the lump that formed in my throat again. Mariyah took hold of my arm, concern clear in her eyes. I shook my head and forced my lungs to draw breath. "He said Tempest is so large because he's a wild eagle."

Whatever Mariyah was going to say about Talon must have left her mind the moment I said Tempest was a wild eagle, her eyes widening. "What in the world happened while you were gone?"

"Come tell us, Zara," Ama said, beckoning me into her pavilion with Queen Jazela beside her.

I took a step inside, and I had to close my eyes for a breath. It was nothing like the palace, all vibrant colors and soft light and plush furnishings, and it made me want to curl up in the bed I knew was still in the other room waiting for me. Instead, I moved into the throne room, where Ama and the others waited.

I walked over and sat down beside Ama.

"Before I tell you what happened at the palace with the emperor, there's something we need to discuss," I told Ama, holding her gaze.

The welcoming smile she had on her face slipped away, and after a moment, she nodded somberly. The others sensed the shift in mood and silently watched us.

Everything I had learned about myself galloped through my mind then. I thought of the Devourer's attacks and how it was after my power, the talks with the wind spirit, my failed attempt to destroy Ozul, and finally, bonding with a wild eagle. But even though I had learned so much, there was still a critical piece of information missing.

I took a deep, steadying breath and took Ama's hand. "I think it's finally time you told me the truth about my father."

ACKNOWLEDGMENTS

Deo gratias.

Writing may be a lonely enterprise at times—lost in my own head, dreaming up scenes and untangling plotlines—but publishing a book requires the help of a whole team of people. And I am so thankful to every single one of you.

For my husband, who makes sure I have everything I need so that I can live my dream of writing books for a living. I love you forever and always.

For my six children, who keep my imagination alive with bedtime stories, wild ideas, endless artwork, and the kind of wonder that reminds me why I write. I hope one day you read this and know that you are my highest calling.

For my parents, who weren't horse people, but became them out of love for their daughter. You bought me my first horse, gave up weekends for shows, and poured time, money, and heart into my dream. You supported me then, and you continue to support me now—thank you for always being there.

For my extended family, who are always so supportive and willing to buy multiple copies of any book I write. My military uncles—Frank, Kevin, and Jim—generously let me pick their brains for battle insight; any mistakes are entirely my own. And to my cousin Kelsey Cox, especially—my first writing partner, my lifelong friend, and now a published author herself. At last, *both* our childhood dreams are coming true!

For my agent and writing partner, David Purse, who wears many hats and somehow excels at all of them. You believed in this story from the start and gave so much of your time and heart to help bring it to life. Thank you for always having my back.

For my editors, Elizabeth Vinson and Cindy Hwang, who fell in love with this book and worked tirelessly to make sure it was the best version it could be. Thank you so much for believing in Zara and Talon's story—and in me.

For Ariana Abad, Hillary Tacuri, Megan Elmore, Angelina Krahn, Julieanna Turner, Olivia Trzaski, and everyone at Ace for all their hard work on this book—and most especially to Sam Hadley and Tyriq Moore for the gorgeous cover that was everything I could have hoped for and more.

For all my friends, especially Jennifer, Angela, and Susanna, who are always willing to listen to plot twists and half-formed scenes while our kids play sports, hang out, or run wild around us. Your support, laughter, and encouragement mean more than you know. And to Bridget Howard—one of the first people to believe this story belonged in the world. Thank you for your early encouragement, and for everything you've done to help bring it to readers.

And to you, dear reader—thank you for opening these pages, for taking flight with Zara and Talon. I'm so grateful you chose to spend your time in this world I created.

The idea for this story began the first time I rode across an open field with the wind in my face on a little Arabian mare, very much like the one in this book. To everyone who has shared this journey with me—thank you.

Keep reading for a sneak peek at the next book following *Daughter of the Wind*!

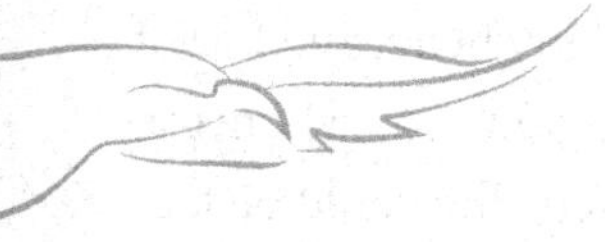

TALON

I couldn't stop thinking of her.

Zara's face, her voice, the feel of her lips on mine—they haunted the silence like a ghost I didn't want to banish.

Alone in the dark, the stone walls pressing in, I had only memories for company. I'd never minded solitude. But here, in the deepest part of the dungeon we reserved for the worst criminals, my mind lay siege to me. Every mistake I made cycled through on an endless loop. The last battle replayed again and again. I should have commanded an entire battalion of Eagle Riders to face the Devourer—and damn the consequences when the emperor found out. Maybe then my closest friends would be alive. I refought that battle a thousand times in my mind, each version a different strategy. All of them better than the shitstorm it had actually led to.

There were no windows down here. No way to tell time except for the sparse meals they brought me twice a day. I ate only to keep up my strength. By counting meals, I figured several days had already passed since I last saw Zara. Anything could have happened in that amount of time. The Devourer could have already unleashed its power upon the world outside, and I wouldn't know . . . but for the fact that the meals kept coming.

Did you bring this First Daughter to me as an offering?

The echoes of the Devourer's voice filled my head, and I tried to shake free. I couldn't let myself spiral again—not when the thought of losing her still felt like being gutted. She could be facing any number of enemies now, and I was powerless to protect her.

Something scratched in the straw near the corner of the cell, jerking me back to the present. The only sounds were the rat I shared this prison with, my own breathing, and the occasional shift of my body.

A guard shoved food through the slot in the metal door without a word. I'd stopped trying to speak to the guards after the first day. I hadn't spoken to Neo in days, either. The silence stretched too long, the bond too quiet. The worry sat in me like a stone: What if he had been injured, captured . . . or worse?

I tried again to contact him, reaching through our mental link. I could feel the bond that tied us together—an unbreakable tether—but it disappeared into darkness. He was beyond our range of communication. Knowing he was alive always eased some of my anxiety, but with each passing day, I became more desperate to talk to him.

I had two goals in this dungeon. Escape, and don't lose my mind in the process. So far, I wasn't sure which was the hardest task.

After beating me bloody and bruising my ribs, the guards threw me in this cell with the promise that I would be executed. I had wasted a full day and night lying on the stone floor, unable to move. But eventually, I had forced myself to get up, to eat, and most importantly, to search for a way out. I ran my hands over every inch of stone, searching for a vulnerability. After a full day of searching, I finally found a crack in the mortar. I used a femur of some long-lost former resident of the cell to chip away at the crack until I widened it inch by painstaking inch.

After two days, I'd carved out maybe three inches—just enough to almost wedge my fist into it. Not exactly an escape route. I glanced down at the bone with a frown. The edge was starting to splinter, and soon I'd be out of tools. But I wasn't digging aimlessly. This wall shared a corner with the guard passage, if my memory of the dungeon's layout was right. If I could widen the hole enough, maybe I'd hear something. Learn something. Maybe even find a way through eventually.

I knew that last possibility was a long shot, but when your choices are digging or losing your mind, you dig.

My bruised ribs groaned in protest as I grabbed the leg bone and resumed digging the hole I'd made in the corner. I dug until my hands and arms ached, but I kept going, welcoming the pain. Pain was good. Pain meant I was still alive.

When the blisters burst and bled, I leaned back on my heels to gauge my progress. Same depth, but a few inches wider.

I'm never fucking getting out of here.

I dropped the femur in disgust. Just as despair tightened its grip, something shifted—a prickle of awareness along the tether between Neo and me, faint but unmistakable.

You know, I never thought you'd be such a quitter, a familiar voice said in my mind.

I scrambled to my feet. *Neo? Where are you?*

I couldn't get close enough before to be in communication range, but something happened and the patrols dropped off suddenly. Like they're busy with something else.

My stomach bottomed out. I could think of several reasons

that might recall Eagle Riders from patrolling—none of them good.

I've been in the dark here. They have me so deep in this dungeon I haven't heard a soul—no voices, no other prisoners. Only the rats and the occasional guard.

Anger on my behalf surged down the link from Neo to me. *Are they feeding you?*

Yes, they're keeping me alive. For now.

The fact that I was still alive gave me a sliver of hope—that Altair might still retain some shred of himself, despite the Devourer's growing influence. I had always been something of a security blanket for my cousin, and I knew he would struggle to order my execution.

He doesn't seem opposed to leaving you to rot in the dungeon, though, Neo added wryly.

It doesn't look like I can hope for a fair trial, no, I said. *And speaking of leaving me to rot . . . what's the situation out there?*

In answer, he sent a stream of memories through our link, showing me everything he had experienced since the moment I freed him from the net. I got an eagle's view of the mountains below as Neo flew high and fast, quickly putting distance between him and the palace guards. He had gone about fifty miles into wild eagle territory when he finally landed on a rocky outcropping on the side of a mountain. There he waited, feathers ruffled against the cold, his eyes constantly searching—he wasn't about to let another wild eagle catch him off guard the way Tempest had.

Once night fell, he returned to the palace. A battalion of riderless giant eagles guarded the palace in a fifty-mile radius, preventing Neo from getting close enough to communicate with me. Neo had flown sharp and evasive patterns, probing their defenses—but curiously, they never gave chase for long. Eventually he gave up for the time being and returned to wild eagle territory. There, he hunted and slept, biding his time.

Every day, he returned to the palace at different times. Daybreak, the middle of the night, and throughout the day. An entire squad of giant eagles waited to rebuff him every time. I noticed, though, that their riders never accompanied them. I could think of two possibilities. One was that the giant eagles—sacred to our people—had been tasked with policing their own kind. It was clear orders had been given not to harm Neo; no one made a move to strike him. We were trained to go to great lengths to protect our giant eagles.

It made me think of Falcon and his eagle giving their lives to protect Shazeera before we could reach her. The fact that Falcon's eagle had been killed was likely due to it getting in the way of an arrow meant for him.

The other possibility was that the Eagle Riders had fallen to the Devourer and were wandering the palace now as undead corpses.

Let's hope it's not the latter, Neo said. *Though I hate to say I think it might be.*

I frowned. *What do you mean?*

You haven't gotten to the most important part of my memories . . . how I'm able to talk to you now.

When Neo flew within range of the palace today, he was immediately flanked by other giant eagles. Only these three were his closest allies. Aero, Storm, and Orion pumped their wings, hovering in front of Neo. I didn't have to wonder why these three particular eagles flew alone.

It was because their riders—Zamir, Baz, and Kestrel—had been killed by the Devourer. Their deaths flashed through my mind–my failure to reach each of them as they were pulled under a wave of undead. An echo of the same grief I felt hummed beneath the surface of their eagles' thoughts, carried like a shared ache across the bond. Regret over their loss settled heavily on my shoulders, and I sank down onto the cold floor.

I was wondering when you would show, Neo said, eyeing each of them in turn.

We're sorry it took so long, Aero said.

Storm, Baz's eagle, spoke next. *We've been under watch for days, but the situation has changed. Now they are distracted.*

Distracted how?

After Commander Talon's arrest, the Eagle Riders demanded to speak to the emperor but were turned away. Now Emperor Altair hasn't been seen in days, and worse, riders are disappearing, leaving their eagles with damaged bonds–like they've become incapacitated.

Or undead, Neo said.

Aero, Zamir's eagle, stayed silent, her pain over the loss of Zamir casting a shadow over her thoughts that could be felt across the lines of communication.

We need Commander Talon free, Orion said. *Our riders gave their lives to stop the Devourer, and we refuse to let their deaths be in vain.*

Then we will need help on the inside, Neo said. *Is there anyone left we can trust?*

Many are awakening to the realization that the emperor they serve has been lost to the enemy, Orion replied, and both Aero and Storm let their agreement be felt across the communication link.

What was their first clue? Neo said with a sardonic tone. *When they killed not only Falcon but his eagle, or when they beat Talon bloody and threw him in the dungeon?*

I think it wasn't until their own riders began to disappear that they accepted the possibility that the emperor has been replaced by a demon, Orion said.

We saw evidence of it when Talon was captured, Neo said, feathers ruffled. *I must talk with Talon, but I will need you three to try and contact eagles who have riders willing to commit treason.*

We will make inquiries, Orion promised. *But for now, we will stay on patrol nearby to give you time to talk to your rider.*

Neo's memories faded. *Which brings us to the present,* he said. *Any names come to mind?*

Before I could answer, footsteps in the hall outside my cell dragged my attention away from the conversation with Neo. It wasn't time for a meal. Quickly, I shoved the pile of straw in the corner to hide the hole I had been working on.

I froze at the screech of metal on metal as the bolt was pulled back from the door. A soldier I had never met stood in the doorway, chains dangling from his hands.

"On your feet, traitor," he said. "The emperor wants a word."

Photo by Redmon Photography

NORA CARMODY lives in South Carolina with her husband and six kids. Before she became an author, Nora worked as a psychotherapist. An avid horsewoman, she grew up riding and competing on her Arabian mare. Her horse-riding days may be over, but she's still a horse girl at heart! When she's not writing or spending time with her family, Nora takes care of a constantly growing menagerie of pets, including (but not limited to) two dogs, four cats, eleven chickens, and a bearded dragon.